Invisible,
as Music

BOOKS BY CAREN J. WERLINGER

Novels:
Looking Through Windows
Miserere
In This Small Spot
Neither Present Time
Year of the Monsoon
She Sings of Old, Unhappy, Far-off Things
Turning for Home
Cast Me Gently
The Beast That Never Was
When the Stars Sang
A Bittersweet Garden
Invisible, as Music

Short Stories:
Twist of the Magi
Just a Normal Christmas
(part of *Do You Feel What I Feel?* Holiday Anthology)

The Dragonmage Saga:
Rising From the Ashes: The Chronicles of Caymin
The Portal: The Chronicles of Caymin
The Standing Stones: The Chronicles of Caymin

Invisible,
as Music

CAREN J. WERLINGER

CORGYN
Publishing

Invisible, as Music
Published by Corgyn Publishing, LLC.

Copyright © 2019 by Caren J. Werlinger
All rights reserved.

e-Book ISBN: 978-0-9982179-5-6
Print ISBN: 978-0-9982179-6-3

E-mail: cjwerlingerbooks@yahoo.com
Website: carenwerlinger.com
Blog: cjwerlinger.wordpress.com

Cover design by Patty G. Henderson
blvdphotografica.wixsite.com/boulevard

Cover image credit: Dreamstime

Book design by Maureen Cutajar
www.gopublished.com

For all those who dare to love

Acknowledgements

Love comes in many forms, expressed in many ways. That exploration, what it is that draws people together, is a bottomless well of inspiration for stories. Most of my books aren't romances in the accepted sense, but they're all love stories. This novel is such a story.

To tell it, I've drawn on many things: my past experiences as a caretaker for a woman who was my model for Henrietta, thirty years working as a physical therapist, and the inexhaustible curiosity of watching people and wondering what their stories might be—and making up my own versions of their stories.

Most of my books have some kind of soundtrack that helped inspire me. This novel's soundtrack was a trip down memory lane.

Thank you to my editor, Lisa. No matter how clean and complete I think the manuscript is, she always finds ways of asking me to look at the story a little differently. Her suggestions and questions make my stories so much better.

Thank you to my Beth. Without you, I don't know if I could write at all.

And thank you, as always, to my readers. Your support means everything!

Chapter 1

HENRIETTA POURED A LITTLE water into a bowl and stirred it into the gesso she'd already spooned in. Picking up a well-used brush, she applied the mixture to a new canvas. Sunlight diffused indirectly through the floor-to-ceiling windows forming the north wall of her studio, where the trees beyond—not quite ready to turn—beckoned and begged to be captured. Again. Though she'd seen these same trees—birches with their starkly white trunks, majestic oaks more than a hundred years old, spreading maples whose leaves would become brilliant crimson and orange in a few weeks—go through this same cycle every year for nearly forty years, it never failed to stir her.

She tried to ignore the thumps coming from the front of the house and the repeated openings and closings of the front door. She tried, too, to ignore the nervous feeling in her stomach. It was going to be a bad night. Probably a bad month or two before things calmed down again. But the calm never lasted long. And then she'd go through this same cycle, just like those trees.

While the prepped canvas dried, she picked up a sketchpad and pencil and laid out a composition to be transferred to the canvas later. She sketched in a view of the pond below as it would appear when the leaves began to fall, with the meandering flagstone path from the house, down the hill, to the pond itself.

She paused. It had been a while since she'd been down there. Maybe later today...

She stiffened at a timid knock on the studio door behind her. A thin voice said, "Miss Cochran? I'm all packed."

Setting her pad down, Henrietta swiveled on her stool.

"I'm sorry to leave you—"

"No need to apologize, Amanda," Henrietta cut in.

"It's just my grandma needs someone, you see." Amanda's pale, watery eyes flitted about the studio, her hands twisting the strap of her purse as she looked anywhere but at Henrietta.

It was a reaction Henrietta was accustomed to. "I understand."

"I've made you a turkey sandwich." Amanda waved a hand in the direction of the kitchen.

"Thank you."

A long silence stretched out between them until Amanda shuffled back a step. "I'll just be going then." She waited a moment, but when Henrietta said nothing further, she said, "Good-bye."

Henrietta swiveled back to the windows, listening to the fading sound of footsteps tapping over the kitchen's linoleum floor, then silence on the living room carpet, then more taps on the foyer flagstones. When the front door thudded shut for the last time, she sat staring out at the trees, but no longer seeing them.

After a while, she picked her pad up. Her pencil rolled off and fell to the floor. She plucked another from the can on her table and continued sketching. Ignoring the rumbling of her stomach, she continued working as the light gradually shifted. She set the pad on a tabletop easel and opened a tin of watercolors. Over the next few hours, the sketch blossomed. Pushing back to scrutinize it, she made mental notes about what to change when she turned it into an oil painting.

Her hands tremored with the hours of work and lack of food. Pushing stiffly to her feet, she reached for her crutches and made her way to the kitchen, where Amanda's sandwich sat on a plate on the table along with a glass of tea, the ice long since melted.

On the kitchen counter was a key. Amanda's key. The key that had been issued to and returned by more companions than she could now remember.

She briefly considered making something fresh, a hamburger maybe, but instead lumbered to the table. Settling herself at her accustomed place with its view of the country club golf course across the road, she ate her stale sandwich and drank her watery tea. This late in the day, there were only a couple of solitary golfers wandering around out there.

As she ate, she ran through an inventory of sources to check with tomorrow. Amanda hadn't been stimulating company—the woman hadn't any more than a high school education and considered Harlequin romances to be literature—but she'd been pleasant and reliable.

When she was done, Henrietta shuffled first her plate, then her glass to the counter where she could push them nearer the sink to wash them and place them in the drainer. She paused as she left the kitchen, undecided between going to the living room to watch television or going to the bedroom to read.

The ache from her body decided for her. She checked that the front door was locked and then made her way down the short hall to her room.

Following a ritual honed over decades, she closed the door, drew the curtains, turned down the bed, and then went to the bathroom. When she was done with her nightly routine in there, she returned to the bed and sat on the edge of the mattress, carefully placing her crutches within easy reach.

She bent over to untie her shoes and unbuckle the lowest straps on

3

her leg braces. Laboriously, she unbuttoned her blouse and skirt, her fingers fumbling with the buttons and zipper. She wriggled out of her clothes and folded them neatly on the chair beside the bed. With the clothing out of the way, she tugged on the leather straps binding her back brace. As soon as it was off, her spine partially collapsed under the weight of her slight trunk.

She undid the higher straps on her leg braces, grasping the metal uprights on either side to free her feet and legs from the restraints. Her thick hose were always difficult to don and doff, but they were an essential barrier between her skin and the braces. She groaned a little as she rubbed the indentations in her muscles left by the straps.

Reaching for the nightgown on the chair, she slipped it over her head. Grasping first one leg, then the other, she swung them onto the bed and pulled the bedclothes up to her chin. She picked up her book, Danielle Steel's newest, and read until her eyes were too heavy to continue. Certain she'd be able to sleep now, she reached over and switched the bedside lamp off.

Darkness and silence settled on the house, but she was instantly wide-awake. Every whirr of the air conditioning unit, every creak and groan of the house, every outside noise that filtered through the windows startled her. She rolled over to turn on the radio on the bedside table, twiddling the dial until she found a station playing soothing classical music, but the noise only served to heighten her anxiety as she imagined other, more sinister sounds being masked by the radio. She turned it off again and lay there, listening.

She fought the familiar rise of panic, forcing herself to concentrate on her breaths, visualizing her lungs pulling air in and expelling it under her own power. In, out. In, out. She heard Una laughing, her beautiful face smiling down at her.

It took ages, but the panic faded. Knowing sleep would not be hers that night, she switched the lamp back on and picked up Danielle Steel again.

~

LOADED DOWN WITH AN olive-green army duffle over one shoulder and a guitar case in her other hand, Ryn stood on the sidewalk, looking up at a three-story Victorian. She shrugged the duffel straps higher on her shoulder and climbed the porch steps. Before she could knock, the front door opened, and she was nearly run over by a young woman. Ryn had a quick impression of big hair, bigger earrings and short shorts before the woman muttered a quick "Sorry" and teetered down the wooden stairs as quickly as she could in heels.

Shaking her head, Ryn stepped through the open door and reached back to push the door shut behind her. From upstairs, she could hear music coming from a stereo—no, make that two or three stereos.

A door at the far end of the hall swung open and an older woman bustled through from the kitchen beyond, wiping her hands on a towel.

"Yes?" asked the woman. "May I help you?"

"I'm Meryn Fleming. Are you Mrs. Middleston?" Ryn held out a hand.

Mrs. Middleston took it in a dainty fingers-only grip, looking Ryn up and down through her wire-rimmed glasses. "You're the new professor at the college?"

Ryn beamed. "I am."

Mrs. Middleston looked doubtful. "Yes, well, your room is up on the third floor."

She led the way up the wide staircase, flanked by an ornate, carved bannister. As Ryn followed her up and around a second-floor landing, then up to the third floor, she thought she heard mutterings of "since when are they hiring twelve-year-old boys". Apparently Mrs. Middleston, despite what her plumpness and silver-blue hair would suggest, was in better shape than she appeared if she had enough breath to mutter, because Ryn was huffing by the time they got to the third-floor landing with its eyebrow window giving a bird's eye view of the street below and the village beyond. Two rooms opened off this landing, and Mrs. Middleston gestured into the room on the right.

Sunshine spilled onto plain, white matelassé bedspreads on the two twin beds, one piled high with stuffed animals and rumpled clothing.

"I insist on all the girls making their beds every day," Mrs. Middleston was saying as Ryn looked around. "Sheets and towels are laundered every Saturday. See that yours are downstairs by nine that morning, and the clean ones will be ready by three."

The one dresser's top was littered with bottles of perfume, jars and tubes of makeup, and more bottles of nail polish, along with about six hairbrushes.

"I understood I was to have a room to myself," Ryn said.

"Oh, well, when you called, I didn't have another girl, but since then, I do," Mrs. Middleston said, fussing with a wrinkle in the empty bed's cover and straightening the neatly folded towel and washcloth sitting at the foot of the bed. "You'll like Vanessa. She's a very nice girl. Three of those drawers are yours."

Mrs. Middleston looked Ryn up and down again, sighing in a disapproving way at the cut-off Levi's, black Converse high-tops, and T-shirt emblazoned with a peace sign. "Yes, well, curfew is ten o'clock during the week, eleven on weekends. And I warn you, I'm very prompt with locking the door. You will have a shelf in a cupboard in the kitchen and may use the refrigerator for milk or lunchmeats. No food in the rooms. That is an absolute. I don't want mice. And no alcohol on the premises."

She moved toward the hall. "I'll leave you to unpack. You've already paid your first month's rent, so your next payment isn't due until the first of the month."

Ryn set her guitar down and let the duffle fall from her shoulder onto the bed. There was a pause in the clatter of Mrs. Middleston's shoes on the stair treads.

"Oh, and no men!" she called from the stairwell.

Ryn snorted. "Fat chance of that." But she mumbled it under her breath, certain that Mrs. Middleston's hearing was as sharp as her appraising gaze.

She had hoped for a desk, but maybe it was better that there wasn't one. She had a feeling she wasn't going to be doing much more than sleeping here. She checked the dresser but, contrary to what Mrs. Middleston had said, there were no empty drawers. Ryn unceremoniously tugged open the three drawers on the left, closest to her bed, and scooped the contents onto Vanessa's bed. She refilled them with her clothes from the duffel. She had to wrestle a few hangers free from the back of the stuffed closet to hang her teaching clothes—khakis and white shirts.

The floorboards vibrated with the bass thumps coming from a room below her on the second floor. She hoped Mrs. Middleston's curfew extended to limits on playing loud music. With her unpacking done, she went downstairs to the ground floor where she found Mrs. Middleston in the kitchen.

"Can you tell me how to get to the campus from here?"

Mrs. Middleston looked up from her scrubbing of her already spotless stovetop. "You're teaching there and you don't know where it is?"

"My interview was over the telephone."

"Well, it's hard to miss. You could probably walk all of Bluemont inside half an hour. We're on the south side of the village. St. Aloysius is on the north. You can go either way on this street. If you turn north, you can't miss it."

"Thank you."

Ryn jogged down the porch steps and went to her car—a 1972 AMC Hornet. She reached into the back of the little station wagon to retrieve a backpack stuffed with textbooks and notebooks. When she closed the hatch, she pressed down the curling corner of a *Re-Elect Carter* bumper sticker adhered to the glass alongside many others.

Giving the fender a pat, she said, "You stay here, Nelly."

She shrugged the backpack straps into position as she walked down the tree-lined street. When she rounded the corner, a stone church steeple poked into an impossibly blue sky. As Mrs. Middleston had said, she hadn't walked more than fifteen minutes before she found herself in the village's small town center—complete with a tree-lined square and statue to some past war hero. Cars parked diagonally on the streets surrounding the square, and people wandered up and down the sidewalks, entering and leaving the little shops lining the streets.

Ryn took in the quaintness of the scene. It was right out of a Norman Rockwell painting. So different from Pittsburgh.

Another few minutes brought her to the campus of St. Aloysius College. It was just as picturesque as the village—four main buildings of gray stone arranged around a grassy quad, a few mature oaks scattered around to provide some shade on this warmish late August day while one tall fir tree stood like a sentinel in the center of the space.

She scanned the signs on the buildings and found hers, Rayburn Hall. According to the little signs fastened to the wall at the base of the stairs, the history department was on the second floor.

Sweat beaded on her forehead by the time she found the department secretary's office.

"Hi," she panted, dropping her backpack onto a wooden chair inside the door. "I'm Meryn Fleming, the new history professor."

The owlish woman behind the desk blinked at her a few times through enormous eyeglasses that magnified her eyes. "Good Lord."

Ryn nodded solemnly. "Yes, she is." She glanced down at the sign on the woman's desk. "Beverly. Could you point me to my office?"

Beverly got to her feet, and Ryn realized she must have had her desk chair cranked to its highest position, because she was hardly taller standing than she had been sitting. She reminded Ryn even more of a bird as she led the way with short, staccato steps. Down the corridor, around the corner to... what looked like a converted broom closet. A desk and chair and one bookshelf had been crammed inside, but there was a window overlooking the hills beyond the campus. The bookshelf already contained what she recognized as the textbooks she'd be teaching from.

"You should have had Professor Aldren's old desk, but he shared an office with Professor Geary, and Dr. Talbert thought you'd prefer being by yourself."

Beverly peered up into Ryn's face, searching as if trying to make up her mind about something. She crooked her finger, and Ryn leaned down obligingly. "I shouldn't say this," Beverly whispered. "I mean, I just met you, but you're the only other woman in the department, and a young one at that. Stay away from Professor Geary. He has a reputation as..." She blushed. "Well, he likes the girls. The younger, the better."

Her flared nostrils and pursed lips indicated just what Beverly thought of Professor Geary.

Ryn grinned. "Thanks. I'll keep that in mind." She nodded toward her cubby. "And thank Dr. Talbert for me. I appreciate both of you thinking of me that way."

"Oh, well." Beverly blushed and smiled. "You're most welcome. I'll leave you to set your office up as you like. I'm sure you'll want to get started on the classes you'll be teaching. I've placed the current syllabi on your desk. If you need anything, just ask. Professor."

Beverly's heels clicked away down the corridor, and Ryn dropped into her office chair, twirling around. She ran her hands through her short hair with a happy sigh. She was here. Her first teaching job. At a Catholic school in the middle-of-nowhere New York. But it was a start.

"Thank you, Goddess."

~

9

"AND WAIT UNTIL YOU see the way this new floor cleaner works on the kitchen floor. I hope you don't mind I went ahead and bought some to use here. I know how you like everything to be spic and span. But don't worry, I know it can't be too slippery for your crutches. Oh, and wait until you hear what my sister told me about the college!"

Normally, Bonnie's non-stop chatter on Wednesdays irked Henrietta, who considered her cleaning day a wasted day as far as getting any painting done. But the silence in the house since Amanda's departure had been so oppressive that Henrietta had taken to leaving the television or the radio on just to have some noise.

Bonnie really was a God-send, a tiny whirlwind of a woman who gave Henrietta a full day's work—dusting, vacuuming, stripping and laundering the sheets and remaking the bed—all the things Henrietta couldn't easily do for herself anymore. If Bonnie talked a bit too much, well, it was a small price to pay for having someone who didn't leave after a few months. While Bonnie gabbed, Henrietta paid bills and balanced the checkbook—things she could do with only one ear tuned to the conversation.

Henrietta paused in the middle of writing the check for the gas company. "How long have you been with me now?"

Bonnie straightened from where she'd been mopping the kitchen floor with the new cleaner. "Let's see, Miss Cochran. It must be going on twelve years. Yes, it is. Because I remember Kevin was just starting junior high school when I decided to take on work. Twelve years. Can you believe it?"

And she continued chattering about all that had happened in those twelve years as she resumed mopping and telling what she'd heard about old Patrick Rooney, who had gotten drunk as a skunk at the bingo hall at St. Rita's, not noticing that Henrietta had stopped writing.

Twelve years. How was that even possible? Henrietta stared at the framed painting above the desk—one of her finest, in her opinion—a view of the house from the hill on the other side of the pond, a view she hadn't seen in person since the day she sketched it for this oil.

She might as well have painted herself into the composition—a figure stuck in one place for all time, never leaving the confines of her house. It wasn't technically true, of course. She went to church most Sundays, and the country club for bridge on Thursday mornings. But when was the last time she'd gone anywhere unscheduled?

"Bonnie," she called. "Maybe we could—"

She was interrupted by the doorbell at the back door into the breezeway between the kitchen and the garage.

"That's Denny with the groceries," Bonnie said, going to let him in.

The young man from the grocery store carried three boxes of groceries into the pantry, just as he did every Wednesday. He called out a good day to Henrietta, taking care not to walk on Bonnie's still-damp floor.

Bonnie waved him off and brought the receipt to Henrietta. "I'll make us some sandwiches for lunch and get a nice roast going for your dinner. How does that sound?"

Henrietta nodded absently. The grocery receipt was itemized, list-ing the same items as it did every week. The same food. The same routine. She couldn't remember the last time she'd actually set foot in the market. It was easier to stick with her staples since the market staff was boxing it up for her. The only surprises were the seasonal changes in fruits and vegetables. She hadn't any idea what new products might even be on the shelves. Only when Bonnie or one of her friends brought her something new they'd discovered did she try foods that might or might not make it onto the list.

The afternoon passed as most Wednesdays did. She stretched out on the sofa after lunch to rest her back and maybe nap a little while Bonnie cleaned the bedrooms and bathrooms. The aroma of the roast in the oven started to fill the house.

By four o'clock, Bonnie had dinner served—Henrietta always ate early on cleaning days. The rest of the tender meat, potatoes, and carrots were packed into the refrigerator in small serving containers that Henrietta could lift with one hand to warm up over the next few evenings.

"Thank you, Bonnie."

Bonnie, washing the roasting pan at the sink, stopped with a shocked expression. The surprise on her face shamed Henrietta. Was it so rare for her to say thank you?

"You're most welcome, Miss Cochran."

Bonnie dried the last of the dishes, putting them away before getting her purse. "Are you sure you're all right here by yourself?"

Henrietta got to her feet, slipping her hands into the cuffs on her crutches. "It's only been a couple of weeks. I'll find someone soon."

Bonnie opened her mouth as if to say something further but then just nodded. "I'll see you next Wednesday then." She opened her purse and inserted the check Henrietta had written when she was paying the other bills.

"Have a good week."

Henrietta stood at the door while Bonnie backed out of the drive. It looked like a nice evening. The undulating fairways and greens of the golf course, empty of golfers, looked pretty in the slanting sunlight, long shadows being thrown by the trees. She considered walking out to the end of the driveway just to stretch her legs. She gave the storm door a shove and then propped it open with one crutch while she stepped over the threshold onto the covered front porch, its two comfortable chairs freshly dusted by Bonnie earlier that morning.

But what if she fell? Who would see? Who would help? She backed up, letting the storm door close before pushing the front door shut. For a moment, she leaned against it, her heart hammering in her chest. With a flick of her wrist, she fastened the locks.

"TIME FOR YOUR TEA, milady."

Ryn had discovered that she and Beverly shared a liking for tea and a dislike of coffee. Beverly had a hot plate that could make water hot enough, and Ryn had brought in a tin of exotic teas. Of course, anything not bearing a Lipton tag was exotic to Beverly. Ryn had decided not to tell her that Celestial Seasonings could be purchased at the health food store downtown.

"What would you fancy today?" Ryn asked, putting on her best British accent, which was just a bad imitation of an English butler.

Beverly giggled. "Surprise me."

Ryn produced two bags of Red Zinger and placed them in the mugs while Beverly poured. Ryn dropped into the wooden chair beside Beverly's desk and closed her eyes as she inhaled the aromatic steam from the mug.

"How are your classes going, Professor?" Beverly asked, dunking her teabag up and down.

Whatever her misgivings had been upon their first meeting, Beverly had finally accepted Ryn's position, even if she still eyed a woman in pants with suspicion. Still, after Ryn had scandalized her by asking if she could teach in jeans and T-shirt, Beverly seemed satisfied that the khakis were at least presentable.

"I've told you to call me Ryn, or I'll be forced to call you Ms. DiSorbo." Ryn opened her eyes and wrung out her teabag.

"I'll try, Prof—I'll call you by your Christian name, Meryn." Beverly looked a little taken aback at her daring.

"Good enough." Ryn wagged her head to one side. "Seeing as how September 1st was just yesterday, and today is Friday of Labor Day weekend, classes are going spectacularly. All two days of them thus far." She took a sip. "The kids are nice. Respectful. But I still want to teach more than just the seminar classes. Has Dr. Talbert said anything more about the class I suggested on the history of American women?"

Beverly glanced over her shoulder toward his office—though it was clearly empty—and leaned forward to whisper, "I heard him mention it to Professor Geary."

Ryn frowned. "Why would he do that? It was my idea. If that guy—"

She stopped abruptly when Beverly's eyes opened wide, staring past Ryn to the office door.

"Hello, lovely ladies."

Ryn stiffened as Bradley Geary came into Beverly's office.

"Tea time? May I join you?" He laid a casual hand on Ryn's shoulder.

She resisted the urge to break his fingers, instead bending down to pick up an imaginary bit of trash off the floor. She stood to drop it in the trashcan behind the desk.

"Sorry, just used the last two bags."

She met his gaze, knowing he didn't believe her, but she didn't care. The guy was even creepier than Beverly had intimated. Once handsome, she supposed, with his sandy hair and toothy grin, he was used to getting his way by lying and smiling and charming people, especially women. In truth, he was a lazy ass. She hadn't been here more than a week, but Ryn could already see that, with his tenure secure, he intended to dump as much work on her as he could get away with.

"I need to..." Ryn picked up her tea mug, leaving the sentence incomplete and hurried past Geary and out to the corridor beyond.

She didn't look back to see if Geary was following her to her office, but she heard Beverly ask him a question to detain him, and thanked her lucky stars for Beverly DiSorbo. The woman might be tiny, but she saw everything. Ryn was glad to have her as an ally. She had a feeling she was going to need allies if she had to keep dealing with that male chauvinist pig.

Her classes were done for the week, so she quickly grabbed a few books, locked her office, and nearly ran out of the building. The afternoon was beautiful—sunny, pleasantly warm with an almost cloudless sky. A few students lounged about on the quad, but most were leaving campus for Labor Day.

She made her way back to the boarding house. Parking on campus was tight, so Nelly had spent most of the week parked on the curb. She gave the car a pat on her way by.

"I promise we'll go for a drive this weekend."

Upstairs, thankfully with no sign of Vanessa, Ryn changed her clothes, carefully hanging her khakis and shirt to keep them as wrinkle-free as possible. After tugging on some jean shorts, her high-tops, and a T-shirt, she went downstairs and found Mrs. Middleston sitting in a rocker on the front porch, snapping a large bowl of green beans.

"How are things going?" the older woman asked.

"Pretty well." Ryn sat on the porch. "My classes aren't very challenging yet, but I hope to add more interesting ones next semester."

She hooked a thumb toward the rear of the house. "What's out that way?"

"Away from the village? Not much. The country club, a few houses, and then mostly farms."

"And how far are we from Syracuse?"

"Oh, not an hour. Bored, are you?"

Mrs. Middleston's sharp eyes were focused on her beans, but Ryn had the feeling she still saw more than most.

"Not bored. Just wondered is all." She stood and dusted off the seat of her cut-offs. "Think I'll go for a walk. See you later."

"Remember the curfew's eleven tonight," Mrs. Middleston called after her.

Ryn gave a wave to show she'd heard and set off down the block, turning away from town when she got to the corner.

She sauntered along, taking random roads, confident she'd be able to find her way back. Nothing around here was big enough to get truly lost in. She found a road that stretched into the distance, lined with large trees whose branches overarched the street, shading it from the westering sun.

ﾊ

A street sign told her she was on Country Club Road, and she could see the golf course stretching out to her left, miles of manicured grass and undulating hills, the holes separated by more mature trees.

A noise from the house on her right distracted her. The garage was open, with a station wagon parked inside. A figure seemed to be struggling with the door. She paused, watching a woman with crutches get out of the car and make her way around to the rear hatch where she was trying to pull out what appeared to be grocery bags.

Ryn jogged down the driveway. "May I help you?"

The woman started and gave a little yelp as one bag tumbled to the ground, its contents scattered all over the garage floor.

"Sorry. Didn't mean to scare you."

"I didn't hear you," the woman said.

Ryn got on her hands and knees, gathering up assorted cans and packages of food, almost lying on the garage floor to retrieve the cans that had rolled under the car. She stood up, holding the shredded paper sack. "The bag is ripped." Her arms cradled the items. "Can I take these straight inside for you?"

The woman looked up at her, fixing her with steel-gray eyes that were cautious as she stood, balanced on her two crutches, both legs locked into metal braces. Ryn smiled, trying to seem disarming.

A can of something slipped out of her arms. She ducked, trying to catch it, but everything in her grasp clattered to the floor.

"Crap!" She glanced at the woman. "Sorry," she muttered as she squatted down to pick it all up again.

"Wait," the woman said. She pointed with one crutch toward a set of shelves against the garage wall. "Get one of those baskets."

Ryn did as she asked, placing all of the groceries in a rattan yard basket probably meant for hauling leaves. She followed the woman through the door into a small hallway and then into the kitchen.

"I'll get the other bag," she said, hurrying back to the station wagon. She had no idea how that woman thought she was going to get this stuff into the house. Or how she drove the car. She closed the station wagon's hatch and brought the bag into the kitchen.

She placed the bag on the counter and then set out all of the things in the basket. "I'll put this back."

She nested the basket with the others on the garage shelf and then hesitantly returned to the kitchen.

"Can I help you with anything else? Put these away for you?"

"No." The woman turned to her, her crutches and braces making small metallic clicks with each step as she maneuvered. "I can take it from here. Thank you for your help."

"You're welcome. Bye."

Ryn let herself back into the garage and trotted out to the street. Glancing toward the house, she saw the woman standing in the garage. Ryn gave a last wave as the garage door started to lower.

Chapter 2

HENRIETTA'S STOMACH GURGLED LOUDLY, followed by a belch. She paused her painting to take a sip of ginger ale. Maybe the new foods she'd thought to experiment with hadn't been such a good idea. Especially the Mexican. Too spicy for her stomach, which was proving to be more sensitive than she'd realized.

What she hadn't been prepared for was the firestorm her last-minute stop at the market had caused. She'd just been driving by and decided to pull in and do a little shopping. Why should that have created such a stir? But by that evening, Mike MacGregor, the owner of the market, had called to see if there was a problem with Denny's delivery, or had the boy been rude, or had he delivered the groceries in less-than-satisfactory condition. And the next morning, poor Denny himself had come to her door, shuffling from foot to foot and apologizing if he'd done anything wrong. Even Bonnie had come by Saturday afternoon to see if she was all right, or if there was something wrong with the leftover roast she'd cooked up on Wednesday.

After reassuring everyone that there was nothing wrong with the market's service or Denny's delivery or Bonnie's cooking, Henrietta had retreated to her studio.

Even at church this morning, people had stopped to ask if she was all right. It was comforting in a way that so many people were watching out for her, but Henrietta felt more boxed in than ever, when even a change in her food shopping habits was enough to get the entire village's attention.

Giving up for the day, she cleaned her brushes.

She left the studio and paused in the breezeway. Instead of turning toward the kitchen and the living room, she went to the back door. Stepping through it, she was greeted by a glorious September evening. She sniffed. Someone was grilling something. The driveway stretched before her, looking much longer than the fifty feet or so it actually was. That young woman who had helped her pick up her groceries had jogged it so effortlessly. Henrietta dreamed sometimes of what it had felt like to run and skip and play, but she couldn't really remember.

As always when she recalled those days, she thought of Una, wondering where she was, what she was doing. Probably back in England, married, maybe with grandchildren by now.

Taking a deep breath, Henrietta struck out, first one step, then another and another until she found herself at the end of the driveway. One of the golfers across the street waved to her from a green.

"You okay, Miss Cochran?" he bellowed.

She nodded and released one crutch handle to wave. She looked left and right along the road, but everything was quiet. No cars. No young woman walking by.

She turned and made her way back to the house. Once inside, she realized she was trembling.

"I did it," she said aloud to the empty house.

She locked the door and went to get a glass of iced tea. A few minutes later, she collapsed into her usual chair at the table. Jubilant at her daring, she considered going for a drive, but, as she reached for the tea, her unsteady hand knocked the glass over, spilling tea across the tabletop. Struggling to her feet again, she got a sponge from the sink, along with a bowl, and mopped up the spill, squeezing one spongeful at a time into the bowl. By the time the table was clean, she was exhausted and deflated.

Standing at the kitchen sink to rinse out the bowl and the sponge, she had a view through the window of the driveway she had just walked down. Suddenly, the drive and the world beyond looked impossibly far away. Her eyes stung with tears that went unshed.

Henrietta had stopped crying a long time ago.

~

RYN RAN A TOWEL roughly over her damp hair as she climbed the stairs from the second floor bathroom. The third-floor rooms may have had the best view, but they also collected all of the heat in the un-air-conditioned house. Entering her room, she tripped over a stuffed Eeyore. She gently nudged him aside with her foot and hung her towel up on one of the towel bars Mrs. Middleston insisted they use—"I do not want mildew!"—before flopping onto her bed.

She fanned her T-shirt and hiked up her cut-off sweatpants to take advantage of the stream of air created by the fan whirring from the top of the dresser. She'd quickly discovered that a cold shower in the evenings and going to bed with damp hair helped the fan cool her down enough to sleep. Of course, it made for interesting hair in the morning.

Vanessa flounced into the room. Even with her eyes shut and in any other part of the house, Ryn could have identified that noisy entrance.

"Can you believe they gave us homework our first weekend of the semester? And it's a holiday!" Vanessa hopped onto her bed with a squeak of the springs.

21

Ryn didn't bother opening her eyes. "Yes, I can. Because I gave homework, too."

Vanessa may have made her bed each morning as per the rules of the house, and picked up all of her Winnie-the-Pooh animals to let them have the bed to themselves during the day, but the moment she entered the room, everything seemed to go flying.

"Yeah, but you're cool, so I bet nobody minds."

Ryn couldn't help grinning. It was impossible not to like Vanessa. With her wild blonde curls and enormous baby-blue eyes, she was like a wind-up version of Shirley Temple—very wound-up. Ryn gave another quick prayer of thanks that she didn't have Vanessa in any of her classes, though there were other boarders here who were now her students. It hadn't occurred to her when she applied to Mrs. Middleston for a room that she'd be the only faculty among students. It wasn't exactly awkward... yet. But she could see how it could quickly become weird if any of her students didn't do well.

"I was reading all the bumper stickers on your car. You're really political. My folks voted for Reagan. You have Carter stickers."

"We're all going to be sorry Reagan was elected. Just wait."

"And that purple one. The sticker with the two-bladed axe. What's that?"

"It's called a labrys." Ryn hesitated. *Do you want to open that door?* "It's a... goddess symbol."

"It's the same as the silver necklace you wear." Vanessa lowered her voice to a stage whisper. "Are you pagan?"

Ryn chuckled, fingering the labrys under her shirt. "Something like that."

"Cool." Vanessa shifted on her bed. "Tell me more about Pittsburgh and your family."

Ryn had purposely been vague—again, that whole teacher-student thing, but, "We don't actually live in Pittsburgh," she heard herself say. "I went to Pitt, but we live in Uniontown."

"And your dad worked in the steel mills."

Apparently, Vanessa had decided that a weekend stuck in Bluemont meant it was a good time to share.

Ryn gave up and turned on her side, facing Vanessa, who was lying on her back, holding a large Pooh. "Not exactly. He was a bookkeeper for a mill. When it closed down, he got a job with an accounting firm. Now, he does business taxes. Boring, but steady, I guess."

Vanessa sighed. "I know what you mean. My dad's a lawyer in practice with his brother. Not criminal like Perry Mason. Wills and estates and stuff like that. Feldman and Feldman. Couldn't be more boring."

"How—" Ryn wasn't sure how to ask this. "You told me your mom is an alumna of St. Aloysius from when it was all-women, but your last name sounds Jewish."

"It is. My mom is Catholic, but my dad is Jewish. I'm not really either one. They told me I could choose when I was old enough, but I've never had any of the sacraments or my bat mitzvah. My grandparents on both sides keep trying to get me to pick one or the other, but my parents never pushed. They just want me to stay a virgin till I'm married. That's why I'm here instead of a dorm, now that there are boys on campus." She rolled her eyes. "So now I'm stuck at a small school that's still mostly women, living in an old woman's house that's like a women's prison. Class of 1987. That's forever from now! This is going to be the longest four years of my life."

Ryn smiled at Vanessa's dramatics. It suited Ryn perfectly that St. Aloysius was about three-quarters women, but Beverly had told her that, in the few years since men had been admitted, the college had seen a shift in the makeup of student council and honor court and other organizations as the males took over. Beverly hated to see it change, and Ryn was inclined to agree. Men ruined everything.

Vanessa flopped onto her stomach, hugging Pooh under her chest. "Tell me about your brothers and sister."

"Told you as much as there is to tell. My sister is a sophomore at West Virginia now, and the boys are juniors in high school. They'll probably go to college on basketball scholarships, at least, that's what my dad is hoping."

"I wish I had brothers and sisters," Vanessa said. "I hate being an only child."

"They're okay," Ryn admitted. Sharing a room with Vanessa was almost like having a pesky younger sister underfoot again, but she didn't say that.

Vanessa got off her bed to change into her nightshirt. She had no sense of modesty at all. Ryn felt her face heat up at the sight of those full breasts when Vanessa's bra went flying, her slender waist sweeping into the curve of her hips. Ryn rolled over to face the wall, trying not to think of Ashley.

We both knew it was going to end when we graduated. Forget her.

"Won't you play your guitar?" Vanessa asked.

"Not tonight. I'm tired." Ryn punched her pillow into shape under her head. "Turn the light off, will you?"

～

A SLIGHTLY BUILT, TWEEDY man with half-glasses suspended around his neck on a jeweled cord moved from painting to painting, leaning close to squint at them, and then stepping back to see them from a distance, his head lowered to look over his glasses. The light coming in from the windows showed the landscapes off to their best advantage.

"Yes, yes, yes." He brushed his index finger back and forth over his precisely trimmed moustache. "Yes, I think we'll take these four. The same agreement as last time."

He turned to Bonnie, pulling a leather-bound wallet from the inside pocket of his jacket. "This is a check for the sale of the last group of paintings we sold."

Bonnie accepted the check, her eyes widening at the amount.

"Are you certain Miss Cochran isn't available? I would dearly love to meet her. We're beginning to think she doesn't really exist."

"She does exist, but she is indisposed today," Bonnie said primly, smoothing her hands over her floral-print top and slacks.

He eyed her, his eyes sharp over the half-glasses perched on the end of his nose. "Are you sure you're not the artist?"

Bonnie goggled at him for a moment. "Me? Goodness gracious, no, Mr. Taylor. I am merely here to represent Miss Cochran."

"Well," he said, bending over the counter to write up a consignment form for the four paintings, "our patrons in the city quite enjoy her quaint country scenes. Please extend my regards to her."

He carried the canvases out to his car, carefully wrapping each in a quilted blanket before driving away. Bonnie watched from the driveway until his car disappeared. When she went back into the studio, Henrietta was standing there.

"You heard?" Bonnie asked.

"Quaint country scenes indeed," Henrietta bristled.

Bonnie chuckled. "Well, it's your own fault. If you would let them meet you, see you."

"And have them take my work out of pity? No thank you."

"Still, that's Albany again on top of galleries in Buffalo and Rochester. Soon, you'll be in the big galleries in New York."

Henrietta snorted, smiling in spite of herself. "Thank you for coming over on such short notice. He caught me off-guard when he called yesterday."

Again, that double take of surprise.

"Can you stay for lunch?" When Bonnie didn't answer immediately, Henrietta quickly added, "I know it's a holiday and you probably have plans."

"No, no plans. Frank was just going to barbeque some frankfurters and hamburgers this evening. But that's not till later."

25

"We can go to the club. To celebrate the sale."

"Oh, goodness gracious, I'm not dressed fancy enough for that place." Bonnie went into the kitchen to check the refrigerator. "How about I make my egg salad with some of the eggs I hard-boiled? Egg salad sandwiches and dill pickles."

Henrietta smiled again. "My favorite. And you know it."

"I do know it." Bonnie chuckled. "You sit down now."

She poured two glasses of iced tea, setting one in front of Henrietta, and then peeled half a dozen eggs. "Any luck finding a new live-in?"

"No. I've called all of my bridge friends and the secretary at St. Rita's. I even called the school board to see if they had hired any new teachers who might need someplace to live, but they said the women already have apartments. There was one male teacher, but I don't want a man."

"I don't blame you. They're an awful mess. Even my Frank. God knows I love that man, but he does make a mess. It's like having another child." Bonnie chattered away as she scooped some mayonnaise into the bowl and mixed it with the eggs, stirring in some mustard and paprika.

A few minutes later, she set two plates on the table, each with a sandwich and a couple of dill pickles.

"Well, someone will turn up."

They ate in silence for a bit.

"I know I'm difficult." Henrietta focused on her sandwich.

"Nonsense. You just have standards, that's all. It's your house, you have a right to set rules."

"Well, no one seems to want to live with my rules more than a few months." Henrietta munched on a pickle. "I used to be able to find single women who needed a situation, but I suppose it's gotten easier for single women to be on their own."

"I could check with my sister," Bonnie offered. "She works at the college."

"A student?" Henrietta frowned as she took a drink. "Students are so unreliable. The last one tried to sneak her boyfriend into her room."

"Well, that was a bad fit from the get-go." Bonnie's nostrils flared her disapproval. "She was a Protestant."

~

RYN SAT BACK AND stretched. The clock on her office wall told her she'd been at this too long. Though she was teaching mostly the freshman seminar courses, even she found them boring. So she was trying to spice up the material she'd been handed with tidbits to make the history come alive for her students. A few seemed to have caught her excitement. History to her had been nothing more than droning on of dates and names until one teacher in high school, Mr. Black, had shown them letters written by Civil War soldiers to their families and wives. Those pages, penned over a century before, had made their story come alive in ways that nothing else had. From that semester on, she'd known this was what she wanted to do.

She stacked up the transparencies she'd been working on for next week's lectures.

"Still at it?"

She froze for a moment. "Just finishing for the day. It's been a long Monday."

Bradley Geary leaned in her doorway, one hand braced against the opposite jamb, effectively closing her in her own office. Far from making him look debonair—the effect she supposed he was going for—the posture opened his jacket, revealing the gap where his shirt buttons strained over his paunch.

"How about a drink?"

Here we go again.

She busied herself rearranging the books on her desk needlessly. "No, thanks."

"Dinner?"

Obviously, subtlety wasn't going to work, as she'd declined his invitations a handful of times already. Ryn straightened and met his eye. "No. I do not want to have dinner or drinks or anything else with you."

She saw immediately that her directness, far from discouraging him, only provided more of a challenge. Rather than stay and argue, she tucked the books she needed into her backpack and slung it over her shoulder. At the door, she wondered just for a moment if he was going to move. With a tilt of her head, she met his gaze again. He smiled a smile that did not reach his eyes. The coldness she saw there caused a chill to run down her spine, but she refused to blink or look away. At last, he lowered his arm, letting her pass. She pulled her office door shut behind her and walked off, knowing he was watching her.

At the end of the corridor, she peered into the department chair's office, wondering if anyone was still there. Beverly's desk was empty, but beyond, she saw that Dr. Talbert's light was on. She ducked in and tapped a knuckle on his door.

"Excuse me, Dr. Talbert."

He looked up over his glasses, the sparse hairs on his head glinting silver in the glow from the old-fashioned banker's lamp on his desk. He tapped the ash from his cigarette into an overflowing ashtray. "Yes, Meryn?"

"I don't mean to bother you, but I wanted to see if you'd given any more thought to the class I proposed? The one on American women? It would be a wonderful addition to our curriculum, and I could have it ready to teach next semester."

He sat back, inhaling deeply on his cigarette and then regarding her pensively through the smoke as he exhaled. "I discussed it with Professor Geary, and he doesn't seem to think there's enough material there to warrant an entire class. Perhaps a subunit within a larger context would be more..."

He left the thought dangling while Ryn fought to keep her temper. Her fist tightened on the strap of her backpack. For a second, she considered complaining to him about Geary, telling him that pervert had no business weighing in on anything to do with women, but Beverly had confided to her that Talbert had his eye on a dean's position. He wanted no boat-rocking that might make him look bad. She was on her own.

She gave a cursory nod, but he had already returned his attention to whatever he was working on. She backed out of his office. In the hall, Geary was thankfully nowhere to be seen. She pushed through the door into the stairwell and, a moment later, escaped into an overcast afternoon.

She stormed back to the boarding house, mumbling to herself the entire way. In the stairwell, she paused and listened. No sounds of Vanessa in their room. She seemed to have decided that Ryn was going to be the big sister she'd never had. Between her here and Geary at the office, Ryn was running out of places she could get work done and have some peace and quiet.

She quickly changed into jeans, sneaks, and a T-shirt. She repacked her backpack with a few other books and a notebook, stuffing in a sweatshirt in anticipation of the coolness of the evening, and walked back downtown.

Hidden on a side street with little foot traffic, she'd found a small sandwich shop that served hoagies and pizza. A few tables arranged in a back corner provided a relatively quiet place to eat and work. She wolfed down a tuna hoagie and began outlining the lecture sequence for her course. She'd show Talbert—and Geary—that there was more than enough material on women to fill five courses.

~

THE CHECK FROM THE art gallery sat propped against the salt and pepper shakers on the table. Henrietta knew she should get it to the bank soon, but she wanted to savor it for a few days first. Her parents had left her well off—a house built just for her needs, sizeable life insurance policies that had taken care of her after they passed, along with the proceeds from the sale of her father's construction business. But it was nice to think she could earn some money herself. It wasn't enough to live on, and she had no crazy desire to be a starving artist, but still, this was money she'd earned through her own work.

She finished the last portion of leftover soup that Bonnie had made for her and transferred her dishes—first her bowl, then her glass—to the sink to wash them.

Daylight was fading a little earlier each evening. In the living room, she turned the lamp on after drawing the curtains at the picture window. All the little things she had to do for herself now without a companion in the house. Little, but they still cost energy. Every extra step, every extra task—it all added up to being so tired she couldn't muster the enthusiasm to paint the past few days.

She had spent most of the afternoon staring out her studio windows at the woods and the pond below. Maybe tomorrow she'd take a sketchpad down there. If she got several sketches done, she would have enough material for paintings to carry her through the winter when the path was too snowy and icy to navigate safely.

She clicked on the television—she'd been the first of her friends to have one with a remote control. It was so nice to be able to click through the channels from the sofa without having to stand at the set and rotate the dial manually. She found the evening news and got her legs situated on the towel she kept there to protect the upholstery from her shoes before settling back on her pillow.

Before Dan Rather signed off, she was asleep. She was startled awake by the hiss of the TV as CBS went off the air for the night. She struggled to sit up, annoyed with herself for falling so deeply asleep. It was tempting to just stay where she was, but she knew, if she didn't get her braces off for at least a few hours, she'd end up with skin breakdown. Her last trip to the hospital for skin issues had turned into a six-week stay before they could get the sores on her back to heal sufficiently for her to be able to wear her braces again. That was five years ago, and she felt she was still trying to come back from that episode in terms of her strength and stamina.

Half an hour later, she lay back in bed, unfettered for the night. Again, as soon as she lay down, sleep seemed to elude her. She mentally ticked through her nightly checklist: stove off; doors and windows locked; lamps off; front and back porch lights on.

The panic wasn't as frequent now as it had been when Amanda first left. Night noises seemed more normal, and her friends knew to check on her each morning if they didn't hear from her.

But just the knowledge that she couldn't get out of the house quickly once her braces were off—it was almost as bad as the iron lung had been.

Against her will, images came to her, things she tried desperately not to remember. Fevered memories of being whisked to a hospital, wanting to talk to Una, but not being able to breathe. Row upon row of the huge tanks in the ward, only heads visible as each patient lay there, completely dependent upon the machines to keep air moving in and out, in and out. Working down the ward, the nurses wheeled curtained panels into position around each of the machines to screen them as they rotated the lung to change diapers or bedpans and bathe what parts they could. Occasionally, crying family members gathered, and the panels would be positioned again as the lung was turned off to "let nature take its course" if the doctors had deemed that the patient would not regain the ability to breathe independently.

Polio.

That one word invoked terror every summer. People disappeared—children mostly—and people whispered the word, as if saying it aloud might invite it to visit their house.

Then, after emerging—emaciated and wasted—from the iron lung, months and months of painful, tortuous rehabilitation.

31

Henrietta pressed her hands to her face, trying to calm her racing heart.

"It's over," she whispered. "Forget it. I can walk. I can breathe. I survived."

Chapter 3

SUNLIGHT BROKE THROUGH THE clouds and pierced a gap in the curtains. Ryn opened one eye. Across the room, Vanessa was buried somewhere under a heap of sheets and blankets. All Ryn could make out was a tangle of blonde curls and Roo. She rolled over and stretched. Wednesdays were her only day with no classes. She'd dutifully spent the first few Wednesdays of the semester in her office in case students came by, but after the confrontation with Geary two days ago, she had no desire to spend more time there than she had to.

She slipped out of bed and quickly changed clothes. She needn't have been so quiet; Vanessa slept like the dead. But Ryn didn't want to take a chance on a tag-along. She packed her backpack with a fun book—not a textbook—and enough layers to get her through into the evening, along with her wallet and car keys. She slung the straps over her shoulders and, at the last minute, reached for her guitar. Holding her breath as the door creaked open, she made her getaway.

Downstairs, only Mrs. Middleston was up as she left her backpack and guitar in the foyer long enough to pack some food and eat a quick bowl of cereal in the kitchen.

"Where are you off to?" Mrs. Middleston asked.

"Not sure." Ryn spooned up some Cheerios. "Just want to get away for the day. Are there any lakes or rivers near here?"

"No lakes unless you go to the Finger Lakes, but there's Jordan's Pond."

Ryn jotted down the directions Mrs. Middleston gave her, made a peanut butter and jelly sandwich wrapped in wax paper, and poured a Thermos of hot water from the kettle on the stove.

Nelly almost trembled with excitement as Ryn loaded her up and turned the ignition. With a pat on her dashboard, Ryn pulled away from the curb.

The sun came and went from behind the clouds as she followed Mrs. Middleston's directions. They took her out of the village and onto an unnamed dirt track that she passed once, having to turn around and retrace her path. Nelly bumped and bounced over the ruts and humps in the dirt road until they came to a dense stand of trees surrounding a pond. Ryn parked in the grass on the side of the lane and whistled.

"Looks like something Thoreau would have loved."

Huge willows grew along the banks, their roots loving the water, their delicate weeping branches sweeping the pond with each breath of wind. Birches also grew in abundance, their white bark gleaming when the sunlight struck it. Other trees—mostly oaks and maples—populated the area around the pond. The pond itself was quite large—apparently large enough to row on, as there was an old kind of pier with a dilapidated rowboat tied to it. It looked as if there was a faint path meandering down a hill on the far side of the water where a small flock of ducks paddled around.

With another pat to Nelly's roof, Ryn gathered her backpack and guitar and set out around the bank, making her way toward the dock.

Mists rose off the water as the sun warmed the morning. Bugs hovered there, and every now and again, a splash broke the stillness of the water's surface as fish rose to take them. Birds flashed down, snatching more bugs. Leaves fell from some of the overhanging trees, spinning acrobatically as they descended to land softly on the glassy surface of the pond.

She sat cross-legged on the weathered gray boards and dug her Thermos and a teabag out of her backpack. While her tea steeped, she wrapped her arms around her knees, listening to... nothing. Except it wasn't nothing. What seemed like silence at first, with no voices and no traffic, was full of sound. Birds called, and bug wings whirred near her, and turtles crawled out onto rocks to sun themselves. Somewhere in the weeds, frogs croaked, and the ducks quacked in reply.

She sipped her tea and breathed it in.

The air warmed, and she peeled her sweatshirt off. Reaching for her book, she lay back, using her sweatshirt as a pillow, and read, *Six of One*, one of her favorites. Her eyes soon drooped, and her book fell to her chest as she dozed off.

The sun was higher when she woke. She sat up, startling a turtle who had crawled onto the dock to share it with her. It dropped into the water with a plop. She stretched and tucked her book into her backpack.

"I am not going to waste the day sleeping."

She opened her guitar case and cradled the guitar in her lap. The vibration of the strings seemed to echo into the morning. Turtle heads turned in her direction. The ducks paddled nearer, quacking softly as she sang.

She played her way through several of her favorite songs—Joan Baez, Peter, Paul & Mary, John Denver, Cris Williamson, Meg Christian.

While she played, the rowboat bobbed in the gentle waves created by the ducks as they paddled by. She tilted her head, considering.

"What's the worst that can happen? I can swim."

She put her guitar back in its case and went to the end of the dock. Squatting down, she reached for the rope anchoring the rowboat to the piling. Some murky rainwater sloshed around in the bottom when she pulled it alongside the dock. She rocked it to and fro. The boat seemed sturdy enough. Gingerly, she reached one foot down onto the seat, waiting to see if the boat would begin to sink. When it didn't, she stepped in with her other foot. Under the seat was an old rusty coffee can. She used it to scoop the rainwater out of the bottom and then untied the boat from the post. Giving it a shove, she slipped the oars into the locks and rowed out into the middle of the pond.

"This is harder than it looks," she muttered when her oars skipped too close to the surface or dug too deeply, spinning her in erratic circles.

Before long, she got the hang of it, and struck out across the water. She followed the circumference of the pond, rowing in and out of shade thrown across the water by the surrounding trees. More turtles slipped off half-submerged logs and rocks, taking refuge under the surface of the water as she rowed by.

She laughed. "This was just what I needed. Screw you, Bradley Geary."

~

"DO YOU HEAR MUSIC?"

Henrietta suspended her bill paying as Bonnie emerged from the unused guest rooms with her duster. They both paused, listening. Bonnie had insisted on opening all of the windows that morning.

"It's a glorious day, and it's past time this house was aired out!" she'd declared before throwing the sashes open.

They both listened now, but Bonnie shook her head.

"I don't hear anything."

"I don't now, but I could have sworn..."

Henrietta finished the last of the bills and got to her feet. She found Bonnie cleaning the bathroom. "I think I'm going to pack up a sketchpad and go down to the pond."

Bonnie straightened. "Really? I can't remember the last time you went down there. That's a wonderful idea. Let me make you a sandwich real quick."

She waved off Henrietta's protests and packed a ham and cheese sandwich, along with a bottle of water, putting them with a sketchpad and pencil case into a canvas bag with a long strap that Henrietta could drape over one shoulder and carry down the path.

"You sure you don't want me to take this down for you?" Bonnie fussed, rearranging the bag so it hung on Henrietta's back where it wouldn't interfere with her crutches.

"No. I'm fine. Thank you, Bonnie."

"Well, you have a good time. Just holler if you need me. I'll keep an ear peeled."

She opened the sliding glass door to allow Henrietta to step out onto the rear patio and closed the screen behind her.

Henrietta walked to the far edge of the stone patio and hesitated. She couldn't remember the last time she'd been down this path. Bud, the yardman, was supposed to keep it clear and raked, but she had no idea if he did. She glanced back once to see if Bonnie was still there. She waved from behind the screen. Feeling foolish—like a girl afraid to ride her bike without training wheels—Henrietta set off.

The flagstones were mostly clear of debris. A few small sticks and early fallen leaves littered the path, but nothing that barred her way. The downhill angle and hairpin turns built into the path to lessen the severity of the slope slowed her progress, but the pond drew closer as she descended the hill. Halfway down, she heard it again. Singing.

Curious now, she waited for the trees to thin as she got closer to the small landing that had been built along the bank of the pond. A couple of covered lawn chairs sat where they always were. Henrietta's property extended all the way down to the water, and she didn't relish trespassers. Few people knew about the pond, and even fewer actually came out this far.

That old boat—no one really knew who had put it there—was in the middle of the pond, being rowed by... was that the same young woman who had helped her the day she dropped her groceries? She sang as she rowed, some song Henrietta had never heard. Her voice was clear and pleasant to listen to, if not well-trained.

The boat skimmed along in a lazy circle, powered by the girl's pulls on the oars, until she came around to where Henrietta was standing.

"Oh." The girl stopped singing when she saw Henrietta. Her face turned bright pink. "Sorry if I was disturbing you."

She glanced up the hill. "I didn't realize... We're below your house."

"Yes." Henrietta didn't know whether to be amused or annoyed at finally getting down here to find she wasn't alone. Her eye was caught by a flicker of movement on the seat next to the girl. She tilted her head. "Friend of yours?"

"Sorry?" The young woman looked around.

Henrietta pointed with one crutch to where a slender black snake with yellow stripes running along its length lay coiled on the wooden boat seat.

In an explosion of sound and movement, the girl yelled and lurched sideways, the boat rocked violently, and the snake went flying into the water just before the girl went overboard.

Through tears of laughter, Henrietta watched the snake swim gracefully across the pond's surface while the young woman sputtered and coughed, cussing when she could finally speak.

She grabbed the boat's rope and waded ashore, dragging it behind her. She crawled up onto the landing where Henrietta stood, propped on her crutches, still laughing. She hauled the boat halfway out of the water and tied the rope to a tree before collapsing on her back.

"Scared the shit out of me," she gasped.

"Probably scared the shit out of the snake, too," Henrietta agreed, reaching up to wipe her eyes. "It was just a ribbon snake. They eat frogs and small fish, so there are lots of them around the pond. Yours was probably already in the boat when you kidnapped it."

The girl sat up and looked at her soaking wet clothing. "I just washed these."

She got to her feet, still breathing hard. She bent over and braced her hands on her knees. "I'll get out of your way, just give me a minute."

When her breathing slowed, she straightened.

Watching her fumble with the rope to untie the boat, Henrietta considered. "You did come to my rescue the day I dropped all of my food. The least I can do is return the favor. Come up to the house. We can wash and dry your clothes."

The girl gazed across the pond. "My stuff is all just sitting there."

"I doubt anyone will bother it. No one comes here." Henrietta waited a beat. "Normally."

The girl grinned. "Leave it to me to be abnormal. I'm Ryn. Meryn Fleming, but I go by Ryn."

Henrietta turned to make her laborious way back up the path. "I'm Henrietta Cochran. No more talking from me until we're back at the house."

"At least let me carry your bag."

Henrietta paused. It grated on her to let anyone else think she needed help, but she hadn't been off her feet since beginning the trek down to the pond. She grudgingly agreed, taking it off her shoulder to hand over.

The pencil case rattled when Meryn slung the bag over her shoulder. "What were you down there for?" When Henrietta glared at her, she said, "Sorry, I forgot. No talking."

Even without the extra weight, Henrietta was panting by the time they got back to the house.

"What happened? I thought you'd be sketching for a couple of hours. Why are you back so soon?" Bonnie peppered Henrietta with questions before she even got the screen door opened. She pulled up short. "And who do we have here?"

Meryn stared hard at her. "Have we met?"

Bonnie looked from one to the other. "I don't believe so. Though I imagine if we had, you probably looked a bit different."

Meryn glanced down at herself, bedraggled and wet, and grinned. "I suppose so. It's weird though. You look so familiar." She introduced herself and held out a damp hand.

"I'm Bonnie Chambers," Bonnie said, taking her hand gingerly.

Henrietta stepped inside and made her way to the kitchen where she lowered herself into her chair with an exhausted sigh.

"Would you mind washing her clothes for her, Bonnie? She can shower and wear a robe from the guest room."

Bonnie gaped for a moment as if she wasn't sure she'd heard correctly. "Of course, Miss Cochran."

~

BONNIE FUSSED, FORCING A cup of hot tea into Ryn's hands as she sat at the kitchen table with Henrietta Cochran.

"Catch your death of cold," she muttered, laying out a plate of shortbread for the both of them while she made sandwiches.

Ryn tried to point out that it wasn't a chilly day and she'd had a hot shower, but Bonnie glowered at Henrietta.

"That pond should have been drained and filled in ages ago," she said, slapping two plates on the table, each with a ham and cheese sandwich. Her nostrils flared and her mouth opened as if she was dying to say more, but she changed her mind, huffing and muttering and banging pans as she started a pot of soup.

She was a little woman, but she sure made a lot of noise. She got out a cutting board and bags of potatoes and carrots.

Bewildered, Ryn took a bite of her sandwich and glanced from Bonnie to Henrietta, but the only sign that Henrietta had made sense of Bonnie's cryptic statement was a slight tightening of her lips.

Ryn, wrapped in a thick terrycloth bathrobe, sat back with her tea. It was kind of nice, almost like being back home. The instant the thought came, she was hit by a pang of homesickness. This—the fussing, the clucking—this was exactly what her mom would have done.

Had done, Ryn remembered. When she and her best friend Rebecca were nine, they'd fallen off an old log that stretched over the creek behind the Fleming house, and Rebecca was panicked because her hysterical mother would have a fit over Rebecca's wet clothes. Ryn's mom had calmly plopped them both into a hot tub and then sat them down with cups of hot cocoa, wrapped in thick fluffy bath towels while she washed Rebecca's clothes.

"Dear?"

Ryn started, realizing she'd been smiling into her tea and not listening. "Sorry?"

"I said, are you a student at the college?" Bonnie asked from the stove where she was chopping up potatoes to drop into the pot.

"No. I'm a teacher. New this year. In the history department."

"You're the one!" Bonnie exclaimed.

Ryn's eyes widened. Henrietta looked just as startled.

"I'm the one what?" Ryn asked.

"You're the one my sister told me about. Beverly," Bonnie added when Ryn simply stared.

"Beverly DiSorbo is your sister?" Ryn laughed. "That's why you looked so familiar to me."

"She said you're trying to shake up that department."

Ryn wasn't sure if that was a compliment or not. Bonnie must have read her mind, because she quickly said, "In a good way."

Ryn combed her fingers through her damp hair. "Well, it's not easy. The men there have been doing the same thing forever. They don't see any need to change."

Henrietta, who had been eating her sandwich but saying nothing, now asked, "You're working for Jerry Talbert?"

"Yes," Ryn said. "You know him?"

"Oh, yes. Jerry and his wife are club members. We play bridge occasionally."

Ryn quickly replayed anything she might have said that could be misconstrued as an insult to Talbert.

Henrietta studied her. "What have you been shaking up?"

"Well," Ryn felt she was walking on delicate ground. "The department teaches history—and I mean every single course—purely from the perspective of men. There's not one single offering that focuses on women. I minored in women's studies in my undergrad degree, and I was able to include an emphasis on women's history in my masters. I'm trying to get Dr. Talbert to approve a course on the history of American women. If we can start there, maybe I can get him to sign off on others. European women—in art, politics, music— we could do ten courses there alone. Africa and Asia. There's so much. We could create an entire major focusing only on women's history."

Ryn realized she was getting carried away. She stopped and sipped her tea.

"And he's not willing?" Henrietta asked.

"He and Geary—that's Bradley Geary, the other history faculty— don't think there's enough interesting material for a semester's course, but there's more than enough."

From the stove, Bonnie harrumphed.

Henrietta shifted in her seat. "What?"

"That one, Geary. Beverly's told me about him." Bonnie's chopping of the carrots became more staccato. "He's deflowered more than one poor girl."

Henrietta turned back to Ryn, who was trying not to laugh at the old-fashioned term. "Is this true?"

Ryn shrugged. "I'm brand new, so I can't say for sure. But from what he's been trying with me, I can believe it."

Bonnie abandoned the carrots for a moment, brandishing her knife. "And what's he tried with you?"

"Nothing I can't handle," Ryn said quickly. "Keeps asking me out, trapping me in my office. That kind of thing. But Beverly keeps an eye out for me as much as she can."

Bonnie huffed again, scraping the carrots into the pot.

Ryn changed the subject. "Bonnie said you went down to the pond to sketch, Miss Cochran—sorry I interrupted that, by the way. Are you an artist?"

"Is she an artist?" Bonnie spoke up before Henrietta could reply. "You walked past her work. And it's in galleries all over the state!"

"Bonnie," Henrietta said.

Ryn glanced out into the living room where she now noticed several framed paintings on the walls. "May I?"

Henrietta nodded. Ryn padded out to the living room, moving from one painting to the next, mostly landscapes—views from this house: the woods, the pond, the golf course. She recognized a few renderings of the village square with its statue and storefronts. Hanging over the piano in the corner was a landscape of a lake Ryn didn't recognize. She knew next to nothing about art, but she liked these.

"You're really good," she said, going back into the kitchen. A distant beep signaled the end of the dryer cycle.

"That'll be your clothes," Bonnie said. She disappeared and came back into the kitchen a moment later, flapping Ryn's jeans and T-shirt to shake the wrinkles out. "I could iron these."

Ryn cracked up laughing at the thought of ironing jeans. "These are already way better than they usually look after the dryers at the Laundromat."

Henrietta looked up at her. "Where are you living?"

"Mrs. Middleston's. Do you know her?"

Henrietta and Bonnie shared a knowing glance.

"We know her," Bonnie said, still eyeing Henrietta.

"You get dressed," Henrietta said. "I'll drive you to your car."

Not sure what that reaction was about, Ryn accepted her clothes from Bonnie. "You don't have to drive me. I can row to that dock."

"Yes," Henrietta said wryly. "Your slithery friend would probably appreciate a ride back."

Ryn rolled her eyes. "If that snake is waiting for me to row it home, then it's a darn lazy snake. It's probably hiding at the dock, waiting for me to bring its boat back."

She went into the bathroom to change, leaving her robe on the hook behind the door. When she returned to the kitchen, Bonnie was pulling wadded-up newspaper from her sneakers.

"These are still damp, I'm afraid."

"No problem." Ryn sat down to lace her high-tops up. "Thanks so much, Bonnie. It was great meeting you."

"You, too. I'll be sure to tell Beverly we met."

Henrietta and Bonnie led the way to the back of the house. This time, Ryn noticed the art studio and let out a low whistle.

"Wow. You really are set up nicely here. That view is something."

"We like it."

Bonnie tutted. "Like it. Miss Cochran pretty much lives in here, creating her art."

Ryn slid the screen door open. "Well, it was nice to meet you. Again." She plucked at her T-shirt, now smelling of Downy. "Thanks again."

She gave a wave and trotted down the path to the pond where the boat was waiting—and empty of any uninvited stowaways. She pushed it into the water and hopped in to row back to the dock where her guitar and backpack were just where she'd left them. She slung the pack over her shoulder and reached for her guitar. Straightening, she peered through the trees in the direction of Henrietta's house. Not sure if they could see her or not, she gave one last wave.

～

UP AT THE HOUSE, Bonnie and Henrietta watched Meryn's progress.

"Are you thinking what I'm thinking?" Bonnie asked.

"I doubt it."

"Don't you take that 'I don't know what you're talking about' tone with me. You know perfectly well, she could be the answer to your prayers."

Henrietta scoffed. "That's a bit dramatic. She's like a human tornado. She would drive me crazy."

"Hmmm." Bonnie pulled a cloth from her pocket and dusted as she moved around the studio. "Or she might blow some fresh air into this place."

Chapter 4

THURSDAY MORNING, AS DID most Thursday mornings, found Henrietta playing bridge at the country club. Bridge was serious business among this crowd, and conversation tended to be sporadic and light, usually of the gossip variety, something all ears could be attuned to without distracting from the game.

When the cards were cleared away to make room for luncheon, Henrietta carefully maneuvered to sit next to Genevieve Talbert.

Genevieve, in the midst of lighting a cigarette, looked displeased at the seating arrangement, and extinguished the flame on her silver lighter, slipping the unlit cigarette back into the matching case. It was an unspoken courtesy that no one at Henrietta's table smoked due to her delicate lungs. Henrietta suspected it was spoken of plenty when she wasn't about, and the smoke from neighboring tables still bothered her, but one could only expect so much.

"I hear Jerry hired a new professor," Henrietta said conversationally as their waitress served her an iced tea and Genevieve a gin and tonic.

Genevieve took a sip of her drink before replying. "How did you hear that?"

"My housekeeper is sister to Jerry's secretary."

"Oh, yes. I forgot. Yes. He had a hard time finding anyone qualified and this girl's advisor—where was it? Philadelphia, I think. Anyway, the advisor is an old friend of Jerry's, so he put in a call to Jerry and recommended her. Said she's working out all right but, like all the young ones brandishing their new degrees, they think they know everything. He'll get her in line. Or she'll leave. One or the other."

Henrietta waited until the salad plates had been passed out. "But surely, if she's good, he'll want to hang onto her."

Genevieve shrugged. "I don't think he really cares. Word is..." She looked around, but everyone else was busily chatting. She leaned near and whispered, "Jerry is expecting to be promoted to dean next year, so staffing the history department will be Bradley Geary's worry."

Naturally, as soon as her voice dropped to a sibilant tone, all the other women were immediately listening.

Henrietta frowned. "Bradley Geary would become chair? Automatically? Wouldn't they do a search?"

Genevieve took another drink. "I doubt it. And who cares, really? It's just history."

She deliberately turned to speak to the woman on her other side, leaving Henrietta to eat her salad. From the little Henrietta knew from Bonnie, if Jerry moved up and this Geary fellow became chair, Meryn Fleming would most likely not be sticking around.

If Henrietta decided to ask the girl if she was interested in becoming her companion, it looked as if this might be another short-term situation. Still, it had been nearly a month since Amanda had left. She really needed someone and soon.

An hour later, she made her way out to her car—driven up to the clubhouse for her by the club manager, as the parking lot was some distance away—and drove into the village. She pulled up in front of a familiar Victorian and parked behind a small station wagon whose back end was plastered in bumper stickers: *Pass the ERA, Re-Elect Carter, Young Democrats.* There were Goddess stickers and one with a pink triangle, another with a two-bladed axe. Henrietta had no idea what those meant, but she had a feeling her country club friends would frown if they saw them.

"Dear God," Henrietta muttered. She'd only caught a glimpse of an outline of a car among the shadows yesterday at the pond but, somehow, she was certain this was Meryn Fleming's car.

For a moment, she considered simply driving home. But there was something so genuine about that young woman. Her open face, her easy laugh—including at herself—her kindness. Even if she was rather... radical.

Henrietta clambered out of her car and made her way up the walk to the porch steps. As she stood there, pondering how to climb them, Sally Middleston emerged from the front door.

"Henrietta."

"Hello, Sally."

"What brings you here?" Mrs. Middleston flipped her dishtowel over her shoulder and stared down at Henrietta.

Henrietta had wondered if Sally would make this hard or easy. Apparently, she was opting for hard.

"I wanted to speak with you about one of your renters, Meryn Fleming."

"What about her?"

"You may have heard, but my companion left to take care of her grandmother. I'm in need of someone else to live-in. I've met Miss Fleming and am considering her as a candidate. But I wanted to ask you for a reference." Henrietta ground her teeth for a moment. "And, if satisfactory, ask your permission to offer her a position. I realize this could inconvenience you if you lose a boarder."

Sally Middleston planted her fists on her hips. "Since when have you cared if you inconvenienced anyone? Always thought the world revolved around you just because of those braces and crutches. You and your parents. Well, it doesn't. My Gilbert was a good man. Your father had no cause to fire him."

Henrietta's hands clenched on the handles of her crutches, but this did not seem to be the time to argue that Gilbert Middleston had been fired after being found drunk on the job, not once, but five times. And that he had drunk himself into an early grave.

"I'm sorry you feel that way, Sally." Henrietta struggled to keep her voice even. "Of course, the girl is neither your prisoner nor your property. I'm here as a courtesy. If she and I come to an agreement, naturally, she'll give you proper notice. Thank you for your time."

Henrietta turned to make her way back to her station wagon. From behind her, Sally called, "Don't think I won't warn her what she'll be getting into!"

In the car, Henrietta started the ignition, wondering if all of those bumper stickers reflected the independent thinker she hoped Meryn Fleming really was.

WHEN RYN DISMISSED CLASS, a small knot of students lingered, waiting for her to gather her books and notes. This little gang of five—three women and two men—had become their own history club, wanting to engage more deeply. They also gave Ryn extra protection from Geary, a fact she gave silent thanks for when they accompanied her to her office and she saw Geary there, prepared to ambush her. He turned on his heel and stalked away as she retrieved her backpack and locked her office, arguing with them about what might have happened to North America's course if the Iroquois had allied with the French rather than the Dutch and British.

The day was chilly but clear, a gorgeous autumn day. Across campus, the bells rang at the chapel, signaling the daily noon Mass. Ryn excused herself, leaving them to continue the argument, while she made her way through the quad to the chapel. She'd promised her mom she'd attend Mass weekly. She figured Friday was as good as Sunday.

The chapel was simple and small, built to hold maybe a hundred people arranged in an intimate circle around a central altar. She took a seat in a middle row, joining about a dozen others. She saw a few familiar faces, including three of the young nuns she'd seen around campus. She wasn't certain if they were students or faculty, but they always nodded hello when she happened to meet them.

Ryn didn't think of herself as a religious person, and the male dominance of most churches—especially the Catholic church—drove her crazy. But there were times when she felt something bigger and kinder wrapping around her like wings, protecting her. That was what she prayed to—funny how it always took a feminine form.

Not funny at all, she realized as she gazed at the stained glass windows. Her comfort had always come from women.

When Mass was over, she was starving. She sat on the granite steps of Rayburn Hall, enjoying the sun while she ate a peanut butter and banana sandwich. She had one lecture that afternoon—the last one before the first exam in that class, so she was fairly certain the students would all be there, hoping for any last minute hints as to what she'd be testing them on. The sandwich was good, but she needed something to wash it down with. She folded and stuffed her wax paper back into her backpack and zipped it shut.

Upstairs, she found Beverly at her desk. Talbert's office was dark. Dangling a couple of teabags, she went in and set her pack on the floor.

"Ready for some tea?"

"Of course." Beverly had her kettle warming on her hot plate and poured two mugs of water for them. "Sit down, Meryn. I need to speak with you."

"Okay." Ryn took a chair opposite Beverly's desk. "Am I in trouble?"
Beverly's mouth twitched. "Perhaps. But not the way you mean."

"In what way, then?"

Beverly didn't answer immediately, allowing the suspense to build as she let her teabag steep for precisely four minutes—Ryn had started counting.

"I understand you met my sister."

"Bonnie. Yes. She and Miss Cochran helped me out after I fell into that pond below the house."

"Did they say anything to you about Miss Cochran's situation?"

Ryn thought for a moment. "I know she's an artist, and she obviously has leg braces and crutches, but..." She raised her mug to drink, feeling she was better off letting Beverly fill in the gaps.

"Miss Cochran had polio when she was a girl. Since her parents passed—I think her mother died nearly eight years ago—she has needed a live-in companion. Someone to be there at night, in case something happens, maybe do some light cooking—although my sister always makes a big batch of some dish to provide leftovers when she's there on Wednesdays—maybe some light chores. In return, Miss Cochran offers a private room and bath at no charge."

Ryn choked on her tea. "No rent?" She frowned. "That sounds too good to be true. What's the catch? Why doesn't she have a waiting list of people?"

Again, Beverly didn't reply immediately. She delicately took a sip of tea and cleared her throat. "Miss Cochran is... particular. Obviously, she has to be cautious about whom she invites to live in her house. And she can be... difficult."

"Difficult."

Beverly met her gaze through her glasses, and Ryn was struck again by the similarity between the sisters. "Miss Cochran is not the easiest person in the world to get on with. Bonnie has been with her longer than anyone. Companions have tended to leave after a few months, which begins the process all over again."

52

Beverly set her mug down. "I don't wish to speak ill of anyone, but you need to know what you'd be in for."

"In for." Ryn felt like a parrot, repeating Beverly's words again as she tried to see where this was leading.

"Miss Cochran has decided that she would like to speak with you about this position. I've been asked to pass along a message that she is inviting you to have lunch with her to discuss it. Tomorrow, if you're available."

Ryn slumped back against her chair. "Wow. Really?" She raised her mug and drank. "Sure. I'll have lunch with her. What's the worst that can happen?"

~

HENRIETTA MADE ONE LAST tour of the guest wing of the house—the part that used to be her parents' until their deaths—to make sure everything was in order. The two twin beds were freshly made, and the bathroom was clean and neat. Bonnie had seen to it on Wednesday as she always did, but after Meryn's unexpected visit, she had given the rooms a little extra polish. Henrietta smiled at the artistic arrangement of pillows and towels. Bonnie wasn't exactly subtle.

Out in the kitchen, the table was laid with two place settings of the nicer china. Henrietta couldn't recall the last time she'd used it. She tended to use the Corelle dishes for everyday. They were more forgiving when dropped.

She heard a knock at the back door. "Coming," she called.

Outside, a boy from the club held a large hamper.

"Come in," she said, stepping back. "Just there, in the kitchen."

"Yes, ma'am."

He set the hamper on the counter and reached inside to lay out containers of food. He handed her a chit for her signature. "Is that everything, Miss Cochran?"

"Yes," she said, scribbling her signature and handing it back to him. She lifted the corners of each container. "This is perfect. Thank the chef for me."

"Yes, ma'am." He reached for the hamper.

"Wait a minute. Let me have that chit again."

He looked on anxiously as he handed the slip of paper back to her. His face lit up when he saw that she'd added a ten-dollar tip.

"Thank you for bringing it all the way here."

His freckled face split into a wide smile. "Yes, ma'am! Any time, Miss Cochran."

He grabbed the hamper and let himself out the back door to trot down the drive and across the road to the club's long entry.

Not sure what Meryn might like, Henrietta had ordered a variety: chicken salad, fruit salad, steamed shrimp, turkey, ham. The chef had included fresh rolls to make sandwiches, or they could just dish it out onto plates and eat it that way.

She exhaled. "Why am I so nervous? You'd think I'm the one being interviewed."

But she was. She now had to accept that she was on the receiving end of this arrangement, which put her in an unfamiliar—and undesirable—position. If Meryn didn't like her, didn't feel welcome, didn't choose to take her up on her offer, she wasn't sure where to turn next.

When the battered station wagon with the radical bumper stickers pulled into the drive, she couldn't help but smile. She noticed Meryn was wearing slacks and a dress shirt rather than the shorts or jeans she'd worn on their previous encounters—even if they were unplanned.

So, she put some effort into this as well.

For some reason, that made Henrietta feel a little better. When Meryn hesitated in the driveway, uncertain which door to knock on, Henrietta opened the back door to call to her.

"Thank you for inviting me," Meryn said.

"Thank you for coming."

54

Henrietta led the way into the kitchen. "I didn't know what you like to eat, so I arranged for a few different things."

Meryn's eyebrows raised when she saw the table. "I've been living off peanut butter and Cheerios. This is a feast. Thank you." She picked up the two empty glasses. "May I pour us something to drink?"

"There's a pitcher of iced tea and another of cold water. Or milk if you prefer. I'd like iced tea."

Henrietta sat while Meryn poured iced tea for both of them. Meryn joined her at the table, taking her cues from Henrietta, waiting for her to spoon some chicken salad onto her plate before helping herself to some of the fruit and a few shrimp. They passed the serving dishes back and forth.

"This is really good," Meryn said. "Did Bonnie make this?" She immediately blushed. "Sorry, I didn't mean to assume you didn't..."

Henrietta chucked. "I can mix a can of tuna or make a sandwich, but I can't stand long enough to do all this. I ordered it from the country club." She shrugged. "I have to use up my quarterly food minimum there anyhow, so this wasn't an inconvenience."

She eyed Meryn, noticing her manners—napkin on lap, no elbows on the table, no unnecessary clatter of silverware against the plate—those little things that could drive her crazy on a daily basis.

"How old are you?"

Meryn, caught chewing some chicken salad, swallowed and dabbed her mouth with her napkin before saying, "Twenty-three."

Henrietta paused with her fork halfway to her mouth. "Twenty-three. I thought you were an instructor at St. Aloysius."

"I am. I graduated with my master's in May."

"How can you have finished your bachelor's and master's at such a young age?"

Meryn grinned. "Well, I'm not any kind of prodigy if that's what you're thinking. When I enrolled at Pitt—the University of Pittsburgh—they had a minimum number of hours you had to maintain to be a full-time student." She leaned forward and dropped her voice conspiratorially. "But they didn't have a max. I figured I could get more for my money if I took more classes. So, I enrolled for between twenty-one and twenty-four credits every semester, plus summers. I finished my undergrad degree in two and a half years, and went straight to grad school."

She held up both hands. "And here I am."

She sat back and picked up her tea. "But why am I here?"

Henrietta reappraised her in light of this new information. "Because I require live-in help, which I have been without since the end of August." She tilted her head. "Did Beverly tell you anything about the position?"

Meryn set her glass down and picked up a roll. As she buttered it, she said, "Yes. A bit. She said you need someone here at night. Maybe a little light cooking and chores."

Henrietta nodded.

"She also said you could be difficult."

Henrietta's bite of shrimp nearly flew across the table as she coughed. Meryn half-rose from her seat, but Henrietta waved her back down.

"Sorry to be so blunt, Miss Cochran," Meryn said when Henrietta's coughing stopped, "but I'm not good at beating around the bush."

Henrietta stalled by taking a drink. No one had ever talked to her like that. Maybe this wasn't such a good idea.

"I don't mind difficult," Meryn was saying. "It means you know what you want, and you like things to be done a certain way. That's how I got so much done so quickly. I understand that."

"Are you always so opinionated?" Henrietta rasped when she could speak again.

Meryn shrugged. "I'm afraid so. So, you're difficult and I'm an opinionated dyke."

Henrietta's mind whirled. What did a floodwall have to do with anything? "A what?"

"A lesbian." Meryn waited a moment to see what reaction this revelation would elicit.

Henrietta blinked at her.

"It means—"

"I know what it means!" Henrietta snapped. "I just never... Are you really?"

Meryn threw her head back and laughed. "I am. Really."

"And... do they know this? At the college?"

Meryn raised one shoulder in a careless shrug. "Probably not. It hasn't come up in conversation. But I won't hide, and I won't lie. If we're to live together, you might as well know what you're in for. And I'm very political. With next year's election, I will be getting involved. You'll probably have to put up with my griping about Reagan at least three times a week."

She did a double take at the look on Henrietta's face. "Don't tell me you voted for him."

Henrietta felt herself blushing. "All of my friends... You're living in a very conservative area."

Meryn popped a shrimp into her mouth. "I can see I'll have my work cut out for me."

Henrietta opened her mouth but then closed it. This was not going at all the way she'd planned. "So does that mean you accept my offer?"

"Does that mean the offer is still on the table?"

Henrietta paused to consider. This girl was unlike any other companion she'd ever had. If it didn't work out, they'd drive each other mad. But somehow, she had a feeling it might work out. She held out her hand.

Meryn smiled and shook it. "Now, I have to deal with Mrs. Middleston."

"Oh, yes." Henrietta sobered. "Sally Middleston does not like me."

Meryn snorted. "So I gathered. I got an earful this morning when I told her where I was going."

"She'll expect a month's notice. I'll pay your next month's rent so that the month will be covered as she advertises for another boarder."

Meryn looked as if she wanted to argue but then changed her mind. "That sounds fair. Thank you. When do you want me to move in?"

"Is tomorrow too soon?"

Meryn stared for a moment. "I can do that." She raised her glass. "To our new adventure, Miss Cochran."

"I think we can be on a first-name basis, don't you?"

Henrietta was as shocked as Meryn to hear those words issue from her mouth. She'd never been on a first-name basis with any of her help—not the companions, not Bonnie, not her yardman.

"That," she would say to herself much later when she thought about it, "should have told me then and there that this would not be like it had ever been before."

Chapter 5

RYN PLACED A LAST hanger in the closet and gave the shirt on it a tweak. An entire closet and dresser to herself. A large, airy room. A bathroom all her own. And no thumping music from three different stereos! The house was blissfully quiet.

Vanessa had been heartbroken when Ryn got back to the boarding house yesterday and began packing.

"What'll I do?" she'd pouted.

"Well, until you have another roommate," Ryn had said, stooping to gather up Pooh, Eeyore, Roo, Kanga, Owl, and Piglet, "your friends can have this bed, and you won't have to pick up the room every day."

Vanessa had thrown herself down on her bed, hugging Rabbit and Tigger. "This place will be awful without you."

Ryn sat down beside her. "This is a great school if you take advantage of everything it has to offer you. Maybe I'll take you to Syracuse one of these weekends."

Vanessa had brightened at that, impulsively hugging Ryn good-bye.

This morning, Ryn had made a point of seeking Mrs. Middleston out—finally finding her out back, hanging towels on the line—to thank her.

"You're making a mistake," Mrs. Middleston said with a dismissive sniff. "But you'll figure that out soon enough. When you do, don't expect I'll have an empty bed for you."

"Thanks anyhow," Ryn had said, trying to make a graceful exit. "I'll see you around. It's a small town."

When she'd arrived at the house, Henrietta was just pulling her station wagon—a Chrysler Town & Country—into the garage. She was wearing her typical skirt and blouse with a lightweight coat as she maneuvered her crutches into place.

"Good morning," Ryn said. "Is this an okay time?"

"It's fine," Henrietta said. "I'm just coming back from Mass at St. Rita's. Come in."

She left the garage door open for Ryn to follow her inside.

"You can bring your things in here or through the front door. And I have a key for you."

From the feel of the key—the smooth edges and the weight of the brass—it was old.

"When you're done, we can have lunch if you like. There's plenty left from yesterday."

Now, Ryn folded her empty duffle bag and placed it on the top shelf in the closet. With a last satisfied look around, she went to find Henrietta, who was standing at the fridge, transferring containers to the counter. She noticed that Henrietta had changed into a different skirt and blouse. She supposed slacks weren't practical with the leg braces. Maybe these were her equivalent of everyday clothes.

"I can do that," Ryn said, reaching for the refrigerator door.

"I'm not helpless."

Ryn pulled up short, uncertain if she'd managed to do something wrong before she'd even been here an hour. "I know you're not."

Henrietta glanced at her and then shuffled away. "If you'll pour tea and get plates down for us, I'll put these on the table."

Ryn had to open a couple of cupboards before she found the right one. Henrietta pushed the containers of food, one by one, along the counter until she could stand and move them to the table. Ryn had both glasses poured and the plates set before Henrietta finished with the last of the leftovers, but busied herself at the silverware drawer.

"This food really is good," Ryn said as they both helped themselves to portions from each container.

"The club's chef does a nice job," Henrietta agreed. "Is the room satisfactory?"

"It's great," Ryn said. "A room to myself. What a treat."

"You shared at Sally's?"

Ryn nodded. "A nice girl, but... And at home, I shared with my sister."

Henrietta spread some chicken salad on a roll. "Tell me about your family."

"I've got a sister two and a half years younger, and twin brothers in high school. My dad is an accountant and my mom's a stay-at-home mom, but I think she'd like to go back to work now that the boys are old enough."

"And you live in Pittsburgh?"

Ryn shook her head as she chewed. "Uniontown. My sister's attending West Virginia University now; it's closer to home, so she can drive back and forth. I stayed in Pittsburgh. There was more going on there."

"Politically, you mean?"

"Yes..." Ryn wondered how much to say. "And more social life."

"Oh."

Ryn hid a smile at the blush that colored Henrietta's cheeks. "How about you? Any siblings?"

"No. I was an only child. My father owned a construction business. In fact he built some of the buildings on campus. We had a big house in the village, but... after I got sick, stairs were difficult. He built this house in 1950, anticipating my needs."

With Henrietta's eyes lowered, focused on her plate, Ryn had a chance to study her. In their first couple of accidental meetings, Ryn hadn't realized how slightly built Henrietta was. Now, she noted the hollows in Henrietta's hands between thumb and forefingers, giving her hands a claw-like grasp; her dark hair, streaked liberally with silver, was cut short with severe, straight edges. Her eyes, when they weren't shuttered, were a steely gray. In fact the word "steel" seemed to apply to a great many things about Henrietta Cochran.

"How old are you, if you don't mind my asking?"

Henrietta raised her gaze. "I'm fifty-three."

"And how old were you when you got polio?"

Those gray eyes flashed for a second, and Ryn had the feeling she was stepping where few dared to go.

"Fifteen." Henrietta nudged a bowl. "Have the last shrimp."

Ryn decided it was a good time to follow Henrietta's lead and change the subject. "Would you like to go down to the pond after lunch?"

Henrietta met her eyes again. "The pond?"

"Yeah. My little adventure kind of got in the way of your sketching the last time. Would you like to go back? It's a nice day."

Henrietta swallowed a last bite as she thought about it. "That would be nice."

"I'll carry your stuff if you'd like. I can bring a book and read. You won't even know I'm there." Ryn paused in the midst of folding her napkin. "If you want company, that is. I don't mean to invite myself along. I can easily occupy myself up here."

"You're more than welcome. You could bring your guitar."

"Really? The noise wouldn't bother you?"

"I enjoy music."

"I noticed the piano in the living room. Do you play?"

"No. It was my mother's. It hasn't been played in years." Henrietta angled her head. "Do you play piano, too?"

"Not well, but yes."

Henrietta started to pick up her plate, but Ryn held out her hand to take it. "I can do the dishes quickly while you pack your sketching supplies."

For a moment, she wasn't sure Henrietta would let go, but she did. Ryn carried the dishes to the sink and ran some hot water while Henrietta went to the studio.

Ryn heaved a deep sigh as she washed the lunch dishes. Living with Henrietta Cochran was going to be like navigating a minefield.

～

THE SCENE ON THE canvas was taking shape—a view across the pond toward that old dock. It had been a long time since Henrietta had seen it or sketched it from the landing her father had built. And she hadn't been on that dock since... She closed her eyes.

Una's bright copper hair, catching the sunlight as they lay side by side, holding hands and talking...

"When the war is over, I'll probably have to go back to England."

"I don't want you to go," Henrietta said, *squeezing Una's hand.*

"And I don't want to. But my aunt says my mum will need me." Una *propped up on her elbow. "But don't let's think about that now."*

"No." Henrietta *stared up into Una's beautiful eyes that were the color of the sky. She wanted to stay like this forever.*

Una leaned over her, closer and closer, until their lips met—

Henrietta caught herself. Her eyes, when she opened them, were misted. She had to blink a few times to clear them. She touched a finger to her lips and realized her fingers were trembling.

This was ridiculous. She hadn't thought about that day—hadn't allowed herself to think about it—for years. Decades. There was no point in remembering. Or dreaming. But her dreams the last few nights had been filled with memories of Una.

It was this girl, this Meryn, with her boldness, her laughter, her defiance of the rules Henrietta had lived by her entire life, stirring things up in unwelcome ways. She glanced at the clock.

If it's so unwelcome, why are you waiting for her to come home?

Frowning, she reached for her sketchbook, flipping through the pages from Sunday. She'd gotten the views she wanted of the pond, the trees, the house up on its hill—but there were also quick sketches of Meryn: sitting with her guitar in her lap; leaning over to poke a stick into the weeds at the water's edge; lying nose to nose with a turtle.

It had only been a few days, but it felt as if things in this house had been turned upside-down, or—what was it Bonnie had said—*"she might blow some fresh air into this house."*

What about Meryn was so different compared to her other companions? Henrietta stared at the sketch and could picture Meryn turning to her, another of her interminable questions on her lips, her dark eyes probing as they met Henrietta's—the sketchbook slid off her lap, falling to the floor with a flutter of pages.

She looks at me.

Henrietta thought hard, trying to recall the color of Amanda's eyes. Or Joyce, the companion before her. Or any of the others. She couldn't. She could picture them vaguely, in sketchy outline, but not fully formed. In her memories of them, her interactions with them, they were always busily doing something or looking elsewhere, anywhere but at her. They never seemed to want to see her.

Or is it you who doesn't wish to be seen?

More unwelcome questions Henrietta couldn't quiet. But they were forcing her to think about the ways in which she'd walled herself off ever since she'd gotten sick. It had been bad enough at the sanitarium, but at least there, she was one among many cripples. If they had to put up with patronizing doctors or sympathetic murmurs from visitors, they could commiserate with one another later. But after she'd come home, seemingly the lone polio cripple in this town—or at least the only one to return—it had felt the entire village's eyes were focused on her every move. Even if she sometimes needed their help, she didn't need their pity.

But there was no pity in Meryn's eyes. There was curiosity—not about her physical limitations—it was more a desire to know her. Now that she thought about it, Henrietta could see Meryn's amusement as she ignored Henrietta's rather pointed attempts to keep her at a distance. She didn't simply refuse to stay outside Henrietta's wall, she barged right through it.

Her thoughts were interrupted by noise from the front of the house when the door opened. Henrietta got up from her stool, bracing one hand on the counter to lean over and retrieve her sketchpad.

"Hank! I'm home."

Meryn's entrance was like that tornado as she stomped through the house toward the studio. "Hi. Whatcha working on?"

Henrietta reached for her crutches and carried her brushes to the sink.

Meryn came over to study the half-finished painting on the easel. "The pond." She leaned closer. "Wow, I love the colors. If I were painting this, I would have just used gray or blue or something. You've got an entire rainbow here, and it's perfect."

Henrietta shook her head as she gently worked soap into the bristles. "Clouds aren't white."

"I guess they aren't. You make me look at things differently. I like that."

Henrietta paused and couldn't help a small smile, which she immediately erased. Shaking the extra water from the brushes, she said, "Am I mistaken, or did I hear you address me as 'Hank'?"

Apparently immune to the ice in Henrietta's voice, Meryn grinned sheepishly. "Yeah. I think four syllables is unreasonable for one person to be saddled with on a daily basis. Takes too long. Especially when

I'm hungry. HEN-REE-ETT-AH. See? Hank is quick and easy. And we can eat sooner. I can have dinner fixed in the time it takes me to call you by your full name. How about hamburgers tonight? I'm starving." Without waiting for an answer, she headed toward the kitchen.

At the sink, Henrietta stared after her. "Hank," she murmured. With another unwilling smile, she laid the brushes out to dry.

⁓

THE CLOCK TICKED CLOSER to ten till the hour.

"Make sure you read the next chapter before Friday," Ryn said over the noise of backpacks zipping and chairs scraping the floor. "I'm pretty sure there will be a quiz."

There were a few groans and some grumbling as the students filed out of the classroom. Ryn gathered up her notes and headed up the back stairs to her office. On the landing, she paused to peer through the glass. Damn. Geary's door was open and the light was on. She pulled the stairway door just wide enough to slip through, catching it as it closed to muffle the thump that would betray her presence. Walking as quietly as she could, she made her way to her broom closet to swap notes for her afternoon lecture, but before she could escape, he was there.

"If I didn't know better," he drawled, taking up his favorite position of leaning against the doorframe to block her in, "I'd think you were trying to avoid me."

She didn't glance up. "You give yourself too much credit."

His voice lost the drawl and became more clipped as he said, "You do realize, by next year, you're going to be working for me."

She straightened. "I can pretty much promise you, that is never going to happen."

A befuddled expression settled over his face. "What do you— Have you heard something?"

"Hi!"

Geary jumped at the voice behind him.

"Vanessa, hello," Ryn said.

Geary immediately sucked in his gut. "And who is this lovely young thing?"

Ryn was about to tell him off, but Vanessa smiled up at him.

"Vanessa Feldman. And you're Professor Geary."

Ryn rolled her eyes as he gave Vanessa a toothy smile and reached for her hand.

"Guilty as charged." He held her hand in both of his. "Nice to meet you, Vanessa Feldman."

Ryn took advantage of the distraction to exit her office, pulling the door shut behind her.

"Walk with me, Vanessa."

"Bye," Vanessa said, reluctantly tugging her hand free and giving Geary a little wave.

Ryn led the way down the hall toward the front stairs. "Stay away from him."

"Why? Is he—Oh. Sorry."

"Sorry? What are you sorry for?" Ryn glanced at her as they descended to the foyer of the building.

"I don't want to trespass."

"Trespass." Ryn stopped and laughed so hard she thought she might pee herself. "You think I want that lout? No. I just don't want him messing with you."

"I think he's kind of cute."

"Cute? He's old enough to be your father. Hell, he's old enough to be my father." Ryn shivered at the thought.

Outside, a few students were tossing a Frisbee on the quad, while others stretched out in the sun, reading or talking.

"Anyway, what brings you by?"

"I miss you," Vanessa said. "Things at Mrs. Middleston's are so boring. Won't you come back?"

Ryn shook her head. "I like it where I am. Do you have a new roommate?"

"God, yes," Vanessa said melodramatically. "All she does is read and study. It's awful."

Ryn hid a smile. "Maybe her study habits will rub off on you."

"That's what my mother said." Vanessa sighed. "I'm going crazy in this town."

Ryn considered. "I was thinking about going to Syracuse this weekend. Want to come?"

Vanessa grabbed her arm. "You mean it? Really?"

"Really. Saturday, nine o'clock sharp. We'll have lunch, do some shopping."

"Oh, that sounds wonderful." Vanessa impulsively threw her arms around Ryn. "Thank you so much!"

Vanessa bounced off. Ryn stared after her, shaking her head. She turned and realized the three young nuns—all wearing black dresses and short veils—were standing nearby, watching her. A fourth young woman, an athletic blonde, was with them. Ryn didn't recognize her, but she gave them a quick nod and headed toward an adjacent hall for her next class. At the base of the stairs, she looked back and caught the blonde watching her. There was a little extra jaunt in her step as she took the stairs two at a time to her classroom.

～

"REFILL?"

Meryn got to her feet to pour Henrietta a second cup of coffee. She claimed she found the aroma of coffee enticing, but insisted she couldn't stand the taste. One shelf of the cupboard above the stove was now stocked with more types of tea than Henrietta had ever seen. She'd even tried some, but for a morning pick-me-up, she needed her coffee.

"Thank you."

"I still think you should come with us," Meryn said.

"Not this time." Henrietta stirred a bit of milk into her cup. "I'm going to a fall flower show with some friends."

Meryn opened her mouth as if to reply, but then apparently decided to fill her mouth with a bite of her peanut butter-and-jelly toast.

"You think that sounds stuffy?" Henrietta guessed, smiling behind her cup.

Meryn shrugged. "Just not my thing. If Vanessa weren't going, I'd bug you more about coming along, but I promised her. Not sure what got into me. She's nice, but she'd drive you crazy."

Henrietta raised one eyebrow. "You think you know what would drive me crazy?"

Meryn set her toast down and bounced in her seat, wagging her head from side to side as she put on a higher-pitched voice. "Oh, my God, this town is so boring. I'm stuck here for four years. My life will be over by the time I can escape from here."

Henrietta stared wide-eyed. "Thank you for sparing me this... adventure."

"Plus, she'll probably bring her stuffed animals for a ride," Meryn said mournfully.

Henrietta snorted, startling herself. "And you associate with this individual?"

"She's sweet despite the immaturity. And I remember how I felt at that age, busting to get out of my small town, where everybody knew me, and I couldn't do anything without my parents hearing about it before I even got home."

Meryn flung an arm out for dramatic effect. "Thus, I got me free and made for yon fair city." She dropped her arm. "Except Pittsburgh is anything but fair."

She finished her breakfast and quickly washed the dishes for both of them. "Not sure when I'll be home, but it'll be before supper."

She bent to pick up her backpack and gave Henrietta's shoulder a squeeze. "Have fun at your flower show, Hank. See you this evening."

The door banged shut behind her, but Henrietta sat like a statue, her shoulder throbbing as if it had been burned. No one touched her. Ever. The last person who had, had been her doctor, listening to her lungs last spring when she'd caught a cold.

This is dangerous. Why are you allowing this to happen?

Things had been so much better in the couple of weeks since this girl moved in. Meryn kept her door partially open in case Henrietta called out for her in the night, so that Henrietta was actually sleeping through the nights. She'd left little thank-you notes in her wing of the house on Wednesdays, notes that delighted Bonnie and shamed Henrietta, who had never thought to do something so whimsical and kind. She called Henrietta from her office to see what she was in the mood for for supper, in case she needed to pick something up at the market on her way home.

Home.

She called this house home. None of Henrietta's other companions had ever done that. To them, this position had clearly been a job. Though Henrietta had never realized it, that arrangement had left her with an underlying feeling that she had to treat them as employees in order to not feel indebted. But when she tried to think of Meryn that way, the image just swirled away, like a dab of watercolor dropped into a bowl of water. The same way the girl was wriggling her way into Henrietta's life, tinting what had been nothing but black and white and shades of gray, bringing bursts of color... and joy. It was already difficult to remember what things had been like before she was here.

What happens when she leaves? You know she will. They all do.

Henrietta looked at her watch. Her ride would be here soon. She got to her feet to gather her things. She needed to regain control of this situation. Now. Before it was too late.

RYN SAT BACK IN her chair, reading over the proposal she'd typed up for the women-and-history course. She'd spent most of yesterday compiling her notes and putting everything together. Satisfied, she hit the print command and saved her work to a floppy disk before scooping her notes from where they'd spread out around the computer she was using. Technically, she was supposed to have access to the department computer, but that was in Geary's office, sitting on the empty desk of the professor who had retired. No way in hell was she going to work in there. So, she came to the computer lab at the library.

She stuffed her notebook into her backpack and went to the staff desk, where the printer was located. Students apparently could use up printer ink more quickly than the cartridges could be refilled, and so had to pay for any printed pages. The dried-up old woman behind the desk looked as if she might disintegrate into dust if a stiff breeze blew through the building. She squinted from Ryn's faculty ID to her face several times, as if certain it must be a forged document to avoid paying. At last, apparently satisfied that Ryn really was faculty, she grudgingly handed the pages over.

Ryn thanked her and walked from the library to Rayburn, taking the steps two at a time. Peering around the door, she saw that Talbert's office was dark, but Beverly was at her post.

"Is he due back today?" Ryn nodded toward the empty office.

"I believe so." Beverly got up to check that the corridor was empty. "He's meeting with the dean." Her dismissive sniff gave a clear indication of what she thought of that news.

Ryn held up her papers. "I have my proposal for the class I want to teach."

Beverly's eyes lit up. "The one on women?"

Ryn nodded.

Beverly opened a file cabinet in the corner. "Let's present it in its best light." She produced a bright yellow folder and a hole punch. In a few seconds, she had the papers punched and neatly ensconced inside the folder. She quickly typed up a label with the title of the course and Ryn's name and degree. Peeling off the adhesive backing, she positioned the label perfectly on the front of the folder.

"We'll place this right on his desk so he can't miss it."

"Thanks so much." Ryn bent down to pick up her backpack but then paused. "Do you have a second?"

"Certainly." Beverly gazed at her through her thick glasses. "Do we need tea for this?"

Ryn chuckled. "We may."

Beverly quickly made tea for both of them. "Now," she said, handing one mug to Ryn. "What's on your mind?"

Ryn frowned into her tea. "Have I— Do you know if Henrietta has said anything to your sister... Have I made her angry?"

Beverly sat back. "Not that I know of. Why do you ask?"

"Well, things seemed fine until this past weekend. I went to Syracuse, and she was going to a flower show. But ever since I got back, she's been really cool and distant. I'm not sure if I did something to upset her. Dinners have been pretty quiet the last few nights, and after, she's gone straight to her room to read until bedtime. It's like she's avoiding me."

"Bonnie hasn't said anything. And she was just there yesterday." Beverly sipped her tea, thinking. "Miss Cochran is not usually one to pussyfoot around things that have displeased her. She hasn't said anything to you?"

"No," Ryn said, tapping a finger on the side of her mug. "But I've been calling her Henrietta—her suggestion that we go by first names. And..." She paused. "I've actually started calling her Hank. Do you think that bothers her?"

Beverly choked and sputtered past the gulp of tea that seemed to have gone down the wrong pipe. "You call her what?"

Ryn lifted one shoulder. "Hank. Henrietta just seems so formal."

Beverly goggled for a moment. "Heavens to Betsy."

"Too much?"

When Beverly didn't reply, Ryn's shoulders sagged. "Yeah, that's what I figured." She drained her mug and sat up straight. "Guess I'll apologize."

She washed both mugs in the women's restroom and brought them back. "Wish me luck," she said as she shouldered her backpack.

She kicked at acorns and crunched through leaves as she walked. She drove if the weather was bad, but walked most days, though Henrietta's house was more than twice as far from campus as Mrs. Middleston's had been. The trek gave her more time to think. Today, her thoughts were not just of Henrietta but this growing restlessness she'd been feeling the last week or so.

In Pittsburgh, there were a couple of gay bookstores that carried a few lesbian novels, stuck in a dark corner in the back. And just last year, Wildsisters had opened, giving the lesbian community a place to gather to listen to music and dance. She and Ashley had gone nearly every weekend and sometimes during the week. Her search for something similar in Syracuse had been fruitless, hampered by Vanessa tagging along everywhere she'd gone that day.

As much as Ryn liked Bluemont and the college, she was feeling the need to be around other women, other lesbians. It was like an itch she couldn't scratch. Adding to the itch was the fact that she'd written Ashley a couple of times, but hadn't heard back. She knew, surrounded by jocks in her work as a trainer for a college in Oregon, Ashley had almost certainly met someone else.

"We said it was fine to move on," she reminded herself. "No promises. No commitments."

But it still hurt that three years together could be tossed aside so easily.

By the time she walked up the driveway, automatically giving Nelly a pat, she was in a foul mood. She unlocked the front door and went on through to her room without saying anything.

She tossed her backpack onto the spare bed, kicked off her shoes, changed her clothes, and flopped on her bed, staring up at the ceiling. She wasn't ready to deal with Henrietta just yet. She didn't even turn on her new boom box with a double cassette player—her one splurge since she was no longer paying rent.

She had no idea how much time had passed before she heard the click of crutches.

"Meryn? Are you there?"

Ryn sighed and sat up. "I'm here."

"Are you ill?" Henrietta asked when Ryn emerged from the room.

"No. Not ill." Ryn moved past her toward the kitchen. "What would you like for supper?"

"We can warm up some of the chicken and dumplings Bonnie made for us yesterday."

Ryn nodded and went to the kitchen. She got out a pan and spooned some of the leftovers into it, placing it on medium heat.

Henrietta followed her, getting down bowls and glasses.

"How was bridge this morning?" Ryn kept her back to Henrietta, occupying herself by stirring the contents of the pot unnecessarily.

"It was fine."

A definite chill filled the space in the kitchen.

"Meryn, are you upset about something?"

Ryn bit her lip for a few seconds. "That's supposed to be my question to you."

"I'm sorry?"

Ryn turned around. "Have I upset you? Are you angry at me for calling you Hank? Have I done something else that bothers you?"

Henrietta blinked a few times. "No. Why would you ask that?"

Ryn felt her throat tighten. *Dammit.* She turned back around, unable to speak for a moment. She did not want to cry in front of Henrietta Cochran, especially when it was only half-tied to her.

"You've been different this week," she said when she could talk.

"Cool. Distant. So I wondered if I'd done anything to make you angry. If I have, I'm sorry."

The silence stretched on so long, she wondered if Henrietta had managed to leave the kitchen without making any noise.

"No."

Ryn froze. *What did that mean?*

"You haven't done anything wrong. I'm..." Henrietta paused. "I've been... distracted."

Ryn sniffed. "Do you want me to leave?"

"No."

She faced Henrietta. "Do you want me to address you as Miss Cochran, like Bonnie does?"

Henrietta's mouth opened and closed a couple of times as she seemed to struggle to find words. "I want us to go back to the way we were. I'm... I'm sorry if I hurt your feelings."

Ryn stared into her eyes for a few seconds and then smiled. "Thank you. And I'm glad you feel that way." She stirred the chicken and dumplings again. "Dinner will be ready in a few minutes."

Only later, lying in the dark and thinking about everything, did Ryn realize that Henrietta's gray eyes looked as bruised and guarded as hers felt.

Chapter 6

TOO MUCH YELLOW. IMPATIENTLY, Henrietta dabbed a bit more ochre into the mix on her palette and tried again. Sitting back, she tilted her head. Better.

The fall flower show had given her ideas for new still lifes. She'd stopped at a farm market to purchase a selection of colorful gourds, and had arranged them artfully around a basket filled with anemones, chrysanthemums, goldenrod, celosia, some purple Michaelmas daisies, a few cheerful pansies.

The vibrant colors stirred her. Almost against her will, her eyes flicked toward a draped canvas leaning against the wall—the unfinished painting of the pond. The feelings it had roused—things Henrietta hadn't felt for years—were just too much. Better to put them away, push them back down where they belonged. It was harder to stop the dreams, but she would. She could control this. She had to.

Her brush lowered. She wasn't sure she'd survive if she allowed herself to remember too clearly the disappointment—it was too mild a word, but she couldn't think of a word strong enough—of coming home at long last to find Una gone, without a word, without a good-bye. Even now, every memory of Una—the way she looked, her smell, the touch of her hands, the sound of her voice and her accent—they were all like knife wounds, straight to Henrietta's heart. Most people didn't think she had one. Even she wasn't so sure some days, but the way it hurt right now proved them wrong.

Speaking of hurting hearts, the look on Meryn's face last evening...

"Oh, posh," she muttered in exasperation, setting her brush and palette down.

She'd never meant to hurt the girl. She hadn't thought her efforts to put some distance between them would even be noticed. Evidently, she was wrong about that, too. The girl saw everything. And she felt everything.

Henrietta stared out the windows, wondering what it would be like to simply show what one was feeling, without censoring, without weighing consequences or the probability of being the target of gossip afterward. She shook her head. It was too risky, in too many ways.

Still, she'd hurt the girl's—*call her by her name*, a voice inside scolded—Meryn's feelings, and she felt she needed to make up for it.

She put a few finishing dabs of dark brown on the rattan strips of the basket in her painting, deepening the shadows and enhancing the contrast with the colors of the flowers.

She had everything cleaned up by the time Meryn got home.

"Sorry I'm so late. Gave an exam today, and I was trying to get started on grading."

"Would you like to have dinner at the club tonight?" Henrietta asked as Meryn hung her jacket on the hall tree.

Meryn looked at her in surprise. "Uh, sure. If you'd like."

"I know it's a little on the early side, but the club gets busy later on the weekend evenings, so we could go in a few minutes, if that's all right with you."

Meryn gestured at her teaching clothes. "These are the best I have. Is this acceptable?"

"You look perfectly fine." Henrietta sat on the sofa and reached for the phone. "Take your time. I'll call them."

"I can drive," Meryn said over her shoulder on her way back to her room to deposit her bag.

"I'll drive," Henrietta said quickly.

Meryn's head reappeared around the corner. She just looked at Henrietta with a knowing quirk of an eyebrow.

"It's just that the club staff park my car for me," Henrietta stammered. "They're familiar with my vehicle."

"I'll pretend I believe that."

Henrietta wasn't certain, but she thought she heard muffled laughter.

A half hour later, they were seated in the club's dining room. Meryn had been fascinated by the hand controls in Henrietta's station wagon.

"It's ingenious," Meryn had said, leaning over to study the scissor mechanism attached to the steering column that allowed Henrietta to push on the handle to press the accelerator or pull on it to push on the brake pedal.

"This allows for regular foot operation of the pedals also," Henrietta said. "When anyone else has to drive."

As Henrietta had predicted, one of the staff hurried out to hold the car door for her and park the car.

"I could have done that, you know," Meryn said.

"I didn't think of that," Henrietta admitted. "This is just what I usually do."

Inside, they were greeted by the hostess, who ushered them to a table near the wall.

"I prefer to be out of the stream of traffic," Henrietta said. She leaned her crutches against the wall, where they weren't in anyone's way.

A server immediately showed up to pour water. "Anything else to drink tonight, Miss Cochran?"

"Just iced tea for me."

Meryn waited just a beat, and then said, "I'll have the same, please."

Henrietta picked up the menu as he left to get their tea. "You could have ordered a drink."

"I rarely do. I don't really like beer, and wine goes to my head."

When the waiter returned with their drinks, Henrietta was still perusing the menu, but she heard Meryn say, "Thank you, Jeremy."

"You're welcome, miss. Are you ready to order?"

After he took their orders and left, Henrietta asked, "Do you know him? Is he a student?"

"No, why?" Meryn squeezed a wedge of lemon into her tea.

"You called him by name."

Henrietta never forgot the look Meryn gave her at that moment.

"I called him by his name because he's wearing a name tag. I say please and thank you because it means a lot when you've been waiting tables all night, and someone acknowledges that you're a real human being, not some nameless servant unworthy of even being seen."

She hadn't said one word in direct rebuke, but Henrietta's face burned as she realized she'd done to that boy—and countless others— exactly what people did to her.

Meryn gazed around at the huge wooden plaques emblazoned with the men's and women's golf champions, going back years, surrounded by photos of club members at various functions.

"Are you in any of these?" she asked.

"I'm not sure. I never checked."

"Is it okay if I do?" Meryn scooted her chair back. There were no other diners in the room. "It's not against the rules or anything?"

Henrietta gave her a droll smile. "I don't believe there's a rule against looking at photos."

Henrietta watched her as she wandered along the wall, perusing the photos, and wondered again how this girl could have turned her carefully structured life upside down in just a few short weeks.

"You are in a few," Meryn said when she returned. "Playing cards?"

"My bridge group."

"Henrietta?"

Meryn jumped to her feet as Jerry and Genevieve Talbert approached their table. "Dr. Talbert."

"Professor." Jerry glanced from her to Henrietta and back. "I'm surprised to see you here. I didn't realize you knew each other."

"Is this your new live-in?" Genevieve asked, her cigarette held in one hand and exhaled smoke issuing from her mouth in puffs as she spoke.

"Your..." Jerry Talbert's eyes narrowed a little. "Dear, this is also my newest faculty member. Meryn Fleming, my wife, Genevieve."

"Nice to meet you," Meryn said, extending a hand.

Genevieve took it, studying Meryn from head to toe. Henrietta knew that sly smile, and could see the wheels already turning in Genevieve's brain. The news of this would spread through the club's gossip machine before the bar closed tonight.

"Have a nice dinner," Genevieve said in a sickeningly sweet voice as they moved to the bar.

Meryn sat back down just as the waiter brought their dinners—fried fish for her and salmon for Henrietta.

"Thank you... Jeremy," Henrietta said.

The boy beamed at her.

Meryn murmured her own thanks to him. When he left, she said in a low voice, "We don't have to stay here. We can take this to go and eat at home."

Henrietta noted the downcast eyes as Meryn stared at her plate. "We're not going anywhere. Enjoy your dinner."

She tried to ignore the furtive glances from the bar as they ate. "I was thinking of taking a drive tomorrow. The leaves are nearing their peak, and I'd like to paint. Would you like to go along?"

Meryn looked up at that, considering. "That sounds nice, but I have that stack of exams I really have to finish grading this weekend."

"Next weekend would do just as well. I know a quaint inn with a wonderful restaurant and a beautiful view of Owasco Lake."

Meryn brightened. "That would be perfect. I've never been there."

She tucked into her dinner and, to her surprise, Henrietta found the salmon suddenly tasted much better.

⌒

THE FOLLOWING WEEK WAS the week from hell for Ryn. She did manage to get her exams graded and returned to the students, with a firm resolve to make her exams simpler to grade in the future—no more essay questions. It didn't help that five of her students had failed the exam. Of course, there were nearly a dozen excellent papers, but it still felt like a reflection on her teaching that so many had done so poorly.

On top of that, Dr. Talbert seemed to be avoiding her. Every time she tried to catch him to ask if he'd had a chance to look at her proposal, he was busy or with Geary. Even Beverly couldn't give her any idea if he'd read it or what he was thinking.

Discouraged, she went to the chapel on Friday for the noon Mass and plunked herself down in a middle pew, sitting with her elbows on her knees. She'd gone to St. Rita's the previous Sunday with Henrietta, but the ornate décor, the ostentatious stained glass, and the engraved plaques of church donors set in prominent places—it all turned her off. Not to mention the craning of necks to see who was accompanying Henrietta Cochran. Ryn had a creepy feeling that some bizarre game of "telephone" had been initiated after their dinner at the country club. This chapel suited her much better.

She looked up in surprise when the three young nuns slid into her pew to join her.

"Hi," whispered one.

"Hi." Ryn sat up and shifted over.

A few minutes later, their friend, the athletic blonde that Ryn had seen with them before, entered the chapel and, after a moment's hesitation, sat with them.

The one sitting beside her leaned over and whispered, "We've seen you around campus. I'm Roberta Salvecchio." She pointed to the others. "Francine, Steph, and our friend, Tamara."

"Meryn Fleming."

"We—"

But the priest entered the sanctuary at that moment, cutting off any further conversation. Ryn felt self-conscious, sitting next to nuns. She was very aware of the blonde casting furtive glances down the pew in her direction.

When Mass was over, she followed them outside.

"Are you a student?" the tall, lanky nun asked. Ryn thought she was the one called Francine.

"No. Teacher. History. What about y'uns?"

Roberta pointed to the three in habits. "We're with the Sisters of St. Joseph. Tamara is an aspirant. She'll be joining the order next year."

"We're having a potluck Sunday to watch the game," said the third nun, Steph.

Ryn looked at her blankly. "Game?"

"Buffalo Bills," Steph said. "We'd love to have you join us."

It was hard to imagine a bunch of women in habits meekly cheering on a football team. Something of her doubt must have shown in her face.

Roberta grinned and held up the corner of her veil. "We won't be in these. Civvies on weekends." She dug into her purse and pulled out a scrap of paper and a pen. "Here's the address. One o'clock is when most people will start showing up. We'd love to have you join us if you can make it."

"Thanks." Ryn accepted the slip, and watched them walk away.

Again, Tamara turned once to look back. Ryn felt a little flutter somewhere in the vicinity of her stomach. "What are you getting into?"

~

THE TREES WERE INDEED just about at their peak—the maples were a brilliant mix of reds and oranges, while the birches and ashes and elms threw in their yellows and golds. Behind them, the dark green of pines provided a gorgeous contrast. The leaves on the road swirled in little whirlwinds as cars flew past.

This time, Henrietta did allow Ryn to drive. "It'll free you to watch the scenery more," Ryn had pointed out. "Besides, Nelly needs some exercise."

"Nelly?"

"Sure. Don't you name your cars?"

"No."

Ryn had patted Nelly's fender hopefully.

"All right," Henrietta consented. "But I insist on buying lunch and filling your tank when we get back."

"Deal."

They packed a bag of painting and sketching supplies for Henrietta, along with a few books for Ryn—"no textbooks," she promised. "This is a fun day."

The drive to Owasco Lake took them through state forest territory. They spotted a few hikers and fishermen.

"Have you ever been to the Finger Lakes?" Henrietta asked from the passenger seat.

"No. We went to Niagara Falls when I was a kid, but that's as far as I ever made it into New York until now."

"I think you'll like it."

Henrietta gave directions as they followed mostly small two-lane highways, and they listened to Ryn's music. She popped cassettes into the player: Dan Fogelberg, Holly Near, Creedence Clearwater Revival.

"You have an eclectic taste in music," Henrietta commented.

"Is that a good thing or a bad thing?" Ryn asked.

Henrietta didn't answer immediately. "Good," she finally decided.

Ryn turned the volume up.

They drove on for a while, enjoying the scenery and the music. It was nice to be with someone who didn't need to talk all the time, very unlike Ryn's last road trip with Vanessa.

The inn was ideally situated on a bluff that gave an incredible view of the lake down below.

"Wow," Ryn breathed. "Are all the Finger Lakes this pretty?"

"I think so." Henrietta stood beside her on the inn's porch. "They're long and narrow, and very deep."

"Like Scottish lochs."

"Yes." Henrietta glanced at her. "Have you been to Scotland?"

"Not yet. How about you?"

"No."

Bewildered, Ryn watched Henrietta's face change as if someone had pulled a shutter over a window. She disentangled herself from the grip of her crutches, and sat down on one of the chairs on the porch. Ryn set her art bag beside her, leaving her to unfold her easel and pull out what she needed while Ryn went farther down the porch. She dragged one of the rockers into a patch of sunlight and sat with her books.

The inn's owner came outside to greet Henrietta. "Miss Cochran, I was delighted to get your call. It's been too long." She turned to Ryn. "And I see you've brought a friend. How nice."

Henrietta introduced them. "Meryn Fleming, Phyllis Vann. She makes the most wonderful apple pie I've ever had."

Phyllis laughed. "The secret's to use our New York apples. It's a little chilly to work outdoors. Would you like some coffee or tea?"

She brought them both large mugs—coffee for Henrietta and hot tea for Ryn—to ward off the autumn bite in the air. "I'll have your table ready for you whenever you're ready to eat, Miss Cochran."

She left them to enjoy the view. A steady stream of other guests came and went, pausing on the porch to enjoy the beauty of the lake on their way in or out of the inn for lunch. Ryn glanced up and nodded at a few of them, definitely feeling underdressed in her faded jeans and hooded sweatshirt. Henrietta hadn't suggested she change, though she was wearing a heavier flannel skirt and a wool sweater.

Ryn read for a while, but the sunlight glinting off the trees and the lake were too distracting. She lowered the book to her lap and rocked, watching the people wandering the gardens around the inn. After a while, she found herself studying Henrietta.

Perhaps it was the leg braces, perhaps it was her intense focus on her canvas, but people really did avoid her. Where normally, Ryn would have expected people to stop and watch or chat with an artist who was painting, they gave Henrietta a wide berth.

She tried to picture Henrietta as a girl, but found it difficult to erase the rather severe haircut, the frown lines on her face, the hard edge of her jaw.

Henrietta sat back to assess her work and glanced over to catch Ryn watching her. "I'm sorry. You must be starving."

"I'm fine. We can eat whenever you're at a good stopping point."

"I can stop now."

Ryn got to her feet. "Mind if I look?"

Henrietta turned the easel a bit.

"Hank, that's gorgeous." Ryn dropped a hand to Henrietta's shoulder. "Even these places that are just a few sketchy brush stokes, you've captured the scene perfectly. How do you do that?"

Henrietta busied herself wiping her brushes clean on a cloth. "I've made a lot of mistakes over the years. Trial and error."

"Would you teach me?"

Henrietta paused as she capped her acrylics. "Teach you?"

"Yes." Ryn gestured toward the canvas. "Teach me to paint."

"If you like."

"I would. And I am starving. Ready to eat?"

Henrietta started to take down the canvas and easel.

"Leave them," Ryn suggested. "You might want to work a little more after lunch. And people can enjoy what you've done so far."

Their table was near a window so that they still had a view of the lake. Phyllis brought them fresh mugs of coffee and tea and took their orders.

"Did you do this with your other companions?" Ryn wondered.

"Do what?"

"Take trips like this."

"No."

Ryn leaned her elbows on the table, cradling her tea in her chilled hands. "Why not?"

"I usually prefer to paint alone, and..."

Ryn waited.

"They preferred not to be with me more than they had to be." Henrietta kept her eyes focused on the view outside the window as she spoke.

Ryn started to protest that she was certain that wasn't true, but she wasn't so sure. "Well, I'm glad you asked me to come along."

Henrietta didn't say anything for a few seconds, and Ryn began to wonder if she would have preferred to be alone this time as well.

"You're different."

Ryn snorted. "I'm not sure how to take that, but I'll grant I'm different."

"No, I didn't mean—" Henrietta fumbled for words. "You're easy to be with."

"Thanks." Down on the lake, multiple boats were out, including what looked like a tour boat. Ryn nodded in that direction. "Have you ever done one of those?"

"When I was a girl. My parents used to bring us here."

"Us?"

There it was again, the shadow that dropped like a curtain over Henrietta's face.

"When I was growing up, there was a girl, Una. Her aunt lived in Bluemont. Una used to come visit from England for the summers, and then, during the war, she was sent to stay, to get her out of London."

Ryn watched Henrietta's face carefully, the way she kept her eyes lowered. This was thin ice. "You were close?"

Henrietta nodded. "She was my best friend."

"What happened to her?"

Henrietta sat back as Phyllis brought their sandwiches. "Thank you, Phyllis."

It seemed Henrietta wasn't going to answer the question as they began to eat. Ryn hesitated but then prompted, "Una?"

"I don't know what happened to her." Henrietta's face was a stony mask. "We went swimming in the pond. I got sick a few days later. It was nearly a year before I got home. Una was gone. I wrote several times, but never got an answer. My mother said it was probably for the best."

Ryn's heart ached for her, for the pain so evident in her clipped words, but one didn't simply hug Henrietta Cochran. Even an expression of sympathy wouldn't, she was sure, be welcome. Ryn was just beginning to see the myriad layers of armor Henrietta had donned in an effort to protect herself.

"This chicken salad is great," Ryn said. "Think we could talk Phyllis into giving us her recipe?"

Henrietta seemed to breathe a sigh of relief at the change of topic. "I can ask her."

"If you can get it, I'll make it for us."

They both turned their attention to the scene below as they ate. All around them, the dining room was filled with a pleasant buzz of conversation. Out on the porch, people did stop to admire Henrietta's canvas.

"What you told me..." Henrietta began, "...that first day..."

Ryn frowned, trying to make sense of this cryptic comment. "The day I fell in the pond?"

"No." Henrietta carefully kept her eyes on the lake. "The day we met to discuss your living-in with me. When you told me you'd heard I was difficult..."

Her voice trailed off. Ryn waited, but no more came. "Yes?" she prodded. "We talked about a lot of things."

Henrietta's cheeks colored, but she couldn't seem to meet Ryn's eyes. "We talked about how opinionated you were. You said you didn't mind difficult if I didn't mind..."

Ryn smiled. "That I'm a lesbian."

"Shhh." Henrietta glanced around.

Ryn leaned a little closer. "I don't think anyone is listening to us. What about it?"

Henrietta's mouth seemed to have trouble forming the words she obviously wanted to ask. "Is there... anyone? You never bring anyone to the house."

"Oh." Ryn sat back in her chair. It was her turn to stare at the trees, but she could feel Henrietta's eyes boring into her. "There was someone. In school. But we both knew we were headed in different directions with our careers and... I haven't heard from her."

Phyllis appeared at that moment with two plates filled with enormous pieces of apple pie.

"I'm sorry," Henrietta murmured after she left.

Ryn nodded. The pie, though it was delicious, tasted just a little bitter in her mouth.

They finished eating and went back out to the porch, but Henrietta packed up.

"I think I'm ready to go home."

Ryn didn't argue. The ride back to Bluemont was silent except for the music, but even that wasn't the comfort it usually was. *Funny how much space ghosts can occupy.*

Chapter 7

WHATEVER RYN THOUGHT THE nuns' house might look like, she didn't expect a perfectly ordinary bungalow with a big Buffalo Bills flag hanging from the porch. Before she could even climb the porch steps, Roberta came out to greet her. At least, Ryn thought it was Roberta. It was hard to be certain that this brunette in jeans and a Binghamton Patriots sweatshirt was the same person who had been in a dress and veil on Friday, but the moment she spoke, Ryn was sure.

"We're so glad you could make it." Roberta jogged down the steps to take her by the elbow and lead her into the house.

Francine, taller than anyone one else in the room, greeted her. "We were hoping you'd come."

Without her veil to tame it, her bushy brown hair was an unruly nest.

Ryn held up a ceramic dish. "I made some potato salad."

"That sounds great," said Tamara, appearing at Ryn's elbow. "Bring it into the kitchen."

The table and counters were packed with bowls and platters over-flowing with food, stacks of paper plates and plastic utensils. On the floor was a large washtub filled with ice and—Ryn almost choked—cans of beer and soda.

Tamara grinned at the look on her face. "What were you expecting? Communion wine?"

She took the bowl from Ryn, letting her fingers linger a bit longer than necessary when they made contact, and then found space for the bowl in the packed refrigerator.

"Want something to drink?" Tamara asked.

Ryn bent over the tub and chose a Dr. Pepper. "What?" she asked at the look on Tamara's face.

"Nothing," Tamara said with a wry smile. "Not a beer drinker? Or you don't trust yourself to drink around nuns?"

"I've never been a beer drinker. But the nun thing is a little... weird."

Tamara chose a Rolling Rock and popped the top. "Nuns are nor-mal people."

Ryn followed her out back where hamburgers and hotdogs were sizzling on a grill and a football was being tossed around the yard. She had to admit, this looked like any other gathering of lesbians she might have attended in Pittsburgh, but then caught herself. Just because there weren't any men, she supposed she shouldn't assume they were all lesbians. *Can lesbians be nuns anyway?*

"Where do you live?" Francine asked from where she was flipping the burgers.

"Out near the country club."

"Do you rent a place out there?" Tamara asked.

Ryn shook her head. "I stay with a woman who needs a little help around the house. It works out for both of us."

The football came flying in their direction. Tamara caught it and dragged Ryn into the circle.

"What do you teach?" Stephanie asked, throwing a perfect spiral.

"History." Ryn tossed the ball to someone she didn't know but whose face looked familiar, probably from campus. "Mostly freshman seminar classes. What are y'uns studying?"

"Education for Roberta, Franny, and me," Steph answered. "Our order is mostly a teaching or nursing order. If we'd wanted to go into nursing, we'd have been sent to SUNY."

Ryn watched Tamara pass the ball, stepping into it and throwing a bullet. "What about you?"

"I'm majoring in business."

Steph laughed. "Not for much longer."

Ryn was about to ask more questions, but Francine called out that the burgers and dogs were ready, and everyone headed inside.

A few minutes later, Ryn was crowded into the smallish living room along with about seven other women, cradling a plate loaded with food as she sat cross-legged on the floor.

As Buffalo kicked off against the Dolphins, Roberta leaned near and said, "Our motherhouse is near Buffalo. We probably should have asked if you're a Miami fan."

Ryn wiped a bit of mustard from the corner of her mouth. "Grew up outside Pittsburgh and went to Pitt. What do you think?"

There was sudden silence. Roberta made the sign of the cross over Ryn's head. "We forgive you."

Ryn's snort was muffled by the howl of laughter from around the room. She sat back against the couch between two sets of legs, enjoying the ribbing and the jokes. Except for the noticeable lack of swearing, this really was like any other gathering she might have attended in Pittsburgh. That ache she'd been carrying around—the empty place only women could fill—it began to ease a bit. Over on her right, Tamara caught her eye and smiled. Basking in the warmth of it all, Ryn relaxed and drank it in.

~

HENRIETTA POINTED WITH A crutch. "Could you cut back those roses, too?"

Bud had just finished raking up the leaves that had fallen from the maple and elm trees in the front yard. The trees were only about half-done, but Bud didn't like to let the downed leaves sit on the grass too long.

Henrietta had joined him to do their fall survey of the yard, deciding which bushes to trim, which trees to prune. He'd picked up a case of bulbs to plant for the spring, and had a trailer of mulch to lay over the flower beds to protect them through the coming winter.

She enjoyed the scent of leaves in the air, the cool air and the still-warm October sun. It wouldn't be much longer, and she'd be ready to hibernate. It seemed the last few years, she'd felt the cold more acutely.

"Not enough exercise. You need to keep your blood circulating," Dr. McCourt said sternly, but he didn't understand how scary it was to walk outside when the pavement was snowy or icy. One bad fall, and she'd be in bed for weeks. Every time something happened—like the cold that threatened to turn into bronchitis last year—it took longer for her to recover, and it seemed to sap more of her strength.

But lately she was walking more, moving more. And she was pleasantly surprised to find that the more she pushed herself, the less winded she was. Even Bud was surprised when she accompanied him down the path to the pond to see what had to be cleaned up down there. She needed to catch her breath a few minutes before she could talk with him, but it was definitely an improvement.

As he bent to pick up an armful of fallen sticks and branches, she had a thought.

"Could you build me a place to have a fire in?"

"Down here?" He dropped the sticks beyond the edge of the stone landing and looked around. "Sure."

He stepped into the underbrush and started digging up random stones. "There's plenty of rock here. I'll make you a nice, safe fire pit. Nothing too big, now."

"No. Just enough to enjoy on a cool evening, maybe roast some marshmallows."

His eyes reflected his surprise, but he just tipped his grimy cap and nodded. "I'll take care of it."

Henrietta left him there to begin planning the fire pit while she made her way back up the trail to the house. The fire pit would be a nice surprise for Meryn. She felt an unfamiliar sensation in her chest and stopped to rub at her breastbone for a few seconds before going on to her studio.

The painting she'd started at the lake was nearly done—one of her best, though she hadn't voiced that thought to anyone else. She tilted her head as she studied it. Yes, just a few little touch-ups here and there. This would be one to show a gallery the next time a rep came to call. Maybe a series of these...

She was distracted by noise from out front. She went through to the garage, which was open for Bud to come and go as needed. From the front yard came the sound of laughter. Making her way down the driveway, she stopped, her mouth open.

An abandoned backpack was sitting in the driveway next to the Hornet, and Meryn was lying in the pile of leaves, flinging them into the air as her arms and legs flew about.

Henrietta walked out to where she could stare down at her.

"Oh, hi." Meryn sat up, bits of leaves clinging to her hair and sweater. She picked up handfuls of leaves and tossed them into the air. "It was just too tempting. Couldn't help myself."

"So I see."

She clambered out of the leaf pile, sweeping her hands down her sleeves and pant legs to clean them. Henrietta couldn't help chuckling.

Meryn craned her neck over her shoulder, trying to see her behind. "Could you do my back?"

Henrietta hesitated a moment, and then plucked leaves from Meryn's back, brushing her hands over her shoulders. She reached up to pull a few crumbled leaves from her dark hair.

"Thanks." Meryn gave her a crooked grin. "Guess I should clean up my mess." She reached for Bud's rake and gathered the leaves into a neat pile again. "Gosh, that was fun. Haven't done that for a long time."

"Me, either." But instead of echoing Meryn's note of wistfulness, Henrietta's voice rang with bitterness.

Meryn retrieved her backpack and followed her inside. "Are you okay?"

"I'm fine."

"What would you like for dinner?"

But Henrietta walked straight back to her room without answering. She closed the door and leaned against it for a moment, pressing a hand to her chest and wondering if something could be wrong with her heart.

She jumped at a faint tapping on the door.

"Henrietta? Are you okay?"

"I... I told you I'm fine. I'm just not hungry."

"Okay."

Henrietta closed her eyes against the hurt tone of the girl's voice.

"Let me know if you change your mind. I'll warm something up or scramble you some eggs. Whatever sounds good, all right?"

But Henrietta couldn't answer. She moved to her bed and collapsed onto it. She looked at her hands, feeling again the warmth of Meryn's back, the sweep of her shoulders, the softness of her hair. Struggling to hold back her sobs, she pressed both hands to her mouth as she rocked. Darkness fell, but she didn't turn a light on. She curled up on her side, staring at her hands.

~

"GOOD JOB, EVERYBODY," RYN said to her class as she dismissed them. "Enjoy your fall break, but remember to study. The midterm exam will be that Wednesday we come back."

A few groans greeted this reminder, but most of the students grinned and gave her a wave as they bolted from the classroom to begin a long weekend. She didn't blame them. She herself was looking forward to a couple of days off. It wouldn't be a complete break, as she had some assignments to grade, but still.

She was feeling the itch to go somewhere, do something. Maybe another trip to Syracuse... Distracted, she plowed into someone as she descended the stairs and turned the corner onto the stairwell landing.

"Sorry."

When she looked up, Tamara's face was inches from her own.

"Hi."

"Hi," Ryn said, clutching at her notebook to keep it from hitting the floor.

"Imagine running into you."

"Literally." Ryn's heart lifted at the smile on Tamara's face. "What are you doing here?"

Tamara pointed up the stairs. "Last class of the week. Can't wait for the weekend."

"I know what you mean." Ryn stepped aside to let Tamara continue on her way. "Are you doing anything? This weekend?"

"Nothing set in stone." Tamara's eyes met hers. "What did you have in mind?"

Ryn shrugged. "Nothing, really. Just wanted to get out of town. Go for a drive. Interested?"

Tamara's smile widened. "Definitely interested. Tomorrow?"

Ryn nodded, suddenly too tongue-tied to speak.

"Give me your hand."

"Excuse me?" Ryn blinked stupidly.

Tamara clicked a pen. "Give me your hand." She held Ryn's left hand in hers and wrote on her palm. "My address."

"You realize I now will not be able to wash this hand until I pick you up tomorrow."

Tamara released her hand slowly, letting it slide from her fingers. "I'm sure you'll manage somehow. What time?"

"Ten?"

"Ten. See you then."

Tamara climbed the stairs, turning to look back at Ryn until she rounded the next landing and disappeared from view.

Ryn hopped down the rest of the stairs to the second floor. She was relieved to see that Geary's office door was closed and no lights were on. She went to her office to pack her bag with the things she would need for the weekend. Pulling the door shut behind her, she went to Beverly's office.

"Hey—"

She stopped short as Beverly's head snapped up, eyes enormous behind her glasses. Beverly jumped out of her chair and hurried around her desk, taking Ryn by the arm.

"This isn't a good time for—"

Just then, Dr. Talbert's office door opened and three men emerged. A very rotund priest was shaking hands with Bradley Geary.

"Ah, Professor Fleming," Talbert said, looking flustered to see Ryn standing there. "I didn't realize... Ah, do you know Father Croson?"

She'd met the president of the college once, at a beginning of the year reception for the faculty and staff. "Of course. Hello, Father."

Father Croson took her hand in both of his pudgy ones. "Hello, Professor. I'm hearing excellent things about you. Yes, indeed."

Ryn's heart leapt. "My course," she started to say, but Father Croson turned to the other two men.

"Your idea for that women-and-history class is excellent, Bradley. Yes, indeed. Just the kind of innovation we need from a future department chair." He still held Ryn's hand, which was the only thing that kept her from trying to wrap her hands around Geary's throat.

"You're lucky to work with two such progressive colleagues, Professor." Croson wagged a finger in her face. "Pay attention and learn from them."

The floor felt as if it were tilting under her feet. Beverly grabbed her by the arm and pulled her out of the office, saying, "Excuse me, Father, I need a word..."

"But," Ryn sputtered.

"Not now," Beverly hissed, leading Ryn down the stairs and into an empty classroom where she pushed the door shut and backed Ryn up to a chair. She sat heavily, dropping her backpack to the floor.

"You're white as a sheet, Meryn." Beverly pulled another chair near. "I'm so sorry. I heard through the door, and I knew what they were doing. I was going to come find you, but..."

Ryn's eyes filled with angry tears. "How could they just steal my work?"

A distant part of her brain knew this happened all the time—faculty advisors stole and took credit for their grad students' research, passing it off as their own—but she'd never expected to be on the receiving end of such conduct. Not here. Not teaching something as benign as history at a small, Catholic college.

"I'm so sorry," Beverly said again, taking Ryn's hand and patting it. "I'm so angry, I could spit. I've a good mind to quit! I could retire right now, you know. It would serve them right."

Ryn rubbed her free hand over her face, wiping her wet cheeks.

"Oh, dear," Beverly said. "You just smeared ink all over your face. Come with me."

Hoisting the backpack onto her shoulder, she kept hold of Ryn's hand and led her to the women's restroom down the hall. A quick look in the mirror confirmed that Ryn had streaky blue splotches all over her face. Her palm was a blue smear as well.

"You wash up, now. Splash some cold water on your face. We do not want to let them see that they got to us."

Beverly pulled some paper towels out of the dispenser. After Ryn rinsed the soap from her hands and face, she took the paper towels and pressed them to her eyes. Blotting her cheeks dry, she sniffed.

"You can't quit. What would I do without you?"

Beverly's nostrils flared. "Well, I'd still like to give them a piece of my mind."

Ryn took her backpack from Beverly and slung it over her shoulders. "Thanks." She tried to smile but couldn't quite pull it off.

Beverly had to reach up to put a motherly arm around Ryn's shoulders. "You get out of here. Go home and try not to think about it."

Ryn nodded numbly, knowing she wouldn't be able to do anything but think about it.

~

HENRIETTA PULLED INTO A parking space at JT's Bar and Grille. It wasn't a place she frequented, but they did the best fish fry in Bluemont. She rolled down her window when a young woman in a JT's T-shirt and apron came out carrying a large brown-paper bag, mopping her sweaty face with a paper napkin.

Henrietta jabbed her thumb at the back seat. "Could you put it on the floor? Please."

The woman deposited the bag behind her seat as requested, and Henrietta handed her a twenty.

"No change."

The woman's flushed face broke into a smile. "Thank you, Miss Cochran."

It was a generous tip, but she was feeling generous. The past few days, ever since that shameful episode of losing control and shutting herself in her room, she'd been forcefully cheerful, hoping that Meryn would forget it had happened. To further make up for it, she'd planned a bit of a surprise for the evening. This fish fry for dinner, next to the fire pit Bud had completed yesterday—she was hoping this could put things right.

Not that Meryn had brought up her embarrassing lack of composure. Quite the opposite, there had been a careful avoidance of the topic. If there was one thing Henrietta knew she was good at, it was avoiding things she didn't want to talk about. She was just grateful the girl had followed her lead.

When she got to the house, the Hornet was just pulling in. She pushed the button on the garage door opener and drove inside. When she emerged from the car and got situated with her crutches, Meryn was just standing beside her car, staring at nothing.

"Could you help me?"

Meryn started. "Sure."

"In the back seat."

Meryn retrieved the bag. "What's this?"

"Fish fry." Henrietta led the way into the kitchen. "I thought we could eat down at the pond. Have a picnic."

She turned when there was no reply. The girl was standing at the counter where she'd set the bag, again just staring.

"What's wrong?"

Meryn burst into tears. Henrietta couldn't have been more shocked if she'd thrown her arms and stomped about in a tantrum. And she was just as ill-prepared for how to handle this. She pulled out a chair at the table.

"Sit down and tell me what happened."

Her authoritative tone had the desired effect. Meryn sat, tugging a napkin from the holder and using it as a handkerchief to wipe her eyes and blow her nose.

"Sorry." She hiccupped a little.

Henrietta sat also. "Now. Tell me what happened."

The story came spilling out, all about how Meryn had worked to put together the proposal for the class, written it all up. She'd even prepared a syllabus and had most of the lecture outlines planned, week-by-week.

"And they stole it!" Her eyes were bright again, but this time with anger, not tears. "They didn't just say 'I think Geary might be the better person to teach this class', they presented it as if it were their idea! Talbert and Geary both."

Henrietta's own jaw clenched. She felt this inexplicable urge to reach out and take the girl's hand. She sat back and clenched her hands in her lap.

"I'm sorry this happened. What are you going to do about it?"

Meryn raised her eyes. "What do you mean? What can I do about it?"

"I'm not sure. Yet. But you need to have a plan in mind. This isn't over. And you're going to have to continue working with them."

The girl's shoulders dropped at this reminder.

"But not tonight. It's Friday. You have a long weekend, away from those idiot men. We're going to celebrate."

Meryn dabbed at her nose again. "Celebrate how? And what did you say is in the bag?"

"Dinner. The best fish in town. I've got a hamper packed with drinks. Go change clothes."

Meryn's dark eyes fixed on her in that way she had that made Henrietta's heart feel funny.

"Go on now. Before the fish gets cold."

A few minutes later, they were on their way down the path as dusk settled over the pond. The sky's pink and purple hues were reflected in the still water. Frogs croaked and squirrels hopped around in the fallen leaves, searching for acorns and seeds.

"When did all this happen?" Meryn asked when she saw the dry-stacked circle of stones, already laid with a small tangle of wood ready to be burned. Off to one side was a large stack of smallish logs and branches, all cut to the same length.

"Bud built it this week."

"Why?"

Henrietta felt caught in Meryn's gaze. "Well..." She broke the stare and busied herself scooting a chair into a different position, drawing it closer to an old card table she'd had Bud carry down for her. "I don't use this landing enough. And I thought we might enjoy being able to have fires down here, now that the nights are cooler."

She sat and pointed with her crutch. "There are matches in the hamper, too. And some newspapers."

Meryn opened the basket and looked up with a grin. "And marshmallows. You thought of everything."

She quickly crunched up and stuffed several sheets of newspaper in between the sticks at the base of the fire. When she held a lit match to them, they caught quickly. Within a few minutes, a cheerful fire was crackling.

"Come and eat."

Inside the brown-paper bag were two baskets of fish and fries, wrapped in more newspaper. There were cold bottles of Coke in the hamper, along with utensils and napkins.

"Oh, my gosh, this is good," Meryn said at her first bite. "Why haven't we done this before?"

"I forget about that place. It's not much in the way of atmosphere."

"Who cares about atmosphere when they fry fish like this?"

They dug into their meals, neither speaking until they were done. Meryn got more wood from the pile and added it to the fire, poking it with an old crowbar Bud had left. She sat down, stretching her legs out.

"Thank you, Henrietta. I needed this tonight."

Henrietta felt that strange sensation in her chest again. "You're welcome."

She watched the girl, the firelight flickering over her face, and she could see the emotions running wild over her features as she thought. "Have you decided how you're going to handle them?"

"Not yet."

"The only way not to deal with them is to quit, in which case, they win by default."

Meryn glanced at her. "You're right. I just don't know how to face them. My emotions always get the better of me."

Henrietta smiled grimly. "That's something no one has ever said of me."

Meryn shifted her chair. "What would you do?"

Henrietta considered. "I'd act as if nothing at all had happened. Be as sweet as you can." She smiled again when Meryn made a gagging sound. "I didn't say it would be easy. But one of these days, something is going to happen that will give you your chance. You just have to be patient enough to wait. And your not reacting will drive them crazy."

Meryn stared into the flames, mulling this over. "You may be right."

They sat, listening to the night sounds of the pond, occasional splashes as a fish broke the surface. A mist materialized like magic over the water as the evening air cooled. The fire slowly burned down, and the dimming firelight let them see the stars dotting the inky sky.

Henrietta gave an involuntary shiver in the cold. The girl must have seen.

"Let's go up."

She went to the fire to knock the embers apart. Bud had also left an old metal trashcan lid that she settled over the ashes to smother them and prevent an errant breeze from blowing a burning ember into the woods.

While Henrietta got to her feet, Meryn gathered up all the rubbish and found the flashlight packed in the picnic hamper. She lit the path as they made their way up to the house.

Meryn quickly emptied the hamper of the dishes and trash, taking the fishy paper out to the can in the garage. She returned to the kitchen and turned off all the lights. After quickly checking the lock on the front door, she met Henrietta in the hall, looking a little embarrassed.

"Hank, I'm glad I had you to come home to tonight."

Without warning, she flung her arms around Henrietta in a hug, holding her tightly for a few seconds. "Good night."

She went down the hall to her rooms, leaving Henrietta frozen in place. Slowly, Henrietta made her way to her bedroom. When she stared at her reflection in the mirror, it was almost a shock to see the same sour face staring back at her.

"Don't be foolish," she muttered to herself.

But, as she got undressed, she couldn't help the small smile that kept flitting over her face.

~

RYN MUTTERED TO HERSELF as she drove slowly down Washington Street. It was the only part of Tamara's address she could remember, since the rest had been washed away in her stupid crying jag yesterday. Her jaw clenched just thinking about Talbert and Geary's stunt—

"Stop." She took a deep breath and let it out. She did not want today to be tainted by those men.

Nelly ambled several blocks until the street dead-ended. Ryn turned her around and they crept back the way they'd come, hoping for some sign.

Like a slender blonde standing in the middle of the street, holding her thumb out to hitch a ride.

Ryn grinned, admiring the view, and braked Nelly to a halt. Tamara trotted to the passenger side and got in.

"You washed your hand, didn't you?"

Ryn nodded. "I tend to do that for special occasions..." She held up two clean palms.

Tamara nodded. "Good recovery. So where are we going on this special occasion?"

"How about Cortland? I haven't been there. Have you?"

"No."

"Buckle up. Cortland it is."

Ryn threaded her way through Bluemont's streets, heading east and south. "Where are you from?"

"Cuba."

Ryn did a double take. "Cuba."

Tamara scoffed. "Cuba, New York. Blink and you'll drive right through and not even know you were there. Between Buffalo and Olean. Rinky-dink town I couldn't wait to get out of."

Ryn laughed. She couldn't help it. At Tamara's indignant expression, she said, "I'm sorry, but Bluemont isn't exactly a metropolis."

A reluctant grin tugged at Tamara's mouth. "Okay, I'll grant you that. But it's still better than Cuba."

"It's only better because it's not where you're from."

"You might be right," Tamara conceded. "How about you?"

"Uniontown, PA."

Tamara shifted in her seat. "Do you miss it?"

"Not a bit. I miss my family, but not Uniontown." She waved at the colorful trees lining the road and the hills beyond. "It's nothing like this."

Tamara nodded. "We'll see if you still say that after digging out from under three feet of snow."

She opened the console. "Wow, you have a lot of music. Do you mind?"

"Not at all. Pick something out."

Tamara shuffled through the cassette cases. "I don't know most of these. Do you have a favorite?"

"Try *The Changer and the Changed.*"

Tamara found that tape and slid it into the stereo. As the strains of the opening song played, Ryn opened her mouth to say something but saw the look on Tamara's face. She remembered how that album had—true to its name—changed her life. She turned back to the road, letting the music fill the car.

They listened to both sides of the tape on the drive to Cortland.

"I think that's the best album I've ever heard," Tamara said.

"It's one of my favorites," Ryn agreed, scanning the streets. "I bought the record album first, but needed a portable version."

She found a parking space on what looked like the main street. While she checked the meter to see if she needed to pay on a weekend, Tamara was reading all the bumper stickers on Nelly's rear end.

She eyed Ryn with a slightly wary expression as they walked down the sidewalk. "You have a lot of interesting stickers."

"Mmmm hmmm." Ryn waited a beat. "Which ones did you find most interesting?"

"Well, the goddess ones are intriguing."

Here we go, Ryn thought, this game of tiptoeing around the one topic they most wanted to discuss, yet found the scariest to initiate. She decided to just take the plunge.

"I'm lesbian, if that's what you're wondering."

Tamara burned a brilliant scarlet, and she looked as if she'd like to crawl under the pavement.

"If that's not what you were trying not to ask me—"

"It was," Tamara said quickly.

To shut me up. Ryn remembered how hard coming out had been, but it felt almost like a different lifetime, four whole years ago, when she was a freshman and had met a group of women she desperately wanted to be part of.

"Sorry if I was too blunt," she said.

"It's okay." Tamara frowned as they walked, her hands shoved into her jacket pockets. "I've just never met anyone who's so... open."

Ryn waited to see if Tamara would reciprocate about herself, but nothing more came. She sighed and pointed to a bookstore. "Let's go in there."

The shop was quaint, carrying a variety of current bestsellers, history, biography. But no women's section that Ryn could find, and certainly no lesbian or gay titles. They left without buying anything.

"Did you—" Tamara struggled to find words. "Did you think... I mean, do I seem...?"

The unspoken question hung between them. Ryn remembered this as well. This delicate balancing act of wanting to be recognized, but only by other lesbians, without being too obvious to anyone else, and yet still not being comfortable calling yourself a lesbian.

"I hoped," she said gently. "But it's okay if you're not. I'm not prejudiced."

That brought a smile. "Sorry." Tamara glanced around to make sure no one was near enough to overhear. "I've just never been around anyone so comfortable with it."

"Well, how about we just concentrate on getting to be better friends. Nothing like a road trip for learning all of your deep, dark secrets."

Tamara's eyes got big.

"Like, what's your favorite cookie?"

Tamara stopped in the middle of the sidewalk. "Cookie."

"Yes." Ryn nodded toward a bakery. "Must have cookies."

It worked. Tamara laughed, and the tension dissipated.

A few minutes later, fortified with a bag of cookies—chocolate macadamia for Tamara and oatmeal with chocolate chips for Ryn—they continued exploring Cortland.

She learned that Tamara didn't mind being called Tam, "but *never* Tammy! My brother sang that stupid song from that stupid movie so many times."

Ryn listened to Tam talk about growing up with an older brother who teased her something awful, but who also taught her to throw a baseball and play a tough game of one-on-one—both of which got her on her high school softball and basketball teams and led to a basketball scholarship. With her parents divorced, and her mom working long hours, she and her brother were close, despite the teasing.

They'd wandered into a clothing store, where Tam was sorting through the sale rack.

"Wait, you're at St. Aloysius on a basketball scholarship?" Ryn asked.

Tamara flushed again. "No. I went to SUNY Syracuse on a basketball scholarship, until I hurt my knee my sophomore year. I was never first-string material, so they cut me. I was looking for something else to... That's when I met some of the sisters. I went to their motherhouse a few times, and decided to become an aspirant. They're helping with my tuition now."

They left that shop and continued along the street. Ryn wanted to ask more about the whole nun thing, like what in the world would prompt someone to make that choice, but she couldn't think of how to phrase it so it didn't sound like a challenge.

"What about your family?" Tamara asked.

Ryn sighed. "My family is great. I'm just realizing how much I miss them. I want to hear how my sister is doing at WVU, and I wish I could see my brothers play basketball. It's their junior year, and I may not get to see them play again."

They looked for a place to eat and entered one nice-looking restaurant, but as they headed toward a table, Ryn grabbed Tamara's arm. There, in a back corner, Bradley Geary was seated with... *shit.* Vanessa.

"Not here," she muttered.

"What's wrong?" Tam asked, following her outside.

"Nothing. Let's find someplace quieter."

They found a little sandwich shop on a side street. Ryn's mind was still seething over Geary taking advantage of Vanessa. They placed their orders and took their meals to a table, but she was only half paying attention when Tamara asked in a low voice, "Does your family know? You know, about you?"

Ryn held up a finger as she chewed and swallowed her bite of sandwich. "We haven't had a formal conversation, but they met my—" She suddenly wasn't sure what to call Ashley. "My girlfriend. I mean, I didn't introduce her that way, but my mom's pretty smart, even if my dad's head is in the clouds—or with his birds—most of the time."

Tam shook her head. "My mom would disown me." She seemed to have suddenly realized what she'd said. "I mean... if I was, you know..."

Ryn decided it was time to steer the conversation to other topics. They wandered around Cortland for another hour or so. Ryn found the Cortland SUNY campus, pretending she was just curious. Truth be told, she was already making contingency plans for where she'd apply if she had to leave Bluemont. Seeing Geary today had only reinforced for her that staying at St. Aloysius might not be an option.

Back in the car, she let Tamara pick more music for the ride home to Bluemont. A couple of times, she felt Tam watching her, but if she was that closeted—*and planning to be a nun*, Ryn reminded herself—then this wasn't going anywhere.

Still, it was nice to have a new friend. *Just a friend,* she told herself sternly.

Chapter 8

UNLIKE MOST WEEKS, WHEN Henrietta tried to ignore Bonnie's chatter as she cleaned, this week, she listened acutely, alert for any mention of the college. She knew Bonnie and Beverly talked nearly every day. Sure enough...

"And that Professor Geary," Bonnie said as she ran a dust cloth over the living room furniture. "What he and Dr. Talbert pulled against poor Meryn. Beverly is ready to spit nails, she's that angry."

As this was the first day classes were back in session after the fall break, it was also Meryn's first day having to face those two.

"Yes, she was quite upset on Friday."

Bonnie stopped dusting and stared. "She told you?"

"Of course." Henrietta remembered how Meryn had burst into tears. "I don't think that girl could hide her emotions if her life depended on it. We had a picnic down at the pond and talked."

Bonnie's mouth actually hung open. "You. Had a picnic. And talked."

Henrietta couldn't help a smile. "Stop it. I do talk to people sometimes, you know."

Bonnie closed her mouth. "Of course you do, Miss Cochran."

"As you've been with me for twelve years now, Bonnie, don't you think it's time you called me Henrietta?"

"If you wish, Miss Cochran. I mean, Henrietta." Bonnie looked a little startled, but she was humming to herself as she resumed dusting.

As per the usual routine, Henrietta sat at the desk to pay the bills and balance the checkbook while Bonnie ran the vacuum in the bedrooms. The telephone trilled. Bonnie must have heard because the vacuum went quiet.

"Hello?"

"Is this Henrietta Cochran?" asked an unfamiliar voice.

"Yes. May I ask who's calling?"

"This is June Fleming. I'm Meryn's mother."

Henrietta paused, not sure how to respond. Was the woman calling because the girl had complained about something Henrietta had done? "What can I do for you, Mrs. Fleming?"

Bonnie wandered out into the hallway where she could listen to Henrietta's end of the conversation.

"Well, I hope you won't think this is too bold of me, or an imposition, but Ryn's birthday is November 23rd, the day before Thanksgiving this year, so we were thinking about coming up there to celebrate."

"Coming here. The entire family?"

"Oh, no!" Mrs. Fleming must have heard the panic in Henrietta's voice. "I mean, yes, all of us coming up there, but we'll stay at a local hotel. What I wanted to ask you is, would you mind if we brought Thanksgiving dinner to you, there? We'll bring everything, and I'll do all of the cooking. You won't have to do a thing. Meryn speaks so highly of you. It would be nice for all of us to be together, don't you think?"

Bonnie must have heard every word. She was mouthing something and flapping her hands.

"Just a moment," Henrietta said, putting her hand over the mouthpiece. "What?"

"Don't you dare say no." Bonnie placed her fists on her hips. "That girl should have her family with her for her birthday. And you don't need to spend another Thanksgiving alone. I'll make the pies."

"Ah," Henrietta stammered into the phone. "That would be lovely. And if you will do the cooking, I'll have the food delivered."

"Oh, thank you so much, Miss Cochran. Don't tell Meryn about this. We'll surprise her, okay?"

"Certainly."

Henrietta hung up, and Bonnie beamed.

"I'll get out the leaves for the dining table. They haven't been used in ages and ages. They'll need a good polishing. And the extra china. I'll make sure it's all washed and ready to use."

She reached for a pad and pencil, making herself a list as she talked. "See? Things are changing around here." Bonnie went back to her vacuuming, leaving Henrietta to stew.

Things certainly were changing. Her housekeeper was now telling her what to do, and her live-in's entire family was about to descend on her nice, quiet Thanksgiving, usually spent with a take-out meal from the club.

Usually? When was the last time you did anything other than spend the day alone?

Bonnie always invited her, and Henrietta always said no. Some of her other friends had invited her to their homes over the years, but after one or two awkward Thanksgivings many years ago at houses with ten porch steps to enter or gregarious dogs wanting to knock her down, she'd declined the invitations until, these days, no more came.

Her entire day would be disrupted by this horde. She huffed in exasperation as she turned back to her checkbook.

After a few minutes, she found herself wondering what Meryn would like for her birthday.

~

WITHOUT HAVING SAID A word, the battle lines were drawn. Beverly and Meryn had their afternoon tea in Meryn's office, leaving the men to wonder what they were talking about behind the firmly closed door.

"I don't want to get you in trouble," Ryn fretted.

"I never take the breaks I'm supposed to get," Beverly said. "And I get more done in the hours I work than three other people. As they'll find out when I do retire."

She sat back, sipping her tea with a satisfied smile. "That's a very useful tool to hold over them. Just knowing I can walk away at any time. And your office smells so much nicer than mine."

"It's the potpourri," Ryn said, poking a finger into a bowl of cinnamon, dried apple slices, cloves, and who knew what else. "It smells like autumn."

Beverly raised her arm and sniffed at her sleeve. "I am sick and tired of going home smelling like a cigarette butt."

"I'm beginning to think I've been a bad influence on you."

Beverly's bespectacled eyes glinted over the rim of her mug. "Perhaps you have, Professor."

Ryn had taken Henrietta's advice and forced herself to smile when she walked into Rayburn Hall the Wednesday after fall break.

"Hello," she'd said to Dr. Talbert on her way to her first lecture. "Had a good break?"

She could feel his gaze boring into her back as she chuckled to herself.

As for Geary, she could barely tolerate even hearing his voice, much less making herself interact with him, but she glued another benign smile on her face whenever she did run into him. She kept an eye out for Vanessa, determined to at least have a talk with her. On such a small campus, how was it possible not to see that girl?

She did see Francine and Roberta, who gave her a big wave on their way to a class. It was kind of funny to see them back in dresses and veils now that she'd seen them hanging out at their house in jeans and sweatshirts.

When Friday arrived without her having encountered Vanessa, Ryn made up her mind. She closed her office and walked to Mrs. Middleston's. Now that she didn't live here, she didn't feel comfortable just walking in and going up to Vanessa's room, so she knocked.

Mrs. Middleston's expression soured when she opened the door and saw who was there. "I told you I most likely wouldn't have a room for you when it didn't work out with Henrietta Cochran, and I don't, so—"

"I'm not here looking for a room," Ryn cut in. "I wanted to visit with Vanessa. Is she here?"

"How should I know? I'm not the keeper of every girl who rents a room from me."

Ryn was fairly certain Mrs. Middleston always knew precisely who was and wasn't in the house at any given moment, but she didn't argue. "May I go up and see?"

"I suppose so." Mrs. Middleston shuffled back. "And if she is, you talk some sense into that girl. She's missed curfew three times now."

"I'll try."

Ryn ascended to her old room on the third floor. The temperature was much more comfortable now than it had been. When she got to the landing, the door was shut. She knocked and listened.

"Vanessa? It's Ryn."

The door flew open, and Vanessa flung herself into Ryn's arms.

"I've missed you so much!"

Ryn sputtered, her mouth blocked by mounds of blonde curls. She wiped the hair out of her face and said, "I've missed you, too."

Vanessa released her and dragged her into the room, closing the door behind them. "Don't sit there!" she exclaimed when Ryn dropped her backpack to the floor and started to sit on her old bed.

Vanessa pulled Ryn over to her bed. "My new roommate is a neat-freak. If there's even a wrinkle in her bedspread, she has a fit. And she runs to Mrs. Middleston like she's in kindergarten or something."

Ryn settled on Vanessa's bed, scooting several stuffed Pooh friends out of the way to sit with her back against the wall. Vanessa cradled Eeyore in her arms.

"How's your semester going?" Ryn asked casually.

Vanessa sighed. "Not great. I bombed my midterms. My mom is really angry with me and keeps threatening to make me come home if I don't bring my grades up."

"Why are your grades suffering?" Ryn asked, resisting the temptation to lecture, knowing it wouldn't accomplish anything.

Vanessa picked at a loose thread on Eeyore's tail. "I don't know."

"Are you going to classes?"

"Most of them."

"How about your homework? Your reading for your classes?"

Vanessa shrugged. "Sometimes."

Ryn weighed how to continue. "Is the work too hard?"

"No!" Vanessa's head lifted. "I'm not dumb."

"I know you're not." Ryn held her gaze. "So why are you failing?"

Vanessa's smooth cheeks pinked under Ryn's scrutiny.

"I saw you." Ryn shifted to face Vanessa squarely. "With Geary. Last weekend in Cortland."

Vanessa blanched. "You won't tell anyone, will you?"

Ryn's jaw clenched. "Vanessa, he's using you."

"No, he loves me." She reached for Ryn's hand. "He told me. He's going to get me an apartment next semester. So we can be together more."

"He doesn't love you," Ryn said fiercely. "He does this. I heard about it my first week here."

Vanessa yanked her hand away, her cheeks colored again by angry scarlet patches. "You're wrong! Even if he... No one before matters. I know he loves me now."

116

She swung her legs over the side of the mattress. "If that's what you came here for, you can just leave." She stood. "I love him, and I'm not giving him up."

Her expression changed as she scowled at Ryn. "He told me about how you're jealous of him. How you try to take credit for his work." She jabbed a finger at the door. "I think you should leave."

Stunned, Ryn bit back all the retorts trying to escape from her mouth and clomped down the stairs. *That couldn't have gone any worse.* She didn't bother seeking Mrs. Middleston out to say farewell. She trudged home to Henrietta as the early evening began to settle over the village.

Despite the cool air, she was warm and sweating by the time she unlocked the front door. Seeing the empty living room and kitchen, Ryn deposited her bag in the hall and poked her head around the door into the studio. Henrietta was sketching.

"You're going to hurt your eyes, working without better light," she said, reaching for the switch.

"Don't turn it on, not yet." Henrietta's eyes flicked back and forth between another still life she had prepared and her sketchpad. "The shadows are just where I want them."

Ryn came over to stand behind her, watching the pencil fly over the paper, shading and sketching as the scene came to life in Henrietta's hands.

"I wish I could do that."

Henrietta pointed. "There's an extra pad and some pencils."

"What? I wouldn't know how to start," Ryn protested.

"You start by picking up a pencil and paper," Henrietta said tartly. "Don't think about it. Just start making lines."

Ryn still hesitated, not sure where to begin. Henrietta flipped to a fresh page in her own pad.

"Like this." She laid out quick, whispery lines that quickly became the rough wooden table, the basic outline of the old apple crate, the pumpkins sitting inside it. "You don't need detail. Just suggestions of what's there."

Ryn tried it. Her perspective was completely off, but it looked like a box sitting on a table. Kind of. If she tilted her head just so. "I think I'd better leave this to the artist in the family." She set the pad down.

Henrietta was looking at her, her face half in shadows.

"What?"

Henrietta shook her head. "Nothing. You're right. It's too dark. We'll try again tomorrow."

She slid off her stool and reached for her crutches.

"What're you in the mood for for dinner?" Ryn asked, leading the way back out to the kitchen.

"What's wrong. You look upset."

Ryn turned with some surprise to Henrietta. "How could you tell that?"

Henrietta rolled her eyes. "What's the problem?"

Ryn stared at the floor for a moment. "It's Geary again."

"I think I may need to sit down for this." Henrietta lowered herself into her chair at the table.

Ryn joined her. "He's having an affair with a freshman. My former roommate at the boarding house. I saw them in Cortland last weekend. I just tried to talk to her, but she says she loves him."

"He's having a relationship with a student?" Henrietta's voice was brittle.

Ryn nodded. "She's a nice girl, but so sheltered and so gullible and naïve. I don't know what to do. Beverly hinted when I first came here that he does this, and I should stay away from him." She scoffed. "Like I'd go anywhere near that pig."

She glanced up. "What do you think I should do?"

Henrietta pursed her lips for a moment. "I think, as unfortunate as it is, there is nothing you can do. Not given your relationship with Jerry Talbert. The girl is, I presume, of legal age?"

"Yes, but—"

"I know this is not what you want to hear, but I think you have enough to worry about with your own position without getting involved in something like this."

Ryn sighed. "I suppose you're right."

She got up and opened the refrigerator. "Chicken and rice leftovers for dinner?"

Henrietta didn't answer.

"Hank?"

"Yes?" Henrietta's head snapped up.

"Chicken and rice?"

"That sounds fine."

But something in Henrietta's voice didn't sound fine.

~

HENRIETTA WENT BACK INTO the bathroom to fuss with her hair a bit more, wetting the brush to make an unruly lick of hair lie flat. Why did it have to have a mind of its own today? She hadn't time enough to shower and wash it to make it behave.

"This is a mistake," she grumbled to the mirror.

"Ready, Hank?"

The girl had talked her into attending Mass at the campus chapel today, rather than going to St. Rita's as she'd been doing her entire life.

"It's really nice there," Meryn had wheedled. "And I'd like you to meet some people."

Henrietta had grudgingly agreed, but now wished she hadn't. She gave her suit jacket an extra tug and went out to the living room where Meryn had her coat ready for her.

"I think we should take my station wagon," Henrietta said. "In case I need my chair."

It grated on her to have to use her wheelchair, but she knew this chapel was in the middle of the campus. She'd been there only one time, and she remembered it being quite a distance from any of the parking lots.

She held out the keys.

"I can drive?" Meryn asked, her face lighting up.

"You know the campus better than I do."

The girl took the keys and hurried out to the garage. Henrietta checked her purse to make sure she had some tissues and cough drops. Sometimes, when she got winded, her throat got so dry it set off coughing spells.

She looked up at a loud thump from the general direction of the garage. The thump was followed by a series of crashing noises. She made her way to the garage where the Town & Country was idling and the girl was scrambling about, picking up plastic flower pots and wicker baskets which were rolling all over the floor. The set of shelves that normally stood in front of the car was leaning precariously.

Henrietta watched with a bemused smile. "Those hand controls are tricky, aren't they?"

Meryn's face was very red. "Yeah. You make it look easy."

She stood the shelves back on all four feet, and hastily restacked all the pots and baskets on them.

Henrietta got into the passenger seat.

"You still want me to drive?" Meryn asked as she slid behind the wheel.

"With the foot pedals, if you please."

Meryn gave an embarrassed half-laugh. "Foot pedals. Got it."

She drove them to the parking lot nearest to the college chapel. The lot was only half-full.

"What do you think?" Meryn asked as she pulled into a space. "Do you want your chair?"

Henrietta got out of the car and eyed the bronze cross she could see on the chapel's roof, probably a good quarter mile away. "Let me try walking it."

"There are benches. If you need the wheelchair, I'll come and get it."

Together, they walked the paved paths that meandered among the campus buildings.

"Where is your office?" Henrietta asked.

Ryn pointed. "Rayburn Hall."

Henrietta nodded. "That building housed the English and language departments when I was here."

Ryn stopped abruptly. "You went to school here?"

"Only a few classes. When I got home, my parents hired some of the instructors to tutor me. I finished my high school and then college degrees." She surveyed the campus. "I would have attended more classes here, but I couldn't get to the upper floors."

"There are elevators," Ryn said.

"There weren't in the late forties," Henrietta said drolly. "So I got a college education in a somewhat unorthodox fashion."

"How did I not know this?" Ryn asked.

"You never asked." Henrietta resumed walking.

Ryn hurried to catch up. "Has it changed much?"

"There are some new buildings. And the trees are much bigger than they were the last time I was here," Henrietta remarked.

"How long ago was that?"

"Twenty years ago, this December second."

Meryn looked at her. "How do you remember that date so precisely?"

Henrietta didn't answer immediately. She was slightly winded and paused to catch her breath. "Because my father's funeral was held in this chapel."

She walked on, leaving Meryn to follow silently.

When they entered the chapel, the click of her crutches echoed a little, causing a few people to turn and see who it was. Meryn waved to a few young nuns sitting in a pew near the front.

"Let's sit with them," Meryn whispered.

Henrietta started to protest, but the nuns gestured and scooted down to make room for them.

As Henrietta followed Meryn and sat, the nuns whispered greetings to them.

"This is my friend, Henrietta," she whispered back.

They smiled and nodded in Henrietta's direction. A trio of guitar players began a song just then, cutting off any further conversation, which was a good thing, because Henrietta's throat was suddenly tight.

She couldn't recall any of her other companions ever referring to her as a friend. And, she realized, it had been mutual.

The hymn they played was unfamiliar to Henrietta, but the young people all seemed to know it. Meryn's clear voice rang out. Henrietta had almost forgotten how musical the girl was. *She hasn't played her guitar for weeks.*

The rest of the congregation stood for the processional, but Meryn placed a hand on Henrietta's knee and remained seated beside her.

This Mass was certainly more informal than she was accustomed to at St. Rita's—two young people, one male, one female—served as acolytes. At the sign of peace, she was flustered when the people around her actually offered a hand to shake or placed a warm hand on her shoulder to wish her peace. Meryn smiled and wrapped an arm around her for a second, giving her a squeeze before letting go.

The Communion bread was not the thin wafers Henrietta was accustomed to having placed on her tongue, but a flat loaf of actual brown bread, blessed and broken into pieces to be offered when the congregants walked up to the altar. Henrietta saw the others holding out their palms for the bread. It was a little more awkward for her, as she had to brace herself and let go of one crutch, but then she followed the nuns as they shuffled sideways to where the acolytes held chalices with blessed wine.

Back in the pew, as the priest finished distributing Communion and then cleaned up, Henrietta recalled her father's funeral Mass. The space had changed but little. New tapestries and banners, but she supposed they switched those out seasonally. She bit her lip and, a moment later, felt Meryn's hand settle on her arm for a few seconds.

When Mass was over, Meryn completed the introductions.

"We were planning to have a brunch," said the dark-haired nun, Roberta. "Won't you both join us? Nothing formal. Please come."

Meryn turned to Henrietta quizzically.

"If you wish," Henrietta heard herself say. *What is wrong with me?*

Meryn grinned and said, "We'll be there in a few minutes."

When they were out of earshot, Meryn asked, "How are you? Do you need your wheelchair?"

"I'm fine. Let's walk." Henrietta's mind was whirling as they returned to the car. "So you're friends with nuns?"

Meryn laughed. "Yeah. Surprised me, too. They're pretty cool. The three in habits are junior nuns, completing their education degrees. Tamara, the one not in a habit, will probably be joining their order next fall."

Henrietta wasn't sure how to ask what was running through her mind. "And are you...?"

Meryn burst out laughing. "Hell, no. Sorry, I mean, no. I like them. They're really nice, but I have no desire to enter a convent."

For some reason, that released a small knot of fear that had started to tighten in Henrietta's chest.

When Meryn parked on the curb in front of a small house on a quiet street, Henrietta frowned out the car window at the porch steps. Seven steps.

"Shoot," Meryn said. "I'm sorry. I didn't even remember those. Do you want to leave?"

Before Henrietta could answer, a tall young woman emerged from the front door and came out to them.

Henrietta stared up at her. "Aren't you—?"

"Franny," she said with a grin, squatting so she was at eye-level with the car. She looked down at her jeans and sweatshirt. "Got out of uniform as soon as I could." She pointed down the driveway. "The back door only has two steps into the kitchen. If that would be easier, pull into the driveway. We parked down the block to leave it for you."

"Thank you," Henrietta said, taken aback by such unexpected thoughtfulness.

Meryn maneuvered the station wagon into the drive, leaving extra room for Henrietta to swing the door completely open. With the use of a sturdy handrail, Henrietta made her way up the two steps and into the kitchen, where a chair was waiting for her at the table.

"Coffee?" asked one of the blonde ones.

"Yes. Please." Henrietta leaned her crutches in the corner where they would be out of the way.

"I'm Tamara," said the young woman as she set a large mug on the table.

"Henrietta."

The kitchen was a beehive of activity, with the one called Roberta mixing up waffle batter while Franny cracked a dozen eggs into a bowl to scramble.

"Here," said the plump blonde, setting a bowl of apples on the table and handing Henrietta and Meryn each a peeler and a section of newspaper. "If you two will peel these, I'll make an apple strudel."

"Anything for your strudel, Steph," Meryn said fervently.

Stephanie laughed. "I grew up on this. My grandmother's recipe."

"God bless Grandma Messner," said Roberta. The others intoned their agreement with a murmured "Amen" and continued their work.

Henrietta peeled her apples, listening to the banter and the laughter. None of the gatherings she attended with her friends was anything like this. Apparently, something was happening later in the day that involved bison and horses. She realized Meryn was grinning at her.

"You have no idea what they're talking about, do you?" Meryn asked, reaching for another apple. "It's the football game today. The Buffalo Bills are playing the Colts."

"Oh."

Roberta cradled her bowl and stirred the batter. "Ryn tells us you're an artist."

Henrietta flushed as everyone turned to look at her. She nodded.

"She's not just a hobby artist," Meryn said. "Her work is in galleries all over the state. You should see her paintings. They're beautiful."

"We'd love to see them," said Franny.

"Maybe we can have you all over sometime," Meryn said with a hopeful glance.

"That... that would be lovely." Henrietta heard the words and nearly looked around to see who had spoken them.

A couple of hours later, Henrietta stretched out on the sofa at home, exhausted but surprisingly happy. She pulled the throw off the back of the couch.

"Thank you." Meryn stood over her and helped position the throw over her legs.

"What are you thanking me for?"

The silly girl stood smiling down at her. "For being part of my circle of friends. For letting them get to know you a little. For not yelling at me when I drove your car into the wall."

Henrietta couldn't help chuckling as Meryn went back to her room, singing one of the hymns from church.

Chapter 9

A STEADY PATTER OF rain hit the office window, and the murky November sky made it feel much later than three o'clock. Ryn adjusted her desk lamp as she bent over one of her old notebooks from school, searching for a specific passage. Finding it, she kept her place on the page with a finger while she jotted down the information on a new pad of paper. When she'd been handed the course material for her freshman seminar class, she'd almost fallen asleep trying to get through it.

"Who wrote this stuff?" she'd asked Beverly, and Beverly's wry expression had told her everything she needed to know.

This was probably the last real work Geary had done. He'd been teaching from the same old, tired material for years without refreshing it or looking for ways to make it more interesting. "It's history; it doesn't change," she'd heard him say a dozen times. Presumably, he put more effort into the upper level courses he and Talbert taught.

Here, she was digging through her old notes on George Washington as a teenager, when at age sixteen, he was surveying the western

127

reaches of the Virginia colony. The same age she'd been when she first learned of it. This was the kind of detail that had made history come alive for her, and she hoped she could pass some of that along.

She stiffened at the familiar sharp rap on the door. For a moment, she debated ignoring it, but she was sure he'd seen the light glowing through the pebbled glass.

"Come."

The door opened and Geary assumed his typical posture, leaning against the frame. "I'll need your notes."

Ryn turned back to her desk. "What notes?"

"The syllabus you made on that woman course," he drawled. "Your lecture notes. I need your material."

She bit her lip and continued to write—though her hand was clutching the pencil so hard it shook, making the squiggles nearly illegible. "I don't have any material."

From the corner of her eye, she saw him straighten. "What do you mean?"

"I mean," she said, careful to keep her tone calm and neutral, "that I wrote a proposal. That's all."

He stepped into the office, and the hair on the back of her neck stood up. "Beverly told Jerry you had almost the entire course put together. I need it. Now."

So that's why he did it. Not only could he take credit for an idea that wasn't his, but he thought he could teach it without doing any work.

Ryn kept her head down, but all of her focus was on his movements in her peripheral vision, her entire body tensed, ready to react if he made a move toward her. She had a very sudden certainty that looking him in the eye would provoke an attack—like making eye contact with an aggressive dog.

"Dr. Talbert misunderstood." She wasn't going to sell Beverly out. "I told Beverly I was going to work on putting the course together once it was approved. Since it got handed to you, that's now your job."

Her eyes flicked to the side just enough to see his clenched fists.

"But I don't— I don't have—" Geary stammered, and Ryn could hear the panic in his voice.

"The new semester starts in just a couple of months," she couldn't help saying. "If I were you, I'd get started."

For a few awful seconds, she was sure he was going to hit her, but he turned on his heel, slamming the door behind him so hard that the glass rattled.

She waited, frozen over her papers, until she heard another door slam farther down the corridor. Slowly, she exhaled and sat back. Her hands were still trembling, but whether it was from the fury that was nearly choking her, or the fight part of the fight-or-flight response that had kicked into high gear, she wasn't sure.

She got up and went to the door, opening it to see if the corridor was really empty. A couple of her students walked by and said hi. She nodded to them and closed the door again. Pulling open her desk's file drawer, she quickly pulled out several manila folders stuffed with her lecture ideas for the women-and-history class, her syllabus, the weekly lecture outline she had prepared, and transferred them all to her backpack. She might not be able to stop him from taking credit for her idea, and she couldn't stop Talbert from giving her course to that jerk, but she'd be damned if she was going to just give him all of her work to make the class a success.

Zipping the pack shut, she looked at the George Washington notes lying on the desk but gave up getting any more work done today. She tugged on her rain jacket and shrugged the backpack straps into position. She didn't even tell Beverly good-bye.

Her hood kept most of the rain off her face, but she wished that she'd driven as she trudged through the campus. Keeping her head bowed against the rain, her vision was blocked by her hood, so she didn't immediately see the car that slowed to roll at her pace.

"Hey."

She lifted the edge of her hood. Tamara sat behind the wheel of a rusty seventy-something Datsun.

"Can I give you a lift?"

"I'm soaked," Ryn said. "I'll get your seat all wet."

Tam laughed. "Nothing can hurt this vinyl. Get in."

Ryn hesitated. She wasn't fit company for anyone at the moment, but this cold rain was miserable. She slipped the straps off her shoulders and got in, tucking the backpack between her feet.

"Thanks."

"What in the world are you doing walking in this?" Tamara asked, reaching over to crank up the heat.

Ryn slid her hood back. "I usually like to walk, but I should have paid more attention to the weather forecast."

Tamara put the Datsun in gear. "You said you live out by the country club?"

"Yes."

They drove through the village streets, the slap of the wipers the only sound. Overhead, trees stretched their naked branches to the leaden sky.

"What's wrong?" Tamara asked.

Ryn blinked hard, willing herself not to cry. She hated it when she got so angry that she blubbered instead of hitting something. "Argument with a colleague," she said curtly.

She felt a warm hand smother her cold one.

"Want to talk?" Tam asked.

Ryn stared down at Tamara's hand. Of its own volition, hers flipped over to clasp Tam's, palm to palm. Their fingers intertwined, and the tears came anyhow.

"Damn it," she muttered, swiping at her cheeks with her other hand.

"It's okay." Tamara pulled over to a curb. "What happened?"

"I had an idea for a new course, wrote it up and gave it to my department chair. And my colleague somehow found out about it. He and the department head not only took credit for the idea, but they gave my course to the colleague. Today, he demanded all of my notes. All of my work on the course."

"You're kidding!" Tamara squeezed her hand. "People really do that?"

Ryn reminded herself that Tamara was a student and reluctantly withdrew her hand, pretending she needed both hands to adjust her wet hood away from her face.

"People do that," she said bitterly. "But it would probably be best if you didn't mention this to anyone."

"Sure."

Tamara put the car in first gear again. "You like living with Henrietta?"

Startled by the change in topic, Ryn pulled her mind away from her office drama. "Um, yeah. I mean, she can be a little acerbic at times, but I like her. Why, don't you?"

"Oh, she was nice," Tamara said a little too quickly. She glanced over. "It just seems like an odd match."

Ryn's mouth quirked into a grin as she remembered her own initial reaction to Henrietta's brusqueness. "I suppose it does." She pointed. "It's that single-story house, just there."

Tamara pulled into the driveway.

"Would you like to come in?"

Tam hesitated a second. "You're sure it's okay?"

"Yeah. Come on."

Ryn pulled her hood back up and fished her key out of her pocket before getting out of the car. Tamara followed her to the shelter of the front stoop. Ryn unlocked the door and called out.

"Henrietta?"

"Back here," came a voice from the rear of the house.

"She's in the studio." Ryn set her backpack down and hung her wet jacket on the coat tree.

"You sure she won't mind?" Tamara asked again.

Ryn gestured and led the way, enjoying Tam's gasp when they entered the studio. The walls and countertops were lined with the still life paintings Henrietta had been doing lately.

"Wow," Tamara breathed.

"Told you." Ryn folded her arms proudly.

Henrietta peeked out from behind another canvas. "Well, hello."

"Tam gave me a ride home. Gotta remember to check the forecast before heading out."

"These are really nice, Henrietta," Tamara said admiringly.

"Thank you." Henrietta wiped her brush on a rag. She looked from Tamara to Ryn. "You're home a little earlier than usual."

"I am." Ryn sighed. "I'll tell you more about that later. We'll let you get back to work, Henrietta."

"Nice to see you again," Tamara said with a little wave as she followed Ryn back to the foyer. "This is a nice house."

"It is. I don't think Henrietta's other companions always got along with her, but I like it here."

"Well," Tamara reached for the door. "I should get going."

"Thanks again for the ride. And for listening."

Tam took hold of her hand, giving it a squeeze. "Any time."

Ryn stepped out onto the front porch, watching and waving as Tamara backed out and drove away. She looked at her hand. "What in the world?"

∼

FOR THE PAST SEVERAL weeks, Henrietta had done her best to avoid being seated at Genevieve Talbert's table during the Thursday bridge games or luncheon afterward, but today, she arranged to be seated next to her when it was time to eat. Genevieve ordered her usual gin and tonic and Henrietta coffee—the temperature outside had plummeted, and she wanted something hot. She ignored the fresh cigarette Genevieve lit in a rather blatant display of displeasure at the seating arrangement.

"We haven't seen you at St. Rita's the last few weeks," Genevieve said, glancing over the menu placed before her. "Have you been ill?"

"Not at all." Henrietta stifled a cough as the smoke wafted in her direction.

Their waitress brought their drinks.

"You forgot the lime," Genevieve said, thrusting the drink away without a glance at the girl.

"I'm sorry, Mrs. Talbert."

"Thank you, Annmarie," Henrietta said, glancing quickly at the girl's nametag. "The coffee smells nice and fresh."

"You're welcome, Miss Cochran. I'll be right back, Mrs. Talbert."

Henrietta used the menu to wave away some of the smoke. "I've been attending Mass at the St. Aloysius chapel."

"Really?" Genevieve's perfectly plucked and penciled-in eyebrows arched imperiously. Henrietta noted the many wrinkles around her mouth as her lips encircled the cigarette to inhale.

"Yes."

Genevieve tapped her cigarette against the ashtray. "With that girl? Your new live-in help?"

The dismissal in her tone struck Henrietta, and she wondered if Genevieve was merely echoing her own past dismissive attitude toward her prior companions.

"Jerry's new professor, yes," Henrietta reminded Genevieve, though she was certain the reminder wasn't necessary. "Her and some other young people I've met there. I'm surprised more of the faculty don't attend church on campus."

Genevieve sniffed. "Please. Jerry has enough of that place during the week. And I wouldn't get too attached to your girl. Word has it that she may not pass muster. You do know, she has to be evaluated each of her first three years. From what Jerry says, she's not a team player."

Henrietta had to clamp her jaw shut to hold back the retort that sprang to her lips. Meryn had shared what that man, Geary, had tried to do, demanding she hand over her work. That on top of his affair with a student. *Keep calm,* she reminded herself.

"Oh, I think she's just trying not to be steamrollered by the men," she said casually.

"Please," Genevieve said again. "That's the way things work. If she hasn't realized that by now, she's in for a rude awakening. And after Jerry gets promoted, she'll be working under Bradley."

"Is he still on track to take over?"

Genevieve forcefully exhaled. "Why wouldn't he be?"

"Oh..." Henrietta let the pause stretch out. "One hears things. It's such a small village, after all."

Genevieve ground out her cigarette. "I suggest you stop listening to idle gossip, Henrietta."

That's rich, coming from you, Henrietta longed to say, but again held her tongue. Instead, "It's not idle gossip if it's true, Genevieve. And I'm fairly certain some of his behavior is also illegal."

She smiled to herself as Genevieve got up under the pretense of needing to talk to Mary Ellen Greene at a neighboring table about something.

When she left the club an hour later, she drove into town. The sky was a flat gray, looking very much like it could snow. *What a dreary day,* she thought, wondering if she wouldn't rather just go home.

"Miss Cochran, what a nice surprise," said the owner of the art supply store when Henrietta pulled the door open, propping it with one crutch. She hurried over to hold the door. "Are you ready for new canvases? I would have delivered anything you need."

She wore a paint-splattered men's shirt over faded jeans, with a colorful bandana tied around her hair. Henrietta often wished she could wear something similar.

"Hello, Sandy. I wanted to come to the store and look things over for myself."

"What do you need? We have a new line of watercolors you might like."

"It's not for me. I need a gift. A beginner's set."

"Painting? Drawing?"

Henrietta frowned. "I'm not sure. Show me what you have."

Sandy led her to the aisle where she had a variety of kits. Henrietta chose one that looked like a wooden briefcase that unfolded to make an easel and was filled with a nice variety of acrylics and watercolors, a few canvas boards to get started with, as well as a sketchpad and a few pencils. They completed the sale, and Henrietta made an additional request.

"Of course I can gift wrap this for you." Sandy checked the calendar. "I'll deliver it on Saturday, the nineteenth after I close the shop." She jotted the details on the sales receipt, and taped it to the box.

"That will be perfect, Sandy. Thank you so much."

Sandy did a double take. "You're most welcome, Miss Cochran."

Henrietta turned to go, but paused. "Sandy, I've been buying art supplies from you for nearly twenty years, ever since you bought this store. I think it's time you called me Henrietta, don't you?"

Sandy smiled. "I'll do that, Henrietta. Have a good day."

"You, too."

Outside on the sidewalk, Henrietta took a deep breath. It wasn't such a dreary day after all.

~

A LIGHT DUSTING OF snow lay over everything, making the campus look like something out of a snow globe, but Ryn barely noticed. She finished her last lecture of the day and grumbled when she realized she didn't have the book she wanted in her backpack. She crossed the quad to Rayburn Hall and dragged herself up the stairs to the second floor.

"Meryn," Beverly called when she walked by without saying anything.

Ryn backed up. "Yes?"

"I didn't expect you back this afternoon."

"I know. I planned to leave after my last lecture, but I forgot something."

Beverly peered at her through her enormous glasses, looking more like an owl than ever. "What's the matter?"

Ryn eyed the dark office beyond Beverly's desk.

"He's not here."

Ryn came in and lowered her backpack to the floor. Sitting down on one of the spare chairs, she unzipped her jacket and slipped out of it, leaving her scarf wrapped around her neck.

"Tea?" Beverly asked.

"I suppose."

Beverly apparently had the kettle already hot. She quickly poured two mugs of water and pulled a couple of teabags from a tin next to the hot plate, then came around to take the other wooden chair.

"Now, what's troubling you?"

Ryn stared into her mug, bobbing her teabag up and down in the water. "Everything. All the garbage going on here. I called my family last night. I was going to drive home for Thanksgiving, but my mom told me they're taking the boys to meet the basketball coach at some college in North Carolina. She said they'd see me at Christmas in a few weeks."

She tossed her teabag into the trash and took a sip, but she had a hard time swallowing. "She's right. I'd only be there for a couple of days and then have to drive right back here. And Christmas is only a month further away. But I think she forgot—" She had to clear her throat. "I just miss them."

Beverly patted her knee. "I know you do. But do try to cheer up. I'm sure you'll have a nicer Thanksgiving here than you expect."

"Thanks." The tea and the conversation were comforting. "I'm sorry. I don't mean to always dump my troubles on you. What are you doing for Thanksgiving?"

"Oh, probably the same as always. My daughter and her family will come over. The men will spend the day watching football while we prepare dinner."

Ryn sat back. "Turkey? The usual?"

"We do a small turkey, but I'll make a big pan of lasagna with garlic bread. Cannoli along with the pies for dessert. It's more Italian than most. Little Billy is four now, so he's more interested in the holidays this year."

Ryn smiled. "Sounds nice." She drained her mug and went to wash it. "Thanks, Beverly." She put the mug in place next to the hot plate and reached for her jacket and bag. "Don't know what I'd do without you."

"You'd be just fine, Meryn."

Ryn smiled. "Have a good evening. I promise to be in a better mood tomorrow."

She went down the hall to her office and nearly jumped out of her skin when she opened her door and found Bradley Geary inside. He jerked upright, caught in the act of tearing through the contents of her file drawer. Papers and folders went flying.

"What the hell are you doing?" she demanded. She dropped her pack and her jacket to the floor with a thump.

His face shone with sweat and his eyes were wide. "Where are they? Where are your notes?"

She was breathing hard as she said, "I told you. You stole my class. I'm not giving you anything."

Quicker than she would have believed him capable of moving, he grabbed her by the scarf, twisting it until it choked her as he pushed her up against the wall. His face was mere inches from hers.

"I will *not* be made a fool of," he snarled. She could smell onions on his hot breath. "Where," he twisted the scarf more tightly, "are those notes?"

His body was at an angle so that she couldn't get a knee to his groin. Her hands flew to his wrist, but he only twisted the scarf more tightly. She felt his thumb rotate into a position on top of the scarf. Without thinking, she grabbed it, yanking it backward viciously.

He yelped and released his pressure on her throat, but she held on, one hand on his wrist, the other forcing his thumb back until his knees buckled and he fell at her feet.

Now it was her leaning over him. "If you ever touch me again, I will break your fucking fingers, one by one."

Scurrying footsteps announced Beverly's arrival before she appeared in the doorway.

"Professors!"

Ryn released him with a shove. Geary cradled his hand against his chest as he got to his feet and rushed past Beverly.

Ryn actually took a step in pursuit, but Beverly stopped her, placing her hands on Ryn's shoulders.

"Let him go." She looked past Ryn at the scattered papers and manila folders. "Let's clean this up."

As the adrenaline left her, Ryn's legs gave out and she collapsed into her chair. "Well, Beverly," she said shakily. "It's been nice knowing you."

Beverly straightened with a handful of papers. She set them on the desk. "I'll tell Dr. Talbert—"

"Don't you see?" Ryn laughed harshly. "Talbert only has his eye on his promotion. When Geary steps in as chair next year..." She ran a hand through her hair. "And I can forget about a reference. I'll be lucky to teach again."

Beverly grabbed her hands. "Now you listen to me." She tugged Ryn to her feet. "This can wait." She led her out of the office, pulling the door shut behind them. Bending over, she picked up the abandoned jacket and backpack. "I am driving you home. No arguments."

Mutely, Ryn took her things and followed Beverly down the corridor to her office to get her own coat and purse, and then out to the staff parking lot. The car was silent as Beverly drove through the village, out to the country club road, and pulled into Henrietta's driveway.

Ryn didn't argue when Beverly got out and accompanied her to the porch. She fumbled with the key a moment before she was able to unlock the door.

"Now, you go lie down," Beverly said, taking Ryn's jacket to hang on the hall tree. "I'm going to have a word with Miss Cochran."

"Beverly, thank you," Ryn managed before her throat sealed itself shut. There was so much more to say, but the words wouldn't come.

Beverly gave her a gentle nudge, and Ryn went to her room.

She dropped her backpack on the spare bed, flipped on the cassette player and curled up on her side on her bed. With Roberta Flack singing *Killing Me Softly*, she tried not to think—about how her family had forgotten her birthday was coming, about how homesick she was, about how much she wished she'd never taken this job.

~

HENRIETTA SAW BEVERLY DiSORBO to the door. "Thank you for bringing her home. And for telling me what happened."

She'd never said more than hello to Bonnie's sister before today. Beverly knew from Bonnie about the surprise Meryn's family was planning, and Henrietta felt just as torn as she did about whether it should stay a secret. Henrietta was rarely undecided about things. Partly because she hadn't the energy or time to waffle about, partly because—as she'd come to realize since September—her life had become so constricted to a rigid routine, that there were rarely any decisions to be made. Not major ones at any rate. Not until this girl turned things upside-down.

More upsetting to both of them was the attack by that man, Geary. She went to the guest wing and stood outside Meryn's door, listening, wondering if she should interfere. All she could hear was music. At last, she raised a hand and knocked.

"Meryn, may I come in?"

It was a moment before a muffled voice said, "Yes."

The room was almost dark. In the gloom, lit only by the lamplight spilling in from the living room, she made Meryn's form out on the far bed—the one that had been Henrietta's father's. She'd wondered which bed the girl had chosen. Henrietta walked around the other bed and sat on the mattress.

Meryn rolled over and clicked the music off. "I'm sorry. You're probably getting hungry."

"I'm not here to talk about dinner."

"Beverly told you what happened."

"Yes." Henrietta paused. "Are you hurt?"

"My throat is a little irritated, but I'm fine."

"Do you want to report this to the police? He assaulted you."

She expected Meryn to immediately refuse, so she was surprised when the girl took some time before saying, "I don't think so. I probably hurt him more than he hurt me."

She took a deep breath. "I'm sorry, Henrietta."

"Why on earth are you sorry?"

Meryn sat up on the side of her bed, her head bowed. "I probably won't have a job at St. Aloysius after this year. I should have just given him what he wanted—"

"Don't you dare!"

Meryn's pale face raised to her.

"There may be some things you can't control," Henrietta said. "Like men taking credit for your idea. That has happened to women forever. But you do not have to do his work for him. And... if that means you'll have to teach elsewhere, then that's what you'll do. We'll deal with that when the time comes. Now, is there anything else bothering you?"

Henrietta was glad the room was still dark as she heard a hitch in Meryn's breathing.

"Nothing important," Meryn said, but it came out barely more than a whisper.

"Of course it's important. You miss your family, and Thanksgiving is coming up." Henrietta sighed. "I'm going to tell you something I promised I wouldn't. Your mother called. They are coming here for Thanksgiving, and for your birthday."

Meryn straightened. "What?"

"Now you must promise to be surprised when they arrive. I didn't want to ruin it, but I can't have you thinking they've forgotten you."

Meryn moved to sit beside Henrietta and clasped her hand. "Really? They're coming here?"

"They have reservations at the hotel in the village, but we'll be having Thanksgiving dinner here. Your whole family."

"Thank you," Meryn said, squeezing her hand gently. "For welcoming my family into your home."

It was Henrietta's turn to have a hard time getting words out. "It's your home, too. Of course they're welcome."

Meryn bounded to her feet. "Dinner. What are you hungry for?"

The girl's change in mood nearly gave Henrietta whiplash. "You pick tonight."

"Pizza," Meryn said immediately. "With pepperoni and mushrooms."

Henrietta immediately regretted letting the girl decide. "Make part of it cheese only."

"You got it." Meryn led the way out to the living room. "I'll pick it up and be back in a little bit."

Henrietta braced herself as Meryn threw her arms around her in a hug. "Thanks again, Hank."

The girl grabbed her jacket from the hall tree and hurried out of the house.

Henrietta watched the headlights as they swept down the drive and out to the road. Rubbing her chest absently, she wondered again about the strange sensations there lately.

"I really need to see the doctor," she said, turning to go to the kitchen and get plates down.

Chapter 10

THE NEXT WEEK FLEW by for Ryn. She caught only glimpses of Geary—wearing a splint on his left hand—but he was making himself scarce. Even Beverly reported that she hadn't seen him other than in passing. By unspoken decree, Ryn kept her office door open, and Beverly found some excuse or other to pass by every fifteen minutes or so when Ryn was in there. If Talbert knew what had happened, he wasn't letting on, and Ryn was certain Geary wouldn't have admitted that he got caught trying to steal her work nor how he'd managed to hurt his hand.

Her classes were going well. As with any requisite class, there were some students who were just taking up space and were probably going to fail, but more than half of her students in each class were excelling, including her unofficial history club, which had continued to delight her with their interest. When she offered extra credit, they dove in enthusiastically.

For her part, she could barely contain her excitement at seeing her family in the coming week. She had to keep reminding herself it was supposed to be a secret, but she was so glad Henrietta had told her. She could laugh now at how silly she'd been, feeling so depressed and thinking they'd forgotten her, but it had been pretty real at the time.

She was gathering up her lecture notes after her last class on Tuesday when Tamara knocked and came in as the students filed out.

"Hi," Ryn said. "Didn't expect to see you. When we saw y'uns at church on Sunday, you said you were going home."

"I am," Tam said. "I'm leaving now. Roberta and the others are leaving in a couple of hours. They'll be at the motherhouse for the holiday."

She shifted her books from one arm to the other, looking nervous. "You're not going home?"

"No." Ryn glanced at her watch and grinned. "My family is coming up here. They should be more than halfway by now."

Tamara nodded. She stared at the board, where Ryn had scribbled some extra tidbits on the Battle of Trenton.

"Is something wrong?" Ryn asked, setting her papers on the desk.

"No," Tamara said quickly. "Not wrong. I just..." Her eyes met Ryn's for just a second and then quickly back down at her shoes. "When we get back... I was wondering..."

She was breathing hard considering she wasn't doing anything. "Could we talk?"

"Sure," Ryn said slowly. "Care to give me any hints?"

Tamara laughed nervously. "Here's a hint." She stepped closer and gave Ryn a kiss on the cheek.

When Ryn's mouth tried to form words, nothing came out. Tamara stepped back with a nod and nearly ran from the room.

Ryn stood staring at the doorway, raising a hand to touch her cheek. In a daze, she picked up her books and almost floated out of the classroom. She'd already given Beverly her Thanksgiving card, so she headed straight to her car, eager to get home and make sure the house was as ready as it could be. She really hoped Henrietta would be okay with her loud, boisterous family invading her usually quiet space. It meant more than she could say that Henrietta had agreed to conspire with her mom to surprise her, even if it wasn't a surprise any longer.

When she got home, she made sure her room was picked up—she knew her mom would want to see it. With Bonnie's weekly cleaning, it never really had time to get dirty or dusty, but she ran a dust cloth over the dresser and night stands anyhow.

Out in the living room, she jumped up every time she heard a car.

Henrietta, from her place on the couch, merely glanced up from the newspaper. "That's not going to make them get here any sooner, you know."

"I know." Ryn grinned sheepishly. "And, I know, I have to remember to be surprised."

"Which will be hard to pull off if you run out the door to greet them the second they arrive."

"You're right." Ryn forced herself to sit down and wait.

When at last the Flemings pulled into the driveway, Henrietta said, "Stay."

Ryn chuckled but stayed put as Henrietta got to her feet and went to answer the doorbell. Ryn tried to pretend she was reading a section of the paper, but when her mom stepped inside, she couldn't hold herself back.

She jumped up and ran to her mother's embrace. "What are you doing here?"

June Fleming hugged her tightly. "You really didn't know we were coming?"

Ryn caught Henrietta's eye over her mom's shoulder. "I had no idea. What a great surprise!"

She hugged her dad, Walt, next and introduced her parents to Henrietta. The twins, ganglier than she remembered, came in behind their dad. "This is Robbie," she looked closely to be sure, "and this one is Roger." She couldn't believe how they'd grown. She greeted them with affectionate punches in the arm.

"And this is my baby sister, Janie."

"You must be tired and hungry after your trip," Henrietta said.

"A little," said June. "But if we could just freshen up, we insist on taking you out to dinner. Then we'll check in at our hotel and leave you in peace until tomorrow."

A half hour later, they were seated at a large table in a restaurant in the village that Ryn had never been to, just a couple of doors down from the hotel. She made sure Henrietta sat next to her so she wouldn't be left out as the conversation bounced around disjointedly. The boys were excited about their basketball season, and Janie was loving life at WVU, with plans to pledge a sorority—"and stay on campus," she added with a worried glance at June—next semester.

Ryn listened happily. She'd missed this so much. Her mom wanted to know all about Henrietta's artwork. Ryn piped up when she thought Henrietta was being too modest.

The twins polished off not only their food, but any leftovers on anyone else's plate.

"Two hollow legs on each of them," June said, shaking her head. "I can't keep enough food in the house."

When dinner was over, Ryn hugged everyone again. "I'll see you tomorrow."

Walking to the car with Henrietta, she said, "Thanks again, Hank, for going along with this. This is the nicest birthday present I could have had."

~

HENRIETTA HAD RETREATED TO her studio at Meryn's urging.

"I know you need some quiet time. It's okay. We've got everything covered out here."

Wednesday morning, Denny had made his regularly scheduled delivery of groceries, except it was about three times as much food as usual. Bonnie was there to receive it, directing the placement of the boxes. She and June Fleming were busy in the kitchen, baking and laughing. Out in the front yard, the children—"it's ridiculous to call those boys children," she reminded herself—threw a football with Meryn while the younger girl sat curled up in a chair, reading.

From the studio windows, Henrietta watched as Meryn's father hung bird feeders up all over her back yard—with suet cakes, sunflower seeds and other mixes of feed to attract and feed the birds through the winter. He placed a couple just outside the studio windows, giving Henrietta a little wave.

"I brought you several bags of feed to replenish them," he'd said. "I hope you don't mind, but I find this very relaxing at home."

All Henrietta really knew of the man was that he was an accountant but, as she watched him move about, there were already birds gathering in the branches, their little heads tilting as they watched and waited for him to leave so they could try out the new treats. Fascinated, she reached for her sketchpad as Walt sat in one of the lawn chairs, motionless. One by one, the birds braved his still presence to fly to the feeders, setting them rocking from their hangers, spilling some seeds on the ground, which got the attention of a few squirrels.

Watching Meryn with her family, she saw that the girl favored her father, with her dark hair and eyes, more handsome than pretty. Someday, when her hair began to turn silver and she needed glasses like him, they would only make her look more distinguished. The younger sister was almost a copy of their mother, pretty and petite, with honey-blonde hair. The boys were a blend, but she could see something of the men they would become.

Muted conversation came to her from the kitchen, and her eyes drifted to her latest painting—a summer scene of the pond. There, on the dock, were two small figures, one with copper hair glinting in the sunshine.

147

Our house used to have laughter and lots of people... but that was the old house, the one they lived in before she got sick. This house, built for her as she was after the polio, had never known that kind of happiness. Though this house allowed her to be independent, it had also, in a way, become her prison.

Her father had built it for her out of love—and guilt. Faced with their new reality of raising a daughter who had come home maimed, never to regain the mobility they had taken for granted or the future they had envisioned, her parents had done the best they could to make her life as easy as possible. It was comfortable, accessible—*but I'm the one who turned it into a prison*, she realized. Shutting herself off from people, especially after first her father, then her mother died; needing live-in companions but keeping them at a distance. Even her friends from the club weren't friends in the real sense. She didn't share confidences with them, didn't invite them into her life, nor did she take part in theirs.

Outside the studio, Meryn and the boys found their father, joining him to talk and point at the birds. She watched Meryn lay her hand on her father's arm with such open affection—*the same affection she shows me.*

As soon as that thought crossed her mind, there it was again, that strange constricting feeling in her chest. She rubbed her breastbone, taking a few deep breaths. She didn't feel ill, but this was happening more frequently. Come Monday, she'd make an appointment with Dr. McCourt and see what was wrong.

For now, she set her pad and pencil aside and went to the kitchen. "Can I help?"

Bonnie turned around, her mouth open, but June brought a large bowl of green beans to the table.

"If you could snap these, we'll blanch them for dinner tomorrow."

She sat down in an adjacent chair to chop an onion. "I want to thank you for offering Ryn such a nice place to live. I wasn't very happy about the boarding house she found originally. It sounded too much like a dormitory to me." She looked around. "This is so much more like home."

Behind June, Bonnie was nodding and flapping her hands.

Henrietta felt a flush creeping into her cheeks. "She's been a delight to have around. I hope she's happy enough to stay for a long time."

June smiled though she was blinking tears out of her eyes. "She seems happy. I'm afraid that means you're part of our family now. We'll have to have you down to visit this summer."

Henrietta tried to ignore Bonnie's beaming face as she dabbed at her eyes with her apron.

~

THE WEEKEND PASSED WAY too quickly for Ryn. Thanksgiving Day had been spent at the house—playing more football, exploring the pond. She and the boys walked all the way around to the dock and got in the old rowboat. Ryn made sure there weren't any critters inside this time, but it was too cold for snakes or turtles. The edges of the pond were skimmed with ice. From the middle, as the boat bobbed, Ryn looked up at the house, clearly visible now through the naked trees.

It made her ridiculously happy that Henrietta had welcomed her family into her home. Ryn knew her well enough now to know what a big deal it was—Bonnie had confirmed that, except for an occasional bridge gathering, Henrietta never had people to the house.

Ryn had kept a close eye on things, looking for signs that anyone was getting on Henrietta's nerves. She'd already warned everyone that the sofa was off-limits, though she was certain Henrietta wouldn't lie down on it while they were there. The boys sprawled on the floor when they were inside, and Janie was content to sit in the chair that Ryn normally occupied and read. When Henrietta learned they were paying for two hotel rooms, she'd suggested Janie stay at the house, sleeping in the spare bed, which would allow the other Flemings to stay in one hotel room with two full beds.

"Why pay for an extra room if they don't have to?" Henrietta had said.

So Ryn and her sister had stayed up late, talking. Janie told her all about WVU and which sorority she wanted to pledge—something completely beyond Ryn's comprehension, but she was happy that Janie was happy.

On Friday, the Flemings spent most of the day exploring Bluemont—"not that that took much time," Ryn told Henrietta later. A light snow fell, making it feel very seasonal as they wandered through the village's small downtown, going into several of the stores. She showed them the campus but, when her mom asked to see her office, Ryn was grateful the building was locked. She liked her broom closet, but it was a little shabby. Henrietta had insisted they all come back to the house for dinner Friday evening.

"Meryn and I will never eat all of this food," she said.

There was little danger of leftovers lasting long enough to go bad with the twins at the table. June ordered the men to do the dishes, but Ryn stayed to supervise the drying and stacking, since they were still using Henrietta's good china.

On Saturday morning, she tried to talk Henrietta into joining them for breakfast in town.

"You go," Henrietta said. "Enjoy your last morning with your family. I'll see you back here later. Please tell your family how nice it was to meet them, and thank your father again for all of the bird feeders."

It was hard to eat, knowing her family was leaving right after they finished, but Ryn's heart was lightened a little when her mother said, "Remember, Christmas is only a few weeks away. Please invite Henrietta to come home with you."

"I will," Ryn promised, but she knew Hank wouldn't come.

She waved them off, thanking them one last time for the new down jacket that they'd given her for her birthday. Blinking back tears, she drove home. When she entered the front door, she just stood there for a moment, listening to the quiet.

"Meryn?"

She followed Henrietta's voice back to the studio.

"They're on their way back to Pennsylvania?"

Ryn nodded. "Yeah."

She looked at what Henrietta was working on and smiled. The sketchpad was full of little drawings of birds. "My dad will be glad to know he gave you new things to paint."

"I had no idea they would be so entertaining."

Ryn went to the window and watched the activity at the feeders. "I think this is my dad's therapy for being stuck in an office staring at numbers all day. I cannot imagine spending thirty or forty years of my life that way."

"You do what you need to for your family."

"I guess." Ryn turned. "Thanks again for my art set. Are you still willing to teach me?"

"I've already been thinking about it. Why don't we begin after Christmas?"

"Okay." Ryn brightened. "Hey, can we decorate this weekend?"

Henrietta stared at her. "Decorate?"

"For Christmas. It's officially the season."

Henrietta's face flushed. "I don't—"

It was Ryn's turn to stare. "You don't decorate for Christmas? Not even a tree?"

Henrietta turned her back, busying herself with the pencils lying on the counter. "It's a lot of trouble, and there's never been any need..." She paused. "We can, if you like."

Ryn frowned, picturing the layout of the house and wondering if there was an attic she hadn't noticed. "Do you even have decorations?"

"Probably in the basement."

"I didn't know this house has a basement."

"Well, it does, and that is where they would be. But they haven't been out of the boxes for years, so I have no idea what condition they're in."

The door to the basement was off the breezeway leading to the garage. Ryn couldn't believe she'd never noticed it. Judging from the cobwebs that caught at her face and hair on her way down the stairs, Henrietta was right. No one had been down here for ages. It was kind of like exploring in a grandparent's house. Who knew what she'd find?

Aside from the cobwebs and dust, everything down here seemed okay. The basement was dry, if musty. There were old buckets and mops and brooms against the wall at the base of the stairs. A few card tables, their legs folded, were propped against the adjacent wall, along with about a dozen wooden folding chairs—presumably used during those bridge games Bonnie had told her about. The harsh light from the three bare bulbs threw shadows everywhere as she moved around.

There were boxes stacked randomly. She leaned over to see if they were labeled at all. She had to keep shifting to get out of the way of the light. Nothing seemed to be marked as to the contents. She opened one box and found bundles of old bank statements. Others held what appeared to be ledgers from Mr. Cochran's construction business. But no Christmas ornaments.

Ryn sneezed at the dust she was raising. Swiping her sleeve across her face, she moved to another grouping of boxes. A Christmas wreath! But it was in pretty bad shape, the bow attached to it crinkled and faded. She set that box aside and opened another. Here, wrapped in newspaper, were ornaments. It was like a scavenger hunt. If she could only find a tree stand, she'd go buy a tree.

She shuffled boxes, finding plenty of ornaments, a set of Christmas dishes, old wrapping paper, and, at last, a tree stand. One box teetered and fell over with a clink of glass, its flaps bursting open and some of its contents spilling onto the basement floor.

"Oh, please don't be anything valuable," she whispered.

Ryn squatted down to pick everything up. Inside were two small lamps of pink crystal in the shape of a lady wearing an old-fashioned gown, with the parasols the lampshades. The broken glass was, luckily, only one of the light bulbs. She set them aside, and stood the box upright to peek inside. Books, a couple of dolls, stuffed animals. She was looking at the contents of Henrietta's room when she was a girl. Ryn was sure of it.

She went to get one of the chairs and unfolded it next to the box. Sitting down, she pulled out handfuls of old books: Nancy Drew, Cherry Ames, The Bobbsey Twins. All original first editions.

Peering into the box, she saw another bundle, tied with a green ribbon. It was a collection of envelopes.

She glanced at the address on the first envelope, figuring it was more of Mr. Cochran's old business correspondence, and was startled to see *Una Marsden* with an address in London, written in what was unmistakably Henrietta's handwriting—shaky and more juvenile, but still hers.

Curious, Ryn tugged on the ribbon. When it fell away, the yellowed envelopes lay in her lap. Turning one of them over, her hunch was confirmed when she saw the return address. It must have been the house the Cochrans lived in before Henrietta's father built this one. Ryn recognized the name of the street, just around the corner from Mrs. Middleston's. Flipping through the envelopes, she saw that they all had uncancelled stamps and no postmark. They'd never been mailed.

One envelope, though, was addressed in a different hand to Bryce and Marla Cochran, from a Wilhelmina Marsden in Boston. Feeling slightly guilty, Ryn cast a glance upward, but this envelope was already open. She gently prized out the yellowed paper inside.

Dear Marla and Bryce,

I write with tragic news. Despite the best efforts of the doctors here, Una died yesterday. They said there was nothing more to be done. Her lungs shut down, and even the iron lung could not resuscitate her.

They said that, had she shown symptoms as soon as Henrietta did, and had we sought medical care more urgently, she might have recovered. As it is, you may have been fortunate to note Henrietta's onset of symptoms so quickly, though, you may now be left with a cripple who will require care for the rest of her life. So, perhaps Una was the more fortunate after all.

I have cabled my brother and his wife, but they do not wish to have Una's body brought back to England amidst all the turmoil there. I am to bring her home to Bluemont for burial.

You may decide for yourselves what to tell Henrietta, but my own thought is that she is so fragile at this time, that this shock may well cause a severe setback for her, and that she ought not be told. Let her think Una returned to England, and let her keep her happy memories.

We shall return within the week.

Best,

Wilhelmina

Ryn sat, staring at the letter, one hand pressed to her chest. She jumped at the click of crutches from the top of the basement stairs.

"Meryn? Have you found anything down there?"

It was a moment before Ryn could say, "Yes. I found some ornaments and a tree stand. I'll be up in a few minutes."

Carefully, she folded the letter back into its envelope. Placing it with the others, she tied the ribbon back in place and tucked the bundle inside her shirt.

THE MAILMAN GAVE THE doorbell a short ring, his usual signal to Henrietta. She was in the middle of dabbling with some watercolors added to her bird sketches, trying to see the effect. The little birds hopped around so quickly that it was hard to see their colors accurately.

They were like flying sketches. She'd found a book on birds on the bookcase in the living room—probably something her parents had purchased—and the colored photos helped her somewhat but, as she sat back and scrutinized the watercolor paper, she realized she liked her indistinct splashes of color better. They gave the feeling of movement rather than something stationary that made the birds look like something a taxidermist had gotten hold of.

She rinsed her brushes and closed up her paints. Making her way out to the living room, she paused at the sight of the eight-foot-tall Christmas tree occupying the place in front of the picture window. Meryn had insisted on the biggest tree that would fit and still allow room for a star at the top.

It was rather festive, she had to admit. She hadn't set up a tree or any other Christmas decorations since the year her mother had been so ill. A stroke, followed by pneumonia, had thankfully taken her mother quickly. If she had lingered, needing care following the stroke, Henrietta hadn't been sure how she would have managed, limited as she was.

Life was forever altered after that. Though Henrietta had been in her forties at that time, it still left her feeling very much an orphan. No parents, no siblings, no cousins anywhere nearby. She thought her father might have family near Saranac Lake, but had no idea if they still lived there. And if they did, so what? She could hardly contact them at that point, alone and crippled, if not destitute.

No, Henrietta had determined to be frugal with her resources and stay as independent as she could, remaining in this house, even if it meant having to bring in someone to live with her.

But none of her other companions had insisted on decorating the house. Of course, none of them had been quite like Meryn. Just the thought of the girl brought a small smile to Henrietta's face.

When she opened the door, she was startled by the large wreath hanging on it. She still hadn't gotten used to it. Out on the front porch, Meryn had also hung a garland around the storm door, lit by a string of lights. Inside, another garland of pine lay over the fireplace mantel. When Henrietta had tried to repay her for what she'd spent, Meryn had refused, insisting this was her home, too, and she wanted to do it.

Bonnie, of course, was delighted. "It's about time this house was properly done up." She had found some old Christmas albums inside the stereo console, and played them while she was cleaning. Henrietta had found herself humming some of the carols while she worked in the studio.

The bridge gatherings were always suspended during this season, as people were busy with their own holiday preparations. Besides, the club was typically booked to capacity, hosting many luncheons as holiday parties for employees of the club members who owned businesses in town.

Henrietta had always felt rather cut off during this period when everyone else was busily running about, preparing for Christmas. With no one to exchange gifts with, other than Bonnie, she had no need to shop. She usually spent Christmas and New Year waiting for them to pass. This year was different in so many ways.

The other thing out of the ordinary this year had been her appointment with Dr. McCourt.

"Are you ill? Have you caught cold?" the nurse had asked when Henrietta called. Colds were always a serious business for Henrietta.

When she assured the nurse it wasn't that, but some strange sensations in her chest, they had worked her in that very afternoon.

After listening to her heart and lungs and doing a thorough exam, Dr. McCourt had pronounced her fit. "I don't know what's causing these flutterings you describe," he said. "But you've never looked better. Whatever you're doing, keep doing it."

His advice had set her mind at ease, though the sensations had continued. They weren't altogether unpleasant and, now that she knew they weren't a signal of an impending heart attack, she could pay them less attention.

She retrieved her mail. The usual bills, several Christmas catalogs, and two envelopes that looked like cards—one for Meryn and... one for her. She smiled when she saw the return address.

Maybe this card from her family would cheer Meryn up. She'd been unusually moody and quiet the last few days. It only lasted for moments, and then she seemed to snap out of it. A couple of times, Henrietta had caught Meryn watching her with a somber expression.

I will not have her feeling sorry for me, Henrietta told herself firmly. The girl would go home for Christmas—"You need to be with your family for Christmas," she'd insisted when Meryn cajoled and wheedled, "and I need to be here." Henrietta planned to pass the holidays as she always did, painting and reading.

But the more festive air in the house this year had also stirred up more memories—of childhood Christmases full of joy and laughter and song when her mother used to play the piano with people gathered round. Una, when she was living here with her aunt during the war years, had had a lovely voice. Henrietta thought she sounded like an angel.

Sometimes, she had sung just for Henrietta, *Till the End of Time.*

They thought they had till the end of time. At fifteen, with their whole lives stretching before them, the war half a world away, they had talked of going to college together, living together, staying together always. They knew it couldn't happen. Una would have to go home to England someday, but...

"Foolishness," Henrietta muttered to the empty house.

Chapter 11

THE CAMPUS WAS FULL again after Thanksgiving, but there was a definite buzz in the air, with only a couple of weeks left before finals and the end of the semester. The quad had been festooned with lights, and the large fir tree in the middle was strung with ribbons and more lights.

As Ryn walked to her classes, she kept an eye out for Tamara, her heart skipping a little at the memory of their last meeting.

It wasn't until mid-week that she saw her, walking toward the chapel at noontime with Roberta and the others. She jogged through the light snow that covered the grass and caught up with them.

"Good Thanksgiving?" she asked.

"Hi!" Franny said. "Yeah, ours was good. It's always nice to get back to the motherhouse. How about yours?"

Ryn nodded, her face warming at the look on Tamara's face. "My family drove up from Pennsylvania to surprise me. It was great to see them." She pointed toward the chapel. "Mind if I join you?"

She fell in beside Tam. "How's Cuba?"

Tamara shrugged. "Same as always. Mom had to work the holiday at the hospital, so it was just my brother and me most of the weekend. I'm glad to be back."

Inside, Ryn shuffled into the same pew with them. She set her backpack in the corner and shrugged out of her new jacket. When she sat next to Tamara, she was acutely aware of the pressure of Tam's thigh against her own. She didn't pay much attention to the Mass. From the corner of her eye, she watched Tamara's hand, lying on her thigh, just inches away. She wished like crazy she could reach out to hold it but, here in church, with the nuns sitting on Tamara's other side... Probably not a good idea. But Tam seemed to have the same thought. At one point, she shifted her hand over, her pinky brushing against Ryn's hand on her own leg.

When Mass was over, Ryn reluctantly gathered her things and accompanied them back outside.

"Will we see you and Henrietta here on Sunday?" Roberta asked.

Ryn frowned at the snow. "I don't know. This might be too hard for Henrietta to walk in. I'll have to see."

"Give her our best," Steph said as they headed toward their next class.

Ryn gave a last wave to Tam before retracing her steps across campus to Rayburn Hall. Up on the second floor, she peeked into the main office, but Beverly wasn't at her desk. She walked down the corridor toward her office and almost plowed into Beverly, nearly hidden behind a tottering stack of books.

"What are you doing? Here, let me." Ryn took the books from her.

"Thank you," Beverly panted, shaking her arms.

"What are all these?"

They walked toward Beverly's office.

"They're for Professor Geary. He asked me to look up some things for him."

Ryn halted in her tracks. "Geary. What kind of things?"

160

Beverly's cheeks were scarlet. "For the new class."

"For—" Ryn stared at her. "Do you want to do this?"

"No, but—"

Ryn turned on her heel.

"Where are you going?" Beverly asked.

Ryn didn't respond. She stomped down the corridor to Geary's office. The door was closed but not latched. She kicked it open. He jumped.

Without ceremony, she dumped the books on the empty desk.

"Do you own work. Beverly is not your TA. You wanted this course; you got it."

She slammed the door behind her. In her office, she found Beverly waiting for her, wringing her hands nervously.

"What did he say? Oh, dear. What if he—"

"Retirement, remember?" Ryn set her backpack on her desk and turned to Beverly. "You can retire, and I'm not going to have a job anyway. Kind of freeing, isn't it?"

Beverly gave a nervous titter. "Yes, it is."

Ryn took her hand. "Would you mind making us both a cup of tea? I think we deserve it."

Beverly trotted away, and Ryn sat with a grim smile. Freeing indeed.

～

MOSTLY SILENT MEALS HAD been the norm in the Cochran house for many years. Henrietta's companions had often had other employment that took them from the house for breakfast and lunch, so that she had been accustomed to eating those meals alone. Dinners, though, had typically been eaten with the live-in, who had either cooked or warmed up something Bonnie had left. Even then, conversation had usually been sparse.

But all of that had changed with Meryn's arrival. Even if she had to leave early for campus, she typically laid out the bread and butter next to the toaster, often with a little note. Henrietta had never admitted—even to herself—how much she'd come to look forward to those bits of paper with just a few cheerful words. And dinners were livelier than they'd been in years. Meryn wasn't content to just sit and eat. She wanted to discuss the news, especially the political news. She was genuinely interested in what Henrietta thought, what she had done during the day, and talked freely about her students and her frustrations with her colleagues.

So it was concerning to Henrietta to watch the girl sit at the table, poking her fork into her stew, pushing chunks of carrot about without speaking. She'd been like this ever since Thanksgiving weekend.

"Are things going well with your classes?"

"Hmm?" Meryn looked up. "Oh, yes. They're all buckling down now that finals are coming up soon. Too late for some of them, I'm afraid."

She returned to eating, frowning a little as she did.

Henrietta cast about for something else to say. "Have you seen the nuns?"

"Yes. I ran into them on campus a couple of days ago. They asked if we'd be coming to Mass on Sunday, but..." Meryn shrugged apologetically. "With the snow now, I don't know how easily you'd be able to get there."

"That's true." Henrietta thought. "Would you like to invite them here?"

Meryn's head snapped up. "Here?"

"We talked about it when we were at their house. It seems we ought to reciprocate."

A slow smile spread across Meryn's face. "I'll ask them. You sure you won't mind having the house full of people?"

Henrietta felt her own insides warm, but curtly said, "If I weren't sure, I wouldn't have offered."

The girl chuckled. Henrietta's brusqueness never seemed to faze her.

"Okay, Hank. I'll ask them."

They finished dinner, and Henrietta helped clear the table. She went out to the sofa while Meryn washed the dishes. Over the drone of the weatherman, predicting heavier snow over the next two days, she heard the girl on the telephone.

It was hard to remember the panic, the loneliness of those nights after Amanda had left. She kept telling herself they would come again. Someday, Meryn would leave, and it would be just as hard to find someone new. But for now, she was happier than she'd been in a long time.

When Meryn came into the living room, she plopped onto the floor to watch the news, waiting until the commercial to say, "They accepted. Sunday at noon. Steph is going to bring her grandmother's strudel."

"I'll telephone the market and ask them to deliver extra bread and eggs."

"No need." Meryn twisted around to look up at her. "I'll stop and pick up what we don't have."

For a moment, the girl just looked at her with that ridiculously happy expression on her face. When she turned back to the TV, Henrietta absently rubbed her chest.

~

THE HEAVIER SNOW DID come. Ryn thought about driving, but she'd first have to dig Nelly out, and she didn't really have time.

"I'll clean you off this afternoon," she promised, giving the car a pat on her way by.

She had an extra pair of shoes in her backpack, her khakis stuffed into tall winter boots. It was harder walking through about eight inches of snow. As she trudged through it, she argued with herself about what to do with the letters. Henrietta had a right to them—*and she needs to know what happened to Una,* insisted one of the many conflicting voices in her head.

But it worried Ryn to give them to her right before she was leaving for Christmas. Though Henrietta kept asserting that she was perfectly fine here alone—"as I have been for years, I might remind you," she'd said pointedly—Ryn just didn't feel right giving her such potentially traumatic news at this time of year. And no matter what Hank said, Ryn was pretty sure she shouldn't be alone when she did finally see those letters.

She was winded by the time she got to Rayburn. No one else was there yet. She stomped as much snow off her boots as she could, but still left little clumps behind her in the corridor. In her office, she unwound her scarf and tugged off her hat and jacket. She hung them all on the pegs attached to the wall and sat to change into her shoes.

She had one boot off when a soft knock on the door startled her. She straightened up to find Tamara standing there.

"Hi."

"Hi." Tamara pointed out into the corridor. "Is it okay I'm here?"

"Sure. Come in."

Tam stepped inside and pushed the door shut behind her.

"Is something wrong?" Meryn asked when Tamara couldn't seem to meet her gaze.

"No." But Tam's usually pale cheeks had a high flush as if she had a fever.

Ryn stood and offered her a chair. "You look like you might fall over."

Tamara shook her head. "It's not... I needed to talk to you."

"What about?"

When Tamara did look her in the eye, the intensity of what Ryn saw there nearly knocked her over instead.

"Oh."

"I haven't been able to sleep. I can't concentrate in my classes." Tam strangled her mittens.

Ryn thought she sounded as if she might cry. "Tam—"

But whatever she'd been about to say flew out of her head when Tamara stepped closer and kissed her. At first, the crush of lips was hard, almost frantic. Tam pulled away just a fraction, her eyes wide and frightened, but Ryn raised a hand to the back of her head and gently held her as they met a second time. This kiss was soft, warm, open. As it lingered, Ryn felt her body responding with sensations it hadn't felt in a long time.

"I've been dreaming of doing that for weeks," Tamara breathed.

Ryn smiled. "I'm glad it's more than a dream now."

Tamara giggled nervously and then clamped her hand over her mouth. "I have to get to my first class. See you later?"

Ryn nodded. "Later."

Tamara fumbled for the doorknob. With a last smile and a little wave, she let herself out.

Ryn dropped into her chair. *What the heck?*

She remained in a fog through her morning lectures—she'd had to go back to the office to change out of her other boot. Half her mind was still on that kiss. She debated going to the chapel at noon, but she wasn't ready to see Tam again just yet—not in front of Roberta and the others. With a start, she wondered what Sunday brunch would be like.

As she left the classroom and turned into the corridor, she collided with someone, almost knocking her down.

"Vanessa!" Ryn reached out to steady her. "I'm so sorry. How are you?"

Vanessa's chin quivered. "I was looking for you..."

"What's wrong?"

From around the corner came the sound of Geary's grating voice. In an instant, Vanessa's face went an ashen color.

"I can't—"

She scurried away before Ryn could say anything. Ryn stood there, watching the door to the rear stairwell swing shut. When Geary rounded the corner and saw her, he stopped.

Ryn recognized the female professor he was talking to, someone from the English department. "Professors," she said with a curt nod.

She had an idea about what had upset Vanessa, and she was willing to bet it had something to do with either that woman Geary was with or some other new fling. From what Vanessa had told her, she'd never been allowed to seriously date. Even her prom date had been the son of a friend of her mother's. She'd most likely never been through a breakup. Ryn was sorry Vanessa was upset, but she'd get over Geary, the skunk. Ryn couldn't help but be glad if Geary was out of Vanessa's life.

Before she got back to her office, Vanessa had receded to the back corner of her mind. Front and center was Tamara and that kiss. That memory gave her the energy to bound up the stairs two at a time. *Sunday is going to be interesting.*

THE BRUNCH PLANS HAD the desired effect. Meryn seemed happier than she had been recently. She came home from the market with two bags loaded with extra eggs, bacon, three different kinds of bread, cheese, vegetables, syrup, as well as another can of coffee.

"I'll make French toast and omelettes. We can fry up a mess of bacon and make regular toast. That way everyone can have something they like."

Meryn accompanied her to church at St. Rita's—where Genevieve and Jerry Talbert didn't acknowledge them at all—and then started in right away when they got home, setting out stacks of plates and glasses and silverware.

When the young nuns arrived—"in our civvies," Franny pointed out—they brought a platter of Christmas cookies in addition to three strudels.

This time, Henrietta was made to sit at the table and supervise while they all jumped in to chop vegetables for the omelettes, mix batter for the French toast, and get the bacon frying. The small kitchen was teeming with activity. Henrietta watched Meryn standing shoulder-to-shoulder at the stove with the pretty blonde one, Tamara, as they got two omelette pans going.

"Refill?" Franny poured more coffee into Henrietta's cup.

"Thank you." Henrietta sipped her coffee, puzzled by the mild stomach upset she was feeling. Briefly, she wondered if she was coming down with something.

Soon enough, they were all eating. The young ones laughed and talked while Henrietta mostly listened. Apparently, Franny and Roberta had taken their first vows two summers ago, and Stephanie was a year behind. Tamara, if she entered the order this summer, would be a postulant for the next year.

"And probably will transfer to SUNY Buffalo, to be near the motherhouse," Roberta said.

Henrietta saw a fleeting frown pass over Meryn's face and felt again that sour sensation in her stomach.

"Not hungry?" Stephanie asked, noticing that Henrietta had hardly eaten.

"This is just more food than I'm accustomed to." Henrietta tried to eat more of her omelette.

After the plates were cleared, Roberta declared she needed to let the food settle before tackling Granny Messner's strudel.

"Would you mind giving us a tour of your studio?" she asked.

Henrietta agreed, leading the way back. The young women were impressed by the work displayed there.

"Did you study with someone?" Steph asked, leaning closer to inspect one of the still lifes propped on the counter.

"One of my tutors was an artist, and he taught me some technique," Henrietta said, "but mostly I've experimented on my own."

"You need to check out the others in the living room," Meryn said, looking at Henrietta warmly.

They stood at the studio windows, gazing down at the now-frozen pond and the snow-covered woods. Birds were flitting to and fro, picking at the feeders, landing on the ground to scavenge some of the seeds that had fallen, littering the snow.

Out in the living room, Franny spied the piano. "May I?"

"It hasn't been played in a long time." But Henrietta nodded her permission.

Franny lifted the lid off the keys, but the piano was so badly out of tune that it wasn't really playable.

"Meryn could get her guitar," Henrietta suggested.

The girl protested, but the others shouted her down. She disappeared into her room for a moment and reappeared with her guitar. Henrietta sat on the couch while they sang Christmas carols. Their voices, young and clear, rang out. Henrietta was suddenly reminded of Una and Christmases gathered around the piano as her mother played and they all sang.

"You're really good," Stephanie said. "We could use another guitar player."

Meryn laughed. "I don't think you want me."

Roberta tilted her head. "Watch out. That's what Tamara said when we met her."

Henrietta saw the look that passed between Meryn and Tamara, but none of the others seemed to notice.

Meryn blushed furiously, lowering her head as she strummed her guitar. "I'm hungry again. How about some of that strudel?"

After another flurry of activity in the kitchen, with fresh coffee and tea, served with generous slices of strudel, the nuns insisted on helping to clean up and then said their farewells.

"Thanks so much for having us over, Henrietta," said Franny. "Your home is beautiful. We can see why Ryn likes it here so much."

With last waves, they said good-bye. When Meryn pushed the door shut at last, Henrietta felt exhausted.

"Hank, that was fun. Thanks a million."

"No need to thank me. This is your home, too." Henrietta turned toward her room. "I'm tired. I'm going to lie down a while."

"You okay? Is there anything you need?"

"No. Just some quiet."

Henrietta made her way back to her room and stretched out on the bed. She felt so odd, with these unfamiliar flutterings in her chest and stomach. She didn't care what Dr. McCourt said. Something was wrong.

~

THE LAST COUPLE OF weeks of classes flew by, and before Ryn knew it, it was mid-December and finals week. Remembering what a pain in the butt her essay questions on her first tests had been to grade, she kept these final exams simple and straightforward. There was a bank of old exams that Geary, being his lazy ass, had used. Beverly had shown them to her, but Ryn was determined to write her own tests.

Beverly had also whispered that the new women-and-history class already had twenty-five students registered for next semester. It gave Ryn grim satisfaction to know that Geary would flame and burn in front of a large class. At least she hoped he would. She doubted he was actually a good teacher, based on what little she'd seen.

She'd barely seen Talbert. He taught his two or three upper-level classes and stayed holed up in his office, presumably planning the décor for his new dean's office.

It was embarrassing how much time her mind spent drifting to thoughts of Tamara. Ryn kept an eye out for her and thought about trying to find out her class schedule, but that felt creepy. Tam wasn't technically *her* student, but she was still *a* student.

It was just a kiss, Ryn said, fighting an internal battle with herself, but she knew she wanted it to be more than a kiss.

169

That made this situation almost as fraught as Geary's with Vanessa. Plus, there was the whole nun thing. She still wasn't sure how that factored into everything. Was Tam changing her mind about entering? Was this maybe-relationship between them just curiosity? Ryn was confused, to say the least.

So, she resisted the temptation to actively seek Tamara out, but she kept hoping there would be another knock on her door.

When the knock came, it wasn't Tamara. Ryn jumped up to see Vanessa standing there, dark circles under her eyes, glancing nervously up and down the corridor.

"I think Geary's in another class," Ryn said, pulling her into the office.

Vanessa nodded. "I know he is. I need to talk to you."

She looked as if she might faint. Ryn guided her to a chair and lowered her into it.

"What's wrong?"

Vanessa looked everywhere but at her.

"Vanessa?"

To Ryn's horror, Vanessa burst into tears, covering her face with her hands. Her muffled words came in bursts, "I'm... I'm pregnant... got to... can you drive me..."

Ryn reached out and gently pulled Vanessa's hands down. "Calm down and tell me."

She kept hold of Vanessa's hands and waited.

Tears streamed from Vanessa's red and puffy eyes. "I've checked. There's a clinic in Syracuse where I can... I have to get rid of it."

She tugged one hand free and reached into her coat pocket to produce a dog-eared envelope. "He gave me money. Told me to take care of it."

"What?" The word exploded from Ryn's mouth.

Vanessa flinched. "Please don't be angry with me."

Ryn fought to control her voice. "I'm not angry with you. Tell me what happened."

170

"When I... when I found out, I told him. He got mad, too. He told me to come back the next day, and he gave me this." She held up the envelope. "He said I was stupid to let it happen, and I needed to take care of it."

Ryn took the envelope from Vanessa. It contained two hundred dollars in twenties. She was so angry her hands were trembling.

"Will you? Take me?"

Ryn set the envelope on the desk and took a deep breath. "How far along are you?"

"Not far. Eight weeks, I think. I got worried when I missed my second period."

"And are you sure you're pregnant?" Ryn was completely out of her element here.

"I've been sick. Almost every morning. And... my body is changing. I'm sure."

Ryn sank back in her chair, thinking hard. "Look, Vanessa, I'll take you if that's what you really want to do, but I want you to be absolutely sure."

When Vanessa opened her mouth to argue, Ryn held up a hand. She leaned forward again to stare into Vanessa's eyes, emphasizing each word as she said, "You cannot undo this. You have to be sure before you go through with it. Please, take this time over the semester break. Try to tell your parents."

Vanessa shook her head violently, but Ryn said, "I don't think they'll be as angry as you think they will."

"You don't know my mother." Vanessa reached for the envelope and shoved it back into her pocket. "Never mind. I'll find another way."

When she stood, Ryn grabbed her sleeve. "Wait. I didn't say I wouldn't take you." She sighed. "Have you called the clinic? Do you have an appointment?"

Vanessa shook her head again. "I'll call today. Can you take me next week? After finals?"

Ryn gave a resigned nod. Vanessa threw her arms around Ryn and held her tightly. "Thank you."

She left the office, and Ryn dropped back into her chair. "Don't thank me yet."

Chapter 12

THE CARDINAL FLASHED BY, a brilliant crimson against the snow as he dove to snatch some sunflower seeds that had spilled. His mate clung to the suet cake swinging from a tree branch. Meryn had refilled the feeders and hung out fresh suet before she left. This pair had become regulars at the feeders, eyeing her cheekily through the glass.

Henrietta sat in her studio with a pencil in her hand, but the tip remained poised over the paper, her eyes staring but not seeing the scene outside.

The girl had been gone for three days, and they felt like the longest three days Henrietta could remember since she'd been sick and stuck in that iron lung for months.

"I hate leaving you," Meryn had said, her raggedy old duffel bag packed and sitting by the front door alongside her guitar case. "I wish you'd come with me."

"Don't be ridiculous," Henrietta had snapped. "I got by before you came here. I'll be fine for a couple of weeks."

But Meryn wasn't put off by Henrietta's bluster. The darned girl had actually smiled. She pointed toward the kitchen. "I made a fresh batch of Phyllis's chicken salad for sandwiches, and I know you placed an order with the club. Bonnie said to call her if you need anything."

Henrietta had waved her off. "Get going. You've got a long trip ahead of you."

Meryn had reached for her bag. "I'll practice the lessons in the drawing book you gave me for Christmas."

"If you can't draw, you can't paint."

Still, Meryn had paused in the driveway before getting in her car, staring back at Henrietta with troubled eyes.

Something was worrying that girl. The brunch had cheered her up for a while, but she'd been brooding again the last few days. Henrietta caught her several times, watching her. Sometimes, she looked as if she wanted to say something, but she always changed her mind. And there was that whole mysterious trip to Syracuse. She'd told Henrietta she'd be gone for the day, but wouldn't say why she was going.

Henrietta gave up sketching. She set her things down and reached for her crutches. Nights had been hard—*just as you knew they would be.* It wasn't just that she was here alone. Meryn had filled this house with more life than it had ever known. As grateful as she'd been to her father for building it for her, it had never been a home brimming with happiness—not like things had been before the polio.

And just last night...

Henrietta made herself a chicken salad sandwich and transferred it to the table. As she ate, the memory of that dream came to her, so strong and clear. Meryn and Una—except this was a grown-up Una, more beautiful than she had been, her red hair spilling over her shoulders—walking arm in arm, holding their hands out to her...

"Don't be ridiculous."

Henrietta finished her lunch and went out to the sofa. The golf course was empty. No new snow had fallen, so there were patches of brown grass visible where the last snow had melted. She reached for one of the three books Meryn had given her for Christmas—*The Frontiersmen* by Allan W. Eckart.

"Promise me you'll read these," Meryn had said. "One of my favorite teachers gave this trilogy to me when I was fourteen. They helped spark my love of history. I'd love to discuss these with you."

The way her eyes lit up, the earnestness in her voice when she spoke—Meryn could hold a class enthralled, Henrietta was certain of it. *She holds me enthralled.*

The thought came so suddenly, so unexpectedly, that Henrietta nearly dropped the book. And she knew.

She'd grown to love that girl. *This will not do.*

~

FROM THE DEN, THE sound of a college bowl game drifted to Ryn, along with her brothers' voices. Her father was out in the yard, hanging a new bird feeder he'd received for Christmas. Ryn watched him through the picture window in the living room where she sat. The sky was a flat, dull gray. It looked like it might snow. The living room was mostly in shadow, except for the tiny, bright lights on the Christmas tree. She sat cross-legged on the floor, her back against one of the stuffed chairs that matched the couch, a cup of tea cradled in her hands. Beside her lay a drawing pad with some very amateurish sketches.

It had been such a great Christmas with her family. She and Janie had commandeered the TV to watch *The Sound of Music*, curled up together under the same blanket, as they'd done for years. They'd heard from all of the relatives who lived in Ohio and Florida now.

She had another two weeks before classes started back up, but she felt restless and irritable. She'd been trying to get into a new book, *The Name of the Rose*, which, any other time, would have completely absorbed her to the neglect of everything and everyone, but she couldn't concentrate.

Vanessa's pale, drawn face kept intruding into her thoughts. Ryn had practically worn a path, pacing in the waiting room of the women's clinic. When Vanessa had emerged, she'd spoken two words. "It's done." The ride back to Bluemont had been silent. When Ryn dropped her off at Mrs. Middleston's, Vanessa had stopped her from walking her inside.

"I'm fine. My parents are coming to get me tomorrow. Thank you."

Watching her walk into the boarding house, Ryn couldn't help feeling that the girl she'd thought of as Shirley Temple was gone forever.

Adding to her irritation was the fact that her day with Vanessa had cost her her last opportunity to see Tamara before they all left the village for the semester break.

"I... I can't," Ryn had said when Tam had finally called her to see if they could have lunch before she left for Cuba. "I promised a friend... I can't."

She couldn't say more, not even to dispel the disappointment in Tamara's voice when she said good-bye.

But even more than Tamara, her thoughts kept drifting to Henrietta—wondering how she was doing, what she was doing, if she was eating and sleeping okay in the empty house. She doubted Henrietta would go into her room for anything while she was gone, but she'd hidden the letters in her duffel and brought them with her, just in case.

"Here you are."

Ryn looked up when her mom entered the living room.

June sat behind her in the chair and tousled Ryn's hair. "Whatcha thinking about?"

"What makes you think I'm thinking about things?"

June chuckled. "Because you've been thinking about things since you were three years old and you asked me what we would look like to the people living in the stars."

Ryn smiled, but it quickly faded.

"What's wrong? You've been so quiet since you got home."

Ryn hesitated. "I know you and Dad love us, but... If, say, Janie, got into trouble, got pregnant and wanted an abortion, what would you do?"

She twisted around to look into her mom's eyes. "And no, it's not me. Someone I know at the college."

June pursed her lips as she thought. "I don't need to tell you what the church's stance is on that, even though it's legal. And I have to say, I would have a hard time not grieving the life that never had a chance, but... I don't believe anyone but the woman and God have the right to make that decision."

Ryn draped an arm over her mom's knee. "I took her. My friend. To the clinic. I asked her to wait and think about it, but she's afraid to face her parents." She paused. "She's a year younger than Janie. And I don't think her life will ever be the same."

"It won't." June laid her hand on Ryn's head. "She'll live with that decision for the rest of her life."

They sat quietly for a long time before Ryn said, "The man responsible is the other professor in my department. And I don't think this is the first time. It's so wrong, but our department chair won't do anything about it. I feel so powerless."

"You're never powerless if you hold to the strength of your convictions."

Ryn met her mom's eyes again. "It will probably cost me my job."

June nodded. "It might."

"And any prospect for a good reference. I may not get another teaching position."

"That's a possibility." June brushed her fingers over Ryn's cheek. "Your room here will always be ready if you need it."

Ryn tried to smile but couldn't. She turned back to the tree. "Thanks, Mom."

~

AS IF MAGIC ELVES had been at work, it seemed that as soon as New Year was past, all signs of the holidays just disappeared from the village. The spirals of artificial garland that had wrapped street lamps, the merry strands of lights that had adorned the village square, the tinny sound of Christmas carols that had shoppers humming along as they wandered the sidewalks—it was all just gone.

This is the hard part, Henrietta thought as she drove through town. Now that the holiday hubbub was over, everyone hunkered down for the rest of the long winter. The country club closed down for two weeks every year to give the staff a break after the crazy holiday catering and party season, so there was no bridge yet. Not that Henrietta was all that eager to see those women.

It was odd how impatient Henrietta had become with their insipid conversation and vicious gossip. She'd never really enjoyed it—she didn't shop for the latest fashions in clothing, and her hair had been worn in the same style for decades, so she had little in common with them in those regards—but they had been her only social circle. Now, though, when she tried to bring up topics like current politics or the failure of the ratification of the Equal Rights Amendment—things she'd enjoyed debating with Meryn—the others quickly changed the subject.

Since Christmas and New Year had been on weekends this year, it felt to her with the start of the week almost as if there hadn't been a holiday. She wondered, as she searched for a parking space that was completely cleared of snow, if it seemed that way to people who worked.

Bonnie kept telling her her art was her work, but it didn't feel like work to Henrietta, not like sitting in an office. She couldn't imagine anything duller, but she supposed some people found comfort in that routine. Working with the same people, earning a steady paycheck—the familiar. That—the need for the steady and the familiar—she knew and understood, knew only too well what a trap it could become. Already, in less than two weeks since Meryn had been gone, she'd been aware that she was falling back into the snare of her routine.

The only thing that had been different had been having the piano tuned.

"What a nice surprise this will be for Meryn," Bonnie had said delightedly.

Henrietta hadn't said she was doing it for Meryn, *but she was right,* Henrietta thought when she sat and touched the keys later.

She found a parking space and made her way to the art store. "Hello, Sandy."

"Miss Cochran! I mean, Henrietta. Happy New Year." Sandy came around from behind the counter. "What can I do for you?"

"I wanted to thank you for doing such a nice job wrapping the art kit at Thanksgiving. It was lovely."

Sandy beamed. "You're most welcome."

"And I need some new colors. I've begun doing some paintings of birds, and I find I don't have colors vivid enough for some of them. I hadn't realized how subdued most of my landscapes are. I suppose I'm as dull as my paintings."

"You're nothing of the sort. Neither are your paintings. But you don't need the same colors for those different types of work. I just bought a new line of oils, over here. I think you'll want oils for birds. The gleam of the paint will set off the subject nicely." She pursed her lips as she thought. "And maybe some watercolors, too, if you're sketching."

She led Henrietta to the oil paints and left her to browse. She brought a basket to set on the floor.

"Just place your selections in here."

"Thank you."

Henrietta wandered the aisle, scooting the basket with her crutch. The shop was small, but nicely stocked. She picked up a few new brushes and some turpentine. When she was done, Sandy collected the basket for her.

"You know, Henrietta, I hope you won't mind, but..." Sandy glanced at her hesitantly. "I was thinking it would be nice to showcase your work. You're a local artist, and most of the village knows you paint, but so few people have seen any of your art."

Henrietta stood there a moment. Her surprise must have shown on her face. "My work?"

Sandy nodded. "I've been thinking about it. I don't have the space here to do it justice, but I've been talking to Maxine. Maxine Adams at the library? They're very interested. What do you think?"

She waited as Henrietta thought.

"Do you really think... Will people want to see my work?"

Sandy smiled. "Of course they will!"

"But most of my canvases aren't framed."

"I'll frame some for you at cost, and we can leave others unframed. It will add interest to the exhibit." She bagged Henrietta's purchases. "So you're willing?"

Henrietta gave a noncommittal nod. "I suppose so."

"Oh, that's wonderful! It will give the village something to look forward to this winter. I'll talk to Maxine again. May we call upon you, say next week sometime?"

"Yes."

"Here, let me carry these out for you."

A few minutes later, Henrietta drove home in a daze. It was one thing for gallery reps to come calling, whisking some of her paintings away to distant cities where no one knew her—*and where you don't have to see them laugh at the village cripple's pitiful work.*

There had always been a sense of safety in her anonymity, but this suggestion—a local showing of her work, here where everyone knew who she was—this was terrifying.

"Why in the world did you say yes?"

She very nearly turned the car around to go back and tell Sandy she'd changed her mind.

"Don't you dare."

The voice that had popped into her head wasn't her mother's, or loyal Bonnie's, or any of her so-called friends. It was Meryn's voice she heard, urging her out of her comfort-zone. With another of those odd tremblings in her chest, she drove home to experiment with the new pigments.

~

BY THE TIME RYN turned off I-86 near Cortland, her butt was numb and she needed to pee.

Saying good-bye to her folks had been hard, but the boys were in school, and her dad was back at work. She and Janie had helped her mom take down the tree and put all the Christmas decorations away right after the Epiphany. Then the restlessness had hit.

"I'm worried about Henrietta being alone all this time," she'd said.

"Of course you should go." June had pulled her into a hug. "Give Henrietta our best."

The drive seemed to be taking longer than she remembered. Mostly because Henrietta wasn't the only one she was worried about.

"Filled your tank and emptied mine," Ryn said to Nelly after a quick stop.

Some fresh snow had fallen, but the roads were plowed and dry. Nelly made good time.

When she arrived in Bluemont, she twitched the steering wheel away from Country Club Road. Parking in front of the boarding house, she bounded up the porch stairs to see if Vanessa had, by any chance, returned early. She doubted it, as there was still more than a week before spring semester started, but she'd had a nagging feeling that just wouldn't go away.

Before she could even knock, Mrs. Middleston was at the door, holding it open for her.

"How did you know?" she asked.

Ryn's mind whirled. "How did I know what?"

Mrs. Middleston gave a sharp upward nod. "Go on."

Ryn ran up the stairs to the third floor, barely noticing the quiet on the empty second floor. At the door to the room she'd shared with Vanessa, Ryn paused to catch her breath. She gave a little knock and stepped inside.

"Vanessa, I—"

She stopped short as a woman straightened from emptying the drawers on Vanessa's side of the dresser. The woman had blonde, bobbed hair and large, blue eyes.

"Mrs. Feldman."

An open suitcase sat on Vanessa's bed, half-crammed with underwear and T-shirts and pj's.

"What happened?" Ryn asked. "Isn't Vanessa coming back?"

"Who are you?"

"I'm sorry. I'm Meryn Fleming. I was Vanessa's roommate at the beginning of the year."

Mrs. Feldman sank onto the bed. "You're the teacher. The one Vanessa told us about."

"Yes." Ryn took a seat on the other bed. "I'm new at St. Aloysius this year, and I didn't have an apartment. Vanessa and I got to be friends."

Those eyes so like Vanessa's filled. "I'm glad she had a friend." Mrs. Feldman looked around helplessly. "I'd hoped that Vanessa would thrive here, like I did. That she'd make friends to last the rest of her life, but—"

Her voice cut off with a hitch.

"What happened?" Ryn's stomach clenched. She asked again, "Isn't Vanessa coming back?"

Mrs. Feldman shook her head. "No. She's going to stay in Albany with us." She fixed Ryn with troubled eyes. "Can I trust you not to share what I'm about to tell you?"

Ryn nodded, her feeling of dread growing.

"Vanessa tried to... She found a bottle of sleeping pills, you see." Mrs. Feldman brushed the tears off her cheeks. "We could tell she was unhappy when she came home, but..."

"Is she—?"

"She's alive," Mrs. Feldman said. "We got her to the hospital in time." She picked up a stuffed Piglet, hugging it to her. "What could have happened?"

Ryn opened and closed her mouth a couple of times before she could say, "Vanessa got pregnant."

Mrs. Feldman's eyes got big. "Preg—" She blinked, frowned. "But why would—"

"She had an abortion."

"No." Mrs. Feldman shook her head again. "No, she wouldn't do that. We could have dealt with her being pregnant, helped get her through it, give the baby up for adoption, but—"

"She did. I drove her to the clinic." Ryn braced herself when Mrs. Feldman pushed off from the bed to close the door.

"Why would you do that?" Mrs. Feldman hissed.

"I asked her to wait, to talk to you," Ryn said miserably. "But she wouldn't. She said if I didn't take her, she'd find someone else who would."

Mrs. Feldman collapsed onto the bed. "But, she's just a baby herself."

They sat silently for a few minutes.

"Do you... do you know the boy?"

Ryn's mind raced, wondering how much more misery to heap upon this poor woman. She shook her head.

"Thank you, for telling me," Mrs. Feldman said. "We'll get Vanessa to a doctor."

Ryn pointed toward the closet. "Do you need any help here?"

"No. No, I can take care of this."

Ryn stood. "I'm sorry, Mrs. Feldman. Please give Vanessa my best. Tell her I'm thinking of her." She took a step toward the door, but then stopped. "Would it be all right if I wrote to her?"

"I think it would be best if Vanessa didn't have any reminders of..." Mrs. Feldman turned back to the dresser.

Mrs. Middleston waited at the bottom of the stairs. If she was hoping for a juicy scoop, Ryn thought, she was going to be disappointed. With a curt nod, she let herself out the door and went to her car.

She pulled away from the curb, her jaw tight. Somehow, she had to find a way to make sure Bradley Geary was held responsible for this mess he'd created.

But for now, she had one more stop to make before she went home.

~

"SEE HOW THE WIDTH diminishes as it recedes into the distance?"

Henrietta pointed to the club's drive across the road. She and Meryn sat in armchairs in front of the picture window, which gave them a wonderful place for a lesson on perspective.

"And there, that cart path does the same thing when it curves out of sight," Meryn noticed.

"Yes." Henrietta pointed. "And note how the light is hitting the trunk of the oak tree in the yard."

Meryn had been home for two days and, for Henrietta, her initial happiness at having her here again was quickly tempered by the fact that something was obviously still bothering the girl.

Instead of the endless chatter Henrietta had expected about her visit with her family—though there had been a bit of that—there had been long periods of silence. She often caught Meryn staring at nothing, biting her lip or worrying hangnails until she made her fingers bleed. There'd been no music since she got back, always a sign something was bothering her.

She doesn't want to be here and doesn't know how to tell you.

That worry nagged at Henrietta, and she knew from the way it made her go cold inside that it was more than simple distress at the thought of having to find a new companion. Much more.

Still, it wasn't fair to hold the girl captive against her will. She glanced over to find Meryn aimlessly running her pencil tip along the outline of the tree she'd drawn.

"Are you unhappy here, Meryn?"

The girl's head snapped up. "Hmmm?"

"Are you unhappy here? Do you want to leave?"

Meryn swiveled her chair to face Henrietta, her dark eyes probing. "No, Henrietta. Why would you ask that?"

Henrietta steeled herself to confront this, whatever it was. "Something has been bothering you since before Christmas. No... actually it dates to Thanksgiving. When your family was here. You've seemed unhappy since then. And I can't help but think you've been wanting to leave here. Maybe leave Bluemont and be closer to them. And I don't want you to feel obligated to me. Obligated to stay here if it's not what you wish to do."

"No." Meryn set her pencil down and reached over to place a hand on Henrietta's arm. "No, Henrietta. That's not it. I'm sorry if that's what I made you think."

She withdrew her hand—though Henrietta immediately wished she'd put it back—and turned to the window.

"I've never been much of a believer in confession as a way of lifting things off your conscience, and I haven't wanted to burden you more than I already have with things from work, but..."

When she faced Henrietta again, her eyes were hard as stone. "Remember the girl I roomed with at Mrs. Middleston's? Vanessa?"

185

Henrietta thought. "The one your colleague was... seeing."

Meryn nodded. "She came to me during finals week."

The entire story came tumbling out. Henrietta struggled to keep up, not because Meryn's explanation was difficult to follow, but because she was incredulous that something so sordid could happen, at St. Aloysius, right under Jerry Talbert's nose.

When Meryn told her about finding the girl's mother packing up her things and why, Henrietta wanted to reach out and comfort her, but she didn't know how.

"I told her mother I wouldn't tell anyone about the pills, so keep this between us, will you?" She leaned forward, her elbows braced on her knees. "I feel guilty. Responsible." Meryn's voice had a hitch in it.

"Why should you feel guilty?" Henrietta demanded. "As you said, if you hadn't taken her, she would have found another way. You tried to warn her against him, but she wouldn't listen. What that man did is wrong, but you are no more responsible for the girl's choices than I am."

Meryn nodded again, her head still bowed under the weight of something. "There's more," she said softly. "Something I should have told you right away, but I didn't know how."

Henrietta's heart raced in fear at whatever it was, but she composed herself and said, "Just tell me."

"Not here." Meryn raised her head. "I need to take you. We'll need your car and wheelchair."

"What on earth for?"

Meryn stood and held a hand out for Henrietta's pad and pencils. "You'll see in a few minutes. And dress warmly."

A short while later, Henrietta sat in the passenger seat of her Chrysler, bewildered as Meryn drove through the village.

"Where are we going?"

"You'll see." Meryn's voice was tight, clipped. That worried Henrietta more than anything.

When they pulled into the cemetery, she was more puzzled than ever. Meryn wound her way along the paths normally reserved for the maintenance crew.

"I want to get us as close as possible."

"As close to what as possible?"

But Meryn didn't reply. She braked to a stop and opened the rear door to retrieve the wheelchair.

"Why do I need this?" Henrietta asked, holding to the car door for support as she got out.

"It's too far for you to walk. And if we wait and get more snow, we can't even do it in your chair."

Henrietta grudgingly lowered herself to the chair and allowed Meryn to push her through the cemetery, winding amongst the headstones and statues. The turf was rough, with tufts of grass and fallen sticks, and she was jostled a good bit. She couldn't suppress a small groan.

"Sorry," Meryn said.

Familiar names flashed by, carved into granite and limestone—names of people Henrietta had grown up with, her parents' friends and business contacts.

They neared a small stone in white granite, almost hidden among the larger, more ornate grave markers surrounding it. Meryn slowed and repositioned the chair to face it. The polished stone was carved with one name—*Marsden*.

Meryn squatted beside her, pulling something out of her jacket pocket. "I found these, when I was looking for the Christmas decorations."

She set the bundle in Henrietta's lap and walked away.

With her heart thudding painfully in her chest, Henrietta picked up the ribbon-bound parcel and turned it over.

Chapter 13

RYN WAS GLAD SHE'D waited. Not that Henrietta let her in; not that she shared what she must be feeling or thinking after learning what happened to Una after all these years. And certainly not that Henrietta was suddenly a puddle of emotion. In fact, she was just the opposite, but Ryn had expected that. She'd prepared herself for the curtness, the sharp words, the coldness emanating from Henrietta whenever they were in the same room.

But she was still convinced she'd made the right decision in waiting until she could be here at the house with her for a few days. Shaken by the news of Vanessa's suicide attempt, Ryn was so glad she hadn't given Henrietta the letters and then left her here alone. Not that Henrietta was likely to hurt herself, Ryn thought. She'd been through so much and was much tougher than most people realized, but Ryn also knew her well enough to know that the armor had chinks, had weak spots. And Una was definitely one of them. What they'd been to each other, Ryn could only guess, but she thought her guess was a good one. Henrietta had been in love with Una. Of that, she was pretty sure. And she figured it was likely Una was the only person Henrietta Cochran had ever been in love with.

So she ignored the barbs and the chill and the attempts to keep her at a distance. She brought Henrietta cups of fresh coffee as she worked in the studio, leaving them without a word. She read or drew or played her guitar quietly in her room, but always with the door propped open a bit so that she could hear Henrietta moving around.

On Wednesday, she asked Bonnie to keep an eye on Henrietta, saying only that she'd been a little under the weather.

She took advantage of Bonnie's company to get to campus and check her office. There were the expected start-of-term announcements waiting in her box. But Beverly was what she most wanted.

"Meryn, how are you?" Beverly said, jumping up to give her a hug.

"I'm okay." Ryn nodded toward the dark office behind her. "Has he been in?"

"Only now and again."

Beverly quickly made two cups of tea.

"What about Geary?"

"No sign of him," Beverly said. "I heard..." She went to the corridor, but it was empty. She shut the office door anyway and handed Ryn a hot mug. "I heard from Evelyn Mills in the president's office—we used to work together in admissions, so she's been here as long as I have—anyway, I heard that the Feldman girl isn't returning. Her mother is very upset about something, and told Evelyn that she wanted to speak to Father Croson."

Beverly's eyes were huge behind her glasses as she shared this news.

"Has he called her?" Ryn sipped her tea.

"I don't think so, not yet." Beverly eyed Ryn over her mug. "Isn't that the girl... Professor Geary—"

"Yes." Ryn's voice was hard. "If they don't do something about him—"

"Tenure makes that almost impossible."

"I know." And because she did know it, Ryn's heart sank. "I keep hoping something will happen to get him fired, or he'll get a job offer somewhere else, and he'll be out of our hair for good."

Beverly shook her head. "No such luck."

They talked about Christmas—Beverly was wearing a new sweater her husband had given her, and Ryn shared some stories about her visit home. She thanked Beverly for the tea.

Outside, she considered driving by Tamara's apartment. *What for?* Even if Tam was back in town, even if she weren't planning on entering the order, even if she might like Ryn enough to explore whatever might be there—"She's a student," Ryn reminded herself harshly. She would not be another Bradley Geary.

She went back to the house. Bonnie was just taking a roasted chicken out of the oven.

"How is she?" Meryn asked as she entered the kitchen.

"Pricklier than a porcupine." Bonnie set the pan on the stovetop. "I'd give her as much room as you can."

She pointed to the refrigerator. "I've got a tray of rolls in there. Put them in the oven at 350 for twelve minutes when you're ready for dinner."

"Bonnie, thanks so much. You're wonderful. I don't know what I'd do without you and Beverly."

"Oh, go on." But Bonnie pulled her into a hug. "You've been good for her. Whether she knows it or not."

She got her coat and purse. Ryn waved her off and closed the door. No matter what Bonnie said, she felt this wasn't the time to give Henrietta more room. Squaring her shoulders, she went to the studio.

Henrietta didn't bother to look around at the sound of footsteps. "Your check is on the desk."

"She got it," Ryn said. "She said she'll see you next week."

Henrietta stiffened but her brush kept laying out wispy outlines of what Ryn recognized as Owasco Lake.

Ryn pulled out a chair and sat. For several minutes, Henrietta kept painting, ignoring her. When it became apparent that Ryn wasn't going to leave, Henrietta lowered her brush.

"What?"

The word lashed like a whip. Ryn took a deep breath.

"We need to talk."

"No. We don't."

"Henrietta, I think I'm right that there is no one else you know, probably no one else you've ever known, who could understand what you felt for Una better than I can. When we talked..." She got up and stood behind Henrietta. Reaching over her shoulder, she pointed to the canvas. "The day we went to the lake and you told me about Una, I could hear the love in your voice. I know what it's like to lose someone you love, but mine is still alive."

She dared to take a step nearer and laid a gentle hand on Henrietta's shoulder. She felt the muscles tense.

"For almost forty years, you believed Una was alive, somewhere in England. Now you know she isn't. That she got sick at the same time you did. You lived, and she didn't. I can't really know what that's like, but I am here for you."

For long seconds, they remained like that, Ryn standing behind Henrietta with a hand on her shoulder. At last, Henrietta partially turned her head.

"When I got back, Wilhelmina Marsden had sold her house and moved. My parents said she went to California, but I don't know now if that's true. She was my last link to Una, and she was gone."

Ryn's heart ached.

"All this time," Henrietta murmured, "I've pictured Una, alive and married, with grandchildren by now. It hurt to think she didn't feel the same way about me, didn't want to correspond and never answered my letters. But I saw her healthy and happy. And now—"

Henrietta's voice hitched and her head bowed. Ryn moved closer and wrapped her arms around Henrietta from behind. She was surprised when Henrietta didn't shake her off or pull away. She didn't dare squeeze too tightly. Holding Henrietta was like holding a bird, so fragile and delicate.

Ryn rested her cheek against Henrietta's head. "I'm sorry."

IT WAS A RELIEF TO Henrietta when the college's classes resumed. Meryn hadn't exactly hovered, but she hadn't wanted to leave the house for more than an hour or so. Only Henrietta needed space, distance—anything to try and forget the feel of Meryn's arms around her. No one had held her like that since before she got polio. She and Una used to lie in each other's arms, and her parents had hugged her when she was young, but afterward, she'd been so sick and weak, only the therapists and doctors and nurses had touched her—clinically, painfully. She still cringed, all these years later, at the memory of the pain.

Henrietta had long ago accepted that she would never know a lover's touch or embrace. She knew Meryn hadn't meant it that way. Even in the privacy of her own mind, Henrietta couldn't let her imagination go beyond a kindly hug, but at moments—"*moments of weakness*," she told herself harshly—she found herself craving that touch, wishing Meryn would hold her again.

This left Henrietta no choice but to avoid Meryn as much as she could, so she'd spent the last few days of the semester break painting madly, isolating herself in her studio. When the girl asked for a lesson, Henrietta set her tasks to work on alone.

But, no matter what she did, the blasted girl seemed to know, without being told, that Henrietta wasn't sleeping well. She'd brought Henrietta one of her herbal teas last evening, knocking on the bedroom door where Henrietta had retreated for the night, trying to read until she was tired enough to drift off.

"This will help," Meryn had said, looking at her with those knowing eyes, except she couldn't know. Couldn't know Henrietta's disturbed sleep wasn't from the usual fear of being helpless without her braces, trapped in the house at night, a fear she had many nights, even when she wasn't alone. But she was far from alone. She didn't tell the girl this, but the nights were altogether too crowded—one dream after another, some of Una, some of Meryn, some of them together.

In her dreams, she was at Una's funeral—she hoped there had been a funeral, mourners who got to do what Henrietta never had, say goodbye. Sometimes, Meryn was standing beside her, a comforting arm wrapped around her shoulders, drawing her close to that warmth.

She longed to get things back on an even keel, to feel she was in control again, and yet... *"You know we love you,"* Una had said in one of the most vivid dreams last night.

"We both love you." Meryn's dark eyes had bored into her, taking her breath.

Henrietta closed her eyes. "Just stop. The girl is thirty years your junior. And Una is dead. Just stop this."

She might not be able to control her dreams, but there was something she could control. At least she could try. She went to her desk and flipped through her address book. Finding the number she sought, she picked up the phone.

Within the hour, she heard a car pull into the driveway. Before the doorbell could ring, she opened the door.

"Leonard."

Father Leonard Croson opened the storm door and stepped inside. "Henrietta." He gave her a warm handshake. "I was surprised to get your call. What can I do for you?"

His face was jovial and his tone light, but his eyes probed her face curiously.

"Hang your coat up. I've made some fresh coffee."

He left his coat and scarf on the hall tree and followed her into the kitchen. She poured, and he carried two cups and saucers to the table, where a plate of Bonnie's pumpkin bread sat.

Henrietta let the suspense build as she cut slices of bread for each of them. She pushed the butter toward Leonard. He waved her off, patting his chest.

"Doc says I have to lower my cholesterol. But I will eat the bread. I'm not a martyr."

Chuckling at his own joke, he cut into the bread with a fork. "So..."

"As I'm sure you're aware," Henrietta began, "when my father passed, his will stipulated that this house and all of his assets passed to me to take care of both me and my mother. And upon my death, his wish was that any unspent assets be bequeathed to the college in thanks for providing me with a degree."

Leonard Croson nodded slowly. "I am aware of that. Has something happened to change things?"

Henrietta didn't answer immediately, taking a bite of her bread and a sip of coffee to wash it down. "That depends."

Leonard paused with his fork halfway to his mouth. "On what?"

Henrietta set her fork down. "Have you spoken to a woman named Feldman?"

Leonard's face flushed. "What about her?"

"Did she tell you what happened to her daughter? What she tried to do?"

He sat back, eyeing her warily. "What do you know about it?"

"I know why the girl, Vanessa, did it. One of your faculty got her pregnant."

"Jesus." Leonard closed his eyes.

"I don't think he'll help you."

He opened his eyes. "How do you know this?"

"That's neither here nor there. The point is, he got her pregnant. And then he gave her cash to go, on her own, and get an abortion."

"Oh, God." He pushed up from the table and paced the kitchen, wringing his soft, pudgy hands. "Are you sure?"

"I'm sure. And that is why this poor girl tried to kill herself. I have no idea how much was heartache over this man treating her so callously or how much was a feeling of guilt over the abortion. Leonard, you have to do something about him."

He sat back down. "Who is it?"

"A history professor named—"

"Bradley Geary."

"I see you're familiar with him."

Leonard wiped beads of sweat from his face. "He's tenured. There's nothing—" He stopped and stared hard at Henrietta. "Who else knows about this?"

"Only a couple of people," Henrietta said, lifting her coffee cup. "So far."

"What does that mean?"

"It means that, tenure or no, you must find a way to get rid of this predator. If you don't, I can promise you, word is going to get out. Not just here in Bluemont—and you know how fast salacious stories spread in a small town—but I'm sure the papers in Syracuse and Rochester and Buffalo would love to get their hands on this story. If that happens, I imagine the archdiocese will be calling."

His face seemed to swell alarmingly. It looked to Henrietta as if his clerical collar were choking him.

"You wouldn't dare!"

"Leonard, this girl's life nearly ended in tragedy. As it is, she will carry this with her forever. And that man is responsible. I will do whatever needs to be done to make sure it doesn't happen again."

She let that sink in for a moment before adding, "And then there's the matter of my will, which may change if things aren't worked out the way they should be."

His nostrils flared as he pushed up from his chair again.

"Not hungry?" Henrietta asked innocently.

"Lost my appetite," he snapped. "Good day, Henrietta."

She sat and listened to him wrestling with the hall tree in the foyer. A few seconds later, the front door slammed and an engine roared out of the driveway.

Lifting her cup, she allowed herself a small smile. "Good day to you."

~

THERE WERE SEVERAL RETURNING students in Ryn's spring semester classes—some because they had to have these courses, but most because they wanted to have her as a teacher again. One class was especially lively in the discussions of European expansion across North America and what that did to the indigenous people here before them.

She wrapped up class on Friday of the first week back. As she left the room, she turned left—away from her office. Beverly had told her where Geary was teaching the new women-and-history class, and she couldn't help being curious as to how it was going. This should have been his third lecture. She paused outside the classroom and listened.

"So you see, with only five of the eighteen women on the *Mayflower* surviving their first winter, you really have to question the wisdom of bringing women along on such an arduous journey to begin with. They're just not cut out for hardship. It's been proven over and over..."

It was all Ryn could do not to charge in and take over. She grumbled under her breath the whole way up the stairs to her office.

"If they'd been allowed off the damn ship, had fresh water and fresh air, and didn't have to take care of all the stupid men who brought diseases back on board..."

She was so preoccupied with her own thoughts that she nearly collided with Dr. Talbert at the top of the stairs.

"Professor..." He stepped back to let her through. "Good break?"

"Yes." Still fuming, she nearly pointed back down the stairs and said, "Do you have any idea what that jerk is teaching those kids?", but she stopped herself. Talbert had conspired against her to give the course—and the credit, she recalled bitterly—to Geary, so let them both hang when it crashed and burned.

Instead, she lowered her head and stalked by him to her office. Dropping into her chair, she stared morosely out the window. The campus was a picture, covered in snow that looked like icing. She thought about going to the noon Mass, not because she was feeling like prayer—though her recent thoughts about Geary might need exorcising—but she really wanted to see Tamara.

And the others, prompted a hopeful voice in her head.

That was true, she mused. Roberta and Franny and Steph—she'd like to catch up with all of them. And if Tam just happened to be with them...

She jumped up and trotted across campus. Inside the chapel, she spied Franny's veiled head, taller than the others. When she walked up to their pew, they all smiled and scooted over, making room for her. Tamara's smile was particularly radiant, enough to warm Ryn's insides all through Mass.

"How was your Christmas?" Roberta asked with a hug as soon as Mass was over.

"It was good." Ryn hugged Franny and Stephanie, too, but hung back when it came to Tamara.

"Just good?" Roberta asked, looking concerned.

Ryn shrugged. "A friend got some bad news. How about y'uns? A good break?"

"Yeah." Stephanie slipped her coat on and reached for her backpack. "It was so edifying to connect with the rest of the community. And we all got home to see our families for a few days."

"How's Henrietta?" Franny asked as they shuffled out of the pew toward the door.

"She's good." Ryn tried to keep her voice neutral. It wasn't technically true, but she couldn't explain without violating Henrietta's privacy.

"Why don't you both come over for brunch on Sunday?" Roberta suggested. "We'd love to catch up with you."

"And bring your guitar," Stephanie said.

Through all this, Tamara hadn't said a word, but Ryn could feel her eyes following her. She didn't dare make eye contact or she was certain the others would see immediately that something was up.

"I'll ask her, but for now, I'll accept for both of us." Ryn looked around. "It's hard for her to get through the snow, so we'll probably go to St. Rita's. See you at your house at eleven?"

"Sounds good," Franny said.

"I'll walk with you." Tamara waved to the others and fell into step beside her as they headed back toward Rayburn Hall.

"You have a class in here?"

"Something like that."

Ryn was puzzled when Tam followed her up the stairs to the second floor. And still more puzzled when Tamara accompanied her to her office.

"What—?"

But whatever she'd been about to ask flew right out of her head when Tamara shoved the door closed with her foot and crushed her mouth to Ryn's. Ryn was bombarded with sensations: the heat of Tamara's mouth on hers; the feel of Tam's arms around her, pulling her closer; the explosion of lust in her own belly. And lower.

Several moments later, she gasped for breath. "Wow."

"I've been thinking of nothing but that for weeks," Tamara said.

When Ryn stood there with her mouth open, unable to come up with something more articulate, Tamara stepped back.

"Was it okay that I did that?"

Ryn came to. "Uh, yes."

"Good." Tamara smiled and moved closer again.

Something clunked into place in Ryn's brain, and she caught Tamara's hands before they could make contact with her face.

"Wait."

Tamara's face clouded. "It's not okay."

"Yes. No." Ryn backed up, pressing her fingers to her forehead. "Give me a second. Let me think."

She exhaled and held her hands up. "Sit down." When Tam stood there, she said, "Please. We need to talk."

Tamara sank slowly into the extra chair in the cramped office. Ryn dropped into hers, her knees still wobbly.

Just as she opened her mouth, Geary's voice came to her through the closed door. For a moment, she thought he was going to charge into her office, but his footsteps receded down the corridor.

"Shit." She felt as if a bucket of ice water had been dashed into her face. "Not now. And not here."

She stood, and Tamara did also.

"We do need to talk," she repeated. "Maybe Sunday? After brunch?"

Tamara nodded, but she looked embarrassed as she backed to the door. Ryn grabbed for her hand.

"Thanks," she said with a crooked grin. "You made my Friday."

Tamara's face lit up with a smile. She fumbled for the doorknob. "See you Sunday."

Ryn let Tam's fingers slide slowly out of hers. When the door closed, she collapsed back into her chair again.

"Perfect," she muttered to the empty room. "You finally meet someone, and there are a million reasons not to see her."

But her mouth quirked into a smile at the memory of that kiss.

~

MERYN WAS AT THE sink, washing the breakfast dishes, when Henrietta entered the kitchen. Meryn glanced up and then did a double take.

"Wow. You look nice."

Henrietta put on her sternest expression. "That implies that I don't always look nice."

Far from being put off by Henrietta's tone, the girl simply laughed.

"You do always look nice. Way nicer than I do. I should say you look extra nice. I haven't seen that suit before. Is it new?"

Despite herself, Henrietta warmed at the fact that Meryn had noticed. She was wearing one of her nicer skirt suits. It wasn't new, but it had been worn so infrequently, it was like new. She'd even put on a little makeup. Only a little. Her face had been so pale and wan when she peered into the mirror, she thought a little color could only help.

Meryn rinsed the sink and dried her hands. "Maybe I should change?"

"You look—" Henrietta caught herself. She felt the heat that flooded her face. "You're perfectly acceptable in your teaching clothes."

Meryn grinned. "Good. Cause I don't have anything nicer than this. I'll have the spiffiest date in the entire church."

"Oh, hush. Go get your coat."

"Want me to drive?"

"No. You'll try the hand controls again, and we don't have time to pick everything up after it crashes to the floor."

Meryn's laughter followed her as she went to collect their coats from the hall tree. Henrietta enjoyed the warm flutter that filled her chest. She still worried sometimes that something was wrong with her heart, but if it was a sign of something bad, it was worth it. The flutter intensified when Meryn held the coat for her, brushing her fingers along Henrietta's arms as she slid the coat up over her shoulders.

At St. Rita's, she was only mildly surprised to see Leonard Croson sitting with Jerry and Genevieve Talbert. They turned at the sound of her crutches, giving her cold nods as she and Meryn passed them. Glancing back, she saw Leonard whispering furiously to Jerry.

She was certain they were putting the pieces together. If they now knew that her connection to the Feldman scandal was through Meryn, that was fine. It didn't change her threats. Geary had to go. Or they would suffer the consequences of enabling him to continue preying on young girls like Vanessa.

Meryn helped her doff her coat. "Did I miss something?" she whispered, turning to regard the Talberts.

"Nothing important."

It would be better if Meryn weren't implicated in what Henrietta had begun. If Meryn were to be questioned, she could honestly say she knew nothing about Henrietta's involvement. The less the girl knew, the better.

When Mass was over, Henrietta noticed that the Talberts and Leonard Croson scurried out ahead of them. She drove over to the nuns' house, entering through the back door, as she had the last time.

Roberta was waiting for them, holding the door for Henrietta and taking her coat before ushering her to the table.

"Coffee?" But Franny already had a cup poured for her.

The kitchen was again a beehive of activity, with everyone doing something. Henrietta was asked to dice red and green peppers. She couldn't help but notice that Meryn and Tamara were side by side at the counter.

The conversation turned to politics—apparently a topic they were all passionately interested in, judging from the vehemence of their opposition to Reagan.

"It's time to get organized," Meryn said.

"I've already contacted the local Democratic chapter," Franny said. "Meeting scheduled for the third Thursday of the month, at the library."

"Speaking of the library," Stephanie said, turning to Henrietta. "I was at the town library this week, and I saw a poster that you're having a show in March."

"What?" Meryn turned around. "You didn't say anything about this."

Henrietta flushed under the scrutiny from the young women. "It's nothing. Probably four—" She quickly scanned the room. "Maybe five people will actually go."

"That's fantastic, Henrietta," Roberta said. "And I'm sure the entire village will turn out for it."

Meryn continued to watch her curiously for a few seconds before turning back to the potatoes she was chopping.

The conversation moved on as they ate, with the others talking about their classes. Meryn sat beside Henrietta, with Tamara on the adjacent corner. Henrietta recalled family dinners with Una and her Aunt Wilhelmina joining them more evenings than not. Henrietta and Una always arranged to sit beside each other, their knees or feet touching under the table. She didn't want to know if Meryn and Tamara were doing the same.

"Henrietta, you're not eating."

She started and looked up at Roberta.

"Is there something wrong with the eggs?"

"No." Henrietta forced a smile and scooped up a forkful. "Everything's delicious. Just wonderful."

RYN HAD THE CAR door open almost before Henrietta braked to a stop inside the garage. She tried not to shuffle impatiently while Henrietta got her crutches out of the back seat and made her slow way into the house.

Racing to her room, Ryn stripped out of her church clothes, tossing on a faded pair of jeans and a sweatshirt. She unfolded the note that Tamara had slipped into her hand while they were cleaning up.

My apartment, two o'clock.

She smiled and tucked the note into her pocket. Padding out to the living room in her socks, she found Henrietta settled on the couch. She squatted in the foyer to lace up her boots.

"I'm going to be out for a while. Anything you need?"

Henrietta's voice was cool as she said, "Where are you going?"

"Um..." For some inexplicable reason, the first thing ready to come out of Ryn's mouth was an excuse—*you mean a lie,* said a sly voice in her head.

She kept her head down, focusing on her laces, as she suddenly seemed to be all thumbs. "I'm going to meet Tamara."

"Oh?"

Though Henrietta's tone was perfectly innocent, warning bells were clanging in Ryn's head.

"Yes, we... um..." Ryn was unaccustomed to this feeling of walking on thin ice. And she never, ever lied, or even felt tempted to. Why now?

"You like her."

Ryn felt the heat that flooded her face. "Well... yes. Does that bother you?"

"Of course not. Why would it bother me?" But the bite in Henrietta's voice belied her reply.

Ryn wound her scarf around her neck. "I'll be back before dinner. Can I get you anything before I go?"

Henrietta pushed to her feet. "I'm perfectly capable of getting myself anything I require. And I doubt I'll want supper after that brunch. I'll probably retire early."

Bewildered, Ryn let herself out the door. She dusted the snow off Nelly's windshield and started her up.

"What was that all about?" she muttered aloud, her words accompanied by clouds of vapor in the cold air of the car.

She'd been honest with Henrietta from the beginning that she was a lesbian. It shouldn't come as a surprise that she might like Tamara.

Unless she thinks it's inappropriate. That stupid voice echoed her own thoughts from over the semester break.

"We're just going to talk."

Like you "talked" in your office?

"Shut up."

She pulled over, battling the conflicting emotions inside her, and confused by the turmoil. Ryn always knew what was right and what wasn't, and she'd never had trouble doing the right thing, but this... She was only now realizing how much she missed being with someone, how much she missed Ashley. There were so many obstacles to a relationship with Tamara.

"You said you needed to talk," she reminded herself. "So go talk. This doesn't mean you're declaring your undying love. Just talk."

With that resolve, she put Nelly back in gear. When she pulled up to the curb in front of Tam's apartment, she found Tamara standing outside, waiting for her.

She got into the passenger seat. "Hi."

"Hi." Ryn's heart beat a little faster, in spite of herself. "Aren't we going in?"

"I thought we could take a drive, if you don't mind."

"Okay." Ryn turned Nelly around. "Where to?"

"I don't care. Anywhere. Out of the village."

Ryn did as she asked, heading west, toward the state forest. For a while, they rode in silence.

"Are you all right?" Ryn asked at last.

Tamara nodded. "I wasn't sure you'd come."

"Why?"

"Figured Henrietta would talk you out of it."

Ryn glanced over sharply. "Why would she do that?"

Tamara shrugged. "I don't think she likes me much."

"Where'd you get that idea?"

"She kept giving me the evil eye while we were in the kitchen."

"No, she didn't."

Tamara laughed, but she didn't sound amused. "You didn't see her. I think..."

She paused. Ryn waited, but nothing more came.

"You think what?"

Tamara shook her head. "Nothing. I'm glad you agreed to come today."

Ryn took a deep breath. "Well, like I told you Friday, we need to talk."

From the corner of her eye, she saw Tamara's clasped hands tighten in her lap.

"What about?"

Ryn gave a half-laugh. "All kinds of things. I'm not sure what exactly to make of this thing that's developing between us."

Tamara frowned. "Why do we have to analyze it? Can't we just go with it?"

"Under other circumstances, yeah, maybe we could."

"What makes these circumstances different?"

Ryn glanced over to see if she was serious. She was. She turned off the main road onto a small lane that wound deep into a stand of forest. She found a pull-off area adjacent to a stream that tumbled between ice-covered rocks.

Twisting in her seat, she said, "First and foremost, what about you and the Sisters of St. What's-His-Name?"

"St. Joseph. And what about it?"

Ryn stared at her for a second. "Aren't you supposed to join up this summer?"

"Yeah," Tam said with a nonchalant wag of her head. "But nothing's set in stone. It's not like I've been drafted or anything."

"I think Roberta and Franny and Steph might have a different idea about that. And, not that I'm an expert or anything, but isn't the decision to enter supposed to be some kind of calling from God?"

Tamara frowned. "Well, I'm looking at things differently now." She reached for Ryn's hand, stroking a finger along her palm. "I've never felt like this about anyone before. It's making me look at everything differently."

She tugged on Ryn's hand, and Ryn allowed herself to be tugged, even while that stupid voice in her head screamed, *No!*

She ignored the voice, letting herself fall into a deep kiss, completely absorbed in exploring the feel of Tam's mouth, her face. When Tamara's fumbling hands unzipped her jacket to reach inside and run a hand over her breasts, Ryn couldn't hold back a moan. She'd never had sex in a car but, for a few seconds, she thought about it.

Reluctantly, she drew away, her body complaining bitterly. "There are still things," she said, trying to remember what they all were.

Tamara's mouth quirked into a resigned smile. Ryn found herself watching those lips, realized they were moving, saying something.

"What?"

"I said, what things?"

Ryn sat back, pulling free to scrub both hands over her face. For a moment, she thought about going to dunk her head in that icy water gurgling by out there.

"The college for one. You're a student, and I'm an instructor. A first-year instructor with no job security."

"But I'm not your student."

"I know, and if you were, that would be an absolute. This makes it grayer, not better." She ran a thumbnail along the pebbled texture of the steering wheel. "I know of another professor who was sleeping with a student—"

"Who?"

"That doesn't matter. The point is, when I look at that situation, there is no gray. It's completely black and white. The only thing that makes this thing between us," she waved a hand, "gray is the fact that part of me wants it."

"Only part of you?" Tamara's voice was cool, and it reminded Ryn of Henrietta.

"Okay, a big part of me," she conceded. That made Tam smile. "But still."

Tamara sighed and settled against the car door. "What else?" Her tone indicated clearly that she'd decided to just let Ryn get this all out of her system.

"Well, for another thing, when I first told you I was a lesbian, you couldn't even say the word. And you just about bolted at the thought that I might have guessed you're one, too."

Tamara squirmed in her seat. "It's just... that word."

"That word is my identity. At least part of it."

"But do you have to scream it out loud to the world?" Tamara's eyes flicked down to Ryn's chest. "That silver axe-thing you wear. All the bumper stickers. Can't you be who you are without all that stuff?"

Ryn watched her carefully. "Can you accept who you are without hiding it from the world?"

"But I'm not—"

They didn't need the icy water from the stream outside. The air in the car had a sudden and very definite chill.

Something else clicked in Ryn's brain. "Is this why we didn't go into your apartment? Why we had to leave the village?"

Tam shifted to face the front. "I think we should go back."

Chapter 14

WINTER SETTLED OVER THE village with a mantle of gray—flat, cloudy skies that sprinkled a nearly constant coat of snow, just a few inches at a time, but never with gaps long enough to allow any kind of melt. The snow, which might be pretty under a cloudless, sunny sky, took on varying shades of gray. It seemed the whole world was dull and colorless.

Ryn stumped to and from campus, avoiding Tamara—which wasn't hard. She simply didn't go to the noon Mass. It was a sure thing Tam wouldn't be coming by her office again. Ryn kept telling herself it was for the best. She didn't need to get involved with someone so closeted and messed up about what she wanted. The last thing she needed was to become someone's experiment, and then, when it ended badly—as it inevitably would—have the college somehow find out about them.

Forget her.

The sad part was, she really did miss the others. Franny had a wicked sense of humor, and Roberta was a keen observer of people. Steph was just a really kind person—with a great strudel recipe.

At the college, Ryn's own classes were going okay, she supposed. Beverly told her about a quarter of the students had dropped the women-and-history class.

"Serves him right," Ryn grumbled, but it pained her to see those students soured on what could have been a fantastic course.

At home, things weren't any better. If she was pissy, Henrietta was pissier. They barely spoke, sitting through mostly silent dinners, and then going to their separate rooms after. Ryn wasn't sure what had happened between them, but she didn't have the energy to sort it out.

She wrapped up her last lecture and went to her office to drop off her notes. Sitting down to stuff her pants into her boots, she was bent over to lace them when a shadow fell across her door.

The small hairs on the back of her neck prickled, but she didn't look up.

"It seems you've been busy." Geary's voice was low, meant to be heard only by her.

"I've been busy doing my work." Ryn's eyes darted around, looking for something, anything that might serve as a weapon if needed.

"You know what I'm talking about."

She straightened up slowly. "Care to enlighten me?"

His lips were stretched thin, his fists balled up. "If I go down, I'm taking you with me."

For a few seconds, he stared into her eyes before turning and going to his own office, where he slammed the door.

"What the hell was that about?" she whispered. Her heart was pounding more than she cared to admit at the undisguised hatred in his eyes.

She finished dressing for the walk home, pausing at Beverly's office to see if she knew what Geary was talking about, but her office was dark.

She thumped down the stairs in an even sourer mood. When she got to the house, Bonnie's car was still in the driveway, parked beside

Nelly. Ryn remembered, with a little stab of guilt, that she hadn't left any little notes for Bonnie the last couple of Wednesdays.

As she unlocked the front door, she heard voices coming from the back of the house. Leaving her boots and jacket in the foyer, she padded through the house to find Bonnie and Henrietta in the studio.

"What's up?"

"Time to get all the paintings together for the show at the library," Bonnie said cheerfully.

But Ryn noticed she glanced worriedly at Henrietta as she said it. Henrietta was scowling at a lineup of paintings propped along the counter and on the floor, leaning against the cabinets.

"I don't like any of them," Henrietta snapped. "None of them are good enough."

"Now that's just silly," Bonnie said. "They're beautiful."

"What're you talking about?" Ryn asked. "These are great."

"What do you know?" Henrietta clanked out of the studio. A moment later, her bedroom door closed with a loud slam.

"Seems to be my day for slamming doors," Ryn muttered. She turned to Bonnie. "What was that all about? I thought galleries have taken her paintings."

Lowering her voice conspiratorially, Bonnie said, "Henrietta has never let anyone at those galleries know who she is."

"How can that be? I thought her work was all over the state?"

"It is." Bonnie's gaze flicked in the direction of Henrietta's room, and she waved Ryn out into the breezeway near the garage. "When the gallery people come, she always asks me to deal with them."

"But why?"

"Because she doesn't want them to take her paintings out of pity."

Ryn's mouth hung open for a moment.

Bonnie nodded vigorously. "I know! I feel the same way. It's just plain silly, but she thinks if they knew she was handicapped, they would look at her work differently. Not judge it the same way. So they have no idea who she is."

"Oh." Ryn looked in the direction of the bedroom, understanding. "And now, with a show here in the village, where everyone knows who she is..."

"She's scared. Plain and simple. But do you think she'd admit it?" Bonnie's pursed lips answered her own question.

Ryn bit her lip as she thought. "Do you think you and I can pick out the paintings for the library show?"

Bonnie wrung her hands. "Oh, dear. That's a lot of responsibility, but I'm afraid if we leave it up to her, she won't think any of them are good enough."

"Come on."

An hour later, the back seat and trunk of Bonnie's car were loaded with about two dozen carefully wrapped paintings. They picked a mix of Henrietta's still lifes, local scenes of the village square and the pond and golf course—"people will enjoy seeing scenes they recognize," Bonnie said—as well as some of the paintings Henrietta had done of Owasco Lake.

"You take these to the art store," Ryn said. "If Henrietta absolutely doesn't want some of these in the show, I'll bring others."

"If you're sure," Bonnie said.

"I am."

She waved Bonnie off and then braced herself. The house was filled with the aroma of the ham and sweet potatoes Bonnie had made for them. A pan of green beans simmered on the stove. On the counter was a loaf of bread Bonnie had baked at home and brought that morning. Ryn's stomach growled its appreciation, but first things first.

Standing at Henrietta's door, she stood with her hand in the air. Sympathy was not the way to go. She gave the door a sharp rap.

"Dinner's ready, and it smells good enough to make me want to eat all of it."

When there was no reply, she said, "Bonnie said you didn't eat lunch, so if you don't come out, I'm gonna have to force feed you. No hunger strikes on my watch. I'll give you five minutes, and if you're not out, I'm coming in."

She went to the kitchen and pulled the ham and potatoes out of the oven. As she was getting the plates down, she heard Henrietta behind her. She set two glasses on the counter next to the refrigerator.

Without turning around, she said, "Just water for me, please."

She dished out some of everything onto their plates and cut a few slices of bread, bringing them to the table with the butter.

A quick glance told her Henrietta hadn't been crying, not that she expected her to. She knew how tough the armor was most of the time.

"When was the last time you went to a museum?" she asked.

Henrietta paused in the middle of buttering her bread. "What kind of question is that?"

"A simple one." Ryn stabbed her fork into a chunk of sweet potato. "When was the last time you went to a museum or gallery?"

Henrietta frowned. "New York City, 1953. We went to visit a specialist in polio cases. While we were there, we visited the Metropolitan Museum of Art."

Ryn tried to hide her surprise. She figured it hadn't been recent, but this caught her off-guard. "What do you remember?"

Henrietta chewed for a moment, thinking. "It was overwhelming. So huge, so much to see. Too much. So many people."

"So you're probably not a very good judge of how your work stacks up."

"Excuse me?" Henrietta's fork lowered.

"I haven't been to New York, but when I used to hang out at the museums and galleries in Pittsburgh—"

"You spent time in art galleries in Pittsburgh?"

Ryn couldn't help grinning at Henrietta's dubious tone. "Yeah. It was a good place to pick up women."

Henrietta snorted, and Ryn continued, "I was mostly interested in the older stuff, not more modern artists. I wanted to see the historic details, what clothing was like, the furniture, china, stuff like that. But the point is, I've seen a lot of more modern paintings. And I can tell you, art critic that I'm not, your work is better than ninety percent of what is in those galleries."

Henrietta stared at her for a moment. Ryn met her gaze openly, letting Henrietta see that she meant what she said.

"I won't lie, Hank. Not even to make you feel better."

Henrietta lowered her gaze to her plate and cut another bite of ham.

"I think," Ryn went on, sparing Henrietta the need to respond, "that we need to take a trip to Rochester or Albany. Someplace where they've shown your paintings, and see how they stack up. I think you'll be surprised."

Henrietta kept her eyes lidded as she considered. "No picking up women."

Ryn chuckled. "Who needs any other women when I have you as my date?"

❧

HENRIETTA FRETTED ABOUT WHICH paintings had been chosen for the exhibit, but, she reasoned, since she hadn't been able to make up her mind at all, perhaps it was better this way. No matter what Meryn said, it was always nerve-wracking to show her work to others. Even when the gallery reps came to the house, she couldn't bear to be within hearing distance of whatever they might say, but she couldn't help herself from eavesdropping. It was maddening.

"Are you ready?" came Meryn's voice through the bedroom door.

Henrietta jumped. "Almost."

Four of her suits lay on the bed, but she was only dressed in her camisole and a slip. Deciding it didn't really matter which of the four sets of gray or brown tweed she chose, she picked one and quickly pulled the skirt on. Standing up to tuck her blouse in, she inspected her image in the mirror. Hardly the picture of creativity.

"You are more old school-marm librarian than artist," she said to her reflection.

But when she stepped out of the bedroom, Meryn glanced her way and said, "You look great."

Henrietta glowered at her. "I thought you said you don't lie."

"I don't." Meryn smiled. "You really do look nice. How about me?"

The girl twirled, dressed in khakis and a white blouse. When Henrietta just stared, Meryn looked hurt.

"Hank, these are new pants. You didn't even notice."

She grinned when Henrietta tried to swat her with a crutch. She picked up Henrietta's coat from where it lay on the back of the sofa, giving her shoulders a squeeze as she helped her into it.

"This is going to be fun."

Henrietta could think of lots of other words for it, but fun wasn't one of them. She took a deep breath and walked toward the garage as if she were marching to her doom.

But within a couple of hours, even Henrietta had to admit the exhibit was a success. Sandy and Maxine Adams—who, in her flowing batik gown and headscarf most definitely did not look like a stodgy librarian—had outdone themselves. The paintings were set up all around the library, so that visitors had to roam the aisles to follow the trail, which served the dual purpose of spreading the crowd out and getting people to wander throughout the space, perhaps seeing some books they might want to borrow as well.

A table of refreshments was set up near the front, where a chair was reserved for Henrietta when she needed to sit and rest.

She was overwhelmed by the number of people there, so many it was actually hard to move around, despite the spread-out nature of the exhibit.

215

"Miss Cochran?"

She turned around to see a middle-aged man with a thin moustache and glasses.

"I'm Randall Taylor. I represent the McGovern Gallery in Albany. I
selected a few of your paintings this past autumn. I was beginning to
doubt you really existed."

He shook her hand with a slight bow. She waited for the curious
gaze down to her braces, but his eyes never left her face.

"I do exist, Mr. Taylor."

He smiled. "And I'm delighted to meet you at last. You received
our check last month?"

"I did," Henrietta said. "Thank you."

He pulled a card from his pocket. "Today is hardly the time to discuss details, but I would like to call upon you to discuss a similar
exhibit at our gallery. Would you be interested?"

Henrietta accepted the card, blinking a couple of times. "Yes. I
would."

"Excellent. I'll call within the week. Congratulations on such nice
turnout."

He left her as Bonnie brought her a cup of punch, her husband in
tow, looking distinctly uncomfortable in a suit and tie.

"Wasn't that the gentleman from the gallery? The one I dealt
with?"

Henrietta nodded, dazed. "He wants to do a show like this. In Albany."

"See? I told you there was no need to hide who you are." Bonnie
beamed at her. "We're so proud. The whole village is. Have you seen
how many people have come in today?"

Sandy came by at that moment. "I agree. This is better than I expected. I think holding this opening on a Saturday was a brilliant idea
of Maxine's. With people off work, and nothing else going on this
time of year, it gives the village something unique to experience."

"Congratulations, Henrietta."

She stiffened and turned to find Genevieve Talbert standing beside her. "Thank you."

"I had no idea you were actually talented."

It was just the kind of backhanded compliment Genevieve habitually handed out to the other women at bridge.

"I'm happy to surprise you," Henrietta said. Just then the four young nuns came in, giving her a reason to excuse herself.

"Henrietta, we're so happy for you," Roberta said. "It's a wonderful way to let the village see your work."

"We feel privileged to have had a preview," Franny said.

Henrietta noticed Tamara scanning the crowd. "I think you'll find Meryn over there," she said to them, nodding toward a display near the windows.

She continued chatting with people who stopped by, but she couldn't help watching Meryn as she greeted the nuns—and the almost-nun. It occurred to her that Meryn hadn't spoken at all about Tamara since the day they had gone out after brunch. Now that she thought about it, Meryn had been quiet in general since that day.

Another group of people came by, distracting Henrietta for a few minutes. When she glanced over again, Meryn was standing alone. The nuns had moved off, and Meryn was watching them with an unguarded expression on her face—wistful, almost sad. She turned from them and caught Henrietta watching her. A slow smile spread across Meryn's face.

A curious buzzing sounded in Henrietta's ears, and it seemed someone dimmed the lights. Suddenly, hands were grabbing her, lowering her into a chair. Someone got a glass of cold water, held it to her lips.

It was Meryn, kneeling beside her, one arm wrapped around her shoulders, the other gently offering her a drink. Henrietta sluggishly wondered how she'd moved across the room so quickly.

"Too much excitement." Bonnie's face swam into view. "I'll stay with her. You go get the car and her chair."

"Are you sure?" Meryn asked. "Shouldn't we get her to the hospital?"

"No hospital," Henrietta rasped. "Home."

Henrietta was surrounded by bodies, crowding her. Sandy and Maxine tried to clear some space, give her room to breathe. It seemed to take Meryn a very long time to get back with her wheelchair. Burning with humiliation, Henrietta wanted nothing more than to get out of there.

"I can walk," she protested.

"Don't be silly," Bonnie said. "Frank?" She searched for her husband. "I'm going with Miss Cochran. I'll call you when I'm ready to come home."

Someone draped her coat over her shoulders as Meryn and Bonnie got her situated in her wheelchair. The cold air outside was like life itself, Henrietta thought. The clearer her head became, the more mortified she was.

They helped her into the car, which was idling outside the entrance. Bonnie got in the back seat while Meryn folded the chair into the rear of the station wagon.

"Let's get you home," Bonnie said.

"No hand controls," Meryn quipped, though her face was pinched with worry.

"Why not?" Henrietta said, closing her eyes and resting her head against the headrest. "Today, I probably wouldn't notice."

◠

DR. GORDON MCCOURT, RYN decided, was a very handsome man, in a "Father Knows Best" kind of way, tall and slender, with his thick silver hair and horn-rimmed glasses. She paced in the living room while he was in Henrietta's room, examining her.

218

Bonnie was making a pot of creamy chicken soup. "Nothing better," she pronounced, though they didn't yet know what was ailing Henrietta.

Ryn had helped cut up some of the vegetables, but she spent so much time looking over her shoulder toward the bedroom that Bonnie finally declared, "You're going to chop a finger off, the way you're going. Go. I can take care of this."

She wished she still had a job of some kind to do, because the waiting was killing her. She tried to sit and read, but all she did was stare at the same page for minutes at a time.

When the doctor finally emerged, Ryn jumped up. Bonnie hurried from the kitchen, wiping her hands on a towel.

"Well?" Bonnie asked.

He shook his head, thoughtfully, his lips pursed. "Not a thing wrong with her physically, other than the usual. She hasn't been getting as much exercise as she was starting to in the fall. But other than that, I can't find a thing wrong."

He eyed Ryn. "You moved in in September?"

She nodded, as did he.

"Hmmm, I wonder," he said, more to himself than her.

Ryn glanced at Bonnie, but she looked as puzzled as Ryn was. "You wonder what?"

Rather than answer, he opened his black bag and dug around, producing a small, brown-glass bottle.

"This is a vitamin formula. Put three drops in her food or drink, three times a day. We'll see if this gives her a little pick-me-up."

He handed the bottle to Bonnie and closed the clasp on his bag. He placed a hand on Ryn's shoulder. "Walk me to my car."

Ryn followed him outside. He placed his bag in the back seat of his Buick and turned to her.

"I've known Henrietta as long as I've been practicing in Bluemont. She's tough as nails. Had to be. But something's changed since you moved in. I have my theory, but we'll see."

219

"What theory?" Ryn asked, more perplexed than ever.

But he only smiled. "I don't know what your long-term plans are, Miss Fleming, but... be gentle with her."

"What the hell does that mean?" Ryn wondered as he backed out of the driveway.

She went back inside to find Henrietta fussing that she didn't need to be served in bed. "I'm not sick!"

"Have it your way, then," Bonnie sniffed. She emerged from the bedroom carrying a tray. "Miss Stubborn won't stay in bed."

Henrietta followed her out to the kitchen and sat at the table. "He said I'm fine. Need more exercise. I won't get that lying around like an invalid."

"No one called you an invalid," Ryn pointed out. "Let's all have some of that soup. Smells great."

But Henrietta frowned at the bowl Bonnie had transferred from the tray. "That's what they're all thinking at the library. All those people. They think I'm too fragile to even stay on my feet for something like that."

Because Ryn understood exactly how she'd feel, she said, "I know. But I've been thinking about it. I think you should use this."

Henrietta glanced up sharply, and Bonnie turned from the stove where she was ladling two more bowls of soup.

"What do you mean?" Henrietta asked.

Ryn held up her hand as if she were following a marquee. "Reclusive artist has emotional breakdown at exhibit."

Henrietta bristled. "I did not have a breakdown."

"Yeah," Ryn said, grinning. "But everyone'll be talking about it for months. More people than ever will want to see your work. And those who were there will get to tell the story over and over."

"She has a point," Bonnie agreed, setting the bowls on the table.

"This could be part of your mystique." Ryn nodded as she spooned up some of the thick soup.

"Mystique, my eye." But Henrietta wasn't frowning so much any more.

Ryn threw a quick wink at Bonnie, who smiled back.

When they were done eating, Bonnie called her husband to come and pick her up. Ryn offered to drive her, but "we shouldn't leave her alone," Bonnie said.

In the few minutes it took Frank to arrive, they got Henrietta settled on the sofa.

"Now, you rest up," Bonnie said, tugging the throw over Henrietta's legs.

A quick honk from the driveway signaled Frank's arrival. Ryn saw Bonnie to the door.

"If you need anything, just call me," Bonnie said.

"We'll be fine. Thanks again."

Ryn closed and locked the door, and then went to sit in her usual chair. "Well, that was an exciting day."

"Hmph."

"Want to tell me what really happened?"

Henrietta didn't answer, but Ryn let the silence stretch out between them until at last, Henrietta spoke. "What happened between you and that girl? Tamara."

Whatever Ryn had expected from Henrietta, it wasn't this. "Nothing happened."

Henrietta didn't glance her way, busying herself rearranging the throw. "I thought you liked her."

"I did. I do. But..." Ryn blew out a frustrated breath. "I just can't. Not when I'm a professor and she's a student. It would make me no better than Geary. And then there's her whole nun thing. I don't get that at all. I'm not sure she really does, either."

She leaned forward, bracing her elbows on her knees. "Hank, I knew I was gay from the time I was little. I didn't call it that, of course, but I knew I liked girls. Tamara... she doesn't know what she wants or what she's comfortable with. Until she figures that out... I hope she finds whatever makes her happy."

Henrietta looked her way. "But today, when you were talking to them, you looked... upset."

Ryn sat back again, hooking one leg over the arm of the chair. "Not upset. More resigned, I guess. Resigned to the fact that I'm probably the only lesbian in this entire town."

For a few minutes, the only sound in the room was the ticking of the clock on the mantel.

"Not the only one."

Henrietta's voice was so soft, Ryn wasn't sure she'd heard correctly. She glanced up and was nearly bowled over by the tenderness in Henrietta's eyes. It only lasted a second, and then Henrietta lowered her gaze, shuttering her emotions back behind that armor.

"I am more tired than I realized," Henrietta said. "I think I'll go to bed."

Ryn started to get up, but Henrietta waved her back down. "I'm fine. I'll call if I need anything."

Dropping back into her chair, Ryn stared after Henrietta's retreating back, her mind teeming with a thousand thoughts, but it kept circling back to that moment, that glimpse into Henrietta's heart.

"Damn."

Chapter 15

TAKING THE DOCTOR'S ADVICE, Henrietta started walking daily, just the driveway. Once Bud—or sometimes Meryn—got the snow cleared, the sun usually dried the asphalt completely, giving her a safe, level surface. The path down to the pond was too treacherous this time of year.

At first, one trip down the drive and back had Henrietta winded and wheezing, as her lungs were unaccustomed to the bite of the cold air. But soon, she could do two and then three circuits of the drive. She felt silly walking in big circles, but there were no golfers this time of year to see her. Sometimes, circling back around to Meryn's car—*who names their cars?* she wondered, but smiled as she shook her head—she stopped to read the bumper stickers. What must it be like to be so free? To not care what others think?

The last thing Henrietta had intended the day of the exhibit was to declare herself a lesbian. The thought was still so startling to her that she shivered with apprehension just repeating it in her mind. But she knew now, she was. She had loved Una Marsden, romantically, even if they were only fifteen. And if things had turned out differently, she would have wanted a life with Una, a home together, as lovers and partners—the life they had so innocently planned.

"We'll be happy," Una had declared as they lay together on her bed while her aunt was away at one of her parties. "Not like Radclyffe Hall and her lovers."

"Who's Radclyffe Hall?" Henrietta had asked.

"Silly. Haven't you read The Well of Loneliness?*"*

"No. What's that?"

"Only the most scandalous book in ages. I found a copy in London and read it. It's not a happy story, but then, I suppose they can't let our kind tell happy stories, can they?"

"What do you mean, 'our kind'?"

Una propped up on an elbow to smile indulgently at Henrietta. Lowering her head, she kissed her on the mouth. "This is what I mean."

Henrietta reached up to pull Una back down, craving the softness of her lips.

Una lay beside Henrietta again, sifting Henrietta's dark hair through her fingers. "I'm never marrying. They can't force me. I want us to stay together always."

"Me, too." Henrietta turned on her side, tracing a finger over Una's lovely face. "Where will we live?"

Una frowned as she thought. "Perhaps New York City. I read there are places there where our kind can live freely. Like Paris was in the twenties. Of course, Paris won't be the same after the war."

"I'd love to live in New York. I could paint, and you could write."

Henrietta stood, staring into the distance as she lost herself in memories. Shivering, she brought herself back to the present and resumed walking.

Life, it seemed, had brought her full circle. Not that she could let herself imagine having Meryn love her in that way, but it was hard to picture life without that girl. And when Henrietta remembered what it felt like to be held by Meryn, to feel the warm embrace of her arms, even if it was in sympathy, it took her breath away.

Henrietta wasn't given to introspection. Introspection led to self-pity, and self-pity led nowhere. But she found herself pondering the puzzling nature of love in all its forms. She'd never truly loved anyone but her parents and Una, so she felt distinctly at a disadvantage. In fact, she sometimes thought her emotional development had been as stunted as her body—stuck in the same place it had been in the summer of 1945. She'd matured, *but have I grown?*

Meryn, though she was thirty years younger, seemed so much wiser about these things. Henrietta admired that.

She thought about this as she walked, wondering how someone so young could be so confident in matters of the heart. She stopped suddenly as it hit her. *She understands love and heart and relationships because she's willing to let herself be hurt.*

That realization shook Henrietta.

She made her way inside to the kitchen, where Meryn had left her a selection of teas with firm instructions to make herself a cup when she came back in. She'd put the kettle on low heat before she went outside. With hot water poured and a tea bag in the cup, she shuffled it to the table and sat.

Her heart was pounding and fluttering in that frightening way. Was it possible for something to be painful and pleasurable at the same time? She'd been hurt so much physically—and emotionally when she thought Una had simply left her—that her default response was to guard against anything that might hurt her. Just the thought of deliberately opening herself to someone, knowing that her heart might be broken...

"I don't think I could do that," she said to the empty house.

～

THE WEATHER BROKE—JUST enough to offer a tease of spring. Days of brilliant sunshine actually melted the snow enough to allow patches of brown grass to show like islands in a sea of white. The trees seemed to stretch a little, reaching for the sunlight. Somehow, most of February had crept by until spring break was only a few weeks away. Ryn was almost as eager for it as the students were.

She sat in a secluded corner of the library where she had a view as she tried to concentrate enough to grade papers—five-thousand-word essays on the War of 1812.

"Why did I do this to myself?" she mumbled for the hundredth time as she circled an incorrect statement and jotted a comment in the margin.

But her gaze kept drifting to the window and the scene beyond. Yesterday, when she'd been here at this same table, grading these same papers, she'd seen Tamara walking across campus. She hadn't spoken to Tam since the reception at the library, and that had been barely two words. It had been so tempting to jump up and run after her, to talk.

But there really isn't anything to say, is there?

She propped her chin on her hand, her other hand playing absently with her pendant. It was kind of funny. As attractive as Tamara was, as much as Ryn had hoped last semester that maybe something was there, she was kind of glad nothing had happened. Drama was over-rated, and she was pretty sure a relationship with Tam would have come with lots of it.

She sighed and returned to her grading.

"Hi."

Ryn looked up to find Franny standing beside her. "Hi."

"Mind if I sit?"

"Not at all."

Ryn slid her pile of papers aside and capped her pen.

"You sure I'm not interrupting?" Franny set her backpack on the floor and sat across from Ryn.

"Believe me, an interruption at this point is very welcome."

"How've you been?" Franny's sharp eyes probed. "We haven't seen you much lately. Actually, we haven't seen you at all since the art reception."

"Yeah, I've been really busy."

Franny tilted her head. "Too busy to come by? Or come to Mass?"

Ryn suddenly found it hard to meet Franny's gaze. She reached for her pen, unclicking the top and doodling on a folder.

"Is there some reason you haven't wanted to hang out?"

When Ryn didn't say anything, Franny reached for her hand, stilling the doodling.

"Or should I say, is there someone?"

Ryn looked up. "What do you know?"

Franny looked as if she was trying not to roll her eyes. "I know avoidance when I see it."

"Sometimes avoidance is the better part of valor. Or something like that."

"Sometimes." Franny released Ryn's hand. "If it helps, I think Tamara's just as messed up."

"I'm not the one who's messed up." Ryn narrowed her eyes. "Has she spoken to you?"

Franny shook her head. "It's more what she won't say."

"Franny, I appreciate this little pep talk, but, no offense, I doubt you'd understand."

Franny glanced around and saw that no one else was near. She startled Ryn by leaning across the table and reaching for her chest, cradling the silver labrys in her fingers.

"Ryn, I found something that means more to me than human relationships. It doesn't mean I never had a human relationship."

Ryn's mouth opened and closed a couple of times. "I... um... Really?"

"Really." Franny released the labrys and sat back. "My last girlfriend was a wonderful person, but, for me, this is what I need."

227

"Wow." Ryn ran her hand through her hair as she absorbed this bit of news. "I like Tam, but I just can't. Not when she's a student and..."

"And doesn't know what she wants." Franny nodded. "It's hard to watch her struggle, but it's her struggle. She needs to figure this out."

Ryn blew out a breath. "And I don't want to be the one she figures it out with. I can't."

"I know."

It was such a relief to know there was someone who understood. "So that's why..." Ryn flipped her hands palm-up. "I really miss hanging out with you guys, but I don't want to make it harder on Tamara right now."

She looked at Franny, her short veil slightly crooked, her tall, gangly body looking out of place in the black habit she wore. Ryn leaned forward and picked up the simple gold cross lying on her chest.

"You've had a girlfriend. What about this? Is this truly enough to make up for never having that again?"

Franny nodded solemnly. "It's hard to explain. I guess it would be like, if you were in a relationship with someone you liked, hoping it might turn into love, and then, wham. You meet the one. And you know. This is what you've been waiting for. And no one else will ever match up, ever come close. Not for you."

Ryn let the cross go, watching it swing gently from its fine gold chain. "But to give up... you know, touch and hugging and sex."

Franny snorted. "I didn't say there weren't sacrifices. That part's hard sometimes. Damn hard. But, overall, it's so worth it. There are lots of kinds of love, Ryn." She searched Ryn's eyes again. "How's Henrietta?"

Ryn blinked at the abrupt change of topic. "She's fine. Why?"

"I was watching you. At the library. Watching her. I think you might understand what I'm talking about better than you know."

She reached for her backpack and stood. "Don't close your heart off to what's right in front of you."

Bending down, she kissed Ryn on the cheek and left.

Ryn walked out of the library in a daze a short while later, Franny's words running around and around in her head. She didn't notice the sunshine or the warmth or the students hanging around outside as she returned to Rayburn. Climbing the steps slowly to the second floor, she opened the stairwell door to shouts coming from the administrative office.

She carefully poked her head around the door. Talbert's door was shut, but the clamor was coming from inside his office. Beverly saw her and waved her away frantically.

"Go!" she mouthed.

Ryn scurried down the corridor to her office. She left the light off and closed the door so it would look as if it were empty. After a few minutes, a small shadow fell across the pebbled glass and there was a timid knock.

Ryn opened the door and dragged Beverly inside. "What in the world is going on?"

"It's Professor Geary." Beverly's eyes were huge. "Father Croson and Dr. Talbert are both talking to him."

Ryn dropped into her chair, her heart thudding. "What did you hear?"

Beverly perched on the edge of the extra chair, her lip caught in her teeth. "I didn't mean to eavesdrop. It's not right, but they were so loud. And then I was afraid to leave, in case Dr. Talbert needed something."

She glanced nervously at the door and leaned toward Ryn to whisper, "I think Professor Geary got a girl in trouble. Father Croson is livid. And I think..." She put a hand over her mouth for a moment. "I think the poor girl got an abortion."

Ryn sat, frozen.

"Father Croson said something about newspapers and the college." Beverly leaned closer and dropped her voice further. "But who could know? How would the papers find out?"

Ryn shook her head. "I don't know."

"I think it must be the Feldman girl. That's why her mother was so adamant about speaking with Father Croson. Maybe she's threatening to tell the story to the newspapers." Beverly wrung her hands. "Oh, this would be just terrible for the college—a Catholic college, of all places."

"More terrible for the girl," Ryn said flatly.

"Oh, of course. I didn't mean—" Beverly stood up. "I should get back. It would be best if they didn't see you here right now."

"Yeah. Let me know."

Beverly nodded and opened the door a crack. The coast was clear, and she let herself out.

Ryn abandoned her papers, locking them in a drawer for the night. Hastily pulling on her jacket, she reached for her backpack and slipped out of the office toward the back stairs.

She paused on the granite steps outside to draw in a breath of clean, almost-spring air. "What a hell of a day."

⁓

FROM THE STUDIO, HENRIETTA heard the sound of the front door opening and closing, and her heart jumped a little. She frowned at her canvas, dabbing a bit more vermillion onto the trees surrounding the pond in her scene. The light began to fade as she worked. Before long, she had to flip on the overhead lights to clean up. She realized she hadn't heard any other noises from the front of the house.

Placing her brushes to dry, she left the studio to find the kitchen empty and dark. She walked into the living room and found Meryn sitting in her chair, staring out the picture window at the gathering dusk, apparently deep in thought.

"Are you all right?"

Meryn jumped, and Henrietta noticed she hadn't changed out of her teaching clothes, something she usually did first thing.

230

"I'm fine."

"How was your day?"

"Just great." Meryn turned back to the window. "Yours?"

"Terrible," Henrietta said.

"That's good."

Henrietta sat on the sofa. "Meryn, what's wrong?"

"Hmm?" Meryn spun in the chair. "I'm sorry, Hank. Just preoccupied."

"So I noticed." Henrietta nodded in her direction. "Since you're still dressed for work, how about we have dinner at the club tonight?"

"Sure."

As it was a Thursday evening, the dining room was nearly empty, with only one other couple seated at a table.

Their waitress, Barbara, according to her name badge, brought them menus and took their drink orders—decaf coffee for Henrietta and hot tea for Meryn. Henrietta waited until the drinks had been brought and their dinners ordered, but Meryn was staring into her tea, her brow wrinkled.

"Something is troubling you," she said at last. "Care to talk about it?"

Meryn shifted her gaze, probing Henrietta's eyes. "Tell me more about Una."

Caught completely off-guard by that request, Henrietta choked on her coffee. She had to cough several times to clear her throat.

"You okay?" Meryn asked.

Henrietta nodded, using her napkin to dab at her watery eyes. When she could speak, she croaked, "Why would you ask that?"

"You said—" Meryn stopped abruptly when Barbara brought their salads. "Thank you."

Once they were alone again, she continued, "I know—at least I think—you loved Una. I'd like to know more about her. About your past."

Henrietta fussed with her salad as she gathered her thoughts. "I told you she spent summers here until the war, then came to live with her aunt."

"What did she look like?"

Chewing slowly, Henrietta let herself remember. "She had red hair, the color of copper in the sun. Her eyes were the most vivid blue—cerulean. When she looked at me, I felt as if I were falling into a pool of the bluest water."

Henrietta caught herself and cleared her throat. "It was a long time ago."

She could feel Meryn watching her.

"I think some memories stay vivid, no matter how much time has gone by," Meryn murmured. "Did she love you?"

"We were children," Henrietta snapped. But when Meryn just waited, she sighed. "Yes. We were going to move to New York together. She wanted to be a writer and poet, and I would paint there." She smiled tenderly. "We had it all planned out."

"Tell me about when you got sick."

"Why are you asking all these questions?"

Meryn's reply was again interrupted by the arrival of their entrées. After the waitress left them, she said, "Because I need to know."

"But why?" Henrietta met Meryn's gaze and immediately regretted it. She'd often watched flies and other insects, caught in the webs spun in the branches of the bushes outside her studio windows, watched them struggle as the spider closed in. She felt like one of those insects now, ensnared by the intense emotions parading through Meryn's eyes.

"Please."

Flustered, Henrietta couldn't reply immediately. She ate a bit of her tortellini and sipped her coffee. "It was June. Back then, every summer there was a rash of polio cases as people swam in infected ponds and lakes and rivers. Not everybody got sick, of course, or, if they got sick, became paralyzed, but we'd been warned not to go into the pond. In those days, there were no houses there. Just the dock. We'd been lying in the sun, planning, talking... kissing."

Henrietta's face burned, and she glanced around to make sure no one else was within earshot. "We got warm, so we decided to go into the water. It wasn't long. No more than half an hour. We got out and dried off on the dock, thinking we were so daring. A few days later, I broke out in a fever. That was the last thing I remembered for ages."

From the corner of her eye, she saw that Meryn wasn't eating. "The doctors here packed me in ice and transported me to Rochester. It was nearly a year before I came home."

Meryn picked up her cup. "And you never saw Una again."

Henrietta shook her head, keeping her eyes fixed on her plate, which was swimming through the tears in her eyes. Her throat was too tight to speak.

"And there's never been anyone else?" Meryn asked softly.

Henrietta blinked several times and gave a curt shake of her head. "Who would there be? Look at me."

"I am."

Her heart pounding so that she thought she might actually pass out at the table, Henrietta gripped her chair, unable to meet Meryn's gaze.

"Is everything all right?" Barbara asked, appearing suddenly.

"We need to have this packed to go, please," Meryn said.

"Is there a problem?" the waitress asked anxiously.

"No problem. We're just not as hungry as we thought."

Barbara scooped up both their plates. "I'll only be a moment."

The ride back to the house was silent. Inside, Meryn put the food in the refrigerator as Henrietta walked through the kitchen to drop her coat on the back of the sofa. She wanted only to escape to her room.

"Henrietta."

Meryn's voice stopped her. Henrietta tensed as Meryn stepped up behind her.

"Thank you. For telling me."

"I've never told anyone what I told you tonight."

"I know."

"Don't make me regret it."

"I won't."

Henrietta went to her room and closed the door. Leaning against it, she closed her eyes. "What am I doing?" she whispered.

But a part of her—a small part that she was ashamed of—wished Meryn would come and knock on that door.

Chapter 16

THAT TASTE OF SPRING turned out to be a cruel trick, as winter wasn't nearly ready to let go. A massive storm system moved over the entire Northeast on Sunday night. Western New York got the worst of the lake-effect snow, but Bluemont still got two feet. Enough for St. Aloysius to cancel classes for a few days. All of the surrounding SUNY campuses also canceled classes while maintenance crews worked to clear parking lots and sidewalks.

Ryn and Bud together got Henrietta's driveway cleared.

"Good thing this is dry snow," Bud said while Ryn huffed and puffed.

People on cross-country skis got out before the plows did, taking advantage of the lack of cars to enjoy the snow, waving a cheery hello to the shovelers as they glided by.

It was pretty. The golf course was an undisturbed canvas of white—"no, not white," Henrietta would have said. "Look at it. There are blues and grays and even pink tones in that snow. Look at it."

Ryn felt she was looking at everything differently. The atmosphere in the history corridor on Friday had been like working in a bomb

235

factory—there was a definite feeling that the slightest spark could set off an explosion. Geary, rather than hiding in his office, made a show of marching up and down the hall, going to Beverly for unnecessary things, she told Ryn. Talbert, though, was holed up in his office, going through three packs a day, judging from the number of cigarette butts overflowing the ashtray on his desk. Beverly came to Ryn's office just to get a break from the smoke that seeped into her space.

"I may not get to retire," she'd complained. "I may die of asphyxiation before that can happen."

"Did you hear any more?" Ryn had asked, closing her door.

"Only a little. Professor Geary thinks he can ride this out, but Dr. Talbert asked me for the department budget. That means he's figuring he'll still be department chair next year."

"So..." Ryn couldn't hide her smile. "Talbert's promotion to dean is on the line. Maybe if he's being hurt by this as well, he'll be more inclined to do something. Did you hear if it was Mrs. Feldman who is threatening to tell the papers?"

Beverly shook her head. "Father Croson wouldn't say, not that I heard anyhow. Do you think she'd do that to her own daughter?"

Ryn sat back. From the short amount of time she'd spent with Vanessa's mother, it was hard to imagine her wanting to splash Vanessa's story all over the place.

"Who, then?"

They were left with that mystery, and it kept running through Ryn's head as she shoveled. That and Henrietta.

She'd always pictured herself in a normal, committed relationship with a woman she'd have mad sex with everywhere—of course, sex of any kind was only a distant memory at this point. For the last several months, the closest she'd gotten was her collection of lesbian novels and her own hand.

But Henrietta had already done so many kind things—the whole birthday and Thanksgiving surprise with her family, asking Bud to make the fire pit near the pond for them to enjoy evenings near the water, trying to make this feel like Ryn's home, too.

Henrietta had a lot of admirable traits—her strength and resilience, her barbed wit, her talent. But it was her vulnerable side, the soft side she hid from everyone, that was what tugged at Ryn's heart the most. When Henrietta spoke of Una or her parents, when she let her guard down enough for Ryn to see deep into her eyes, Ryn did want to hold her. Not to make love, but to comfort and protect her. To promise her that nothing would ever hurt her like that again. And the feeling was so unexpectedly powerful. Was it love?

Damn Franny anyhow. I don't want to be in love with Henrietta Cochran.

"Tired?"

"Huh?" Ryn snapped alive.

"You been leanin' on that shovel like you need something to prop you up," Bud said. "I can finish this."

"I'm not tired." Ryn dug her shovel in. "Just catching my breath."

She didn't dare steal a look at the house. If Henrietta was standing at the window, watching them, she felt certain Hank would know what she'd been thinking.

They refilled all the bird feeders and suet cages. Before they'd finished, a score of birds were flapping and chirping in the higher branches, eagerly waiting for them to leave.

Ryn cleaned Nelly off and started her up, letting her engine idle long enough to warm everything.

When she and Bud returned to the garage, Henrietta was waiting for them.

"Thank you both so much," she said, handing a check to Bud.

"Always a pleasure, Miss Cochran," Bud said with a tip of his cap. "When the snow goes for good, I'll make sure the path to the pond is cleared for you."

He shouldered his shovel and went to his truck while Ryn hung hers on the garage wall and stomped the snow off her boots.

237

"You should get inside," she said when Henrietta stayed there.

"You, too. You've done enough."

Henrietta pushed the button to close the garage door, and Ryn followed her into the kitchen where the teakettle was steaming.

"I'm happy to pay you, too." Henrietta busied herself at the counter with her back to Ryn. "Shoveling snow was not part of your responsibilities in our arrangement."

Ryn stood in her socks. She'd nearly forgotten that this was a business arrangement. But maybe Henrietta hadn't. She got a teabag and poured some hot water. Henrietta had a plate of shortbread cookies already sitting on the table.

"I'll get that," she said as Henrietta tried to get a firmer grip on a cup of coffee to move it from the counter to the table.

They sat, Ryn cradling her hot mug in her hands as she fought a chill that had nothing to do with the cold outside.

"Are we friends, Henrietta?"

Those gray eyes rose to meet hers. "What do you mean?"

"When you offered to pay me a few minutes ago—"

"I didn't mean to offend you," Henrietta blurted.

"I'm not offended, but it made me realize, I don't know what I am, exactly."

Henrietta frowned. "I don't understand."

Ryn reached for a cookie as she struggled to figure out how to word this. "When I remember how things were between us, back when I first moved in, compared to how they are now, I get the feeling that you and I are different from the way things have been with your other companions. Am I right?"

Henrietta dunked a cookie in her coffee. Ryn could tell she was stalling, thinking hard about how to reply.

"You and I are different," Henrietta admitted. "Sometimes, I forget that you're here as my unpaid companion."

"I'm not."

"What?" Henrietta looked startled.

"What I mean is, I haven't thought of myself that way for a long time. And when you offered to pay me for shoveling, I realized, maybe you still do."

For long seconds, they stared at each other.

"How do you think of yourself?" Henrietta asked at last.

Ryn smiled. Henrietta wasn't going to go first. "I see myself here as your friend, as a roommate, I suppose." Now it was her turn to frown. "But that's probably not fair. I don't contribute anything here. Not financially."

Henrietta gaped at her for a moment. "But that's how I've always done things. I need someone to be here, and to expect that person to be willing to stay with me, I've had to offer a room, free of rent."

She paused, her face now a mask. "But all of my companions leave. You've already lasted longer than most."

"That's not what I meant." Ryn set her shortbread down and leaned her elbows on the table. "I love–" She caught herself. "I love living here. I love living with you. But I need to know how you see things."

Henrietta looked flustered. "A minute ago, you said you don't contribute anything. That couldn't be further from the truth." She dropped the shortbread that was crumbling in her fingers and busied herself brushing the crumbs off. "You've brought joy into this house, more joy than it's known since my parents were alive. You've brought me joy, Meryn. I... I would find it difficult to imagine living here without you."

"Then let me feel as if I really share this house with you."

"How? The house is paid for. I've no need to charge you rent. It wouldn't feel right."

"Let me pay part of the utilities."

Henrietta waved a hand in surrender. "Very well. You may pay the water bill, if it will make you feel better, but it's not necessary."

Ryn grinned. "I'll take it."

"Anything else?"

Ryn popped the rest of her cookie in her mouth. "Can I paint my room?"

"You–" Henrietta frowned in bewilderment. "You want to paint the walls?"

"Yeah. Not a mural or anything, although I could ask you to do that, couldn't I? And not like purple or Pepto-Bismol pink. I was thinking a pale green or blue. I hate peach."

"Why didn't you say something before?"

"Because I was just a companion before."

Henrietta allowed herself a grudging smile. "You were never just a companion, Meryn."

WITHIN A COUPLE OF days, the village got the snow cleared and people emerged again. Henrietta drove up to the club for bridge on Thursday, checking to see if the entrance was clear enough for her to walk safely. One of the employees met her at the curb, escorting her inside and then parking her station wagon for her.

It was the first time she'd been there since the opening of her show at the library. Most of the bridge ladies commented on it, congratulating her, though she suspected they probably hadn't been so complimentary when they were speaking to one another.

"Now don't be like that," Bonnie had said just yesterday when Henrietta voiced that thought. "If they are unkind, it's only because they wish they had your talent."

Henrietta doubted that, but she appreciated the loyalty behind the sentiment.

Bonnie had been excited about Meryn's plans to paint. "I can vacuum behind all that furniture while it's moved. You be sure and tell her. I want to do a good cleaning in there."

Between the two of them, Henrietta felt a little as if she was being ganged up on, but, if she was honest with herself, it was comforting. She normally wanted to be in control of everything at all times, but it was kind of nice to trust that she could let them take charge with this.

"What do you look so happy about?"

She turned to see Genevieve Talbert, pressing a tissue to her nose, her eyes red and puffy, taking a seat at her table.

Henrietta quickly hid her grimace as Genevieve blew her nose and reached for the cards. She considered getting up and changing tables, but that would cause a row, as everyone else was already seated.

"Just happy to be out of the house after all that snow." She gingerly picked up her cards, mentally reminding herself not to touch anything else.

Perhaps if Genevieve had a cold, she would forego smoking. But that hope was dashed as the first cigarette was lit. No matter that it made her cough and hack as if a lung were coming up. That was something Henrietta never would understand.

"How are things at the college?" Henrietta asked sweetly.

"Ter—" Genevieve sneezed, and Henrietta recoiled. "Terrible. Some little hussy got herself in trouble and now it's Jerry's problem. Not that he—" Genevieve obviously realized what that sounded like. "But he has to deal with it. It'll probably cost him his promotion. If we ever find out who was behind it..."

Henrietta made a sympathetic noise. So, Leonard Croson hadn't told them who informed him. Perhaps he had more discretion than she gave him credit for. More likely, he didn't trust Jerry not to tell Genevieve and didn't trust Genevieve not to spread it like wildfire. *Smart man.*

"Do you still have that underling of Jerry's living with you?" Genevieve asked.

"You mean his new professor? Yes, she's still living with me."

Genevieve tried to sniff dismissively, but her nose was too stuffy, and she snatched her tissue again. "Is she even Catholic? I notice she doesn't always go to Communion when she accompanies you to church. I thought she might be Jewish or something."

"Oh, it's worse than that," Henrietta said. "She's a Democrat."

"Are we playing or not?" complained Mary Ellen Greene.

By the time Henrietta got home a couple of hours later, she was cursing herself for not getting up and leaving as soon as she saw Genevieve was sick. Despite repeated trips to the ladies' room to wash her hands, her throat was starting to get sore.

She considered calling Dr. McCourt, but she was still embarrassed over the fuss made when she'd had that spell at the library, and she hated to seem like an alarmist over a simple cold. She made herself a cup of tea and poured a dash of bourbon into it. She would just have to ride it out.

She thought about going to the studio, but decided it would be best to rest. She stretched out on the sofa with a book and her throw and promptly fell asleep.

"Henrietta."

She started awake to find Meryn kneeling next to the couch, gently shaking her. She was dizzy and groggy when she sat up.

Meryn steadied her with a hand on her shoulder. "Are you all right? I've been trying to wake you for a few minutes."

Henrietta tried to speak, but her throat felt as if it were full of jagged glass. "I think I've caught a cold. Don't want to make you sick."

"Don't worry about that. Would you like some hot soup?"

Henrietta shook her head. "Just bed, I think."

She struggled to her feet, too shaky to argue when Meryn insisted on following her to her room. She allowed Meryn to lay out her nightgown and turn down the bed while she brushed her teeth and took some cold medicine.

"I'm going to leave your door open just a little bit, Henrietta." Meryn backed out. "Please call me if you need anything."

Henrietta just nodded. She nearly gave up and called for help to unbuckle her braces. Her hands were shaking so she could barely grasp the straps, and her muscles were like mush. At last, she fumbled her way out of them, but she gave up trying to get changed. Wearing only her chemise and underpants, she slid between the covers. She'd started to shiver, and her eyeballs burned hot behind her lids when she closed her eyes. It was going to be a long night.

~

RYN SAT UP IN bed reading, her door also open wider than usual. She kept getting up, tiptoeing to Henrietta's room to listen. Everything seemed to be quiet. It was about midnight before she turned out the light and crawled into bed.

She had no idea what time it was when some noise startled her awake. She sat bolt upright in bed, listening. There was a kind of moan. Leaping out of bed, she ran to Henrietta's room and pushed the door open to peek inside.

It was impossible to make anything out in the dark, but Henrietta's breathing was a ragged whistle. Ryn flipped on the hall light to partially illuminate the bedroom and crept to the bed. Henrietta didn't stir. Ryn laid a hand on her head. She was burning up with fever.

"Shit."

Ryn knelt there for a moment, uncertain what to do. She knew Henrietta hated asking for help from anyone, but her breathing sounded bad.

Ryn hurried to the desk and clicked on the lamp there. The Rolodex was, thankfully, neatly arranged in alphabetical order, and she found Dr. McCourt's number. The dial seemed to take forever to rotate through the numbers.

"Dr. McCourt?" she said quickly when he answered sleepily. "This is Meryn Fleming. I live with Henrietta Cochran."

"What's wrong?" he asked, sounding immediately more awake.

243

She hastily explained the situation.

"I'll be there in a few minutes."

Ryn yanked on jeans and pulled a sweatshirt over her ratty sleeping shirt. She had the front door open for him when he arrived, bag in hand. He hurried through to Henrietta's room where he retrieved his stethoscope to listen to her lungs.

"Henrietta? Henrietta!"

Her eyes opened, but she didn't answer.

"Help me get her to my car."

He tugged the sheet loose and swaddled it and the blanket around Henrietta, plucking her up as if she weighed nothing. Ryn grabbed his bag and followed him, sliding her bare feet into her boots and pulling the door shut behind her.

She opened the back door of his Buick so he could place Henrietta inside. Ryn got in next to her. He started the engine, quickly backed out of the driveway, and roared down the street.

Ryn wrapped an arm around Henrietta, cradling her tightly so that she wouldn't slide around on the slick leather. Dr. McCourt maneuvered around to the hospital's ambulance bay and braked to a hard stop. Without waiting for a gurney to be brought, he picked Henrietta up again and carried her inside, Ryn on his heels.

The small emergency room waiting room was empty in the middle of the night. A handful of nurses rushed out to greet Dr. McCourt, ushering him and Henrietta through a set of swinging doors. One nurse threw out a hand to block Ryn.

"You'll have to wait out here."

Ryn stood there, watching them through the small square of glass in the door until they turned a corner out of sight. A clock on the wall read two-thirty. She dropped into a hard plastic chair along the wall and fidgeted.

By three-thirty, she was pacing circles around the waiting room, but there had been no word. She had no idea if any of the staff even knew she was out there. She went to the window, but no one was at the desk. She knocked on the glass; no one responded.

She zipped her jacket and laced up her boots. Outside, a half-moon lit the way as she walked the empty village streets. No cars passed her on the country club road, and the house was as she'd left it. Sleep was out of the question. She figured she'd just have to wait until daylight to call the hospital and get information.

She left the lights off and opened the curtains covering the picture window. Sitting in her chair, she watched the night and waited. And thought.

The fear that had gripped her—that still gripped her—when she found Henrietta so helpless, so fragile—it had shaken her. Against her will, she found herself imagining the worst. She pushed to her feet and nearly went back to the hospital, but what was the difference between waiting here and waiting there? If she couldn't be with Henrietta, she'd at least feel closer to her here. She stood in front of the window, her arms wrapped tightly around herself.

I love Henrietta.

She had to accept that truth. But where was the line between loving someone and being in love with her? She had no idea.

She sat down again, and must have drifted off, because the ring of the doorbell scared the crap out of her. She ran to the door to find Dr. McCourt standing there.

"I didn't mean to abandon you," he said, looking exhausted.

"Come on in. Coffee?"

"Sounds good."

He hung his coat up and followed her into the kitchen. She quickly made a pot of coffee and poured two cups, forgetting she didn't like coffee. His silence while she worked frightened her, but she couldn't make herself ask.

When she set a steaming mug in front of him and sat, he finally said, "I think she'll be all right. We've got her on antibiotics and oxygen." He paused to take a drink, and she wondered how he wasn't scalding his tongue. "Henrietta knows better. Her colds always turn into bronchitis at best, pneumonia at worst. She should have called me right away."

"I think she just got sick yesterday afternoon. Someone at the club, she said."

He nodded. "I'm going to keep her in over the weekend, until she can breathe easily on room air. She'll need a few things, if you can bring them to her."

"Of course. I'll do it this morning."

He drained his cup. "She's in room 114. Tell the nurses I instructed you to come, even if it's not official visiting hours."

"Thank you."

She accompanied him to the door.

"Tell Henrietta I'll be by later today after my office hours to check on her."

"Okay."

She waved him off and thought about trying to get some sleep, but she knew she wouldn't be able to. She did call Beverly's office number and left a message that she wouldn't be in.

Going to Henrietta's room, she flipped on the light. She made a mental note to try and get the sheet and blanket back from the hospital.

"What will she need?"

Her back and leg braces were lying next to the bed, where Ryn supposed they sat every night. She placed them on the bed and turned to the dresser. Underwear, probably her own nightgown, real clothes for the day she was discharged.

It felt incredibly intimate to be going through Henrietta's closet, through her drawers. She laid things on the bed to be packed in a bag. In the bottom of the underwear drawer, her fingernails scraped against something that sounded like glass. She shifted the undershirts aside to find a framed photo.

Feeling slightly guilty at snooping, she tugged it free and held it under the lamp. Two teenage girls, laughing with their arms around each other, stood in front of a house Ryn didn't recognize. Even in black and white, Una was very pretty, but Ryn stared, transfixed, at Henrietta. Her dark hair gleamed in the sun, her face—full and soft and unlined—stared back with eyes that Ryn recognized. It must have been summertime, because both girls wore shorts and sleeveless blouses. They could have been poster girls for the 40s.

Henrietta's legs were long and slender and shapely. Her young breasts were outlined under her blouse, tucked in to show off a narrow waist, and her shorts hugged her hips.

She was beautiful.

She turned the photo over to see if it was inscribed with a date or place. Instead, she saw, written in an elegant hand, a poem.

> This World is not Conclusion.
> A Species stands beyond –
> Invisible, as Music –
> But positive, as Sound –
> It beckons, and it baffles –
> Philosophy – don't know –
> And through a Riddle, at the last—
> Sagacity, must go—

Ryn dropped to the bed, holding the photo. Tears welled up from nowhere, and she didn't try to stop them. She cried for Una's death and the life she and Henrietta never got to have together. She cried for the tribulations of the girl in the photo, for everything Henrietta had been through, the unfairness of it all. And she cried for herself, though she wasn't sure why.

Chapter 17

THERE WAS NOTHING THAT aggravated Henrietta more than being treated like an invalid—especially when she was. Without her back brace, her weakened trunk sagged sideways, which made it even harder to breathe, but the brace was uncomfortable to wear for hours when she was stuck in this stupid hospital bed.

At least she had her own nightgown to wear. She'd spent months draped in hospital gowns—if she was covered at all—while in the iron lung, and she hated the damnable things. It was slightly mortifying to realize Meryn had gone through her drawers—"it's no different than my going through them to put your laundered clothes away," Bonnie had pointed out when she came by the hospital and Henrietta mentioned it, but it felt different.

Meryn had said little, but had insisted on sitting at her bedside for hours. Henrietta didn't remember most of the first couple of days, as she drifted in and out of awareness. But by Sunday, the antibiotics and oxygen had started to do the job. She was still stuffy and congested with her cold, but she was more than ready to be home.

A nurse came in to chart her temperature. While the thermometer was in her mouth, Meryn arrived in the room.

When the nurse plucked the thermometer from her lips to read it, Henrietta said, "You tell Dr. McCourt that I expect to be discharged today. I will not spend another night here."

"Yes, ma'am." The nurse left.

"What are you grinning at?" Henrietta asked, frowning at Meryn.

"Nothing." But the girl still had a smirk on her face. "It's just the first time you've barked at anyone. Must mean you're feeling better."

"Hmmmph." But Henrietta couldn't hide a little smile. "Good enough to be out of here."

Meryn reached into her bag. "I brought you one of Bonnie's oatmeal muffins."

"Thank you," Henrietta said, holding her hand out, but Meryn snatched it back.

"Before I give you this, you have to promise you'll follow Dr. McCourt's orders once you're back home."

Henrietta glowered at her, but that muffin looked so tempting. "I promise."

Meryn handed her the muffin, along with a napkin and fork. Henrietta rolled her bedside table into a more comfortable position.

Meryn sat on the only chair in the room. "The house has been quiet without you."

Henrietta glanced over at her. "I would have thought you'd be enjoying it. Staying up all hours. Having wild parties with your friends."

"Did that." Meryn shrugged. "Wild parties just aren't as much fun as they used to be."

Henrietta sniffed. "I wouldn't know." She ate a bite and closed her eyes. "Oh, that's so good."

She opened her eyes and caught Meryn watching her with a peculiar expression on her face. "What's wrong?"

"Nothing is wrong."

But there was something in her eyes, something that made Henrietta's heart beat faster. She reverted her attention to her muffin.

Meryn picked up her bag. "I have to go enter my grades. I'll come back in a couple of hours and see if you've been discharged."

Henrietta stared after her. Her memories of the last few days were fuzzy, but among the clear memories was Meryn's face, her hands, so warm and comforting, on Henrietta's arm as she sat beside the bed.

She jumped when Dr. McCourt entered the room.

"How are you?" He tilted his head, looking her over. "You look flushed."

He consulted the chart and then listened to her lungs again. Flipping the stethoscope around his neck, he straightened.

"I'll let you go home this afternoon, but I want you on antibiotics for two more weeks, with a follow-up in my office. No cancelling," he added sternly. "I know you, Henrietta."

She huffed. "All right, all right."

He wrote everything out in the chart. To the nurse beside him, he said, "Have the pharmacy deliver this prescription before lunch."

"Yes, doctor."

"I'll see you in two weeks, Henrietta."

She waited impatiently, picking at her lunch when it was brought. At last, she heard Meryn's voice approaching from the corridor. She entered the room, pushing Henrietta's wheelchair. A nurse's aide was with her.

Meryn picked up a bundle sitting on the wheelchair seat. "I was thinking."

"Now that's a problem."

The aide looked shocked, but Meryn just chuckled.

"It seems like a lot of trouble to get into your braces just to go home and go to bed..."

Henrietta started to protest, but Meryn cut her off. "Because that is where you are going, Hank."

Henrietta closed her mouth.

"Anyway, I brought a pair of sweatpants and a sweatshirt. They'll be a little big on you, but they'll do for the ride home." She waited a beat. "What do you think?"

Henrietta had to admit, she'd been dreading the struggle with her braces. The hospital bed was too soft and too high to sit on the edge as she did at home. She gave a reluctant nod.

"Great." Meryn reached for the braces. "I'll take these out to the car while Wendy here helps you get changed. Be right back."

The aide fumbled and apologized, but she was gentle as she helped guide Henrietta's feeble legs into the sweatpants. Meryn had brought socks as well. Wendy tugged those in place over Henrietta's feet. She helped her to sit up to get the sweatshirt over her head.

"It's like dressing a three-year-old, isn't it?" Henrietta grumbled, but Wendy smiled.

"You're a little easier. At least you point your feet in the right direction."

Henrietta ran her hands over her thighs. She hadn't worn pants of any kind since before she'd gotten sick. Skirts were just more practical, since her braces went all the way up her thighs. The soft material felt good on her skin. She sniffed the sleeve of her sweatshirt. It smelled like Meryn and, for a moment, she longed to bury her face in it and inhale.

Meryn returned in a few minutes. "How shall we do this?"

"Just position the chair next to the bed, and I can slide into it."

Wendy placed Henrietta's folded nightgown in her lap. "Take care, Miss Cochran."

"Thank you, Wendy."

Meryn wheeled Henrietta down the corridor to the checkout area near the entrance. The woman there had all of the paperwork prepared for Henrietta's signature. The station wagon was waiting under the covered drive-up just beyond the doors.

Meryn opened the door and rolled the chair close, but Henrietta's weakened state was already taking a toll. She tried a few times to partially stand, gripping the door, but she couldn't.

"Here."

Meryn backed the chair up and locked it. Bending down, she said, "Put your arms around my neck."

She picked Henrietta up and pivoted her around to the car seat. From there, Henrietta was able to manually lift her legs inside while Meryn folded the chair into the back of the car.

The house was a welcoming sight, as was Bonnie, standing at the door, waiting for them. She hurried out to the garage when Meryn pulled in and parked.

"I've got your bed all made up with fresh sheets," she said, opening the car door.

As much as Henrietta didn't want to go back to bed, she had to admit she was tired.

"This is simpler than getting the chair back out," Meryn said, leaning down to her.

She gathered Henrietta in her arms and carried her into her room, setting her gently on the bed. Bonnie followed with the braces and other items from the hospital.

"I've got a pot of nice hot chicken soup all set for whenever you're hungry," she was saying, but Henrietta was looking into Meryn's eyes, her arms still wrapped around her neck. She slowly let go, wishing she could hold on a little longer.

Meryn straightened and held her gaze as Bonnie fussed with getting Henrietta situated in bed.

"We should get you changed and into a nightgown."

"I'll be just out here if you need me," Meryn said, backing out of the room and closing the door.

Bonnie tugged and rolled Henrietta to get the shirt and pants off her. Henrietta was thoroughly exhausted by the time she was dressed in a clean nightgown and covered up to her chin.

"Leave that," she said when Bonnie started to take the sweatshirt away. "I'll just rest for a while."

"You do that." Bonnie gave the covers a last tuck and left the room.

Henrietta brought the sweatshirt to her face, breathing in Meryn's clean scent. She rolled over and gasped. Sitting on the bedside table was a photo, one she hadn't looked at in years. She dropped the sweatshirt to the floor and turned the other way.

~

IF RYN HAD THOUGHT the weekend was tiring, it was nothing to the following week. Between getting up several times a night to check on Henrietta—who was recovering nicely—calling the house three times a day to see if she needed anything, and dealing with upcoming midterms, she was frazzled and irritable, ready to explode.

Either that or cry at the drop of a hat, which pissed her off even more. She hated being hormonal. It was bad enough in a normal month, but this month felt anything but normal. Her emotions were all over the place, what with the scare of Henrietta's illness and the discovery of that damned photo, and the soul-searching she'd been doing.

So when she went to the library to write up her exams, she cursed under her breath when she saw Tamara sitting at one of the computers. She briefly considered taking her chances with Geary and using the computer in his office, but he'd been exceptionally volatile lately—falsely cheery one minute and then slamming doors the next.

We are adults, she reminded herself. Surely, she and Tam could be in the same space and not have issues.

But one icy glare from those eyes told a different story.

Too bad, she thought with a resigned sigh. She sat down at a console in a corner and dug out her notes. From where she sat, she had a rear quarter-view of Tamara, which allowed her to glance over periodically with only a flick of her gaze whereas Tam had to turn around to look in her direction. She tried to concentrate on her exams—all she had to do was type up the questions she'd already written—but she was finding it difficult to do without making stupid mistakes.

Tamara was as attractive as ever. She was wearing a navy blue sweater that probably looked amazing with her eyes, and her blonde hair was a little longer, tucked behind her ear. Ryn could trace the curve of her cheek and jaw.

But she felt nothing. She lowered her head to her hand and closed her eyes, allowing herself to remember the kisses she'd shared with Tamara, the way she felt and tasted. She was relieved to at least feel a slight arousal of her body, but it stopped there. Her heart, her mind—*nothing above the waist*—none of those parts of her were stirred, not the way they were when she thought of Henrietta.

More pissed off than ever, she jammed a floppy disk into the computer to save what she'd done so far. She zipped all of her things back into her backpack and left the lab without a backward glance.

Her head down, she muttered to herself as she strode across campus back to Rayburn Hall. "Didn't ask for this, goddammit. Why the hell can't I ever do things the easy way?"

At an intersection of the concrete walk, she nearly plowed into Roberta and Franny.

"Hi," Roberta said cheerfully, but Ryn glowered at Franny.

"Sorry. Late for..." She kept walking.

She stomped up the back stairwell and slammed her own door. She tossed her bag down and threw herself into her chair, feeling like a supreme idiot.

A few seconds later, there was a light rap at the door and Beverly opened it to peek inside.

"Are you all right?"

"Fine," Ryn mumbled. She scrubbed her hands over her face. "Fine." She looked more closely at Beverly's worried expression. "What's wrong?"

Beverly stepped inside and closed the door. "Dr. Talbert wants to see you as soon as possible."

"Oh, jeez." Ryn sat up straighter. "What now?"

Beverly only shook her head. Ryn got to her feet, filled with a foreboding feeling that this wasn't going to be good.

"Just perfect."

"What was that?" Beverly asked.

"Nothing."

She followed Beverly down the corridor. Beverly gave her arm a little squeeze as she ushered Ryn into Talbert's office and closed the door.

Jerry Talbert looked up, a plume of smoke drifting from his nostrils. She was a little startled. He looked as if he'd aged several years. There were large bags under his eyes and deep lines along his jowls.

"Sit down," he said without any kind of greeting.

She slowly sat and waited as he ground out his cigarette and sat back.

"I don't know how much you've heard," he began, a heavy crease between his brows. "But Bradley is going to be out on medical leave, effective immediately."

Ryn wasn't certain she'd heard correctly. "Medical leave."

"Yes. He most likely won't be returning to St. Aloysius next year."

It took several seconds for this revelation to sink in. "Can you tell me why?" she asked.

His nostrils flared. "If you don't know, then no. I can't. But something tells me you had more to do with this than I realized."

Ryn's eyes widened. "I have no idea what you're talking about."

He reached for his pack and struck a match. The flame trembled as he held it to the end of a cigarette and inhaled. "No matter. You and I will have to split his classes between us."

"Split?" Ryn felt as if she were struggling to keep her head above water as she tried to keep up with all of these revelations. "Is he on paid leave?"

"No."

She took a steadying breath and braced herself. "Then no. My contract stipulates that I will teach four sections each semester, in addition to the scholarship committee and my advising responsibilities. I'm doing that. If I'm to pick up after Geary, there will have to be additional compensation."

"Why you—" Talbert ground out the fresh cigarette and leaned forward. "You think you're in a position to make demands?"

Ryn regarded him for a few seconds. "If you'd moved on to the dean's position and Geary had taken over here as chair, he'd already made it clear I wasn't going to have a job at this college next year." She held up her hands. "I've got nothing to lose. And if I'm going to be helping pick up after the mess he's made—"

Talbert jabbed a nicotine-stained finger at her. "You do know something!"

"I know he's a pig and should have been fired years ago. I'll help out, for the students' sake, but I won't do it for free." Her brain was whirling. "You'll also write me a letter of recommendation, giving me full credit for creating that women-and-history class. If you meet those conditions, then I'll pitch in to cover his courses."

He looked as if he'd like nothing better than to throw her out of his office, but at last he nodded. She jumped up and left before he could change his mind.

In the outer office, she risked a glimpse in Beverly's direction, not sure how much she might have heard. When Beverly gave her a furtive thumbs-up, she nearly laughed out loud.

Her heart was racing so fast as she ran to her office to get her stuff that she didn't even realize her first thought was, *I can't wait to tell Henrietta.*

HENRIETTA SAT ON THE sofa, a book open in her lap, but she was watching Meryn at work at the dining table. Their routine had changed over the last couple of weeks, ever since Jerry Talbert had announced that other man's departure. Henrietta had listened as Meryn recounted the conversation, and had to give the girl points for so adroitly managing the situation. She had her letter of recommendation, in case she had to seek a new position elsewhere—but Henrietta couldn't let herself think about that.

Meryn had fretted about needing to work on the new courses. "I don't want to leave you alone in the evenings, but I have to prep these. They're a mess."

It had been Bonnie's suggestion to have Meryn use the dining table as a temporary desk. "You hardly ever use it," she'd pointed out. "You always eat in the kitchen."

So, after dinner, Henrietta read while Meryn worked. Where Henrietta had often had the television on in the evenings for noise, she found the silence comfortable—this silence, made bearable by Meryn's presence. It was embarrassing to remember how she'd dreaded the quiet and the alone after her last companion had left. Meryn filled the house—*and me*, Henrietta thought—simply by being there. Of course, it wasn't always silent, as Meryn had a habit of humming while she worked. Henrietta smiled, listening to her.

"Did you return your mother's phone call?" Henrietta asked now.

"Yes." Meryn glanced up. "I told her about all this new work, and that I wouldn't be home for spring break. She was disappointed, but she understood."

Henrietta nodded and looked back down at her book, afraid to let Meryn see the shine in her own eyes. It felt selfish—*it is selfish*, she reminded herself harshly, but she couldn't help it. A week without Meryn in the house would have felt like an eternity.

"Are you sure you didn't have anything to do with this?"

Though the question seemed to have come out of nowhere, Henrietta was prepared. She carefully kept her face neutral. "You've asked me that a hundred times."

"And a hundred times you've avoided actually answering me," Meryn pointed out.

"How could I interfere with your work or the college?"

"See, that's what you do every time. You deflect with another question."

"Aren't you supposed to be working?"

Meryn stared for a few more seconds but then shook her head and returned to her notes with a half-laugh.

But she knew Meryn didn't believe her. Maybe someday she'd tell her the truth, but it seemed best to keep the girl in the dark for now. Henrietta felt sure it would help protect her from any retribution Jerry Talbert might want to mete out.

She allowed her eyes to close. She was pleasantly tired after having spent nearly the entire day painting. Finally, she was sufficiently recovered to have the energy and the concentration to work. It had been ages since she'd gone so many days without being able to paint or draw, and she'd missed it sorely.

"Why do you always draw?" Una tilted her head as she flipped through Henrietta's Latin notebook, looking at the little sketches she'd drawn in the margins.

They were stretched out across Una's bed, supposedly studying for their next exam.

"I just like to."

"Is that me?" Una tipped the page to look at it more closely.

Henrietta felt the flush warm her cheeks, but Una beamed at her. She rolled over on her back, her hair splayed out around her head like a glorious red halo.

"You draw me?"

Henrietta shrugged. She sat behind Una in class, so it was easy to watch her—the way she absent-mindedly ran her fingers through her thick hair, the way she twiddled her pencil when she was bored, the way she pretended to be taking notes when Henrietta knew she was writing a story or poem.

Una nodded sagely. "You need that creative expression. It's like air to you.'
"Then your writing must be like that for you."
"It is. Artistic souls need that outlet. Without it, we'd wither up and die."
Henrietta wanted to blurt, "I'd die without you." But she didn't dare say anything so melodramatic. It's true, she thought, even if she couldn't say it.

The framed photo was still on her bedside table, the first time she'd been able to have it out, seeing it daily, since she'd come home from the rehab hospital. Back then, she'd hated seeing it, that reminder of Una, of when she herself was healthy and whole, of an innocence that she'd never have again. She'd forgotten it was in the bottom of that drawer. Since Bonnie was the one to put the clean laundry away, Henrietta hadn't dug to the bottom of the drawer for years and years.

She could still remember the day that photo was taken. It was just a few weeks before they'd gone swimming in the pond, the first day of summer vacation. Una's Aunt Wilhelmina had taken it in front of their house.

When Una had had it framed and given it to her, Henrietta hadn't noticed the inscribed poem right away. She'd asked Una about it a few days later.

"It's Emily Dickinson, isn't it?"
Una smiled. "Yes."
"But I don't understand it. This world is not conclusion. What does that mean?"
Una had looked at Henrietta in that way she had sometimes—the spells that seemed to come over her now and again, where she focused on something only she could see, almost as if she was only half in this world. It made Henrietta wonder if she could see the future.
"You will understand," Una said. "Someday."

She thought about it now, wondering if there really was something beyond. Would she see Una and her parents again someday? She was nearly fifty-four, more than halfway through her life. The end suddenly felt very near. Her parents had had her, and her father had left a legacy of buildings that still stood.

What will you leave behind? she wondered. *Nothing but a few paintings. No one will miss you when you're gone.*

"What are you thinking about?"

Henrietta's eyes snapped open. "Nothing."

"It didn't look like nothing."

Henrietta colored under Meryn's scrutiny. She squirmed when the girl got up from the table and came over to sit on the coffee table.

"Tell me, Hank."

Henrietta plucked at the fringe of the throw on her lap. "It was silly. I was just thinking of my parents and what they left behind. And how I've left nothing. No children. Nothing of any importance. No one who will remember."

She felt Meryn's gaze, almost as intimate as a caress, and she didn't dare look up.

"That's not true." Meryn braced her elbows on her knees. "Your art is important." She paused. "And you're important. To me."

Against her will, Henrietta slowly raised her eyes. She lost track of how much time ticked by as they stared at each other.

"Your life is just beginning," Henrietta managed to say. "I'll be long gone as you move on, living your life."

To Henrietta's horror, Meryn's eyes filled with tears.

"I may have to go on without you, someday," Meryn said in a strangled voice, "but I'll never be the same. I had time to think about that while you were sick."

She reached out and took Henrietta's hand in hers. Henrietta stared down at them—her ugly ape-like hand, clasped in Meryn's warm, soft grasp. She longed to press that warmth to her cheek.

"Do you think Una knew?" Meryn whispered. "When she wrote that poem to you?"

"I don't know." It was hard to draw breath. "She sometimes seemed to see things."

"I wish I could have known her."

261

Henrietta couldn't help smiling. "She would have liked you."

"But she loved you."

Meryn shifted to lean over the couch and pressed her lips to Henrietta's cheek. She lingered there a moment and then stood, her fingers slowly sliding out of Henrietta's.

There was a tremor in Meryn's voice as she said, "I'm done for the night. Going to bed." She turned but then stopped. "Good night."

Henrietta couldn't speak. She listened to the sound of Meryn's bedroom door closing. And pressed her hand to her cheek.

~

IN THE BEDROOM, RYN lay fully clothed on top of her bed. Tears ran from her eyes into her hair.

When she'd glanced up and seen Henrietta, her eyes closed, her face looking so defenseless with whatever she was thinking about, it had twisted something inside Ryn, wrenching her heart. This was the girl in the photo, the one who should have had a happy life, a life with love and intimacy and laughter.

Without her even being aware, she'd suddenly found herself there, sitting next to Henrietta, wanting to give her those things.

"How do I stop this?" she whispered in the dark.

Chapter 18

OVER SPRING BREAK, YOUR assignment is to read up on Carrie Chapman Catt. I want three thousand words on her contribution to women's suffrage."

Ryn's instructions were greeted with a few groans.

"I have it on good authority that there will be a quiz the first day back," she added, and several of the students grinned.

"This class is so much better now," she heard one of them say as they packed up their books and notes.

Her heart lifted. As hard as it had been, picking up the slack after Geary's mysterious disappearance, all the hours of work were worth it for comments like that. Teaching six classes, with all the peripheral work that went into prepping and grading, was just about killing her. Luckily, Talbert had excused her from the scholarship committee, so all she had to do was teach and meet with her advisees.

And figure out how to deal with Henrietta.

As she packed up and left her classroom, she thought about that. It wasn't exactly Henrietta she needed to figure out, it was her own feelings. Neither of them had spoken of that evening, but something had shifted. Small glances, a slightly different tone of voice, anticipating little things like the passing of the salt.

But the conversation felt forced, both of them deliberately keeping to light topics of no importance. Ryn had no idea if Henrietta was upset by Ryn's encroachment into her space—*you kissed her.* She could not for the life of her explain why or how that had happened. It just had.

Taking the rear stairwell—she'd been avoiding Talbert at all costs— she saw Beverly's head peek around the corner. She must have been waiting for Ryn, because she immediately came trotting to her office.

"News?" Ryn asked.

"Perhaps." Beverly pushed the office door shut. "Dr. Talbert got a phone call from a dean at a college in South Carolina."

Ryn straightened from where she was rearranging things in her backpack. "South Carolina? You think Geary's applying for a position down there?"

"I can't think of any other reason." Beverly wrung her hands and blinked at Ryn through her glasses. "Unless you...?"

"No. I admit, I've been thinking about where else I would apply if I had to, but Talbert hasn't said anything about getting rid of me, so I'm on hold."

"Oh, I'm glad." Beverly patted her arm. "You've been a breath of fresh air around here."

"Thanks. Plans for the break?"

"Anthony and I are going to have Billy for the week. Donna and William are going to a conference his work is holding in New York."

Ryn grinned. "You'll be exhausted. And love every minute."

"I will." Beverly patted her shoulder. "You try and get some rest. You've been working so hard."

"That's not likely this semester. But, if I'm still around next year, this will all pay off. First time teaching a class is always hardest. Is Talbert advertising for a third faculty member in the department?"

Beverly lowered her voice. "Not yet. I overheard him saying on the phone that Professor Geary's position isn't officially vacant yet."

"Of course not. That would be too easy."

She zipped her jacket and swung her backpack over her shoulders. "Enjoy your break."

"You, too." Beverly pulled the office door shut for her and walked with her down the corridor. "And try to get some rest."

Ryn waved to a few students as she crossed campus. Lots of suitcases and duffels were being tossed into cars as they all got out of Bluemont for the week. Ryn felt a bit of nostalgia for the spring breaks she and Ashley had spent in Nags Head, days on the beach, getting way too much sun, nights spent making love without having to worry about roommates walking in on them. Oh, how she missed the feel of Ashley's hands on her. It was a physical ache.

For a brief moment, she thought about calling on Tamara, but "don't be an idiot," she mumbled to herself. "That would be a monumental mistake. For all the wrong reasons."

The air was still chilly for mid-March, but the snow was melting, mostly gray piles of it where it had been plowed or shoveled. She was so ready for this winter to be over. She kicked at the edges of the snow piles as she walked, her mood sinking deeper and deeper, so that she was thoroughly pissed-off by the time she opened the front door.

"Meryn?" Henrietta's voice called from the direction of the studio.

Ryn closed her eyes for a second. Toeing off her shoes, she dropped her backpack in her room and went to the studio. "What?"

Henrietta was at the sink, cleaning brushes. "Are you all right?"

"Fine. Just tired." She went to the easel. "Hank, these cardinals are beautiful."

"Thank you." Henrietta turned around, drying her hands. "It's been a while since you did any painting."

Ryn scoffed. "I'll never be as good as you."

"Does that matter?"

"It shouldn't, but I'll just stick to walls for the time being."

"You picked out the color you want?"

"I think the blue I showed you. I'll get the paint tomorrow."

Henrietta peered at her more closely. "What's wrong?"

"Told you. Just tired."

"Do you want to have dinner at the club tonight?"

"Oh." Ryn leaned against the counter. "I think not. If we ran into the Talberts, I might not behave myself."

Henrietta smiled. "I know what you mean. Genevieve was particularly vicious at bridge yesterday. I was so glad to be at a different table." She hung up her smock and slid her arms into her crutches. "How about fish fry?"

Ryn brightened at that. "That sounds much better. I'll go change."

A few minutes later, feeling more comfortable in jeans and sneaks and a flannel shirt, Ryn drove them to JT's. Henrietta sat at an empty table while Ryn went to place their orders.

The woman at the counter shouted their order to the cooks in the back and filled two cups with Coke.

"Sorry," Ryn said when she set the cups on the table. "Their drink choices are kind of limited here."

"Henrietta!"

They both turned to see Sandy and Maxine standing there.

"How are you both?" Sandy asked, her curious eyes flicking from Henrietta to Ryn and back again.

"We're doing well," Henrietta said. "Just thought we'd enjoy the best fish fry in town."

"Exactly," Maxine said with a big smile. "Though it doesn't come close to a Cajun fish fry."

"Won't you join us?" Ryn asked.

"You're sure you don't mind?" Sandy asked. "We don't mean to barge in on your dinner."

"Please." Henrietta waved toward the two empty seats.

"Be right back." Sandy went to the counter while Maxine sat, arranging the folds of her linen tunic.

"You're from Louisiana?" Ryn asked.

"Yes, ma'am," Maxine said. "New Orleans. Born and bred."

Her flawless mahogany skin was highlighted by the rich colors of the woven headband she wore—purple and indigo and russet.

"What brought you north?"

Ryn followed Maxine's gaze to where Sandy was paying for their dinners.

"Love and money. Sandy grew up in Lake Placid and missed being up north. The library had an opening, and Sandy wanted to try owning her own art store. After twenty years, Bluemont has become home."

Sandy returned to the table and handed Maxine her drink. Ryn felt her mood lighten.

"A few people have inquired after buying some of your paintings, Henrietta," Maxine said. "I told them you hadn't set prices on any."

"Oh," Henrietta stammered, "I wouldn't even know what to say."

"That would be tough," Sandy said. "You don't want to undervalue your work by giving it away, but charging what it's worth, here in the village, will probably give you a reputation for being uppity."

Henrietta chuckled. "I think I already have that reputation."

Ryn snorted her agreement, causing Henrietta to turn to her with a raised eyebrow.

"Sorry." Ryn cleared her throat. "You've sold several through galleries. You could charge the same price they paid."

"There's an idea." Maxine nodded. "You think about it and let me know."

The woman who'd taken their orders brought a large tray to the table, passing out baskets of fish and fries.

Maxine turned her gaze to Ryn. "We got so little chance to talk at the opening. What do you do, Meryn?"

Ryn swallowed. "I teach history. At the college."

Caren J. Werlinger

"She's brilliant," Henrietta put in.

"I'm sure she is," Maxine agreed with a small smile, picking up her fish. "And are you artistic as well?"

"No." Ryn shook her head.

"She's learning," Henrietta said. "But she's very musical. Guitar."

"Really?" Sandy leaned forward, also glancing back and forth between Ryn and Henrietta. "We'd love to hear you play sometime."

It was Ryn's turn to blush and stammer. "As for painting, I'll confine that to walls."

"Murals?" Sandy asked with a tilt of her head.

Ryn laughed. "No. New paint color in the bedroom. That's my project for spring break."

"Do you need help?" Sandy asked.

"You mean it?"

"Sure. I close the store at noon tomorrow. I'll come over and lend a hand."

"And I'm off tomorrow," Maxine said. "I can help."

"Wow, that's really nice of you," Ryn said. "Between us, we can probably get it all done in a day. Thanks."

"What are you working on now, Henrietta?" Sandy asked.

Ryn let Henrietta talk while she basked in the unexpected glow of realizing she wasn't as alone as she'd thought.

∼

HENRIETTA REACHED INTO HER closet and tossed another suit onto her bed to join the three others there. Another dark wool suit to join the tweeds. Custom tailored to accommodate her back brace—long-wearing, durable, sensible.

"And ugly," Henrietta muttered.

Ever since she'd come home from the polio hospital—"oh, I so hoped you wouldn't need those awful things," her mother had moaned when she saw the braces—she'd been dressed basically the same way. But she was beginning to feel as confined by her clothing as she was by her prosthetics.

On Saturday, when Sandy and Maxine had arrived to help with the painting, she'd been envious of Sandy and Meryn's jeans and Maxine's loose-fitting pants, even if they reminded Henrietta a bit of hippie pants. She'd spent the day mostly staying out of their way.

She'd had food delivered from the club again. "The least I can do is feed you," she'd said when they protested.

Henrietta had come to inspect the room, and had to admit the blue-gray color Meryn had chosen was restful. "I had this room painted after my mother passed and never thought about it again. I'm sorry I didn't offer."

"No problem, Hank. But I like this." Meryn, splattered with paint, had proudly regarded what they'd accomplished. "I cannot thank you both enough. It would have taken me a few days on my own."

"Our pleasure," Sandy said. "You had all the hard work done—the furniture moved, taping off the windows and doors."

"We should have you both over for dinner," Maxine had said as they ate.

"That's a great idea," Sandy had agreed. "How about Tuesday?"

Plans had been made and, so, Henrietta found herself grumbling now as she picked an outfit.

"I can hear you," came Meryn's voice from the hall. "What's wrong?"

"Nothing," Henrietta said as she got her skirt zipped. She yanked the bedroom door open and stared enviously at the faded jeans and comfortable-looking sweater Meryn wore.

"You okay?"

Henrietta didn't answer immediately. She walked out toward the breezeway to the garage. "You all look like normal human beings in the 1980s, and I look like a mannequin in a store window. From the 40s."

Meryn placed a hand on Henrietta's shoulder before she helped her on with her coat. "No, you are like an icon of classic fashion that never goes out of style. My only nod to fashion that never goes out of style is my tennies." She held up a foot. "Converse will never go out of style."

Henrietta chuckled in spite of herself.

"Really," Meryn said, reaching around Henrietta's shoulders from behind as she adjusted the coat's drape. "You look..."

For a moment, Henrietta thought Meryn was going to hold her, that she might wrap her arms around her from behind, but she stepped back.

"You look great." Meryn reached around her to get the door. "Shall we?"

She held the car door and swept her arm dramatically. "Milady."

Henrietta swallowed her disappointment as she got in.

Meryn retrieved a couple of bottles of wine from the refrigerator and laid them in the back seat.

"Why didn't you tell me they were a couple?" she asked as she backed out of the garage.

"A—what? Who?"

Meryn paused at the end of the driveway. "Sandy and Maxine. Why didn't you tell me they're together?"

Henrietta frowned. "You mean...?"

Meryn laughed. "You really didn't know?" She shifted gears and drove toward the village.

"No." Henrietta thought. "I've been buying supplies from Sandy for twenty years, but I suppose I never really got to know her personally."

"Don't feel bad." Meryn glanced over. "They've probably learned to hide it well. I didn't pick up on any vibes at your art opening, either."

The house was all one level, to Henrietta's immense relief, with only two steps up to the front porch.

Maxine was waiting to greet them as Meryn, cradling the wine in her arm, took one crutch so Henrietta could use the handrail to help pull herself up.

"Welcome." Maxine took Henrietta's coat for her.

"Your house is beautiful," Henrietta said, taking in the eclectic mix of art—African, Caribbean, ocean landscapes with dunes and surf.

She enviously eyed Maxine's flowing pants, a knee-length kind of vest over a blouse of vibrant turquoise. She was like a walking painting.

"I really like your outfit."

"Thank you," Maxine said, flashing a brilliant smile. A slinky brindled cat with yellow eyes meowed from the back of the chair near the foyer. "I hope you're not allergic to cats."

"No. I'm just rarely around animals."

"This is Cassatt." Maxine stroked the cat. "Shall we open a bottle of that wine?"

Sandy was at the stove when they all walked into the kitchen. "Hope you're hungry."

Henrietta couldn't recall later much of the dinner conversation. She spent most of her time in fascinated observation of Sandy and Maxine's connection with each other—the small touches and smiles they shared—and with watching Meryn as she interacted with them and the cat, which had taken an immediate liking to her, curling around her ankles and lying at her feet, asking to be rubbed. Meryn was always open and friendly—indeed, that had been one of the first things Henrietta had noticed about her—but there was an extra sense of ease around the table that evening.

The three of them clearly shared the same political views as they discussed the need to get Reagan voted out of office. Henrietta mostly stayed quiet, listening to the passion in their voices. She'd never felt that strongly about anything, at least not once she'd gotten sick. It seemed to her now that her world had shrunk as it turned inward. Her physical needs had consumed her family's lives after she'd come home, through the post-war years. Her father built the house for her; her parents had rearranged their lives around her doctors' appointments and further rehab. Even once she was stable physically, her world

271

hadn't expanded to take in things like the plight of the poor or human rights abuses or the injustice of tax cuts that only benefitted the wealthy. Sandy and Maxine volunteered one Wednesday a month at a food pantry in Cortland. She couldn't help but compare these women to the ones from the club she called her friends.

"Are you okay, Hank?"

She caught the quick glance Maxine exchanged with Sandy when Meryn laid a concerned hand on her arm. "Yes." She drew her arm away. "This lentil soup is delicious. So is the cornbread."

Sandy smiled. "I'm glad you like it. It's Maxine's grandmother's recipe."

"Time for dessert. Bread pudding." Maxine rose, but Sandy pushed her back down.

"Stay here, sweetie. I'll get it."

"Let me help you," Meryn said. She took Henrietta's plate along with her own into the kitchen.

"So," Maxine said, angling her head. "Meryn seems like a nice young woman. How long have you been together?"

Henrietta choked and sputtered on the wine she'd just swallowed. Maxine jumped up to help her, but Henrietta waved her back down.

"I'm not," she gasped when she could speak. "We're not... together."

"I'm so sorry." Maxine looked mortified. "We just assumed... You're so natural together."

Henrietta took a gulp of water, her eyes still streaming as she contemplated how to respond. The answer suddenly came to her. "I'm flattered you would think so. But I doubt she—"

"Here we are," Sandy said, sailing back into the dining room with two bowls of warm bread pudding.

Meryn followed with two more.

"What did we miss?" Sandy asked, her sharp eyes taking in the expressions on Henrietta and Maxine's faces.

"Nothing." Maxine accepted a bowl. "Thank you, honey."

Meryn, too, was clearly perplexed.

"Tell us how you two met," Sandy suggested.

"Maybe they don't want to talk about—" Maxine started to say.

"Why wouldn't they?" Sandy asked.

Henrietta hid a smile as Maxine tried in vain to catch Sandy's eye and give her some kind of warning. "It had to do with a snake and a rowboat."

~

RYN SAT AT A table at the small pizza place she used to go to a lot when she first arrived in Bluemont and needed to escape Mrs. Middleston's boarding house. She hadn't needed to find out of the way places like this in months, not since moving in with Henrietta. But with today being Bonnie's cleaning day and the campus pretty much closed down for spring break, she'd needed to find somewhere else to work.

Only her mind was on everything but her work. She propped her forehead on her hand, staring at her notes without seeing them, wondering again what had happened between Henrietta and Maxine. Something had definitely been exchanged between the two of them, but Henrietta had insisted she was imagining things. Except Ryn didn't think so. A few times, she'd caught Henrietta watching her with an odd expression—softer, more wistful than she typically wore.

When they'd returned home last evening, Henrietta had been unusually quiet, even for her.

"Are you sure you're all right?"

Henrietta hadn't answered immediately. "I'm fine. It's just... I suppose I've never been around a lesbian couple."

"Did it bother you?" Ryn had asked, more curious than she would admit.

"No," Henrietta had said quickly, but her voice sounded strange as she said, "I like them both. This evening gave me a lot to think about."

273

Inside, when Ryn had taken her coat for her, her hand had accidentally clasped Henrietta's. They'd stood like that for what seemed a long time, staring into each other's eyes. Ryn had nearly caressed Henrietta's cheek—*God, I almost kissed her*, she thought now, closing her eyes.

But Henrietta... Henrietta had looked almost as if she was expecting to be kissed, as if she wanted to be kissed. It had been Ryn who cleared her throat, who backed away with a murmured "good night."

With a groan, she slapped her notebook shut. "This is pointless."

She practically threw her notes into her backpack and zipped it shut. Outside, a cold drizzle had begun under a solidly gray sky that matched her mood. Luckily, she'd driven and didn't have to walk in this.

Bonnie was just getting her coat and purse when Ryn came in.

"Don't know what's gotten into her," Bonnie whispered, "but she's in a mood. Don't you mind if she snaps at you. There's a pot roast in the oven. Timer's on. Should last you a few days."

"Thank you, Bonnie."

Bonnie gave her arm a motherly pat as she left. Since there was no sign of Henrietta in the living room or kitchen, Ryn figured she must be in the studio. She went to her room to deposit her backpack. The oven timer indicated the roast had another fifteen minutes.

She debated whether to risk entering the lion's den. Peering around the door, she saw Henrietta perched on her stool in front of the easel. Ryn stood, studying her—the angles of her face, the rigidity of her posture, the severity of her simple haircut—all so different from Ashley and Tamara. *So why do I prefer this?*

Her attention shifted to the canvas, where there was a rough outline of...

"The rowboat?" Ryn stepped fully into the studio. "Is that me?"

Henrietta stiffened. "Our conversation last evening got me remembering."

Ryn stepped closer, careful to keep her hands in her pockets. "I suppose it was rather comical."

The corner of Henrietta's mouth twitched. "It was certainly a unique meeting."

"It wasn't actually our first meeting," Ryn reminded her.

Henrietta half-turned. "No. You were very kind. Coming to help me."

For a long moment, neither spoke.

Finally, Ryn hooked her thumb over her shoulder. "Bonnie's roast is about done. I'll get it out of the oven while you clean up in here."

When they were seated at the table fifteen minutes later, Henrietta asked, "Did you get a lot accomplished today?"

"Not as much as I should have."

"Why is that?"

Ryn glanced up at Henrietta and then back to her plate. "Um, just having to rewrite a lot of Geary's notes, I suppose."

They ate a bit in the quiet kitchen.

"This is good," Ryn said, trying to fill the silence.

"Mmmhmm."

"Bonnie said you weren't in a great mood today. Anything wrong?"

Henrietta speared a carrot with her fork, breaking it into smaller pieces. "Not wrong, exactly."

"What, then?" Ryn reached for her glass, noticing the way Henrietta seemed to avoid looking at her.

"Last evening, when Maxine and I were talking, while you and Sandy were getting dessert, she assumed..."

Ryn paused with her glass halfway to her mouth. "Assumed what?"

Henrietta's cheeks were flushed, and she kept her eyes downcast. "She assumed we're a couple."

The silence in the kitchen thickened, the ticking of the wall clock the only sound until finally Ryn forced herself to speak.

"What did you say?"

Henrietta laughed, but it sounded forced. "I assured her we're not."

"Oh." Ryn couldn't decide if she was relieved or hurt by that.

"What a notion."

"Yeah." Ryn's stomach twisted.

"I mean, you're young and vibrant and—"

"Henrietta—"

"It's a ridiculous thing to even think about." Henrietta frowned. "I assured her we're not a couple."

"You said that."

Henrietta looked up, met Ryn's gaze at last. What Ryn saw there hit her like a fist to the gut—the tenderness, the hope and fear. It only lasted a second, and then the wall slammed down.

Henrietta lowered her gaze again, and her voice when she spoke was flat. "Yes, well, I set her straight. She apologized. That's the end of that."

Ryn forced herself to finish her meal, though her appetite was gone. She cleared the dishes and put the leftovers away while Henrietta went to the living room. Flicking off the kitchen light, Ryn stood there in the dark, something writhing inside her, fighting to get out.

"I need some air," she announced. "Going for a walk. Don't wait up. I'll be sure to lock up when I get back."

She grabbed her jacket and left before Henrietta could say anything. Outside, the tree branches gleamed wetly in the shifting moonlight as clouds scudded through the sky. Her breath puffed out before her in the cold, damp night. The only sound was the steady rhythm of her heels pounding into the pavement as she strode down the road toward the village. She tried to make sense of the feelings churning around inside her, but it was like trying to ride out a tornado. Everything kept circling round and round.

With most of the students still gone, the village streets were quiet, only a few cars out, their headlights trying to pierce the mists. She had no idea if Tam was in town, but that wasn't who she wanted now anyway. She found herself standing in front of the nuns' house. Lights glowed inside, but she wrestled with whether to knock or just go away. Almost against her will, she found herself climbing the porch steps. At the first knock, the door opened and Stephanie pulled her inside.

"How are you? We haven't seen you for ages."

Roberta came out from the kitchen and Franny from upstairs.

"I didn't know if y'uns would be back yet," Ryn said awkwardly.

"We all have mid-terms to study for," Roberta said. "So we spent a couple days at the motherhouse and then came back early. How are you?"

"Fine." Ryn's eyes darted toward Franny, and she suddenly felt foolish for coming here. What the hell were three nuns going to do or say to make this better? "I shouldn't have just barged in like this."

"Don't be silly. Come on in," Steph said. "There's cake in the—"

"Steph," Roberta cut in, glancing to where Franny stood on the second step from the bottom. "I don't think Ryn's here for a social call."

"What do you—" Stephanie followed Roberta's gaze to Franny and then back to Ryn. "Oh. Ohhh."

Taking Roberta's hint, she gave Ryn's hand a squeeze and then followed Roberta up the stairs. Franny descended the last couple of steps.

"Tea?"

She led the way into the kitchen and put the kettle on. Ryn took her jacket off and dropped into a chair. Franny didn't ask any questions as she cut two slices of chocolate cake and placed a couple of teabags into mugs.

"Damp night for a walk."

"Yeah," Ryn agreed. She reached for her jacket and stood. "Listen, I'm sorry, I shouldn't have—"

"I think we've already established that you should have," Franny cut in. She took the jacket from Ryn and hung it over the back of a chair. "Besides, I already cut the cake. I can't eat two pieces. If you don't eat it, Steph will, but she shouldn't. So stay put."

When she finally sat down in an adjacent chair and placed a steaming mug in front of Ryn, she simply said, "Eat."

Ryn did as she was told. The cake really was delicious, but it was hard to swallow past the lump in her throat. She ate half the cake and then pushed the plate away, cradling her mug in hands that wouldn't warm.

Franny waited.

"Henrietta," Ryn began, "when she was young, before she got sick, she loved a girl. Una. So it's not like she's straight, but..."

She pressed her fist to her mouth. She really didn't want to cry in front of Franny, who still said nothing.

"I don't know how to love her." Immediately, she raked her hand through her hair. "Shit, I sound like that song from *Jesus Christ, Superstar.*"

Franny gave her a tiny smile. "You're not so far wrong." She slid her plate aside and leaned her elbows on the table.

"You told me," Ryn said, "that day in the library, that there are lots of kinds of love."

Franny nodded. "There are. And no one kind is better than another. If you love Henrietta and she loves you—"

Ryn shoved to her feet. "That's the problem, though. We met another lesbian couple, had dinner with them. They assumed we're a couple, but Henrietta swore we're not, so I don't know how she feels about me. And I don't know what to do with it if she does love me. I don't know—"

She paused, pressing her fingers hard against her eyes. "I just don't know."

"That's a very healthy place to be," Franny said. She reached for Ryn's arm and tugged her back down to her chair. "Not knowing leaves you open to things you might not consider otherwise. Right now, you're probably wondering if you can be in love with someone who doesn't love you back, at least not in that same way."

Ryn wiped at her eyes. "What do you do with that?"

Franny gave her a wry grin. "You've come to the experts." She took a sip of her tea. "Religious life is often a damned slog, dedicating yourself to this being, this idea—it doesn't have physical form; a lot of people say it doesn't even exist; it doesn't offer the physical comfort you'd get from loving another person. So why do we do it?"

Ryn stared at her.

"Because this kind of love, this bone-deep love, won't leave you alone." The grin slid from Franny's face.

"Real love should be hard. People who make it sound easy are wrong. It requires sacrifice and compromise and work. Love that comes easy is love that probably only goes skin-deep and isn't going to last. Real love digs deep and hooks you. It won't let you walk away, even when you want to, even when it seems it's giving you nothing back."

She leaned forward again and grasped Ryn's arm. "That's the thing. The kind of love we're talking about isn't dependent on getting something back. It's there no matter what. Even if Henrietta never loves you the same way, you'll always love her."

"But..."

She let Ryn's arm go and angled her head. "But what about sex?"

Ryn felt her face heat up. "I just never pictured myself in a relationship without it."

"How do you know it won't be there?" Franny waved a hand. "And whether it is or isn't, that doesn't define a relationship. A lot of relationships, marriages even, aren't based on sex."

Ryn frowned at her cup. "I need to talk to her."

Franny stood and reached for Ryn's jacket, holding it out to her. She pulled Ryn into a hard hug. "Yeah. You do."

~

HENRIETTA PUSHED UP FROM the sofa for the tenth time. She kept trying to read or watch some television, but it was no use. Meryn had never just left like this.

But she was hurt. The look in her eyes...

Henrietta opened the door and stepped out onto the front porch. The street was empty and dark.

"I'm just trying to protect her," she whispered to the night.

Maybe she doesn't need protecting. Doesn't want it.

That was too much to hope for. Leaving that possibility open was more than Henrietta was willing to risk. She couldn't even envisage what a relationship with Meryn might look like.

She shivered and went back inside. She opened the drapes over the picture window and turned off the lamp so she could sit on the sofa and keep watch. So she saw as Meryn walked down the road and turned into the driveway.

The key turned quietly in the lock, and Meryn stepped into the foyer, pushing the door shut and flipping the locks.

"Meryn."

The girl jumped. "Damn. Henrietta, you scared the crap out of me."

"I'm sorry. I've been waiting for you."

Meryn hung her jacket up and slipped out of her boots. "I didn't mean to worry you. You didn't need to stay up."

Henrietta leaned toward the lamp.

"Don't." Meryn padded across the living room to her chair, her outline visible against the picture window. "I want to talk with you, and it'll be easier in the dark."

Henrietta's heart thudded against her brace. She and Una used to talk in the dark all the time, but she had a dreadful feeling this wasn't going to be like that.

"Henrietta," Meryn said, "you have known from the beginning that I'm a lesbian. As we've gotten to know each other, as you shared your past with me, you've kind of described yourself the same way."

Henrietta remembered the night she'd said that. Leave it to Meryn to have heard it and to remember it.

"I know, when you and Maxine spoke, and she assumed we're a couple, that that probably shocked you. And maybe insulted you."

It seemed to Henrietta that Meryn was breathing hard for someone who was sitting still.

"I'm not good at hiding my feelings, Henrietta. I... I just want you to know, that I... I do love you."

Henrietta was certain she'd misheard.

"I don't know how you'll feel about that. And I know you may not feel the same," Meryn continued quickly before Henrietta could respond.

She couldn't sit any longer, and began to pace back and forth, her shadow moving across the picture window as if it were a movie screen.

"I don't have any expectations. And I don't want anything to change between us, but, of course, this may change everything. I realize you've got a certain position in this town, certain expectations and obligations, and, if you want me to leave, I will. But, you've changed my life. I just couldn't continue being around you and not tell you how I feel."

She stopped moving and speaking at last, standing there, silhouetted against the faint light from outside. Henrietta couldn't tell if she was facing her or the street.

A war raged inside Henrietta—her heart leapt with a joy it hadn't known in nearly four decades, but her mind sternly demanded that she do the right thing.

"You can't," she heard herself say.

"Can't what?"

"You can't..." Henrietta couldn't say the words aloud. "You can't be tied to me that way. You're too young, too beaut—too full of promise.

You have your entire life to live, and it can't be anchored down by me."

"Henrietta, age doesn't matter—"

"Poppycock," Henrietta snapped. "You've read enough novels to know that that's an argument only the younger person makes, never the older. I'm more than twice your age. I'm older than your parents. By the time you're my age, I'll be in my eighties, if I live that long. Your career is just beginning. Your whole life is just beginning. You shouldn't be trapped in this village forever, and I don't see myself leaving. This cannot be."

To her consternation, Meryn heaved a sigh that sounded like relief as she sat back down in her chair.

"You've given me every excuse but one, the only one that matters," Meryn said softly. "You haven't said how you feel. About me."

Tell her. Tell her you don't love her. Make her leave.

At Henrietta's hesitation, Meryn said, "If you don't feel the same, just say so. I'll never bring it up again. And I'll leave if you want me to."

"I don't."

Meryn's head dropped. "Okay."

"No." Henrietta grasped for words. "I don't want you to leave. And..." She'd never imagined herself ever saying these words to anyone. It was terrifying. "And I do love you. Very much."

Meryn's head lifted slowly. "You do?"

Henrietta was certain she was going to pass out if her heart beat any faster. "Of course I do," she said brusquely. "How could I not? What with you falling out of that blasted boat, and crashing my car into the wall, and turning the entire house upside down with..." Her voice caught. "I do."

Meryn got up and approached the sofa. Petrified, Henrietta sat frozen in place, but Meryn went around to the back of the couch and wrapped her arms around Henrietta from behind. Her cheek, so soft, so warm, pressed to Henrietta's as her arms cradled her gently. Tentatively, Henrietta reached up to clasp Meryn's arms in her gnarled hands.

"Thank you, Henrietta," Meryn whispered.

She kissed Henrietta's cheek, her lips lingering a moment, before she straightened and went to her room.

Chapter 19

NOTHING HAD CHANGED AND everything had changed.

Ryn dove back into the semester. Her routine was basically as it had always been, but nothing was the same. Her increased teaching load felt lighter. Even Jerry Talbert's sour face couldn't dampen her enthusiasm. Most of her students had passed her midterms with good grades—that boded well for her performance evaluation, no matter what Talbert might have against her.

Beverly eyed her suspiciously near the end of the first week back. "What are you so happy about?"

"Nothing in particular," Ryn said, trying not to grin. "Just had a good break. How was yours?"

If Beverly noticed the deflection, she played along.

"Come with me," she said, leading the way down the corridor to Geary's office.

Ryn hung back, but Beverly grabbed her by the hand and dragged her inside.

"He must have come in over break. Cleared out all of his things."

Beverly was right. The office was empty. Geary's desk was clean, his bookshelves empty, all the frames on the wall gone, leaving only the nails.

"Do you want to move your office?" Beverly asked. "I'll help you."

Ryn looked around. This room was bigger, with two windows—"and the computer," she said. "I won't have to go to the library."

She and Beverly spent a couple of hours getting her things moved out of the broom closet and settled in the other office. They rearranged the desks so that she could have one next to a window.

"Thank you so much," Ryn said, sitting at her new desk.

Beverly gave a little sniff. "One more thing." She trotted back to her office and returned a moment later with a can of air freshener, which she sprayed liberally.

"Oh, that's much better," Ryn said. "No more man-smell."

Beverly giggled. "I'll put the kettle on."

She frequently caught sight of Roberta and Franny and Steph across campus, but noticed Tamara wasn't with them as often as she used to be. She kept thinking she should catch up with Franny to fill her in on what had happened after their conversation, but she wasn't sure what to say.

At home, her interactions with Henrietta would have seemed the same to an outside observer, but little changes made it all feel different. Brief touches to shoulders or arm, lingering eye contact—it surprised Ryn how intimate those small things were. She still experienced a thrill inside every time she replayed that conversation in her head. If Ryn had needed any further proof of how Henrietta really felt, it had been how hard Henrietta had tried to push her away, to protect her.

"What are you grinning about?"

Startled, Ryn looked up to see Franny beside her on the campus crosswalk. She grinned. "You must have read my mind. I was just thinking about you."

Franny scoffed. "Whatever you were thinking about, I don't think it was me."

"Well..." Ryn's face burned. "It was indirectly about you."

"You talked to Henrietta?"

Ryn couldn't suppress a smile as she nodded.

"And she feels the same way?"

Ryn's smile widened, and she nodded again. "I mean, nothing... it's not..."

"I'm happy for both of you."

"Franny, I really can't thank you enough. If you hadn't listened, encouraged me to be honest with her..."

The chapel bell tolled.

"Come to Mass with me."

Ryn drew up. It had been ages. "Is Tamara going to be there?"

"Probably." Franny tugged on Ryn's arm. "You and Tamara need to be able to be in the same space without it being weird. Come on."

Ryn allowed herself to be steered toward the chapel. Steph and Roberta waved and scooted over to make room. Tamara's face, though, was anything but welcoming. Ryn gave her a smile and sat, grateful there were three people between them.

The chapel was decorated in somber purples for Lent. She'd nearly forgotten what season it was. She'd been so wrapped up in all of her extra work after Geary left that she hadn't even realized Easter was fast approaching. This whole year was flying by.

What would happen if her position here wasn't extended? She really should be updating her CV and preparing to apply elsewhere, but it was hard to think about leaving this village, these people, Henrietta.

She stole a few glances down the pew to Tam, who met and held her gaze for several seconds. Nothing. She could honestly say that she felt nothing. She sat back. Eight months ago, if someone had told her that her heart would belong to Henrietta rather than Tamara, she would have said they were crazy.

She smiled. *Hooray for crazy.*

~

HENRIETTA STOPPED IN FRONT of the mirror for the fifth time. "You look ridiculous."

She untied the colorful silk scarf she'd added to her outfit and tossed it on the dresser. Surveying her image—drab gray blouse, navy blue jacket and skirt—this was the Henrietta the club women expected.

"What would Meryn urge you to do?" she asked her reflection.

That had become her refrain for so many things over the last few weeks. Though she was still weighed down by her noisy and restrictive braces, she felt she could almost float. She, Henrietta Cochran, had a lover. Kind of.

She honestly couldn't imagine—wouldn't let herself imagine—having Meryn as a real lover, but the confession of their mutual feelings was as good as.

Only that little niggle of doubt kept creeping in. *Is it good enough for her? Will it be forever?*

"But she loves you. She said so."

Feeling more defiant, more confident, she reached for the scarf—a Christmas gift from Bonnie years ago that she'd never worn—and draped it around her neck.

Walking into the club a few minutes later, she got a few double takes and curious glances from the other women as they took seats around the tables set for bridge.

"You look very nice, Henrietta," said Mary Ellen Greene, sitting to Henrietta's right.

"Thank you." Henrietta tried not to blush.

"Yes," said Genevieve Talbert from a neighboring table. "Did you hire a new fashion consultant?"

The benign words didn't hide her waspish tone, triggering a few titters from some of the other women.

Henrietta ignored her as the other two chairs were filled. "Shall we draw to see who deals?"

Though she tried to keep her mind on the game, she couldn't avoid overhearing the bits of gossip from Genevieve and the women at her table.

"My sister went to the city last week. She saw some of the most shocking women, at least she thinks they were women, but with those lesbos, it's hard to tell. They all had short men's haircuts and wore men's clothing. Honestly, how could any woman be attracted to a fake man?"

Henrietta missed a trick. "Henrietta!" Mary Ellen snapped.

"Sorry."

"And..." Genevieve's voice lowered into that carrying whisper that immediately had most of the women craning their necks to listen to her. "They all wear that symbol, that axe with two blades, like some kind of advertisement. It's disgusting how brazenly they parade their abnormality."

Henrietta felt the blood drain from her face. She forced herself to stick it out for the rest of the game, but excused herself from the luncheon.

"I'm not feeling well," she mumbled to Mary Ellen.

Calling for her car, she realized her hands were trembling as she waited in the foyer. Genevieve's comments were aimed specifically at her. She had no idea if any of the others realized it, but she certainly did.

At the bottom of the club's drive, she hesitated. Instead of pulling into her own driveway, she drove on into the village. She found parking in the library's lot.

Inside, her heart fell when she didn't see Maxine at the desk. She turned to leave.

"Henrietta!"

Maxine stepped out from the shelves with an armful of books. "How nice to see you." Her eyes ran curiously over Henrietta's face.

"I shouldn't have bothered you while you're at work," Henrietta said, feeling self-conscious now that she was here.

"Don't be silly." Maxine set her books down. "Sherry, I'm going to be in the small conference room with Miss Cochran."

Henrietta proudly noticed her art still being displayed on the walls as she followed Maxine to the back of the library. From this vantage point, she was able to study Maxine. Her hair, unbound today, had wonderful streaks of silver running through the black curls, and her clothing flowed like air around her as she moved. Everything about her was graceful, feminine, sensuous—*everything I'm not*, Henrietta thought as she clanked along behind her.

Maxine showed her into a room with a small conference table and six chairs. She closed the door and sat across from Henrietta.

"What can I do for you?" Her eyes lowered to the scarf. "That's beautiful."

Henrietta touched her fingers to it, and she wished she'd remembered to take it off in the car.

Maxine angled her head, and she studied Henrietta closely. "But I don't think you wore that for me."

"No. I just came from bridge at the country club."

Maxine's nostrils flared and a subtle coolness settled over her features.

"Is there something wrong?" Henrietta asked hesitantly.

"I didn't realize you were a member there," Maxine said.

"We have been, I mean, I grew up with my parents being members there. And I've just continued." She frowned. "Is that a problem?"

"Not at all." But Maxine's even cooler tone belied her response. Henrietta's confusion must have shown on her face, because Maxine smiled. "It's not your fault."

Henrietta felt completely at sea. "What's not my fault?"

"That club's segregationist policies."

Henrietta blinked a few times. "Its... what?"

Maxine pursed her lips for a moment. "You really don't know, do you? Haven't you ever noticed, there's not a single black or Jewish member at that club."

"That can't..." But Henrietta stopped, trying to think.

Maxine leaned forward. "There are blacks in the kitchen, but you've never had a black server in the dining room, have you? And I can promise you, there are no Jews anywhere on that property."

Henrietta was gobsmacked. "How could I not know that?"

"Like you said, you grew up there. You probably play cards with women who grew up there."

"Yes, some of them. I've known them most of my life. But—"

"I'm sorry," Maxine cut in. "I'm sure you didn't come here to get a lecture from me on the country club's history of discrimination."

"No." Henrietta fingered the scarf again. "But it's all of a piece, isn't it?"

Maxine's eyebrows raised. "What is?"

"They know. Or at least one of the women I play bridge with knows about Meryn. And she's the wife of Meryn's department chair."

"What does she know?"

"I'm sorry. She was making all kinds of crude comments about lesbians being fake men, and she mentioned that symbol, the two-bladed axe—"

"The labrys?"

"Yes. Meryn has that among the many bumper stickers on her car." Henrietta's fingers twiddled with the loose knot on the scarf. "She told me, when I met her, that she was open about... about that. That she wouldn't lie and she wouldn't hide." Her eyes flashed. "And I don't want her to."

Maxine's face softened. "You do love her."

It was one thing, terrifying enough, to admit it to Meryn herself, but... Henrietta nodded.

"After our dinner with you and Sandy, Meryn was odd, unsettled. And I suppose I was, too. She left one evening. For a little while, I wasn't sure she was coming back, but when she did, she wanted to talk."

Henrietta paused. She'd not said it aloud to anyone else. "She loves me, too."

Maxine reached across the table and took Henrietta's hand in hers. "I'm so happy for both of you."

Henrietta looked into her dark eyes and saw nothing but joy and acceptance—all the things she would never see in the eyes of the women she'd considered her friends for decades. It felt as if her life was being flipped upside down.

At her hesitation, Maxine's brow creased. "Aren't you happy?"

"Yes, but..." Henrietta felt like an absolute fool, but there was no one else she could talk to. "Our age difference is so vast, thirty years. And..." She flushed in embarrassment. "Physically, I don't know how to..."

"Henrietta," Maxine squeezed her hand, "there are no rules. And I suspect Meryn would say she has no expectations. Whatever happens—or doesn't—between you, is for you to decide. It's no one else's business."

"But what if she needs or wants..." Henrietta couldn't complete that thought. Even with Maxine, it was too personal.

"Then you'll talk about it. You'll work it out. That's what people in relationships do."

Henrietta stared into Maxine's reassuring eyes again, feeling calmer than she had in a long time. "Would you and Sandy come to dinner this weekend?"

Maxine's face broke into a radiant smile. "We'd love to."

~

"YOUR HOME TRULY IS lovely."

Maxine and Sandy stood in the studio, Sandy squatting to peruse the canvases stacked against the wall while Maxine gazed out the windows.

The April weather had started to hint at spring, with longer days and warmer temperatures, though piles of snow still lay in the shadowed areas that didn't receive any sunlight.

"We could take a walk down to the pond if you'd like." Ryn turned to Henrietta. "I went down with a shovel earlier to make sure everything was scraped clean. It's safe."

Sandy stood. "Could we?"

Ryn got a light coat and held it up for Henrietta. "You should put this on, though."

She caught the glance Sandy exchanged with Maxine as she helped Henrietta. These two were a godsend. It was so nice to have another couple to talk to, to do things with. Ryn had been surprised to come home a few days ago to learn that Henrietta had invited them. After their last dinner with them—the one where Henrietta had sworn she and Ryn weren't together—Ryn hadn't been sure Henrietta would want to see them again.

"Did you ask them if they're vegetarian?" she'd asked when Henrietta told her she'd invited them for dinner.

"Vegetarian?" Henrietta had stared at her. "Why would I ask that?"

"Lots of lesbians are. They served us lentil soup and cornbread. I can't remember what they ate the day they helped me paint my room."

"Oh." Henrietta had frowned. "But they eat fish."

"True." Ryn had pondered. "Let's do spaghetti and marinara sauce. I can make meatballs for anyone who wants them. And we'll do garlic bread."

The sauce simmered on the stove as they headed down the paved walk to the pond.

"What a nice spot, Henrietta," Sandy said. "I can see why you paint this so often."

Maxine pointed. "And that's the famous rowboat?"

Henrietta chuckled. "Probably with the famous snake coiled up inside."

"That would have scared anyone," Ryn grumbled, but she was smiling. "I wasn't expecting a passenger."

"Do you have fires down here?" Sandy asked, noticing the fire pit.

"We do." Ryn bent over to clear some of the fallen branches. "Henrietta surprised me with it last fall. It was our first date."

"Our first—" Henrietta sputtered, blushing. "It most certainly was not."

Ryn shrugged. "I don't know. You brought fish fry home, you had a whole picnic basket packed, a fire all set."

"How romantic," Maxine said with a chuckle. She wrapped an arm around Henrietta and gave her a squeeze.

"You, as I recall," Henrietta glared at Ryn, "needed cheering up. Your work was being stolen from you."

"What's this?" Sandy asked.

"I'd almost forgotten," Ryn said. "I was kind of a mess that night. I'd put together a proposal for a new course, wrote up a syllabus, lesson plans, everything. Then the two men in my department took credit for it, got it approved."

"She's brilliant, and the men are threatened by that," Henrietta said stoutly. "But they got their comeuppance."

At Ryn's questioning stare, Henrietta avoided her gaze and turned to the pond.

"We get beautiful sunsets here. We'll have you back again when we can light a fire."

The sun was already sinking below the hills to the west. Ryn noticed when Henrietta shivered in the chill dusk.

"Let's go back and eat."

Everyone chipped in to do something. Sandy helped prepare the garlic bread while Ryn got the water boiling for the spaghetti. Out in the dining room—cleared of all of Ryn's books and notes—Maxine helped Henrietta set the table.

With the pasta cooked and strained, and all the bowls and platters on the table, they sat.

"So, Henrietta," Sandy asked as she uncorked the wine they'd brought and poured for all of them. "Where is your art exhibit going next?"

"To Albany," Ryn answered for her. "That gallery rep who came to the library has arranged a show there in June."

"Henrietta, that's wonderful," Maxine said, raising her glass. "To a successful show."

They drank to that.

The bowl of pasta circulated around the table, followed by the sauce.

"While we're making toasts," Henrietta said, "I have an announcement to make."

Ryn, spooning a few meatballs onto her plate, glanced from Henrietta to Sandy and Maxine, but they appeared to be as clueless as she was.

"I resigned my membership at the country club today."

A stunned silence greeted her words. To Ryn's surprise, Maxine was the first to react.

"Oh, Henrietta, no," she said, looking stricken. "That's not what I meant. I feel horrible."

"Don't." Henrietta said firmly.

"Henrietta," Ryn said, "I don't understand. Why would you do that?"

Henrietta took a sip of her wine before saying, "For months, I've been questioning why I have settled for such a limited circle of... I used to consider them my friends. I put up with the gossip and the vicious

pleasure they take in cutting others down, though I would like to think I didn't participate. Still, I was a miserable person inside, miserable to be around."

She glanced in Ryn's direction. "When I met you, it was as if someone held a mirror up. And I didn't like what I saw."

"I'm sorry," Ryn muttered.

"No." Henrietta's hand twitched in Ryn's direction, but then she caught herself and pulled back. "You are the kindest, most genuine person I've ever known."

Ryn sat, stunned, by Henrietta's words. It was so unlike her to be this demonstrative, especially in front of others. She was even more shocked when Henrietta did take her hand.

"You've been a truer friend to me in the months you've been here than any of them in the decades I've known them."

She released Ryn's hand and turned to Maxine. "And when you pointed out what I'd been too blind to see—how blatantly racist and bigoted they are—I just can't be part of that any longer. Even if I don't feel the same way, by being a member there, paying dues every month, I sanction that bigotry. So, I wrote a letter explaining all of that, and met with the club manager today to deliver the letter."

Heaving a deep breath, she said, "And I feel so much lighter. Better. And I'm starving. Let's eat before everything gets cold."

Sandy raised her glass. "That does deserve another toast."

"Hank, I'm proud of you." Ryn fought the urge to throw her arms around Henrietta.

"This is delicious," Maxine said.

Ryn noticed with some relief that both Maxine and Sandy had helped themselves to meatballs. No need to worry so much about the menu for future dinners. She had a feeling she and Henrietta would be spending a lot of time with them.

When the evening ended, Maxine and Sandy hugged both Henrietta and Ryn good night.

Ryn stood beside Henrietta on the front porch, waving them off. Back inside, she locked the door.

"That was such a nice evening," she said.

"I like them both, very much," Henrietta agreed.

"Hank," Ryn said, stepping close to Henrietta. "I don't mean to sound patronizing in any way, but I really am proud of the stand you took with the club."

She wrapped her arms around Henrietta, careful not to knock her off-balance. She felt Henrietta's hands tentatively reach up to hold her in return. For a long moment, they stood like that. When Ryn drew away, she searched Henrietta's eyes.

"Good night." She lightly stroked her fingers along Henrietta's cheek.

As they walked to the hallway and turned in opposite directions, Ryn said over her shoulder, "And it was, too, our first date."

~

HENRIETTA LAY IN THE dark for a long time, unable to fall asleep.

"I should have told her," she whispered. "Should have told her it was because of her, because of the things Genevieve was saying about her."

Even so, she hadn't spoken up, hadn't defended Meryn, or gays in general.

That includes me.

Henrietta was slowly coming to accept that that label applied to her. It was still an adjustment, one made easier by having friends like Maxine and Sandy.

The genuineness and camaraderie around the table this evening had felt more real than the kind of guarded, stilted interactions she'd become accustomed to with the country club set. It had been like that with the young nuns, too, she realized. Maybe the club people were the aberration; maybe other people were kind and thoughtful and caring as a matter of course.

Her social circle had been so limited for nearly her entire life. If she and Una hadn't gotten sick, if they'd escaped to the city as they'd planned, her life would have been so different. A part of her wished mightily that she could have lived that life... *but then I would never have met Meryn.*

That was a sobering thought.

When sleep did come, it came with bad dreams—Una took her by the hand, dragging her to the pond despite Henrietta's warnings that they shouldn't go in. Una jumped in anyhow, urging Henrietta to join her. But when she did, Una was gone, and it was Meryn who was splashing in the pond. Meryn's voice changed. She was floundering, calling for help. Henrietta was unable to get to her. No matter how hard she swam, Meryn was beyond her reach. She called and called for help. Genevieve Talbert and some of the other women stood on the dock, pointing and laughing. Henrietta treaded water, begging them to throw a life preserver to Meryn, but Genevieve and the others just turned and walked away.

"*Henrietta,*" called Meryn.

She tried again to get to her.

"Henrietta."

Warm hands grasped her arm, shaking her gently. She woke to find Meryn leaning over the bed.

"What...?"

"You were having a nightmare," Meryn said. "You were crying and moaning in your sleep. I couldn't wake you."

Henrietta wiped at the tears that dampened her face and hair. "I'm sorry."

"Let me get you some water."

Meryn went into the bathroom and returned a moment later with a glass. Henrietta struggled to sit up a bit. Meryn wrapped an arm around her to help support her shoulders as she sipped the cold water.

With a nod, she handed the glass back and lay down. "Thank you."

Meryn set the glass on the nightstand. "What were you dreaming about?"

Henrietta took a shuddering breath. "The pond." She decided not to elaborate.

Meryn sat on the side of the bed, smoothing Henrietta's hair from her forehead. She laid her hand on Henrietta's arm. "You're trembling. Would you like me to stay until you fall asleep again?"

Henrietta stared up at her in the dim light. She wanted that more than anything, but—

Meryn got up, and Henrietta's heart sank. Meryn walked around to the other side of the bed, stretching out on top of the covers. Henrietta lay stiffly. Meryn scooted closer, slipping an arm under Henrietta's shoulders to pull her near.

"There," she said softly. "Close your eyes. I've got you."

Henrietta's muscles were tense.

"Is this hurting you?"

"No."

"Relax." Meryn's free hand cradled Henrietta's cheek. Henrietta let herself nestle into Meryn's shoulder, felt Meryn's warm breath on her hair.

She was sure she'd never be able to fall asleep, but the tension slowly left her shoulders. Her breathing deepened and she felt herself sinking, but this time she sank into warmth and softness, never-ending softness.

When she woke next, daylight was streaming in between the curtains and she was alone. Turning her head, she sniffed. Lingering on the pillow was Meryn's clean scent. If it hadn't been for that, Henrietta was sure she'd have thought she dreamt the entire thing.

She turned into the pillow, breathing deeply and holding tight to the memory of the thing she'd been certain she'd never know.

She held me.

Chapter 20

SPRING ARRIVED IN FULL force the second week of April. Early flowers—Ryn didn't really know all their names beyond the daffodils—burst into bloom in a riot of color in flowerbeds all over campus, as well as in Henrietta's yard. She supposed Bud must have planted a lot of things last fall.

With the warmth and sunshine came a restlessness, an itch to be outdoors, to get rid of the heavy coats and hats, to strip down to T-shirts and maybe even shorts, though that was pushing it a bit. And it wasn't just the students. Ryn felt just as twitchy. She actually held a class outside, her students sitting on the grass of the quad as they argued about the role of the WASPs. Predictably, the women all felt that their role, even though they flew non-combat missions, contributed to the war effort, maybe even shortening the duration, while the men countered that they were nothing more than glorified taxi-drivers, ferrying planes around the country while the male pilots did all the serious work. The women shot back that they did a lot more than that, challenging the guys to fly a plane trailing a target for gunnery practice and see if they came back without having wet themselves. Ryn let them debate. She was happy that they were engaged enough to have an opinion.

On the periphery of the quad, standing in the dappled shadows of one of the trees, stood Tamara. It was harder for Ryn to concentrate with her there. When she dismissed the students, Tam hadn't moved. Taking it as a sign that she wanted to talk, Ryn zipped her backpack and sauntered over to the tree.

"Hi."

"Hi." Tamara's eyes were searching as she scoured Ryn's face. "Looked like they were going to fight for a few minutes."

Ryn grinned. "They feel pretty passionate about the topic. Makes me happy."

"None of my classes get us fired up like that." Tamara shrugged. "Kind of makes me wish I could have taken one of your classes."

Ryn didn't respond to that, certain that her silent *thank God* would not go over well. Instead, she asked, "How is your semester going?"

"Okay." Tamara kicked at a tuft of grass. "More than halfway over. Finals will be here before we know it."

"Yeah." Ryn tilted her head. "Have you decided about entering?"

"Kind of." Tamara glanced around, but they were alone. "You really don't... There's nothing between us?"

Ryn had been half-expecting a question like this. "Tam, there can't be," she said as gently as possible. "I want you to be happy. If that means joining the order, great. I think Roberta and Franny and Steph are fantastic. But if that means taking another path, maybe with another woman, I hope you find someone who can love you the way you deserve. But it won't be me."

Tamara's eyes filled with tears. "It's Henrietta, isn't it?"

Ryn stared at her. "Why would you say that?"

"Because I have eyes." Tamara swiped a hand across her eyes and focused on something on the other side of the quad. "I saw the way she looks at you. And you at her. I don't get it. She's so old. And she's—"

"Careful, Tamara." Ryn's voice was cold. "I'd like to stay friends with you."

Tamara's mouth gaped at the warning. She backed up a step. "Fine. See you around."

Ryn turned on her heel and walked to Rayburn hall. She refused to look back and see if Tamara was still there. She'd been caught off-guard by Tam's comment about Henrietta—*and my reaction to it.*

She was rarely moved to anger that quickly, but she wasn't going to tolerate anyone putting Henrietta down. Hank had had to deal with people doing that to her her entire life.

She paused as she climbed the stairs. Every time she remembered that night last week, holding Henrietta after her bad dream, it filled her with so much tenderness, so much protectiveness, it took her breath away.

It wasn't sexual at all, she'd reminded herself. *Why are you so wrapped up in this?*

But she was. Even if she couldn't explain it.

She was about to stop in to say hi to Beverly, but she saw that Talbert was in his office, standing at the window. He turned to her with an inscrutable expression, a lit cigarette in his hand. She quickly continued down the hall, almost going to her old broom closet until she remembered that wasn't her office anymore.

Taped to the pebbled glass of her door was a folded piece of paper. When she unfolded it, she saw it was a flyer for the upcoming meeting of the Democratic group in town. At the bottom was scrawled,

Hope to see you there. Bring Henrietta.

Franny

Ryn pulled her notes out of her backpack and swapped a different set for her afternoon classes. It was a few minutes before she heard familiar staccato footsteps in the corridor.

"Come on in."

Beverly entered and shut the door. "He was watching you. Outside. Teaching your class."

"Really?" Ryn dropped into her chair and nudged the other with her foot. "Did he say anything?"

Beverly shook her head and sat.

"Then what's the matter?" Ryn gasped. "You're not retiring for real, are you?"

"No." Beverly swatted at her. "At least, not yet." She wrung her hands in a gesture that Ryn knew only too well.

"Tell me."

"Well, Father Croson has received applications for this department. He brought the curricula vitae to Dr. Talbert. I've been asked to type up letters asking four of them to come for interviews."

Ryn sat back. "Huh. For my position? Or Geary's? Or both?"

Beverly looked miserable. "I don't know."

"Okay," Ryn said with a deep sigh. "Good to know. I guess I'd better get serious about looking for something else."

"Oh, Meryn," but Beverly's voice caught. Huge tears shimmered behind her glasses.

Ryn leaned forward and took her hand. "Bev, I'd never have gotten through this year without you. Your friendship. Your tea."

Beverly gave her a watery smile. "You bought most of the tea."

"But you made it. And that made it special."

That did it. Beverly heaved a sob and jumped to her feet. She hurried from the office, but the sound of her crying echoed in the corridor as Ryn stared out the window where it was still a beautiful spring day.

"Oh, well." She stood and swung her backpack over one shoulder. "If my next class is up for it, we're going outside."

～

MAXINE PULLED INTO A parking space. Henrietta sat in the passenger seat, her hand gripping the door handle. "I don't think this is such a good idea."

Turning the ignition off, Maxine said soothingly, "It is. It really is." She unclicked her seatbelt. "Patty's waiting for us. She came in specially for this. No one else will be there."

Henrietta felt as if she were being led to a guillotine as she got out. She followed Maxine into a charming clapboard shop a block removed from Main Street.

"I can't believe I've lived in this village my entire life, and I've never noticed this place."

"Well, you wouldn't, would you?" Maxine held the door for her.

Inside, a smiling woman with impossibly red hair was waiting to greet them. "Hello, Maxine. And you must be Henrietta."

"Yes."

"Henrietta, Patty is the best hairdresser around. Sandy's been going to her since we moved here. She can even do my hair." Maxine pushed at her heavy curls.

Henrietta glanced at her. "But I've been going to—"

"Mmm hmm," Patty interrupted. "I can see exactly who you've been going to."

Henrietta felt like a zoo specimen as Patty and Maxine spoke over her.

"She's nervous."

"I can see why." Patty's fingers sifted through Henrietta's hair. "It's like straw. She's probably never used a conditioner. And these ends! I only know one person in town who cuts hair like this."

"Like a signature?"

Patty laughed. "I can spot it anywhere."

As a matter of fact, Henrietta had been going to the same salon all of her adult life. The long hair she'd had as a girl—the hair Una used to run her fingers through—had been shorn when she got sick. The polio nurses had enough to do with bathing and caring for dozens of patients. Grooming hair wasn't a priority. So hers had been nearly shaved. Her mother had cried almost as hard about that as she had at the braces when Henrietta came home.

"Well, there's no sense in having pretty hair now," her mother had bemoaned. "No boy will ever want to marry you."

She'd let Henrietta's hair grow until the uneven ends had to be trimmed and then taken her to her hairdresser. "Keep it practical, Justine."

Straight bangs, sides and back just down to her jawline. Easy to wash and dry, just run a comb through and be done with it. That's as much thought as Henrietta had given to her hair in decades. When Justine had passed the salon to her daughter, Paula, nothing had changed.

As she lay back at the sink—Patty made sure her neck was comfortably padded—those thoughts ran through her head while Patty shampooed her hair with something that was thick and smelled wonderfully tropical. When she began massaging Henrietta's scalp, she nearly put her to sleep.

"Now," Patty said, gently wrapping Henrietta's head in a towel and leading her to a swiveling chair in front of a mirror. She fastened a drape around her neck. "I'm going to let this conditioner work for at least fifteen minutes." She removed the towel and squirted some thick goo into Henrietta's hair and worked it in. "In the meantime, how about some coffee? Cream? Sugar?"

"Just cream, please."

"I didn't mean to take up your whole day off," Henrietta said to Maxine while Patty went to a back room. She tried to get a glimpse of herself, certain she looked ridiculous, sitting there with that stuff in her hair, but Patty had swiveled it away from the mirror.

"I consider this a challenge."

"A challenge?"

Patty came back with three mugs clenched in her hands. "Cream and extra sugar for yours, sweetie," she said, handing Maxine one of the cups. "Henrietta."

She checked Henrietta's hair and sat down. "Did I hear something about a challenge?"

"Henrietta has presented me with one," Maxine said, surveying Henrietta up and down. "You take care of the hair, Patty. I'll take care of the rest."

By the time Maxine drove back to the house late that afternoon, Henrietta was exhausted. Maxine helped her carry her bags inside.

"Where do you want these?"

"In the bedroom, please."

Maxine returned to the living room a moment later where Henrietta was staring wide-eyed at her reflection.

"I feel like a clown, some kind of impostor."

"You look wonderful." Maxine laid a reassuring hand in her shoulder as they both gazed into the mirror. "Now you leave everything just as it is. Remember, Henrietta," she tapped a fingernail against one of the crutches, "Ryn sees you, not these."

She glanced at her watch. "She'll be home soon." She gave Henrietta a quick kiss on the cheek. "We'll see you both tomorrow night. Sandy's making something special for your birthday, so come hungry."

She backed out of the driveway with a wave. Henrietta went to the sofa to sit and wait. Nervously, she kept running her hands over her hair. Though it was even shorter than she was accustomed to, it felt wonderfully soft and full.

Not content to stop at her hair, Patty had insisted on giving her a facial as well. Though Henrietta had drawn the line at makeup, she had allowed Patty to apply a moisturizer that made her skin feel like silk.

In the bedroom were bags of new clothing unlike anything Henrietta had ever worn.

"Are you sure you want to wear these again?" the woman at the boutique had asked, disdainfully holding up Henrietta's suit and blouse.

"I'm sure."

The hair was change enough for one day, Henrietta thought. Her heart raced when she saw Meryn saunter down the street and turn into the drive. *She is so beautiful, so graceful.*

She held her breath as the front door opened and Meryn entered.

"Hi, Hank."

"Hello."

It took a second for Meryn to notice. When she did, it was almost comical, how she froze mid-step.

"Wow. Henrietta. You look wonderful."

Henrietta's breath hitched. "Really?"

Meryn's answer was in her gaze. She lowered her backpack and came to sit beside Henrietta on the couch. "What prompted this?"

"Maxine."

Meryn laughed and raised a hand to softly touch Henrietta's hair. "Well, I need to remember to thank Maxine." She angled her head. "Do you like it?"

Henrietta searched Meryn's eyes. "I do now."

RYN STOOD IN THE kitchen, shuffling all of the pieces of paper spread on the counter: Bonnie's instructions for heating the ham and making a glaze, her mom's recipe for green beans sautéed with shallots, the list of what everyone else was bringing.

From the village, she heard the church bells chiming.

"Ready?" she called toward the back of the house, checking that her shirt was still neatly tucked in.

Henrietta's crutches and braces announced her arrival.

Ryn gaped for a moment. "Look at you."

Henrietta stood there in flowing slacks of deep blue, with a tunic top in a flowered print of blues and greens.

"Henrietta..."

"It's not too much?" Henrietta's cheeks were very pink. She started to turn around. "I should change."

"No." Ryn went to her, laying a hand on her shoulder. "You look fantastic."

"I feel like a fool."

"You shouldn't. Maxine again?"

Henrietta nodded, a tortured expression on her face. "I can't do this. Everyone will stare."

"Yes, they will, but they'll be staring in envy." Ryn scanned Henrietta up and down. "How's it feel?"

Henrietta couldn't hide the smile that tugged at the corner of her mouth. "It's wonderful. I haven't worn anything but skirts and those awful heavy nylon hose in forever. These cotton hose are so light and comfortable. Of course, they probably won't last as long."

"So they don't last as long." Ryn guided Henrietta toward the garage. "Who cares? Life is too short to be uncomfortable if you don't have to be."

Henrietta cast her a sidelong glance. "That's your philosophy on everything, isn't it?"

Ryn grinned at her. "Pretty much. Can I drive?"

Henrietta got into the passenger seat of the Chrysler and waited until Ryn had managed to back out of the garage—using the hand controls—without hitting anything before saying, "You've been practicing, haven't you?"

"Yeah. They're kind of fun. But the pedals are still safer for me."

"At least our garage is all in one piece."

Ryn smiled at the pronoun. Checking for oncoming traffic at the end of the drive, she said, "Thanks again for letting me put the Democratic signs up in the yard."

Henrietta voice was hard as she said, "Every person turning in at the club will see them."

"Are you sorry?"

"About resigning from there?"

Ryn nodded.

"Not at all. I'm only sorry it took me so long to do it."

"But that was your social circle for a long, long time." Ryn felt a stab of guilt at not having told Henrietta that St. Aloysius was interviewing for the history department. She'd updated her CV and sent it out to some of the surrounding SUNY campuses, wondering if she could do the commute on a daily basis. She couldn't bear the thought of not being here.

Henrietta scoffed. "Too long. And I like my new social circle so much better."

Part of that new social circle was waiting for them at the packed campus chapel, as Franny and the others had saved space in their pew. It warmed Ryn's heart to hear the whispered compliments they all offered Henrietta. She knew how self-conscious she'd feel if she suddenly had to wear a dress—she coughed to cover a snort at the thought—and figured it must be about the same for Henrietta. It was a few minutes before she realized Tamara wasn't with them.

The Easter celebration was joyous—riots of flowers filled the chapel, people sang enthusiastically. When Mass was over, Franny, Steph, and Roberta walked them out.

"We'll be there inside half an hour," Steph called as they peeled off in the opposite direction.

Back home, Ryn hurried to change into jeans and a T-shirt, but she took the precaution of calling to Henrietta, "Don't you dare change."

Sandy and Maxine arrived just as the nuns were pulling into the driveway. They all introduced themselves to one another, so they were a noisy bunch as they entered the house.

In the kitchen, Ryn was happy to yield control to the others and even happier listening to all the compliments Henrietta was paid. Roberta slid a pan of sweet potatoes into the oven next to the ham to warm up.

Maxine and Sandy had brought a hummingbird cake decorated beautifully with sugared violets.

In the midst of the noise and the laughter, she watched Henrietta talking to Stephanie about something. Henrietta glanced over and caught her eye. For a few seconds, everyone else faded away and there was only Henrietta.

"She looks beautiful," murmured a low voice in Ryn's ear.

Ryn jumped to find Franny standing beside her. "Yeah, she does." She peered quizzically up at Franny. "Where's Tamara?"

"She hasn't been hanging out with us as much lately." Franny hesitated, carefully avoiding Ryn's gaze. "I think she met someone."

"Oh." Ryn was kind of relieved. And curious. "How do you feel about that?"

Franny shrugged. "It's not my place to feel any way about it. If she wants to be with someone, she should. She wouldn't be happy with us if that's where her heart is."

"Don't you folks recruit?"

Franny chortled. "I thought that was the main complaint about your people."

Ryn grinned. "I suppose. You know how subversive we are."

Franny nudged her, pointing her chin at Henrietta. "Your newest recruit?"

Ryn gave her a sly look. "Maybe."

"Time to eat," Sandy said, carrying the platter of ham to the table.

As dishes were passed around the table, Ryn kept checking to see if Henrietta had enough food, but she needn't have worried. Between Maxine on one side and Stephanie on the other, they handled the heavy bowls and platters, making sure Henrietta got a bit of everything that came by.

Roberta offered grace. Listening to the heartfelt prayer, Ryn found herself choking up. This gathering of women, the love and companionship at this table—it was all more than she could have wished for when she came to this little village last August.

Henrietta laughed at something Sandy said.

So much more, Ryn thought as she dug into her sweet potatoes.

After dinner, everyone was so stuffed that they opted to walk down to the pond before having dessert. Ryn, anticipating this, had gone down the day before to make sure the path was clear of all branches and leaves, anything that could impede Henrietta. She'd uncovered and cleaned the chairs so Henrietta could have a place to sit and rest once she was down there. She'd even laid wood in the fire pit, just in case.

"What a beautiful place," Sandy said. "Why didn't we ever come out to this pond before we met you?"

"Most people don't really know about this pond," Henrietta said a little breathlessly.

The trees were only just starting to bud. A few early flowers pushed through the loam at the bases of the trees and along the pond's bank. The April sun glinted off the water. A family of ducks, two adults and six fuzzy ducklings, paddled along the far shore near the dock where the rowboat bobbed gently.

Maxine pointed. "Do they know about the famous boat?"

Ryn colored. "I don't think so."

"What's the story?" Roberta asked.

"Let Henrietta tell it," Sandy said with an evil-looking grin.

Henrietta, like a queen ensconced on her throne, regaled the others with the tale of Ryn's misadventures that day.

They hooted and laughed. Ryn nodded, her lips pursed.

"You really enjoy telling that story, don't you?"

Henrietta looked up at her, her eyes shining, her cheeks glowing. "I do. It was the funniest thing I'd seen in a very long time."

For long seconds, she and Ryn stared at each other.

"And," Henrietta added, "it was one of the best days of my life."

Chapter 21

THE BIRDFEEDERS SWUNG WILDLY as birds flittered about, vying for access to the seeds, spilling many in the process. Several had figured out that they only had to wait below, hopping around to snatch the bounty falling to the ground.

Henrietta sketched, making quick splashes of color from an old set of watercolors. She'd work out the details of composition later, fine-tuning the color mixes.

Her art exhibit at the library was over, all the unsold paintings back in her studio. But most of them were going to be part of the exhibit in Albany. Mr. Taylor had been in regular contact, as he would be curating the show. He wanted to come to Bluemont again next month to finalize their selections.

Henrietta's pencil hovered above her pad as she sat, lost in thought. And amazement. The changes in her life these last months were beyond anything she could have dreamt for herself. As much as she had felt her world shrinking, imprisoning her inside walls of her own making—*was that just this past autumn?*—it now seemed her horizons were limitless.

With Meryn at her side, with new friends who were wonderfully open and non-judgmental, it seemed anything was possible.

She touched a hand to the lavender geometric pattern on her sleeve. Strange, how she'd gravitated toward these vibrant colors and patterns—"*so garish,*" said a voice inside her head that sounded a lot like Genevieve Talbert. But she loved them.

The changes, she knew, were as much internal as they were external. It was like a kind of metamorphosis. For decades, she'd been confined, like a seed trapped inside a husk that wouldn't break open to let it germinate. Everything about her—the drab colors she'd worn, the lack of any kind of ornamentation—now felt like part of the shell she'd kept closed in an effort to protect herself.

Then Meryn had come into her life. She couldn't help smiling at the mere thought of that girl. The tornado had become a nutcracker—*and my savior.* She knew Meryn would say Henrietta had saved herself, but it wasn't true. She never would have been brave enough to force that shell open on her own. She wasn't that tough. But Meryn was. Despite everything she'd dealt with at the college this year, she was unfailingly kind and optimistic. Henrietta knew her own reaction would have been to withdraw further, to shut people out even more. But Meryn just turned things around, reached for others. She was like nectar to hummingbirds. Everyone was drawn to her.

"And this is why you are a painter, not a writer," she said aloud, laughing at her sentimentality.

But... she reached for a fresh sheet of paper, her pencil flying over it.

The light gradually shifted, and she realized it was almost two o'clock. She'd been working for hours. Getting stiffly to her feet, she felt odd. Her legs were heavier than usual. She gripped her crutches and turned toward the kitchen.

With a cry, she toppled over, landing on one crutch when it tangled around her arm. She lay there a moment, struggling to breathe. When her initial panic subsided, she gingerly tried moving. All of her limbs worked, and nothing seemed to be broken. She fumbled for her stool and grasped a lower rung. Her leg braces wouldn't allow her legs to bend at the proper angles to get her feet underneath her. She had to push herself up, straight-legged, until she could grip her countertop to steady herself.

She stood there, panting, her whole body trembling. When she thought she was stable, she bent over, keeping one hand on her stool, to retrieve first one crutch and then the other. She made her way to the kitchen where she collapsed into a chair.

For several minutes, she sat, letting her heart and breathing slow. Pulling her sleeve up, she saw the start of a nasty bruise around her forearm.

"That was stupid of you," she muttered. "Too long without eating. Got to be more careful."

~

RYN SMILED WHEN SHE realized her class should have ended four minutes ago, but none of the students had begun the passive signals she typically got: the closing of books and shoving them into back-packs, the pointed glances at the clock, the restless sliding of backsides half off the edges of their seats as the students prepared to bolt.

"Okay, we'll pick up this discussion of Justice Sandra Day O'Connor on Friday. Read. Be prepared to discuss. Go."

When the first students opened the door, she saw that Jerry Talbert and Father Croson stood with a third man in the corridor where they'd apparently been watching the class. Another applicant.

She'd already been introduced to two: a younger guy about her age from Seattle and a middle-aged man from... she couldn't remember where. Apparently Talbert was so desperate to have the history department reeking again of testosterone that women candidates weren't even being interviewed.

That's not fair, she reminded herself, turning her back on them to pack up her notes. She had no idea who had applied. There weren't many women in this field, period. Much less those who wanted to come to a rinky-dink village and a tiny campus like this one. *But I want to be here.*

That's what burned her more than anything. If she were ready to leave, if she didn't want so desperately to stay, she wouldn't give two figs whom Talbert interviewed. Of course, most of why she wanted to remain had nothing to do with the college. She couldn't contemplate leaving Henrietta, and she also couldn't envision Henrietta ever leaving Bluemont. If only something else would open up within commuting distance of this place.

None of the SUNY campuses in Binghamton, Cortland, or Oswego had posted openings, but she'd sent query letters out to all of the central New York college history department heads to see if they anticipated any openings they might not have advertised yet.

"But you don't even know that you won't have a job here next year," Beverly had said, her eyes misting.

Ryn had shrugged. "I haven't been offered a contract for next year. Finals are in two weeks. I can't wait. I'm probably already too late to get something for next year."

"Have you told Miss Cochran?" Beverly had asked.

"No." That omission nagged at Ryn. It wasn't fair not to tell Henrietta, but she kept putting it off, hoping something would happen, some miracle that would keep her employed here, let her make this village her home for good.

But, she mused as she locked her office, she was going to enjoy every minute she had here while she could. Walking across campus, she was still surprised at how late everything was in this part of New York. Back home, the crabapple and cherry trees, the dogwoods and redbud—it all would have been in full bloom by now, and the non-flowering trees would have been fully leafed out. But here, the first week of May was still early. Tender buds swelled on the flowering trees, tiny leaves fluttered from maples and oaks and elms.

She took it all in as she strolled home, waving to a few people she knew. When she got to the house, Bud was just packing up. Judging from the amount of leaves and other debris loaded into the back of his pick-up, he'd had a productive day.

"Got your fire pit all cleaned up today, Miss Meryn," he said.

"Thanks, Bud." She peered skyward. "Might be a good evening to go down there."

He tipped his cap, and she waved him off.

"Saw Bud leaving," she said as she entered the house. "Maybe I should do that instead."

"Do what?" Henrietta glanced up from the desk, where she was sorting through the mail.

"Clean yards. Mow, rake, plant flowers. At least then, I wouldn't have to deal with academic egos and needy students. And I might have a sense of having accomplished something at the end of the day."

"Oh, posh. You're a good teacher, and you know it."

Ryn studied her, her leg braces now covered by loose slacks, and her back brace obscured by a tunic in a woodblock print of greens and browns.

She set her backpack down and went to stand behind Henrietta, running her hands up and down her arms. "This is pretty."

Henrietta sat back. "Thank you."

Ryn bent down to wrap her arms around Henrietta, pressing their cheeks together. When Henrietta more readily reached up to clasp her arm, Ryn smiled.

"I think we should have an early dinner and go down to the pond. Bud said he cleaned up down there. It's nice out."

Henrietta considered a moment, but then said, "We could do that. It won't take long to warm up the soup Bonnie left for us."

Ryn changed clothes, and they ate quickly. Stepping out the back door, she noticed Henrietta seemed a little wobbly. With a small basket in one hand, Ryn stayed a step ahead of Henrietta on the path, making sure there were no acorns or other debris to slide under her crutches, but Bud had done a good job of clearing everything. At the landing next to the pond, she got Henrietta settled in a chair and then turned her attention to the fire Bud had laid for them.

When it was lit, the flames snapping and sparking, she opened the basket and took out a Thermos of hot tea. "Here you go," she said, handing a warm mug to Henrietta.

"Thank you."

She pulled a light wool shawl out of the basket as well and wrapped it around Henrietta's thin shoulders. "It's cooling down. Don't want you to get chilled."

Taking the other seat, Ryn sat back with her own tea, watching the fading daylight reflected on the mirror surface of the pond. For long minutes, they listened to the croaking of frogs, watching birds swoop acrobatically to snatch bugs over the water.

"Do you ever think about it?" she asked softly.

She met Henrietta's eyes.

"Sometimes. More so when I was younger." Henrietta gazed out at the pond. "I used to wonder if I was being punished, or what my life would have been like if only we hadn't gone swimming that day."

Ryn watched as a parade of emotions crossed Henrietta's face, and she could see the girl she used to be.

"I wonder now if Una would still be alive."

Ryn reached out and took Henrietta's hand, not certain her touch would be welcomed. She was ready to withdraw when Henrietta's fingers tightened.

"Does it ever bother you to have this reminder here, just below the house?"

Henrietta shrugged. "It's pointless to think that way. This land was available. My father built a house I can manage in. Where else would I go?"

Ryn felt Henrietta's eyes on her, but she couldn't meet them. "What if we did look for someplace else? Somewhere else."

"Why would we do that?"

Ryn was grateful for the rapidly falling dusk and flickering firelight that obscured the color she knew was in her cheeks. "No reason."

~

SANDY WAS WAITING TO open the back door of her store for Henrietta.

"Are you sure it's all right to park here?" Henrietta asked.

"Of course. I've got four spots and there are only two of us working here. Come on in."

A few customers were roaming the aisles when Henrietta stepped into the shop from the storeroom. They smiled shyly in Henrietta's direction.

"I loved your paintings when they were at the library," one woman said.

Henrietta blinked at her, still unaccustomed to having people comment on her work. "Thank you."

"Jodi," Sandy said to the silver-haired woman behind the counter, "I'm going to lunch. Be back by one."

"Before you go," Jodi said, "can you help me with this special order?"

"Go ahead," Sandy said to Henrietta. "I'll be right with you."

Henrietta wended her way through the store and out to the sidewalk.

"Henrietta."

Henrietta stiffened at the sound of that voice. "Genevieve." She turned around to find Genevieve Talbert, cigarette in hand, looking her up and down.

"Don't you look lovely. So... bohemian."

Henrietta smiled. "Thank you. I'll take that as a compliment."

The smile Genevieve gave her in return was icy.

"Ready? I'm starved." Sandy caught up to them. "Oh, hello, Mrs. Talbert."

Genevieve stared at Sandy for a moment as she took a drag on her cigarette and exhaled. "Running with the artsy crowd these days, Henrietta?"

"Yes, I am. It's such a refreshing change."

"Is your lip bleeding, Mrs. Talbert?" Sandy said, leaning toward Genevieve a little. "Oh, my mistake. Come on, Henrietta."

She led the way down the sidewalk a few doors to a small diner where they got a table near the wall, out of the traffic flow.

"What was that about her lip?" Henrietta asked as she lowered herself to a chair.

Sandy grinned wickedly. "It's just her lipstick bleeding into all those wrinkles around her mouth. She'll obsess about it for weeks."

Henrietta laughed and looked around. "I haven't eaten here in years."

"Maxine and I meet here a couple times a month." Sandy moved the ashtray to an adjacent table and tugged three menus out from behind the fluted glass sugar dispenser. She looked up and waved when the door opened again. "Speaking of."

Maxine joined them. "Hello, lovely ladies."

Henrietta watched as she gave Sandy's hand a covert squeeze under the table.

"Hi, Maria," Sandy said as a waitress appeared, pad in hand. "I'll have iced tea, a chicken salad sandwich, and a bowl of today's soup."

"You don't even know what today's soup is," Maxine said.

"Doesn't matter." Sandy flipped her menu closed and slid it behind the sugar again. "They're all good."

"You're right." Maxine closed her menu, too.

"Make it three," Henrietta said.

"You're making my life easy," Maria said, tucking her pad in her apron pocket with a smile. "Drinks coming right up."

Henrietta took in the old village photos adorning the walls. "This is quaint."

Sandy nodded, reaching for her tea when Maria brought three glasses to their table. "It is. Surprised you don't come here."

Henrietta squeezed a slice of lemon into her tea. "Other than JT's and the club, I suppose I haven't been to many of the restaurants in town." She nodded toward her crutches, leaning against the fourth chair. "I always feel self-conscious."

"Tell me about it." Maxine sniffed as she poured some sugar into her tea.

"What do you have to feel self-conscious about?" Henrietta asked.

Maxine stared at her for a moment. "You're serious."

"Well, yes. I mean, you're attractive, you're able, you're well-known in town. Everyone likes you. What is there to feel self-conscious about?"

"Henrietta," Maxine said, "what kind of reaction did you receive from the others when you and Sandy came in here?"

Henrietta thought. "I guess people glanced our way and nodded before they went back to what they were doing."

"Mmmm hmmm. And when I came in?" Maxine stirred her tea, the spoon clinking rhythmically against the glass.

Henrietta frowned. "I didn't notice. I was watching you."

Maxine paused while Maria served their food. "Well, I can tell you, every single face in here—and they're all white, by the way—every one turned to look at me. They didn't nod. Okay, a few did once they realized it was me. But their first reaction was to notice that a black person had just walked into the diner."

"That's not true," Henrietta protested, glancing around. "Is it?"

Sandy nodded. "It is. It happens all the time."

Maxine took a drink of her tea, watching Henrietta. "Have you ever been the only white person in a store or bank or restaurant?"

Henrietta thought. "No. I haven't."

"Mmmm hmmm," Maxine said again. "Most white folks haven't ever had that experience. It doesn't mean people are being hostile, but they always make you feel obvious, like you don't belong. It's immediately clear that one of these things is not like the others."

"I never thought about it," Henrietta admitted.

"Most of us don't," Sandy said. "I never did until I saw things through Maxine's eyes. When I go home with her to her neighborhood in New Orleans, I'm usually the only white person in sight. Like she said, the stares are mostly curious, but it makes you realize."

"Well, I'm usually the only person with braces and crutches."

"Which makes people sympathetic," Maxine pointed out and then quickly added, "Not that you need or want their sympathy. But it's not the same."

"I suppose not."

"How's Meryn?" Sandy asked, spooning up some of the mushroom and rice soup.

"Fine."

Maxine paused with her sandwich halfway to her mouth. "Why doesn't it sound fine?"

"I think she's just stressed with her extra teaching load this semester."

"What's she saying or doing?" Sandy asked.

"She's been talking about possibly moving. Going somewhere else," Henrietta said.

Sandy and Maxine exchanged a quick glance.

"What?" Henrietta asked.

"This is her first year at St. Aloysius, isn't it?" Maxine asked.

Henrietta nodded.

"I know several of the English faculty," Maxine said. "New faculty members are on provisional contracts for their first three years, renewable annually. Has Meryn's contract been renewed?"

Henrietta stared at her. "I don't know. She hasn't said." She frowned down at her sandwich. "Jerry Talbert doesn't like her. He may not renew."

"Maybe that's why she's been hinting at moving. She might have to search for a position elsewhere." Maxine tilted her head as she studied Henrietta. "Would you go with her?"

That's exactly why she was asking. Henrietta's stomach lurched. "I don't know. How could I leave? Everything I own, everything I know is here."

Sandy lowered her voice and leaned closer. "Maxine did that for me. I know it hasn't always been easy, being so far from family and where she grew up."

Maxine smiled tenderly. "Sometimes love leads us in unexpected directions. The path isn't always clear or easy." Her hand shifted under the table, and Henrietta knew she'd clasped Sandy's hand. "But it's always worth it."

~

RYN GAZED FONDLY AT her students, feeling kind of emotional. Turning her back on them, she pretended to be occupied erasing the notes she'd scribbled on the board. "I hope you all have a wonderful summer. I'll see you Wednesday at eight sharp for the final exam."

For a few seconds there was no sound, but then a few hands started clapping. Startled, she spun around as the rest of the class joined in on the applause.

"This was the best class I had all year," said one young woman. "Thank you, Jesse."

Another said, "I'm going to go home to Vermont and make sure I help register as many people to vote as I can. I never bothered before, but now, knowing how hard those women worked to win us that right, I'll never not vote again."

Ryn's throat tightened. "Then I can't ask for anything more."

Each student came up to shake her hand and thank her. A few of the women offered hugs. A handful of them waited for her, walking her out of the classroom and out of the building.

Waving them off, Ryn headed across the quad toward Rayburn Hall when she saw Tamara. She was walking shoulder to shoulder with another young woman—a butch-looking jock Ryn had a passing acquaintance with. When there were so few lesbians, they tended to notice and acknowledge one another. They spied Ryn. Tamara stopped and stared at her while the other woman grinned. Ryn nodded in their direction and walked on.

So, Tam has found someone else. Looks like God and the nuns lost out on this one.

She paused on the steps of Rayburn, trying to figure out why the sight of Tamara with someone else left her feeling unsettled. She didn't want a relationship with Tam. She knew that and had confirmed it that day in the chapel. So what did it matter if Tam was seeing another woman?

Is it because it's a door closed to you? taunted a voice inside her. *She was always there as a backup, and now she's not?*

Ryn had to grudgingly admit that was a possibility. And, she also had to admit, everything here—her job, her life with Henrietta—it felt as if some cosmic hand was tossing it all around like dice in a cup. And all she could do was wait to see where the dice landed.

The door of the building opened, and Jerry Talbert rushed through, a manila folder tucked under his arm as he shook a cigarette out of a pack. He stopped short at the sight of her.

"Professor." His voice was cool. He flicked his lighter and took a deep drag.

"Dr. Talbert." Ryn kept her voice as cool and even as his. Forget the cosmic hand. The only one screwing around with her future was this jerk.

She walked by him and up the stairs. "Bev," she started to say, rounding into the department office, but Beverly wasn't at her desk.

Grumbling to herself, Ryn went to her office and dropped into her chair. Only then did she notice the envelope lying on her desk. It was heavy stock, embossed with St. Aloysius's seal in the upper left-hand corner and her name, Professor Meryn Fleming, typed across the front. A little note lay beside it.

I hope this is good news, it said in Beverly's perfect handwriting.

She picked the envelope up, her heart pounding. The flap was securely sealed. She started to slip a finger under it, but stopped. Whatever this held, it didn't affect just her.

She emptied her backpack of class notes—probably the last time she'd be teaching the women-and-history course here at this college—and repacked it with a few things she'd need to review for tomorrow. And the letter.

She meant to savor the walk through the village. She meant to notice each moment she had left here, not knowing how many more there might be. But her mind was racing, wondering what that letter said and, before she realized it, she was turning into the driveway. She paused to give Nelly a pat.

"We haven't been anywhere lately. Maybe a drive this weekend."

She imagined the little wagon shivered in anticipation.

Hesitating outside the front door, she tried to prepare herself. Aside from their one conversation at the pond, when Ryn had suggested moving and Henrietta had shot the idea down, they hadn't broached the topic. She had a feeling things were going to be decided, one way or the other, by the contents of that envelope. Her stomach sank at the thought that she might soon be packing to leave. Separating from Ashley had been hard, but they'd both known that day was coming. This felt as if it were ripping her in two. She closed her eyes for a second and unlocked the door.

To her surprise, Henrietta was sitting on the sofa, apparently waiting for her.

"Thought you'd be painting," Ryn said as she lowered her backpack.

"Not today."

327

Ryn sat in her usual chair. "Are you okay?"

"I'm fine."

Only Henrietta didn't look fine. She looked tired, with dark circles under her eyes as she fidgeted, her fingers plucking at bits of lint on the sofa cushion.

"What's wrong, Henrietta?"

Henrietta carefully avoided Ryn's eyes. "I've been thinking..."

Ryn braced herself.

"I called a realtor I know and explained that I might be leaving Bluemont, at least for a while."

Ryn was certain she'd misheard. "Wait. Where are you going?"

Henrietta looked up at that, her face blanching. "You talked about leaving, about going somewhere else. But, if you don't—"

Her voice caught.

Ryn perched on the edge of her chair. "You would do that? You would go with me?"

Henrietta nodded stiffly. "He recommended I close the house up, perhaps rent it rather than sell it. In case..."

Ryn bent down to her backpack, giving herself a minute to get her emotions under control. Pulling the envelope out of her pack, she moved to sit beside Henrietta.

"This was waiting for me today."

"What is it?" Henrietta asked.

"I'm guessing this will tell me whether I have a job at St. Aloysius next year."

They both stared at the envelope lying in Ryn's hands.

"You didn't open it?"

Ryn shook her head. "This affects both of us. I thought we should find out together what it says. But before we do," she reached for Henrietta's hand. "I just want you to know how much it means to me that you would even consider going with me if I had to leave to find work."

With obvious effort, Henrietta forced herself to meet Ryn's eyes. "I can't imagine—I don't want to imagine—my life here without you."

Ryn raised Henrietta's hand to her lips. "Shall we?"

Henrietta nodded.

Ryn pried the flap loose and slid out the folded paper inside. Typed on the same heavy stock as the envelope, the words blurred as she read them.

"They're offering another year," she whispered.

She handed the letter to Henrietta, who read aloud, "Based upon your students' excellent feedback and positive evaluations from colleagues, we are pleased to extend your contract through the 1984/85 academic year, subject to the same provisions as your original contract."

Ryn collapsed back on the sofa. "I don't know if I can survive two more years of this."

The letter fluttered in Henrietta's trembling hand. "I know what you mean."

Ryn eyed her. "You didn't have anything to do with this, did you?"

"No." But Henrietta didn't look at her as she answered.

"I have a feeling you're only telling me part of the truth."

Henrietta's mouth twitched. "Let's just say I helped convince Leonard Croson to clear the path for you. You did everything else yourself."

"I knew it!" Ryn punched the air. "You did do something."

"All I did," Henrietta said, seeming to carefully choose her words, "was to let Father Croson know how devastating it would be for the college if word somehow got out about that poor girl and her situation with your colleague."

"Vanessa. I hope she's okay." Ryn reached for Henrietta's hand again. "Thank you, Henrietta. For believing in me. For being willing to leave this village if we had to."

Henrietta searched her eyes. "I told you. I don't want to think about living here without you."

329

Ryn wrapped her arms around Henrietta and pulled her close. Resting her cheek against Henrietta's head, Ryn's hands gently caressed her thin shoulders. She felt Henrietta melt into her.

"Meryn?"

"Hmmm?"

"I think we should celebrate." Henrietta pulled away. "Call the nuns. Call Sandy and Maxine."

"Pizza and s'mores?" Ryn said excitedly. "Down at the pond?"

Henrietta frowned. "What's a s'more?"

SPARKS FLEW INTO THE night sky when Roberta tossed another log onto the fire. Ryn sat beside the fire pit, roasting a couple more marshmallows for Henrietta, who had discovered she loved s'mores.

"What's up after finals?" she asked Roberta.

"Back to the motherhouse for us. We're all scheduled for retreats in June. But we'll be back in August."

"This village won't feel the same without you guys." Ryn blew out a marshmallow that caught fire.

"What about you? Here all summer?"

"I'm going to go home for a couple of weeks after I turn in grades." Ryn glanced toward Henrietta, who was engaged in conversation with Sandy and Stephanie. "I tried to talk Henrietta into going with me, but she doesn't want to intrude."

"You worried about leaving her alone?"

"Yeah. She's been a little off lately. More tired. I hate to leave her, but I haven't seen my family since Christmas."

"We won't be going right away. We can check in on her."

Ryn pulled the charred marshmallows off the stick and tucked them in between two graham crackers. "That would be great, thanks."

She delivered the treat to Henrietta. "I'm cutting you off at five, Hank."

At the smile on Henrietta's face, Ryn's heart felt as melted as the square of chocolate.

Sandy chuckled. "This was such a nice gathering. And what a great reason to celebrate."

"To Ryn," Franny said, holding up a Coke.

"To Ryn," echoed the others, raising drinks or marshmallows or whatever was at hand.

Ryn's throat tightened. She lifted her own Dr. Pepper, her eyes locked on Henrietta. "To friends and home."

Chapter 22

MUFFLED VOICES FILTERED THROUGH the bedroom door. Henrietta sat on the side of the bed, huffing as she fastened the straps of her leg braces. The young nuns hadn't just checked in on her, they'd been rotating nights, sleeping in the spare bed in Meryn's room.

Though Henrietta had protested that it wasn't necessary, they'd insisted. The argument had been settled when Meryn took her hand before she left for Pennsylvania.

"Please, Henrietta. For me. It'll be so much easier to be away if I know you're not alone at night."

She closed her eyes now, whispering a prayer of thanks for Meryn and her friends. Again, she was reminded how much richer her life was now. Every now and then, that old, familiar negative side of her broke through, taunting her that this wouldn't last, that Meryn would leave, that these new friends would disappear. Sometimes, it was terrifying, letting herself feel so much.

"Stop," she said. "She's coming back. She won't leave you."

She finished getting dressed and emerged from her room to find Franny in the kitchen, talking to Bonnie.

"Well, good morning, Henrietta," Bonnie said, pouring a cup of coffee for her and setting it on the table.

Franny poured milk into a bowl of cereal and joined her. "Sleep well?"

"Yes." Henrietta reached for a slice of toast. "You really don't have to do this."

Franny shrugged. "We don't mind. Your house is much nicer than ours. And quieter."

"Well, I think it's very nice of these young women to stay here," Bonnie offered. "Saves me the worry of wondering if you're all right through the nights."

"I've survived by myself before," Henrietta reminded her.

"Hmmph." Bonnie shook her head. "Need I remind you that you barely slept during those times in between companions."

She narrowed her eyes and peered harder at Henrietta. "Speaking of which, you look awfully tired for just waking up."

"I'm fine," Henrietta said firmly. But she knew better than to think Bonnie would let it go.

"Have you heard from Meryn?" Bonnie asked.

"Yes, she called to say she got home to Pennsylvania safely. It'll be good for her to have a nice long visit with her family." Henrietta spread jam on her toast, trying to feel as positive as she sounded.

Franny finished her corn flakes. "Do you need any help here today, Bonnie?"

"No, dear, but thank you. You run on."

"How about you, Henrietta? Need anything from the village?"

"No," Henrietta said. "I have an appointment in town, but I can't think of anything we need."

Franny took her bowl and coffee cup to the sink and washed them. "Steph will be with you this evening."

"You really don't have—"

"We promised Ryn."

She met Henrietta's gaze in such a frank way that Henrietta felt herself blush. She gave Henrietta's shoulder a squeeze. "You know she'd never forgive herself if anything happened to you while she was gone."

Franny went to get her overnight bag and then said good-bye. "Just call us if you need anything. We'll all see you at church on Sunday."

The warmth in Henrietta's face spread all through her. It had been ages since she'd been so cared for, not since she lost her parents.

"Such nice girls," Bonnie said. "I'm going to change your bed sheets."

"Thank you," Henrietta said. "I'll be back in an hour or so."

She pushed heavily to her feet and went to the garage. She had to sit for a few minutes in the car, waiting for her breathing to slow and her hands to feel steadier on the controls.

Downtown, she turned off Main Street, drove two blocks down Elm and pulled into Dr. McCourt's parking lot behind the gray three-story Victorian that served as both residence and office. Inside, the nurse was waiting for her.

"Come right in, Miss Cochran."

She took Henrietta's vitals and jotted them down. "Dr. McCourt will be with you in just a moment."

Henrietta sat nervously, suddenly feeling foolish for making this appointment. There was nothing wrong with her. She was just pushing to her feet when the door opened.

"Ah ha," Gordon McCourt said, smiling. "I had a feeling you might be planning your escape. Sit back down, Henrietta."

She lowered herself to the chair again, scowling at him. "What gave you that feeling?"

He laughed and pulled a rolling stool over. "Because I know you. You never come to see me as soon as something's wrong. You always wait until even you can't ignore it. So—"

He stopped abruptly, looking not at her face but at the rest of her.

"You look lovely, Henrietta. It's nice to see you in bright colors." He got back to business. "So, if you're here, something is up. Tell me. Still having chest pains?"

"No." She hesitated. It all seemed so silly now. "I've just not felt well."

"In what way?"

"I've been more tired, short of breath, weak feeling. I..." She paused again. "I fell the other day. In my studio. But I'd been working and forgot to eat, so I'm blaming it on that."

"Hmmm." He reached for his stethoscope and listened to her heart and lungs. He asked her to grip his fingers and push and pull against his resistance. With her legs, he asked her to hold while he pushed on her.

He did all this without speaking, turning to jot notes on a pad of paper.

"Well?" Henrietta asked impatiently.

But he pushed a button on his desk. The nurse appeared almost instantly.

"Yes, doctor?"

"I'd like to do blood work, Tina."

She left and returned in a few seconds with a needle and several vials. Henrietta rolled up her sleeve with a resigned sigh.

When the samples had been drawn, the nurse left them again.

"Gordon, stop stalling and tell me what's wrong."

"Henrietta, if I knew what was wrong, I wouldn't need to do blood work."

"You're not fooling me. I know you suspect something."

He shifted from the stool to the desk chair and sat back, crossing his legs. "I can't be certain, but the literature is beginning to document a phenomenon that we don't fully understand."

Henrietta frowned. "What kind of phenomenon?"

"Those of you who survived the worst years of the polio epidemic are all now approaching the same timeframe of having lived with the effects. About forty years, give or take."

"It will be forty years for me next year," Henrietta said. "So what?"

He leaned forward, bracing his elbows on his knees and staring at his folded hands. "It doesn't seem to be dependent on age so much as that post-polio timeframe. A new or renewed onset of weakness." He cleared his throat. "Almost as if it's coming back."

Henrietta blanched and gripped the arms of the chair. "Coming back." Her voice was barely audible.

"Not completely," he said quickly, reaching out to lay a hand on hers. "We haven't seen anyone get to the point of having to be on a ventilator, not like the first time. But there have been too many of these cases to dismiss it as coincidence. They're calling it post-polio syndrome, for want of a better term."

Henrietta forced herself to meet his gaze. "And what's the prognosis? How far does this syndrome progress?"

He sat back again. "We simply don't know. You're all hitting this stage at about the same time. We don't have enough data to go on."

"So, this... this weakness could get worse?"

"Yes," he admitted reluctantly. "Or it could arrest and stay right where it is. We just don't know."

"So the bloodwork...?"

"Just a precaution, to make certain I'm not missing something else."

Henrietta brushed her sweaty palms on her slacks. "Is there any treatment, if it is this post-polio thing?"

He shook his head. "Not that we know of. We could get you back into physical therapy to try and strengthen your muscles."

Henrietta reached for her crutches. "I'll think about it."

"Henrietta—"

"Thank you, Gordon." Henrietta stood. "Let me know when you get the blood work results."

He opened his mouth but seemed to think better of whatever he'd been about to say. He got the door for her. "I'll be in touch."

She remembered nothing of the drive home. Bonnie greeted her when she came into the kitchen from the garage.

"I was just going to make tuna salad for lunch. Are you—" Bonnie stopped when she saw Henrietta's face. "What's wrong?"

"Nothing." Henrietta walked through the kitchen. "I'm not hungry. I think I'll lie down for a bit."

Alone in her room, Henrietta lay, staring at the ceiling. Her chin quivered, but she clenched her jaw, determined not to give in to the emotions roiling inside her. It was so damned unfair. She'd beaten it once. She shouldn't have to do it again.

Maybe Una was the lucky one, after all.

~

INCHING OUT ALONG A stout tree branch, Ryn secured a new bird-feeder. "This good?"

Walt shaded his eyes with one hand. "Lower it a little."

She fed out a little more chain.

"That's about right," he said, reaching up to test that he could refill it.

She fastened the chain and shimmied over the side of the bough, hanging for a second before dropping lightly to the ground. "That the last one?"

Her dad grinned at her. "For now."

She shook her head. "You do know you're also feeding every squirrel in the neighborhood."

"Don't tell your mom." He draped an arm around her shoulders as they walked back to the garage.

"I'm pretty sure she knows."

He gave her a squeeze before veering off to lie in his hammock and enjoy watching the birds—and squirrels—check out the offerings in the new feeder.

Ryn went into the house, pausing to wash her hands in the laundry room. She found her mom in the den, reading in the recliner, where she had a full view of the backyard and the tree Ryn had just been in.

"A new feeder?"

Ryn kept a straight face. "I'm sworn to secrecy."

June shook her head. "That man. He'll never be able to retire at this rate. We'll never be empty nesters."

"A different kind of nest," Ryn said, flopping onto the couch.

"But almost as expensive." June watched him for a moment with a rueful smile.

Ryn bit her lip as she studied her mom. "I got my new contract for next year."

June turned to her. "They'd be foolish not to want to keep you. The other situation, the girl your colleague got in trouble, has that resolved itself?"

"Yeah." It seemed a lifetime ago that she'd spilled her guts to her mom about Vanessa's situation. "He left. No idea where he went, but I'm so glad he's gone."

"And you want to stay?"

"Yeah. It's a small college, but I've made some good friends there. I think I could make Bluemont home."

June's face darkened. "Are you going to look for a house or apartment of your own?"

Oh, crap.

"Nooo," Ryn drew the word out. "I'll stay with Henrietta."

June took her glasses off and closed her book, shifting in the recliner. Ryn read the signals that a talk was coming and sat up.

"Henrietta is a very nice woman," June said, "but don't you think maybe you should have your own place?"

Ryn stared at her hands. "I thought you liked Henrietta."

"We do. And it was one thing when you only needed a room. It's just that, you're kind of tied down while you're with her, aren't you? You can't take off with friends to go to New York City or anything."

"I don't want to go to New York. And if I did, I'd go with Henrietta."

She could feel the weight of her mother's gaze. "But what if you meet someone?"

339

Ryn took a deep breath and forced herself to meet June's eyes. "I have met someone, Mom. I met Henrietta. And I want to spend the rest of my life with her."

A flush suffused June's cheeks. "Ryn, I've always known you were gay. We understood when you brought Ashley home with you. And I know it was hard on you when the two of you went in different directions. But I hoped you'd meet someone your own age. Henrietta is... she's older than your father and I are!"

"So what?"

"It's not just her age." June paused, obviously trying to remain calm. "Her health issues are a real concern."

"They weren't a concern when she hosted all of us for Thanksgiving," Ryn said.

"Henrietta is a perfectly nice woman, and I meant it when I said she was part of the family," June said, enunciating each word. "I didn't mean as your lover!"

"We're not—" Ryn felt the burn in her own cheeks. "It's not like that. That part is no one else's business. Not even yours, Mom."

June pinched the bridge of her nose. "You're going to be tied down. By Henrietta's handicap. By her age. By the health problems she will no doubt have." She sighed and met Ryn's eyes. "She gets a nurse and you get, what?"

A curious ringing filled Ryn's ears.

"Ryn, honey, I'm sorry." June's eyes filled. "I'm just worried about you. I don't want you to be saddled with—"

Ryn found herself on her feet. "I'm going for a walk."

She heard her mom's voice calling to her, but she almost ran for the front door. The sun was harsh and glaring, giving her an excuse to bow her head when a few of the neighbors called to her. She walked aimlessly, with no destination, and found herself at a park. A few mothers with young children were in the playground area.

She veered away from them, making for the covered bandstand. On

Saturday evenings in the summer, local bands played free concerts, but now, on a Wednesday, it was empty.

Pacing around and around the circumference, she ran her fingers along the wooden railing, trying to calm her racing heart.

"You should have known..." she muttered aloud. "Just because our friends in Bluemont are happy for us..."

She hadn't expected her mom to be happy, exactly. She slowed.

"I didn't mean as your lover!"

Ryn groaned and dropped cross-legged onto the wooden floor, leaning against a round pillar. That's what everyone would be secretly thinking and wondering about if they learned what she and Henrietta were to each other. She couldn't blame her mom for worrying, but she sure as hell didn't want to discuss her non-existent sex life with her mother.

If she were really honest, she knew she'd be wondering the same thing if it were someone else in her situation. She'd never have believed she could love a woman this much, in a way that didn't have to be sexual. Didn't mean there hadn't been occasional urges, but those were easily taken care of. Just being with Henrietta was enough most of the time.

But will it always be that way?

She longed to talk to Henrietta, but she couldn't call from home and leave her parents to see the call on their bill. And she didn't feel she could call collect, though she didn't imagine Henrietta would mind.

Another week of this. She'd hardly seen the twins, but their basketball camp was due to end this week, and then they were all supposed to go to Kennywood on Saturday. She'd promised Janie they could partner up for the rollercoasters.

She pushed to her feet. On the way home, she'd reminded herself she hadn't seen her family for almost six months. One more week wouldn't hurt anything.

～

GORDON MCCOURT SAT AT his desk, staring out the window, his hands tented while his index fingers tapped against his lips. In front of him sat the paper with Henrietta Cochran's lab results. The clinic was closed for the evening, and a large stack of charts awaited his notations, but he stood and stretched.

"Tina, I'm going out to see a patient. I'll see you tomorrow."

Startled, Tina immediately began sifting through the messages littering her desk. "But who—"

"I need to speak with Miss Cochran."

Tina stopped her frantic search. "Oh."

He nodded and went out the clinic's back door to the old carriage house now serving as his garage. Within a few minutes, he pulled into Henrietta's driveway, noting that the other car wasn't there. What was that young woman's name? Something unusual.

It took a long time for Henrietta to answer his ring of the bell, but he waited patiently, watching the golfers across the road. Everyone told him he should take the game up. Of course, they also told him he should have a wife. It seemed there was never enough time. Maybe when he retired. For the golf, anyhow.

When Henrietta opened the door, she didn't appear to be surprised to see him. She walked into the living room, leaving him to come in on his own.

She was, he noticed, wearing one of her old, familiar outfits, a dark blouse and skirt. Durable, sensible. And utterly unlike the bold colors she'd been wearing when she'd come to the office. He could almost see her retreating again into her shell.

Henrietta paused on her way to the sofa. "Would you like some coffee? Or something to eat?"

He glanced at his watch and was surprised to see that it was past six o'clock. He frequently worked through what was dinnertime for most people before going upstairs to his living quarters above the clinic to make himself something.

"Have you eaten? How about I whip up some eggs and bacon."

She glanced at him. "Bacon? I thought doctors were opposed to bacon."

He grinned and rolled up his shirtsleeves. "Don't tell anyone."

He was, of necessity, handy in the kitchen. A man living alone had two choices: spend a lot of money eating out, or learn to cook.

Within a few minutes, he served Henrietta a cup of coffee and a plate with two eggs, bacon, and toast.

"How has no woman snatched you up before this?" Henrietta asked, nibbling on a crispy piece of bacon.

He chuckled. "There have been a lot of ill-guided attempts, believe me."

They ate, talking about a variety of topics. He asked about Henrietta's art, and she told him about the upcoming show in Albany. They discussed the likelihood that Gary Hart would get the Democratic nomination over Walter Mondale—"I can imagine that Democratic sign in your yard drives the country club folks mad," he observed—but that, sadly, neither was likely to defeat Reagan.

When they were done eating, and Henrietta sat with her coffee cup cradled in her hands, she said, "This has been delightful, Gordon, but are you going to tell me why you're really here?"

"I've always admired your directness, Henrietta. The way you face things head-on."

"What am I facing this time?"

He sighed. "Nothing. That's the problem. Your blood work came back completely normal. No anemia. No elevated white count. Nothing that would account for what you've been experiencing."

She nodded. "In other words, nothing that's treatable. I suspected as much."

He reached across the table and took her hand. "I'm sorry. I wish this was something I could take care of with a transfusion or prescription."

Releasing her hand, he asked, "Are you living alone?"

"No. Meryn went home to visit her family in Pennsylvania. Some of her friends from the college have been staying with me at night. I'm expecting one of them later this evening."

"But she is coming back. Meryn?"

He tried to make out what was going on in her mind as he watched her face. This was beyond his role as her doctor, beyond even the bounds of professional ethics, but to hell with boundaries. "Henrietta." This time he clasped both of her hands. "Don't let this post-polio diagnosis close you off. Don't let it rob you of the happiness you've found. This girl has been so good for you."

He longed to say more, but stopped himself. Scooping up the dishes, he carried them to the sink.

"You don't have to—"

"It'll only take a minute."

When the dishes were clean, he turned to her again. "Thanks for dinner. And the company."

"You cooked."

"You gave me someone to have a conversation with."

She followed him to the front door. He hesitated again before bending to kiss her cheek.

"Good night, Henrietta."

He got in his car, watching her silhouetted behind the storm door. Until he felt brave enough to have an actual relationship, not just meeting men in the city, he had no right to lecture Henrietta.

Chapter 23

UNLIKE AFTER HER LAST trip home for Christmas, when Ryn had followed a hunch and stopped at Mrs. Middleston's boarding house to find Vanessa's mother packing her room, this time she was determined to go straight to Henrietta's. This separation had been much harder. The long expanses of highway stretched on forever.

The conflict with her mother hadn't helped. Ryn had never had a real argument with her parents. She'd never gotten into trouble as a kid. *Maybe I should have,* she thought as she drove. *Might have prepared both of us.*

Even the revelation that Henrietta had interceded with the college on her behalf hadn't swayed her mom much, though she'd grudgingly admitted it was nice of Henrietta to have done that.

The music that usually soothed Ryn couldn't calm her frazzled nerves as she drove. She kept breaking into muttered arguments while the Alan Parsons Project warbled through the speakers.

"She'll come around," she insisted over and over. "When Mom sees how happy Henrietta and I are together, she'll learn to be okay with this."

It seemed naïve now to believe that, after finding such easy acceptance from Sandy and Maxine, and from Franny and Roberta and Steph, it would be like that with everyone.

"It's her job to be protective of you," Ryn reminded herself. "She's your mother."

But, damn, it was hard, knowing her mom disapproved of something that made her so happy.

When she pulled into the driveway, she threw Nelly into park and ran to the house without even pausing to grab her duffle bag.

"Henrietta!" The living room was empty, the house quiet. Ryn hurried to the studio, but it, too, was empty.

Deflated, she checked the garage. The Chrysler was gone.

"But I told her when I'd be back."

She yanked the back door open and went to collect her things from her car. She unpacked and started a load of laundry. The afternoon turned into evening. She made herself a peanut butter and jelly sandwich and tried to read, but she kept finding herself staring out the picture window, wondering where on earth Henrietta was.

Finally, too impatient and worried to wait any longer, she reached for the phone.

"Roberta? Hi, it's Ryn."

"Hi! How was your visit home?"

"It was... okay. Hey, I'm back, but there's no sign of Henrietta. Do you guys know where she is?"

"Not specifically. She did say something to Steph about cards with some friends tonight. But I don't know where."

Ryn's nerves gave a warning jangle. "Everything go okay while I was gone?"

"Yeah." Roberta hesitated. "Well, it was a little strange."

"What?"

"About a week ago, she suddenly got real quiet. And she went back to wearing the dark clothes she used to wear, you know, the conservative skirts and hose. Not the bright colors she'd been in recently. We all noticed. Don't know what that's about."

"Okay. Thanks so much to all of you for keeping an eye on her. When do you leave for the motherhouse?"

"This weekend. Will we see you before that?"

"I hope so. I'll try to come over tomorrow. Bye."

Ryn hung up. Cards? That made no sense. The only people Henrietta ever played cards with were those women from the country club.

Unless she's regretting giving up her friends from the club. She's known them for years. And me for less than one, Ryn reminded herself.

It was easy to forget that. Sometimes, she felt she'd known Henrietta forever.

It was well after dark when Ryn saw the sweep of the station wagon's headlights and heard the rumble of the garage door as it opened. Ryn jumped up and opened the door to the garage before Henrietta could get there.

Henrietta stopped and stared at her. Ryn tried to read her eyes, but saw only a blank expression. If Roberta hadn't warned her, the sight of Henrietta in her staid, conservative skirt and blouse would have been a shock.

"When did you get back?" Henrietta asked, pressing the garage door button on the wall and stepping inside.

"When I said I would," Ryn said sullenly. "About four o'clock. Thought you'd be here."

"I'm sorry. Mary Ellen Greene called and asked if I could join a bridge party she was hosting at her house. I haven't seen my old friends in a while, so I said yes. Have you eaten?"

"Yeah. Made a sandwich. Do you want anything?"

"No." Henrietta led the way through the kitchen. "I ate at Mary Ellen's."

Henrietta paused. "I'm glad you got your trip over safely. Bonnie washed your sheets on Wednesday, so your bed is freshly made. Good night."

Ryn stood, watching in disbelief as Henrietta turned toward her room. A moment later, the door closed. Henrietta didn't slam it, but she might as well have. All the anticipation, all of the excitement Ryn had felt at getting back here, back to Henrietta—it burned like acid in her stomach now.

Moving like an automaton, Ryn clicked off the living room lamp and checked the front door. She took a quick shower and brushed her teeth. In her room, she lay in the dark, trying not to give in to the tears that welled up in her eyes. This was like some horrible movie, where Henrietta—the laughing, loving, approachable version—had been replaced by some replica, a likeness that was cold and indifferent.

"What happened?" Ryn whispered in the dark.

~

HENRIETTA SAT IN HER studio, watching Meryn down at the landing near the pond, playing her guitar. Her heart felt pinched and empty, where for a blessed little while, it had been full to bursting.

It's the right thing to do, insisted a nagging voice in her head.

But it didn't feel right. Not when she saw the hurt in the girl's eyes. Hurt Henrietta knew she'd caused.

She'd been so looking forward to the summer, to having Meryn free from her classes so that they could travel—back to Owasco Lake or the other Finger Lakes. The show in Albany was due to open in two weeks, and she'd tentatively planned for them to spend a few days there, enjoying the opening and touring the city.

But the house echoed with a cold silence. Henrietta had offered no explanation, and Meryn didn't know what to say. The girl's eyes spoke volumes—unlike Henrietta, she had no skill at hiding her emotions. Everything she felt was right there.

What if she leaves? asked that voice.

It might be better if she did, she replied.

Henrietta knew her own heart would never recover, but Meryn was young. Hers would. And she deserved a whole life, not a half-life tied to... *to someone like me.*

Where Henrietta had once dared to hope that she and Meryn could be happy together, even given the age difference and Henrietta's physical restrictions, that calculation had changed. She'd fooled herself into thinking they could get beyond those barriers, but if her health was going to deteriorate further, she could not, would not, burden the girl with being her nurse.

Resolutely, she turned back to her canvas, but scowled at the painting. It was horrible. Stiff, stilted. *Just like me.*

Giving up, she cleaned her brushes and went to the kitchen. Scribbling a quick note that she was running some errands, she went to the garage.

A few minutes later, she had parked at the library and made her way inside.

"Henrietta," said Maxine from behind the front desk. Her dark eyes swept up and down, but she said nothing about Henrietta's appearance. "How nice to see you. Looking for a summer read?"

"Actually, I needed to do some research." Henrietta looked around. "But I don't really know where to start."

"We can help you with that." Maxine set down the books she'd been holding. She led Henrietta to the reference section. "What's the general category?"

"Medical."

Maxine paused and glanced sharply at Henrietta before leading her around the corner to a desk lined with a row of books. "Then you'll need this set of references. Make a list of any pertinent articles, and we'll see if we have them. If not, we can probably get them through an inter-library loan."

Henrietta felt like a heel, not acknowledging Maxine in a friendlier manner. "Thank you."

Maxine must have read her hesitation. "I wish I could stay to help, but I've got a meeting. I'll send Sherry over in a few minutes to see if you need any assistance."

Maxine left her. Henrietta and Sherry spent the next two hours looking up everything they could find on post-polio syndrome. There wasn't much. The few articles there were seemed to be based on case studies, not actual research. And, just as Gordon McCourt had said, they offered no predictive data on what she could expect.

"I hope your search was productive," Maxine said as Henrietta waited for Sherry to make some copies for her.

"Sherry was helpful," Henrietta said noncommittally.

"Would you and Meryn be available for dinner this week?"

"No." Henrietta realized how sharply that had burst out. "No, we're... I'm busy. But thank you."

Sherry brought the copies, and Henrietta handed over a few dollars for the copying fee.

"Thank you for your help," she said. "Good-bye, Maxine."

In the car, she closed her eyes. *You were so rude.* But it was the same as Meryn, wasn't it? They all needed to be pushed firmly away. If she was indeed going to be dealing with the effects of this syndrome, she would do it her way, with things under her strict control. It was how she'd always managed. This... this circle of people who had worked their way inside those defenses, this was what weakened her.

I will not be weak.

THE SUN WAS FULLY up, slanting through the crack between the curtains, when Ryn opened her eyes. For the last few nights, she'd been staying up late reading, and then sleeping in later in the mornings. It was easier this way. Henrietta would have already had her breakfast and gone to her studio.

For the first week after she got back, Ryn had kept to her usual schedule of getting up early, making breakfast for both of them, trying to engage Henrietta in conversation, but it was like pulling teeth. For the life of her, she couldn't figure out what had changed.

"Are you feeling okay?" she'd asked.

"I'm fine," Henrietta had snapped. "Why do you keep asking me that?"

It was like their early days together, when it had felt like walking on eggshells to be around Henrietta.

But Ryn had seen her—when she was down at the pond or out in the yard refilling the birdfeeders—she'd seen Henrietta standing at the windows, watching her.

It made no sense.

She was trapped. She couldn't go back home to Pennsylvania, not with the way things had been left with her mom. And she didn't want to go, not now that Franny and the others had left for the summer. It would have meant leaving Henrietta alone at night and, no matter what else was—*or wasn't*—happening between the two of them, Ryn still felt protective and responsible.

So, she spent some time on campus, preparing her fall courses and catching up with Beverly, who told her she still hadn't heard which of the candidates had been hired. She tried to question Beverly on whether her sister had said anything about Henrietta.

"No," Beverly said. "Bonnie and I spoke just yesterday, and she didn't say anything. Why? Is there a problem?"

"No." Clearly, there was, only Ryn couldn't articulate what.

The evenings were no better. Dinners were mostly silent. Henrietta spoke stiltedly of the upcoming art show in Albany, but she sounded as if she no longer wanted to go. After four attempts to get Henrietta down to the pond or out for an evening walk, all of which Henrietta declined, Ryn began retreating to her room after the dinner dishes were done. She played her guitar or read or just listened to music.

351

And she thought, replaying those last days before she'd left, trying to figure out where things had gone so horribly wrong. She couldn't find anything that could explain this.

She'd even peered into Henrietta's room, hoping to see some clue that would explain the change in her demeanor. The only thing that stood out was that the photo of Henrietta and Una was missing. Ryn strongly suspected it had been tucked away again into one of the dresser drawers.

Finally, in desperation, she cobbled together all the loose change she could find and walked into the village, looking for a phone booth. She wanted the kind that had a door that closed so she could speak freely without being overheard.

Overhead, heavy clouds moved in from the west. She hoped she could accomplish her mission and get back before it rained.

From her pocket, she pulled a piece of paper with the number to the nuns' motherhouse. Franny had told her to call if she needed anything. Ryn whispered a quick prayer that Franny would be available on a Saturday afternoon.

She dialed the number and deposited the required number of quarters into the slot. When a woman answered, Ryn asked for Francine Mabry and waited for what seemed like forever. She shifted inside the hot, smelly booth while the seconds ticked away. She nervously flipped the metal cover over the returned change slot as she waited.

"Ryn?" came Franny's voice at last.

Before Ryn could say anything, the operator cut in. "Please deposit four quarters for three more minutes."

Ryn quickly jammed the quarters into the phone. "Franny, I don't have much time. Henrietta is completely weird. Back in her old clothes. Won't talk to me. Hardly interacts at all. Do you know what's wrong?"

"No, but something happened that last week we stayed with her."

352

"What?" Ryn pounded a fist against the glass wall of the booth, startling a small dog on a leash just outside so that it yapped angrily.

"I don't know. But we all noticed it." Franny paused. "It changed sometime between my last two nights with her. One day, she was fine, talking and laughing. I think she had an appointment that day when I left. The next time I stayed, she was like she is now. I asked Roberta if she noticed it. She said she did, but none of us knows why."

Ryn flipped the piece of paper over and tugged a pen from her pocket. "When were your last two nights? Do you remember?"

Franny had to think for a few seconds. "Tuesday was my second to last night. I remember because Bonnie was there the next morning."

"Okay, thanks."

"Ryn, don't give up. Remember what I said to you that day. Real love isn't easy. Fight for it."

"I will. Thanks, Franny."

"See you in August."

Ryn hung up and stood there a moment. When she opened the door and stepped outside, she took a deep breath of fresh air.

With her determination renewed, she walked home, where an unfamiliar Chevy was parked in the drive. Just as she approached the front door, it opened unexpectedly and a paunchy, middle-aged man stepped out.

"We hope to see you soon, Miss Cochran."

He nodded in Ryn's direction and got in the Chevy.

"Who was that?" she asked when she stepped inside.

"Tom Bartlett, the manager of the country club," Henrietta said, moving to the couch. "He came to invite me to return."

"To return." Ryn tried not to sound judgmental. "I thought you said you'd realized how biased the club is, and you didn't want to be part of that."

Henrietta carefully avoided looking at her. "I've missed my friends from the club."

"You said they weren't really friends."

"Why are you cross-examining me?" Henrietta asked sharply.

Ryn's patience snapped. "Why are you acting like this?"

"Like what, exactly?"

The icy tone of Henrietta's voice should have been a warning, but Ryn didn't care.

"Like... like you used to." Ryn moved to sit beside her. "All closed up and hard. Hank—"

"My name is Henrietta."

Ryn stood. She felt as if Henrietta had slapped her. When she was able to speak, it was only a whisper. "You said you loved me."

"Yes, well..." Again, Henrietta wouldn't meet her eyes. "I expect I was just caught up, what with spending time with Maxine and Sandy. The idea of... it's preposterous."

Ryn backed up a step. Blindly, she yanked the door open and strode outside, where a light rain had begun to fall. Retracing her steps, she stalked off down the road, not knowing or caring where she was going. She just needed to be away from the house, away from Henrietta.

By the time she got to the village, the light rain had become a steady downpour. Water dripped from her hair, running in steady rivulets down her face and inside the collar of her T-shirt. Her Converse squished with each step. The tears on her face mixed with the rain, and she felt as if her entire body had filled up with tears that brimmed over when they reached the level of her eyes. It was bottomless.

She had no idea what path she took, but she found herself on campus. Only a few office lights glowed through the gloom, and the quad was deserted. For a moment, she considered going to Beverly, but the thought of running into Talbert right now was too much. She couldn't let him see her this broken. Her feet turned of their own accord in the direction of the chapel.

Tentatively, she tugged on the door handle, expecting it to be locked, but it wasn't. The inside was even darker, with only two nearly burnt-out votive candles lit in a small alcove off to one side, their small flames dancing with the inrush of air when she entered. Digging into the pocket of her wet jeans, she found the leftover quarters from her phone call to Franny. She dropped a couple into the change box and tried to light a candle. Her wet hands were trembling so badly, she couldn't strike a match. After mashing three matches, she finally just held a match to one of the lit candles. It flared wildly for an instant. When she touched it to the wick of an unlit candle in the top row, it seemed the illumination grew by a factor of ten.

She knelt at the prie-dieu, tears still welling in her eyes. "Help me," she whispered. She screwed her eyes shut, remembering Henrietta's evolution—the softer hairstyle, the new clothes—all the outward signs of the changes that had been happening inside. Henrietta's hard edges had softened, too. The smiles, the warmth in her gray eyes, the ease with which Henrietta had started to touch her. All gone now.

"What happened? I don't understand."

The only sound was the tiny whicker of the candle flames in the lower votives as they flickered in their pools of melted wax.

She thought of the things Franny had said and pressed her fingers to her eyes. Was this some kind of trial? Some kind of test? To see if she was worthy?

A small puff of air, like a breath, brushed against her cheek, and the two candles guttered out, leaving only her candle burning. She looked around but no one had entered the chapel. Her candle flame blew wildly, fanned by some unseen gust and, suddenly, the wick of the candle next to it caught, burning brightly.

Side by side, those two candles burned, their flames improbably tall, dancing toward each other, blending together into one brilliant light for a moment before separating again.

Ryn gasped and stared at them. Behind her, the chapel door opened, and she nearly jumped out of her skin.

"Meryn?" came a coarse whisper.

"Here." She stood to find Maxine and Sandy standing just inside, a dripping umbrella in Sandy's hand.

"I told you I saw her," Maxine said.

"What are you doing here?" Sandy asked as they approached her. "You're soaking wet."

"And crying," Maxine added, staring intently at Ryn's face.

"What's wrong?" Sandy laid a concerned hand on her shoulder.

Ryn opened her mouth, but the tears started up again, and she couldn't speak.

Sandy wrapped her arm around Ryn's shoulders. "Come home with us."

∽

THE GLOOMY AFTERNOON TURNED into a gloomier evening and then night, and still there was no sign of Meryn. Henrietta kept walking to the front door, stepping out onto the covered porch to stare at the steady sheet of rain falling outside.

You practically pushed her out the door, she reminded herself. *What did you expect?*

She was too ashamed to answer her own question. She wanted the girl not to be tied to her, but what, exactly, did that mean? Maybe she wouldn't be content to stay here after Henrietta unilaterally changed the terms of their relationship.

"We don't have a relationship," she muttered aloud.

But we do, insisted another side of her, the gentler, kinder side that had only emerged with Meryn's presence in her life.

She felt as if she were two people stuffed into one body.

She tried to convince herself to eat something, but her stomach turned at the thought. She sat on the sofa, clicking endlessly through the channels, unable to settle on anything.

Gazing around the living room, she forced herself to remember what it was like, nearly a year ago, when Amanda left and she was without a companion. That interval had been hell, she recalled.

"But that's no reason to keep the girl imprisoned here!"

As she said it, she realized that that conflict summed up the entire problem. She could admit—to herself—how much she loved Meryn, but because she loved her so much, she couldn't keep her trapped here. No matter how much she needed someone to be here, it wasn't fair. It was time. Meryn had to go.

No sooner had Henrietta reached that conclusion than headlights swept through the rain and a car pulled into the drive. She got to her feet and hadn't quite reached the foyer when the key turned in the lock and the door opened.

To Henrietta's surprise, Maxine sailed into the living room, followed by Meryn and Sandy.

"Good evening, Henrietta."

"Maxine." Henrietta stole a glance at Meryn, but the girl wouldn't meet her eyes. She couldn't help but notice how red and swollen her eyes were.

Sandy carried a large pot in her hands. "We brought some chili. We figured you probably hadn't eaten."

"But I don't—"

Ignoring Henrietta's protest, Sandy walked past her into the kitchen where she plunked the pot on the stovetop and turned on a burner.

"I'll be right back," Meryn said, heading to her room.

With Maxine and Sandy both in her kitchen, Henrietta was left with no choice but to follow.

"Have a seat, Henrietta," Maxine said.

It wasn't a request.

"You, too," she said to Meryn when she returned, wearing different clothes.

Meryn sat silently as Henrietta glared at them. Sandy and Maxine moved efficiently around the kitchen, getting bowls and glasses from the cupboards. Henrietta, out of the corner of her eye, saw that Meryn still wouldn't look at her.

The only sound in the kitchen was Sandy and Maxine's low voices as they filled glasses with water and checked to see if the chili was warm enough to serve.

When it was, they set four bowls down and took the two remaining chairs.

"It's not spicy," Sandy said to Henrietta as she spooned up some of the aromatic chili.

Henrietta sampled it and realized how hungry she was. Meryn, she noticed, ate a little but not with her typical relish.

"This is good, hon," Maxine said.

"Thanks." Sandy smiled.

The two of them acted as if this was just an ordinary visit. Henrietta felt unsure about what exactly they were doing here, so just ate a bit more, though her nerves made it difficult to get anything down.

"Well," Maxine said when her spoon scraped the bottom of her bowl, "since it's apparent you two aren't going to initiate any conversation, we'll start."

Henrietta paused her spoon.

"You might wonder how we happened upon Ryn," Maxine continued, sounding as if she were reading a story to children at the library. "We were driving past St. Aloysius, and I thought I saw her walking through the rain. No umbrella, no jacket. We went to investigate."

"And," Sandy picked up the narrative, "we found her in the chapel on campus."

"In the chapel?" Henrietta looked openly at Meryn for the first time.

Meryn's face was red, but she just nodded.

"We pretty much forced her to come home with us." Sandy rested her arms on the table. "And we pretty much forced her to talk to us."

"And now," Maxine said, picking up with what seemed to be a coordinated attack, "we are going to force you to talk to us, Henrietta."

Henrietta dropped her spoon into her chili. "You think so?"

"Told you," Meryn mumbled.

Maxine folded her hands, commanding the attention of the others. "If you two separate, if you don't stay together, it's going to be for a better reason than that you didn't communicate."

She turned to Henrietta. "If you're not going to volunteer to Meryn what you were researching at the library, I will."

Meryn sat up straighter, and even Sandy looked intrigued.

"What business do you have—" Henrietta began, but Maxine held up a hand.

"I don't. Except that Sandy and I care about both of you." She met Sandy's gaze tenderly. "And someone once did the same for us when trouble came a'callin'."

They clasped hands for a moment, but then Maxine returned to her original topic. "So, post-polio syndrome. Explain."

When Henrietta remained stubbornly silent, Maxine said, "Henrietta, I wasn't trying to pry. But the journals you copied articles from were left next to the copier. It wasn't hard to figure out."

"What is she talking about?" Meryn asked, now looking fully at Henrietta.

"I've... I've been feeling strange recently." Henrietta cursed Maxine for putting her in this position. "I fell a few weeks ago. And I've been weaker. I went to see Dr. McCourt. While you were away."

"That's the appointment you had," Meryn said. "What did he say?"

"My blood work is all normal. There's no other obvious explanation. He told me about this syndrome they're starting to find in people, like me. People who had polio thirty to forty years ago."

"Is it coming back?" Meryn asked, reaching for Henrietta's hand.

Henrietta stared at their intertwined fingers. "Not... not like the first time. But apparently, there is some reactivation of the virus, and a new onset of weakness. There is no treatment. And no one knows how far it will go. Yet."

Meryn withdrew her hand. "Now I understand. You decided for both of us that we're not going to be together."

Henrietta swallowed hard. "You shouldn't be burdened—"

"That is about the stupidest thing I have ever heard!" Meryn pushed to her feet and began pacing around the kitchen.

Sandy turned to Maxine. "I think they're talking now."

Maxine nodded. "Time for us to go."

She squeezed Henrietta's shoulder while Sandy hugged Meryn. "We'll call tomorrow."

They let themselves out.

Meryn stood leaning against the kitchen counter, glaring at Henrietta. Henrietta felt her certainty falter.

"Don't look at me like that."

"I can't believe you did this. To us."

"Why can't you see—"

"Oh, I see." Meryn began pacing again. "I see that you think I'm too young and immature and inexperienced to understand what a relationship with you means. I see that you think you can make all the decisions for both of us. And I see that you think pushing me away is going to protect me. Right?"

Her assessment was so accurate that Henrietta couldn't think of any defense.

"You know," Meryn continued, "Sandy and Maxine told me, they said this was the time. If I was going to leave, if I couldn't handle being with you—for better or worse—this was the time to go. When you were already pushing me in that direction. It would never be easier than it would be now, they said."

She paused her pacing. "You know what I said?"

Henrietta stared at her.

"I said, don't you think I've already thought about all of that. Don't you think I've considered that age and health are going to be challenges for us. And don't you think I already decided that none of

360

that matters. That the only thing that matters, is that I've never been happier than I am—make that *was*. That I'm a better woman for loving you, for having your strength and determination as an example for me to try and be worthy of."

"Meryn—" Henrietta was humiliated to feel tears pricking her eyes.

But Meryn wasn't finished. "Henrietta, I don't know how to convince you that my love is real. I couldn't convince my mother, either. I know you all think I'll just 'get over this' or something. Or maybe..."

She stared hard at Henrietta. "Maybe my love isn't what you want. Maybe it never was." She drew herself up. "If so, then this is the time for you to tell me. If you don't love me, just say so, and I'll never bring it up again."

Henrietta couldn't look away. Tears spilled over and ran unchecked down her face. "I can't," she whispered.

"You can't what?"

"I can't say that."

But Meryn was merciless. "You can't say what?" she demanded.

Henrietta swiped her fingers over her cheeks. "I can't say I don't love you. And I can't say I don't want your love. I do."

She put her hands over her face and sobbed.

A moment later, she heard a chair scoot across the floor and felt Meryn's warm hands on her wrists, gently tugging on them. When Henrietta opened her eyes, Meryn's smiling face swam before her.

Meryn leaned near, brushing her soft lips over Henrietta's cheeks, her forehead, her lips. She knelt in front of Henrietta and wrapped her arms around her, pulling her close. Henrietta held on for dear life, her body still wracked by her tears.

"God help me, I do love you," she murmured.

"God help us both," Meryn said.

Chapter 24

D APPLED SHADOWS RIPPLED OVER the rowboat as Ryn lazily rowed a large circle around the pond. Henrietta sat in the bow, trailing her fingers in the water.

To Ryn's surprise, it had been Henrietta's suggestion. It took a little doing to tie the boat securely and stabilize it so that Ryn could guide Henrietta into it and get her seated. Henrietta did acquiesce to Ryn's demand that she wear a life jacket. Ryn's memory of her own unexpected swim that day with the snake made her only too aware of how quickly something could happen, and she wasn't certain—what with Henrietta's braces weighing her down—that she could get to her fast enough if the boat did sink or overturn.

"This is the first time I've been on this pond since 1945," Henrietta murmured.

She gazed around, and Ryn was certain she was seeing ghosts.

"Are you okay?"

Henrietta nodded. "I've been thinking a lot about Una lately." Ryn listened as she rowed. "We were so naïve and innocent with the plans

363

we were making, but now, I think if we'd been in New York or Paris during the fifties and sixties, it would have been very easy for her to fall in with the wrong people."

"Brilliant but tragic? Like Sylvia Plath or Patricia Highsmith?"

Henrietta looked at Ryn. "Exactly."

Ryn angled her head, studying the way the sunlight struck Henrietta's face. "But not you?"

Henrietta smiled, and it warmed Ryn's heart. "I don't think so," Henrietta mused. "I'm not built that way. Too practical. Not brilliant."

"No," Ryn disagreed, shaking her head. "Too strong. Too independent. Which isn't always a good thing."

Henrietta glanced sidelong at her. "Are you ever going to let me forget that?"

"Nope." But Ryn grinned. Her grin faded and she reached for Henrietta's hand. "But if you hadn't pushed us to the precipice, we might not have found our way here."

Henrietta's lips compressed as she squeezed Ryn's hand. She still got very emotional, thinking about that night. Ryn let go and grabbed the oar again.

She took a deep breath, enjoying the scent of the honeysuckle growing along the banks of the pond. The summer was flying past. The art show in Albany had been a huge success, with gallery reps from New York now jostling to get Henrietta to do a show with one of them. She still bristled when they referred to her paintings as "quaint" or "rustic", but Ryn pointed out that they were all of those things.

"I would much rather be surrounded by your paintings than scenes of cities or violence or, heaven help us, modern art," she'd said.

The honeysuckle was full of bees, busily searching for nectar.

Ryn glanced at her watch. "Time to go."

"Not yet," Henrietta protested.

"Yes," Ryn insisted. "If we don't get your exercise in now, there won't be time before we're due at Sandy and Maxine's. And don't think that I don't know that that's your evil plan."

Dr. McCourt had set Henrietta up with a physical therapist who had taught Ryn several exercises they could do to build up the strength of Henrietta's arms and legs. The only part of it that Henrietta liked was the discovery of sweatpants. Although she'd worn a pair of Ryn's home from the hospital, she hadn't really experienced the freedom. She now lived in them almost exclusively in the house.

Henrietta frowned. "You would have made a good physical therapist."

Ryn laughed. "I'll take that as a compliment."

"You would," Henrietta grumbled.

Ryn dug the oars in and made for the dock.

An hour and a half later, both of them still flushed from Henrietta's exercise session, Ryn wrapped up a warm casserole dish of baked beans. It had been an awkward conversation when she'd called her mom to get the recipe, "but it's good you talked," Henrietta reminded her. "It will get easier."

Maxine was waiting for them when they parked the Chrysler. "Henrietta, you're positively glowing!"

Ryn, reaching into the back seat, chuckled when she heard Henrietta say, "Oh, hush. I know this is a conspiracy."

The conspiracy theory was confirmed when Gordon McCourt stepped outside.

"Hello, Henrietta," he said, bending to kiss her cheek as he guided her into the house.

"Hmmmph."

He grinned at Ryn. "She still pretending to be angry with us?"

"Yep. But she's getting stronger. Thanks for your help."

"Any time."

Within a few minutes, they were all seated with wine and overflowing plates of hotdogs, burgers, chicken, beans, corn on the cob, fresh tomatoes and green beans—"my first attempt at a garden," Gordon said proudly.

The food was wonderful, but what really warmed Ryn's heart was watching Henrietta laugh and talk. When their eyes met, the smile that illuminated Henrietta's face made Ryn's heart stop for a moment.

After dinner and kitchen cleanup, they all went to the living room with fresh glasses of wine while Sandy turned on the television.

They'd all been watching the Democratic national convention over the past few nights, but Ryn had been waiting especially for this night. When Geraldine Ferraro took the stage as the Vice-Presidential nominee, they all whooped and clapped.

"It's about time a woman was on a major ticket," Ryn said, standing to clap some more.

Sandy wiped tears from her cheeks. "I never thought we'd see a night like this."

Ryn glanced at Henrietta, who sat stoically. "What're you thinking?"

Henrietta focused on her wineglass.

"You don't think they'll win?"

Henrietta shook her head. "I don't. I think too many rich and powerful people are benefitting from Reagan's economy. Mondale's ideas are too egalitarian for them. I admire his ideals, but I don't think he'll win."

"But we're still going to work for his campaign, right?"

"Oh, yes." Henrietta nodded, adding in an undertone, "I'm all for tilting at windmills."

Ryn narrowed her eyes. "I heard that."

Gordon stood and went to the window, where he jangled the change in his pocket. "Did any of you see Bobbi Campbell's speech?"

The women all exchanged worried glances.

"Gordon, how many friends do you have who have AIDS?" Maxine asked.

He hadn't said anything directly, but it had become an unspoken given that Gordon was gay.

"Have or had?" he asked. "Thirteen have already died."

Henrietta, who had been educated by Ryn on the lack of research and funding by the Reagan administration, asked, "But you're not...?"

He turned and gave her a sad smile. "No. One of the benefits of being so isolated. And so closeted. I'm careful. And it may have saved me."

He pointed at the TV. "But it won't save Bobbi or thousands like him. Just wait. Wait until this epidemic spreads beyond the gay community. And it will. But it'll be too late for too many."

His voice cracked, and he turned back to the window.

Ryn went to him and rested a hand on his shoulder. "We'll do what we can, which, for now, means trying to get Mondale elected."

But the silence from Henrietta, Sandy, and Maxine weighed more than her words.

THE LAKE BELOW WAS dotted with several small boats while the larger tour boats chugged along their routes. Henrietta and Meryn both had easels set up before them, though Meryn chose to stand.

Beside her, Meryn huffed impatiently and stepped back.

"You're being too literal," Henrietta said, frowning at the canvas. Meryn was trying to paint every tree, every undulation of the hills between the inn and the lake.

Meryn had finally expressed a desire to resume her painting lessons, and they'd decided to go back to Owasco Lake for a weekend. Henrietta decided to try a different approach.

"Some of the songs you sing, I've heard other versions of them on the radio—"

She paused when she saw the doubtful expression on Meryn's face. "Oh, hush. I do listen to music, you know. What I'm saying is, you

don't sing the songs as an exact mimicry of those artists. Your inter-
pretation of them is different, uniquely yours. Why?"

"Because I couldn't copy them if I tried," Meryn said. "I'm not
good enough, so I just sing and play for me."

Henrietta simply raised one eyebrow.

"Oh."

"Exactly." Henrietta pointed with her brush. "Now paint what *you*
see and feel, not what you think I would paint."

She reached over and swiped long swaths of white paint over top of
what Meryn had done. The girl yelped, but Henrietta ignored her.
"The beauty of acrylics. They're very forgiving. You can paint right
over anything you don't like and start over."

"Maybe they're forgiving..." Meryn mumbled.

Henrietta chuckled and returned to her own canvas.

The light gradually shifted as the sun moved lower in the west. The
porch fell into shadow, and Henrietta took a peek at Meryn's canvas.

"Much better." She smiled. "I like the colors you chose for the water."

"Doesn't look like the lake," Meryn said, frowning.

"It looks like your vision of the lake," Henrietta corrected. "I'm
hungry. Let's pack up."

Phyllis had a table reserved for them. "And I've already set aside
two slices of my apple pie," she told them as they perused the menu.
"So don't fill up on dinner."

They took a walk through the garden after supper, under an indigo
sky that was rapidly deepening to purple. The tree silhouettes were black
against the fading light, and the first stars were beginning to pop.

"It's a Maxfield Parrish sky," Meryn said.

Henrietta's heart swelled. It wasn't just the interest Meryn took in
art, or the fact that she wanted to spend time doing what Henrietta
loved. It was a million little things: the way Meryn always checked to
see if Henrietta was chilled; the way she automatically scanned for the
obstacles that could trip Henrietta up anywhere they went; the smiles

and glances they shared. She'd never dreamed she could be this happy. And if, every now and again, the niggling doubts wormed their way in, well, she could be forgiven.

She and Meryn often lay together, just holding each other and talking. Sometimes, Henrietta longed to touch Meryn, to explore her beautiful body and give her what she knew she must be missing. But Henrietta's own body was so floppy without her braces. She felt spineless—*in both senses of that word*. She couldn't bring herself to initiate anything so intimately physical. Yet.

She tried to focus on what she did have.

She had a circle of friends who were dearer to her than she'd once thought possible. And she had a love she'd never have let herself believe she wanted.

Or needed.

She could finally admit it, at least to herself. She needed Meryn and her love like she needed air. *No, not air. Like art.* She knew she could survive without love. She had done for most of her life. *But I was only half-alive,* she would have said. Surviving and living, she now knew, were two completely separate things.

~

"SO," FRANNY SAID, STRETCHING out her long legs and crossing them at the ankles, "couldn't help but notice you've kind of turned Henrietta's yard into a Mondale/Ferraro shrine."

Ryn grinned as she poked the pond with a stick. "Think the country club set will change their vote?"

Franny choked on her beer, sputtering as she tried to swallow. "Fat chance," she gasped when she could speak.

Ryn had also redecorated Nelly's rear hatch with new stickers proclaiming her allegiance. She took a long drink from her own bottle of Heineken.

"Can't believe how much better good beer tastes."

Franny laughed. "Told you."

"Gosh, it's good to have you guys back."

"Can't believe classes start next week." Franny pointed her bottle in Ryn's direction. "Your position is secure?"

Ryn shrugged. "At least for this year. If I can survive one more provisional year after this, I'll be more or less permanent. Then tenure."

"Have you met the new guy?"

"Yeah. Met him last week. Andy Webb. Taught at a small college in Georgia, but his wife is from Syracuse, so they wanted to be closer. Seems like a nice guy. Much better than Geary."

"You ever hear what happened to him?"

"Not really." Ryn lowered her voice, though there was no one else around to overhear. "Beverly told me Talbert got a reference request from a school in Oregon."

"Oregon?" Franny chuckled. "Wanted to get far, far away, didn't he?"

"Guess so."

They sat for a long while, listening to the birds and frogs while they watched turtle heads pop up along the edges of the pond in the wake of a pair of mallards paddling in lazy circles.

"Have you had any contact with Tamara?" Ryn asked.

Franny hesitated a moment. "We heard she transferred to SUNY Buffalo and is delaying her postulant year."

"Really?" Ryn considered. "Buffalo will probably be good for her. A bigger campus, closer to home."

"You okay with that?"

"Me?" Ryn took a drink. "I'm completely fine. I wish her well. I really do hope she figures out what will make her happy."

"Me, too." Franny raised her bottle to drink. "I don't think it'll be with us, but..."

Ryn studied Franny more closely. She looked tired, which was something of a surprise.

"Good summer?" Ryn asked somewhat doubtfully.

"Kind of." Franny sat forward with her elbows on her knees. "I told you we had to do a retreat this summer."

"Yeah." Ryn eyed Franny curiously.

Franny picked at the corner of the label on her bottle. "You remember when I told you this life is sometimes a hard slog?"

"Yeah."

Franny heaved a shaky sigh. "Well, this summer has been fucking sloggy."

Ryn wasn't sure what to say or how to help. "In what way?" she asked tentatively.

Keeping her head bowed over her knees, Franny had to clear her throat a couple of times before she could speak. "Have you ever done a retreat?"

"No." And judging by the way Franny was behaving, Ryn was certain she never wanted to.

Franny covertly swiped a hand across her eyes. "Well, sometimes they can be great. Full of light, almost like a really good orgasm."

Not having had one of those in a very long time, Ryn was glad Franny wasn't looking at her. "I'm taking it this wasn't one of those times."

A half-bark of mirthless laughter from Franny confirmed her guess.

"This one dug deep, but not in a good way. It really left me questioning what the hell I'm doing here."

Franny's confession twisted Ryn's heart. "You're not thinking of leaving?"

"I don't know." Franny pulled the rest of the label free. "Maybe."

"No." Ryn scooted her chair closer and laid a hand on Franny's arm. "You're the one who told me real love is supposed to be hard. You said sometimes it takes sacrifice and... and compromise. You said it grabs you and won't let you walk away. Even when you're getting nothing back."

"Damn." This time, Franny's chuckle sounded more genuine. "You really listen to everything I say?"

Ryn grinned sheepishly. "I didn't like it at the time, but this summer... It saved me."

Franny looked up, her eyes still wet and red. "When you called?"

Ryn sat back. "I was ready to give up." Her hands strangled her own beer bottle. "Henrietta was trying so hard to push me away. I didn't know what to do. I ended up in the campus chapel."

She rubbed the back of her neck in embarrassment. "I prayed. Just asked for help. It came."

Franny's eyes reflected her surprise.

"Maxine and Sandy showed up out of nowhere. I don't think that was an accident. They took me home with them. I spilled my guts. They drove me back here and kind of forced Henrietta and me to talk. Turns out Henrietta got a bad diagnosis—her polio might be flaring up—and she was trying to make me go."

She leaned forward again. "My point is, you were right. It is hard. Maybe it has to be, or it doesn't mean anything. I don't know anything about religious life, Franny, but you spoke last spring with so much conviction. You said this kind of love, it's always there, even if it doesn't give anything in return. But it won't be like this forever. I know that. Don't walk away."

Franny sat back and sniffed. "Shit."

~

THE LIBRARY WAS ABUZZ with activity. Henrietta sat at a table where she was registering people to vote. She knew Meryn was outside, corralling passersby, asking if they were registered and, if not, inviting them to come in and do so. Judging from the steady stream of people approaching the table, Meryn was very persuasive.

Henrietta smiled and greeted people, showing them how to fill out the form.

She'd taken great delight in standing out in her front yard among the new garden of political signs proclaiming her allegiance to the Democratic nominees. Waving to the scowling faces behind the wheels of cars turning into the country club, she couldn't help realizing how much happier she was now. She was glad she'd declined their efforts to get her to return.

"Here you go."

She glanced up to find Maxine placing a cup of fresh coffee on the table. "Thank you."

Maxine gave her shoulder a rub. "Thank you for volunteering."

Henrietta scoffed. "You think I had a choice?"

Maxine laughed, and Henrietta couldn't hide her smile.

"Sandy and Gordon are cooking something up between them for dinner, so make sure you're hungry when you come over tonight."

Maxine returned to her library duties.

"Well, Henrietta Cochran."

Henrietta knew that voice before she even looked up. "Hello, Genevieve. Come to change parties?"

Genevieve Talbert gazed down her nose at Henrietta. "I swear, you've become positively communist."

Henrietta's brows shot up. "So it's communist to register to vote in a democratic election?"

Genevieve glanced around. "Most of these people don't even know what they're voting for. They're sheep, doing as they're told."

The tone with which she said *these people* almost dripped with condescension.

"Unlike those who will vote for Reagan despite all the reasons sane people shouldn't."

Genevieve tilted her head as she surveyed Henrietta. "You really have changed."

"Yes, I have." Henrietta nodded toward the stacks. "If you're looking for reading material, I'm sure the library has a copy of *Mein Kampf*."

Genevieve's nostrils flared. Henrietta smiled sweetly and watched her stalk away.

She felt the weight of someone watching her. Expecting it to be another country club person here with Genevieve, she turned with a scowl to see Meryn watching her with a proud smile pasted on her face.

She came to the table and leaned near. "That was brilliant."

Henrietta flushed. "I've put up with her snobbery for years."

Meryn laughed so softly, only Henrietta could hear. Even more quietly, she murmured, "I love you."

The words felt like a caress. Henrietta's heart hammered as it always did when Meryn said something endearing.

Unable to meet Meryn's eyes, Henrietta said, "Go on with you."

Meryn squeezed her shoulder gently and went back outside. Henrietta sat there, remembering when Meryn's touch felt like being branded. She laid her own hand on her shoulder, trying to hold on to the sensation.

"Mmmm hmmm," drawled Maxine as she strolled by to shelve some books. "I saw that."

Henrietta finished her shift at the volunteer table. When she left the library, Meryn was still handing out flyers and trying to steer people inside.

"I'll see you at home in a bit," she said to Henrietta.

When Henrietta pulled into the driveway, the mailman was just walking up to the house. He waited until she got out of the car and opened the door from the garage into the breezeway.

"Here you go, Miss Cochran."

"Thank you."

He tipped his hat and left.

She carried the thin sheaf of envelopes into the kitchen and set them on the counter. "Electric bill, gas bill, water—"

She stopped as she saw the last envelope in the stack. The return address sticker read *June Fleming* in Uniontown. But it wasn't addressed to Meryn. It was addressed to her.

Sitting down at the table, she stared at the envelope for several minutes before reaching for it. Her fingers fumbled with the flap. When she pulled out the slip of paper within, the note inside was polite but terse.

Dear Henrietta,

As you can imagine, I was surprised when Meryn announced that she intends to stay at St. Aloysius and more surprised that she plans to stay with you rather than look for an apartment of her own.

When she shared her reason for that decision, I must admit, I was disturbed.

Her father and I have always trusted Ryn to make good decisions, but I cannot help but feel that her decisions are being clouded by a sense of responsibility to you which, I'm sure you would agree, is not fair to her.

I would like to discuss this with you. I would also appreciate it if you would not tell Ryn about this. I'm sure you can understand that, as her mother, I want what's best for my daughter.

It was signed simply with June's name and a telephone number.

Henrietta slowly folded the note and tucked it back into its envelope. She gazed absently out the kitchen window. She couldn't blame June Fleming for feeling as she did. It hadn't been so long ago that Henrietta had the very same concerns about tying Meryn down here. But how could she explain to Meryn's mother that she loved that girl more than anything? That life would hardly feel worth living without her?

Even as she thought it, she heard exactly how selfish those sentiments would sound to a concerned mother.

She pushed to her feet and went to her desk. She tucked the note in a drawer, pushing it closed as Meryn came in. She saw the envelopes lying on the kitchen counter.

375

"Anything good in the mail?"

Henrietta forced a smile. "Nothing important."

~

THE HISTORY TEA CLUB expanded by one. Turned out Andy Webb was a tea drinker, also. He even bought an electric kettle for the office he now shared with Ryn.

"I miss the whistle of the old kettle," Beverly bemoaned privately to Ryn. "But I suppose this is faster."

"And safer."

But where Ryn and Beverly liked a variety of herbal teas, Andy stuck resolutely to a strong, black English breakfast tea, several cups of it per day, courtesy of a habit he'd developed while at Oxford. Ryn wondered why the guy didn't have caffeine tremors, but she also wondered a lot of other things about him. If he hadn't had a wife and two kids—a son and daughter in junior high and high school—she would have guessed he was gay.

Not particularly handsome, he was a little soft around the edges, with receding dark hair and a moustache left over from the seventies. But he was wickedly funny, highly intelligent, "and he's a Democrat!" Ryn had announced to Henrietta.

In short, he was everything she could have wished for in a colleague—and everything Bradley Geary hadn't been.

"This year is going to be so much better," she said to Beverly.

She dove into her classes, which were full nearly to capacity. Beverly had told her that students were specifically requesting her courses, much to Dr. Talbert's chagrin.

He was still sullen and resentful that his chances of promotion to dean had disappeared, but with two provisional faculty under him, there was no one to step in as chair. Ryn was under no delusions that, when it came time, it would be Webb and not her chosen as Talbert's replacement, but Webb had his Ph.D. and almost fifteen years of teaching experience in Georgia. He would be a logical choice, if he lasted.

"I can't believe I'm back in Yankee territory," he joked.

He'd grown up in Massachusetts, but had been in the South since finishing his doctorate. His wife, Charlene, was sweet, often coming by to drop off batches of cookies or freshly baked pies. With her parents and siblings all in the Syracuse area, they were looking forward to being closer to family.

As nice as the Webbs were, Ryn was reluctant to share too much of her personal life with them. She noncommittally told Andy that she shared a house with a woman, and she supposed Beverly had explained some things about Henrietta's situation, because he mentioned her polio and her art.

When she was younger, in college and grad school, she'd been adamant about being out and open, but things felt different now. Part of it was Henrietta's obvious discomfort with too many people knowing too much about her private life. Part of it was Ryn's lingering tension with her mom. She had thought she'd go home for one more late summer visit, maybe with Henrietta, but after what happened in May, she had no desire to go home. Still, it was weird not to feel like she could just call and talk to her folks as she'd always done. She missed them. This emotional distance nagged, like a pebble in her shoe that she was always aware of.

By the end of her first week of classes, she was starting to learn her students' names. There was one young woman in her freshman seminar who reminded her forcefully of Vanessa.

It was hard to remember how confusing things had been last year, what with Geary and Vanessa and Tamara. Feeling nostalgic, she opened the door to her old broom closet. The rays of sun slanting through the window set alight a cobweb strung across the gap from window to desk.

"Am I that bad?"

She jumped at the sound of Andy's voice behind her. "Huh?"

He pointed. "Beverly told me this was your office last year." He angled his head, studying her. "From what I hear, the chap I replaced was a bit of a... miscreant."

She sniggered. "Okay, I haven't ever heard anyone use the word 'miscreant' in conversation, but, yes, he was." She pulled the door closed. "And no. I'm very happy sharing an office with you."

Vanessa was still on her mind, though. After her last lecture of the day, she shouldered her backpack and went into the village. She bought a bouquet of autumn flowers at the florist shop.

A few minutes later, she climbed the steps of Mrs. Middleston's house. She knocked and waited. When Mrs. Middleston came to the door, she opened it with a puzzled expression.

"You're not here for a room, are you?"

Ryn grinned. "No. I'm still happy with Henrietta, but I was just remembering last year. And I don't know if I ever really thanked you."

"Thank me? For what?"

"For creating a home away from home for so many young women. I know I was a little older than most of your boarders, but it's kind of comforting to have a place like this, with rules and someone to notice if something is wrong."

She held out the flowers. "For you."

Mrs. Middleston accepted them with a dazed expression. "No one has ever..." She cleared her throat. "They're pretty."

"Bye."

With a wave, Ryn hopped down the steps and made her way to her real home.

Chapter 25

HENRIETTA SAT, CALMLY PRETENDING to read the newspaper, as Meryn stomped around the house talking to herself, every now and then blurting something loudly enough for Henrietta to make out things like "can't believe you did that" or "what were you thinking" or "this is just great" which, of course, it wasn't. At least not in Meryn's mind.

When Henrietta had steeled herself to call June a couple of days after receiving her note, she'd deliberately chosen a day when she knew Meryn had a full teaching load and wouldn't pop home unexpectedly. She'd also decided that only so much would be accomplished over the telephone. After a frosty greeting but before June could build up a proper head of steam—if that was her intention—Henrietta headed her off by inviting her and Walt to come to Bluemont for Labor Day weekend.

"If Janie will be back at college, I presume your boys are old enough to stay by themselves now, and it will be a long weekend for your husband. It seems the ideal time for us to sit down and talk."

From the momentary silence on the other end of the line, it seemed June was flummoxed. Henrietta was certain the poor woman had an entire litany of things she'd wound herself up to say, as Henrietta knew she would in her place, but this unexpected invitation had knocked her off-kilter.

Telling Meryn had been an entirely different matter. Henrietta had waited until Friday evening, knowing that she'd most likely need the entire weekend—and the whole of the next week—to come to terms with what Henrietta had done and to prepare herself.

As Henrietta had anticipated, Meryn had stared at her, speechless and open-mouthed, upon hearing of the arrangements. When Henrietta showed her her mother's note, Meryn's face had turned an alarming shade of puce.

After her initial concealment of the letter, Henrietta had realized that, if she and Meryn were to have a real relationship, it couldn't include secrets. "I don't blame your mother," she'd said as Meryn read it. "She's worried about you. Just as I would be in her place. We knew there would be opposition. There are a lot of reasons that people will think this is wrong, and our sex is probably the least of them. We owe her this opportunity, to hear her out, to reassure her."

Naturally, the speechless part hadn't lasted long. Once Meryn had found her voice, she'd been mumbling like this, mostly to herself, non-stop for several days.

As it was now Thursday, and June and Walt would arrive tomorrow night, Henrietta said, "We should discuss sleeping arrangements."

Meryn paused, momentarily silenced again, as the implication of her parents' spending three nights in this house hit her.

"Maybe they could—"

"No hotel." Henrietta's voice was firm. "We need to hash this out, and we can't do that if they're staying somewhere else."

Meryn looked at her, eyes wide.

"Sit down," Henrietta said more gently.

Meryn sat beside her on the sofa. Henrietta took her hand.

"Do you, or do you not, intend for us, for this relationship, to last forever?"

Meryn, whose mouth was already open to argue, was only able to say, "Yes. Of course."

"Then, for better or worse."

Henrietta could see that it took a few seconds for the impact of her words to sink in.

"Better or worse." Meryn's face softened for the first time since hearing the news.

"Your family is now my family. I know in-laws don't always get along or like one another." Henrietta couldn't believe she was thinking of these people as her parents-in-law. It was laughable, but, "You will not be whole or happy if there's strife between us."

Meryn stared at the floor, thinking. "You're right. If I always have to choose between them or you, it'll tear me apart."

She watched Meryn's face. It was like a movie projector, playing her emotions like a film across her features. Her expression shifted, and she turned to Henrietta.

"Did you just propose to me?"

It was Henrietta's turn to gape. She cleared her throat. "I suppose I did."

Meryn leaned nearer, her face a hair's breadth away. Lightly, she pressed her lips to Henrietta's, as she sat frozen, ensnared by the nearness of that beloved face.

After a moment, Meryn pulled away. "I accept."

∼

RYN DID ONE LAST check of her bedroom, straightening the spread on the bed she usually slept in. After much discussion about the pros and cons of the twin beds in her room versus the double bed in Henrietta's, the bathroom layout decided the matter. Henrietta couldn't step over a tub to shower, and her bathroom had extra room and safety bars that the guest bath didn't.

The only sticking point was where Ryn would sleep. She was prepared to sleep on the sofa, but Henrietta asked, "Would you do that if you were with Tamara instead of me?"

Ryn felt herself go red. "That would be different."

"Because you would already be sharing a bed with her every night. And you would..."

This was still an area where Henrietta felt she was depriving Ryn of something she needed.

Reading her mind, Ryn said, "I've told you over and over, this relationship is already giving me more than I've ever had with anyone."

Henrietta gave her a dubious frown. "But—"

"What we are to each other doesn't depend on what other people do or say or think," Ryn said. "We get to make up our own rules. I will sleep with you, as long as it won't disturb you. And my parents will just have to accept it."

Henrietta nodded.

Ryn got a sleeping shirt and a pair of shorts to take to Henrietta's room. Other than the infrequent nights when she heard Henrietta having a bad dream and went to comfort her, they didn't sleep together. It would be interesting to see what the next few nights would be like.

Just as she did last November when she was expecting her family, she couldn't settle as they waited for her parents to arrive. She kept jumping up, looking out the window before huffing impatiently and plopping back into her chair.

"I know you're laughing at me," she said.

"I'm not laughing," but Henrietta's voice definitely had a lilt to it.

It was almost ten o'clock when June and Walt pulled into the driveway. Ryn was out the door before her dad turned the car off.

She threw herself into his arms when he got out. She was more hesitant with her mother.

"Mom," she said, standing awkwardly until June held her arms out.

Ryn moved into them, wishing this hadn't become a barrier between them. She and her mother had never been estranged for any reason. She'd never even been seriously pissed at her parents.

She helped her father with the suitcases, leading the way to the house, where Henrietta stood at the door to welcome them.

"It's so nice to see you again," she said.

"And you," June said, but Ryn heard the forced tone of her voice.

"Are you hungry?" Ryn asked.

"No, we ate in Elmira." June looked around, and Ryn wondered if her mom expected the house to be redecorated with rainbow pillows and lavender drapes.

Her parents took the two chairs while Ryn and Henrietta sat on the couch. A tense silence filled the room, and Ryn thought for a moment they were going to dive right into the purpose of this visit. She suddenly wondered if her dad even knew why he was here.

"I imagine you're tired after your trip," Henrietta said just as June opened her mouth.

"We are." Walt stood. "My back gets stiff these days."

Ryn picked up a suitcase again and led the way to her bedroom.

"You can sleep in here," Ryn said, setting the suitcase on the bed nearest the door.

June followed, frowning. "But where—?"

"This is just fine," Walt cut in. "We'll see you in the morning."

He gave Ryn a smile and closed the bedroom door.

Ryn heaved a grateful sigh and followed Henrietta to her room. She pushed the door shut and stood there uncertainly, realizing she had no idea how Henrietta got herself in and out of her braces. Any time she'd spent in this room had been in the middle of the night after one of Henrietta's bad dreams, after she was already in bed.

"What do you need?"

Henrietta paused, thinking. "Give me twenty minutes?"

Ryn nodded and went back out to the dark living room. No matter where they were emotionally, Henrietta still needed her privacy and her dignity.

Getting comfortable being naked with Ashley had taken a while, and Ryn couldn't help but wonder if that would ever happen with Henrietta, if they ever became lovers in the physical sense.

After giving Henrietta twenty-five minutes, just to be safe, Ryn knocked quietly.

"Come in."

She opened the door to find Henrietta in bed. Reaching for her T-shirt and shorts, she said, "I'll just be a sec."

When she was done in the bathroom, she flipped off the light and padded to the far side of the bed.

They both lay stiffly for several minutes.

"Are you okay? Am I crowding you?" Ryn asked, though she was as close to the edge as she could get without falling out of bed.

"I'm fine." Henrietta reached for her hand. "You don't have to stay so far away."

Ryn shifted closer, taking Henrietta's hand. Henrietta squeezed it.

"Relax. You're not going to break me."

Ryn snorted. Turning on her side, she rested her other hand on Henrietta's shoulder. "If I snore or talk in my sleep, just push me out of bed."

"Deal."

Ryn closed her eyes, listening to Henrietta's breathing as it slowed and deepened. *What would it be like to fall asleep listening to that every night?*

～

BREAKFAST ON SATURDAY MORNING felt almost normal. Meryn and her mother made pancakes and bacon for everyone, and Walt made sure Henrietta's coffee cup was topped off each time it got half-empty. After breakfast, Walt insisted on checking the birdfeeders. With an apologetic glance in Henrietta's direction, Meryn accompanied him, leaving Henrietta alone with June.

"Are the boys excited for their senior year?" Henrietta asked casually, trying to steer the conversation to safe topics.

"Absolutely," June said, seeming equally glad to have something benign to talk about. She went on about the summer basketball camps the twins had attended, and their hopes for scholarships. "Probably only to a mid-level school, but still, a scholarship is a scholarship."

Henrietta wondered, with three days looming before them, if they should tackle the reason for this get-together right away, or if they should pretend it was a normal holiday visit for a while. When Meryn and her father returned, she took the initiative.

"Where would you be most comfortable talking? Here in the kitchen? At the dining table? In the living room?"

Meryn looked slightly panicked at such an upfront approach but, in Henrietta's experience, when something painful was hanging over your head, you'd best get it done with as quickly as possible.

When the other three simply looked at one another, Henrietta took charge.

"Meryn, would you please bring me a cup of coffee?"

While the Flemings bustled about in the kitchen getting fresh cups of tea and coffee, Henrietta headed to the dining table, taking a seat at one end. This was clearly a family that avoided confrontation—or perhaps, Henrietta thought, they've never had reason for a confrontation. She decided this would require some tact.

When the others were seated—Walt at the opposite end of the table, with Meryn and her mother sitting across from each other on either side—Henrietta waited a moment to see if one of them would begin, but seconds ticked by, accompanied only by nervous sips or twirling of mugs in clenched hands.

All right, then.

"June," she began, "I think you had some concerns about Meryn's living arrangement here with me."

"Well..." June paused, her face a brilliant pink. "It's not so much the living arrangement, but, yes." She straightened her shoulders. "I think Ryn should be in a place of her own, if she's to stay in Bluemont."

A puzzled frown creased Walt's brow, and Henrietta had the distinct impression that the poor man had no idea why he was really here.

"Why would she move?" he asked, turning to Meryn. "Do you want to move?"

"No." Meryn glanced at her mother and quickly lowered her eyes. "I like it here. With Henrietta."

"Then—"

"It's not the house," June cut in. "And I'm sure Henrietta is a perfectly lovely person." She couldn't look at Henrietta as she said it. "It's everything else."

Walt looked from his wife to his daughter and back again. "I don't understand."

"I'm in love with Henrietta, Dad."

Henrietta was certain Meryn hadn't meant to blurt it out like that, but there it was. Out in the open.

"Oh." Walt blinked a few times in Henrietta's direction.

"And she's in love with me," Meryn added, which, Henrietta was relieved to note, saved her the necessity of saying it aloud.

"And that's the problem," June said.

"Why is it a problem?" Meryn asked.

The flush in June's cheeks had become splotchy patches of red, and Henrietta wondered if she had a temper like her daughter's.

June's nostrils flared. "I'm sure I don't need to point out the obvious..."

"You're referring to my handicap," Henrietta said.

June gave a curt nod. "Yes." She hesitated. "That and the age difference."

"Mom," Meryn began, but Henrietta interrupted.

"I told Meryn as much myself."

At that, June's mouth opened and then closed. "You did?"

"I did. She didn't agree." Henrietta gave Meryn a small smile. She turned back to June. "I'm not trying to steal your daughter's future."

"Those things don't matter," Meryn insisted stubbornly.

"They will," June insisted.

Henrietta nodded. "Your mother's right. Time is not on our side."

Meryn started to push back from the table. Henrietta knew she needed to pace and move, but she restrained herself and scooted her chair back in. "No one knows how much time they have. A car accident. A heart attack. Cancer. Anything can happen to any of us."

"But the chances of those things are smaller than the likelihood that Henrietta is going to need more and more help." June avoided Henrietta's gaze. "You're going to become her nurse. It's... it's selfish!"

For a stunned moment, no one said anything.

"Mom..." Meryn said, her hurt palpable.

"I suppose it is," Henrietta mused. "It is selfish that the best part of my day is the moment she comes home. I watch the clock, waiting for Meryn to light up this house with happiness it never knew before."

Meryn turned, her eyes shining at this admission.

I should have told her this before now.

"It is selfish that I laugh and smile now, something I haven't done much of since I was fifteen. It is selfish that, through her, I've met a wonderful circle of friends who support us. My world is so much larger for knowing Meryn." *Say it.* "For loving her."

Meryn reached for her hand, and she took it briefly.

She focused on June. "You're absolutely right. It is selfish."

June looked ready to cry herself. "But, beyond a nice house, what can you offer her?"

"Nothing," Henrietta said simply.

"Everything," Meryn said.

In frustration, June turned to her husband. "Walt, say something!"

He gazed out the window for a long moment, watching the activity at the birdfeeders. "Shall I cut her in half, like King Solomon?" he said at last. "June, all we've ever wanted is for Ryn to be loved, to be cherished. I think it's obvious she is. Isn't that enough?"

June's shoulders sagged in defeat. Henrietta felt only empathy for her, but she wasn't certain June was ready for kind words just now.

"If it helps," she said instead, "I promise not to call you Mom and Dad."

Meryn snorted with laughter. Even June couldn't help but laugh through her tears.

Chapter 26

AUTUMN, RYN DECIDED, WAS definitely her favorite season in Bluemont. It wasn't just the brilliant colors of the trees around the house and pond, or the still-new feeling of the school year on campus. This time of year would forever be tied to her memories of meeting Henrietta, moving in with her, of the visit with her parents.

Before June and Walt left, they had elicited a promise from both Ryn and Henrietta to come to Uniontown for Thanksgiving. It was, Ryn knew, a kind of truce between her mom and Henrietta, and she was grateful to both of them.

Her women-and-history class had been so popular last year—once she was the one teaching it—that word had spread, prompting Talbert to suggest offering it fall and spring. The extra course kept her busier than she'd have liked, but she couldn't complain when she was doing what she loved with a colleague she enjoyed.

Andy might have been born in the States, but he had absorbed more than a tea habit from his time in England. His sense of humor was decidedly British—cutting and subtle—and he had Talbert tagged from the get-go.

"He's got his sights set on bigger and better things, hasn't he?" he observed after an attempt at a history department meeting.

"I kind of screwed that up for him last year, and he hasn't forgiven me."

"That chap whom I replaced?"

"Yeah." Ryn shook her head. "He was planning on becoming department chair after Talbert moved into a dean's slot. They had it all lined up."

Andy sat back with his mug of tea. "I take it he got involved with a student?"

Ryn gave a short nod. She didn't want to say too much. Turned out, she didn't have to.

Andy's face darkened. "We all know it happens, but I swear, if any man ever takes advantage of my daughter—or my son—like that, I'll take care of him myself."

He kept throwing little bones like that, little signals that he was perfectly fine with gays, with the possibility his kids could be gay, and Ryn wondered again if he'd had any relationships with men in the past.

She zipped up her backpack. "You guys sure you don't want to come over to watch the debate tonight? Ferraro will grind Bush into the dust."

"Thanks, but the kids will open up more if it's just us. Don't worry, we'll be watching."

"Cheers, mate."

His laughter followed her down the corridor. She waved goodnight to Beverly and hurried home.

Franny, Roberta, and Steph were already there, having taken over the kitchen. They'd decided to just do a kind of potluck buffet. Ryn had already made a vat of beef stew. When she came in and saw all the food on the dining table—three strudels, a potato casserole, and a loaf of zucchini bread—she laughed.

"Well, if the debate's a bust, we can always drown our sorrows in food."

She quickly changed into jeans and a sweatshirt. By the time she emerged from her room, Sandy and Maxine had arrived with a pot of their lentil soup.

"Mmm." She sniffed. "Did you bring cornbread, too?"

"You bet." Sandy grinned. "Can't have lentils without cornbread."

For a moment, Ryn watched Maxine and Henrietta, standing side by side in the dining room. Maxine looked regal in a knee-length tunic of deep plum that highlighted her beautiful skin, while Henrietta had chosen a cozy sweater in a gray-blue that, when she turned and caught Ryn looking, matched her eyes almost perfectly.

"Oh, stop making googly eyes at each other," Maxine said with a deep laugh. "Ryn, make yourself useful and bring those plates to the table, will you?"

When Gordon arrived with a pan of brownies, Ryn gave up.

"I'm going to die happy."

They ate until they were stuffed, waiting for the debate to begin.

"I have got to walk some of this off, or I'll never sleep tonight," Franny said.

Ryn jumped up and grabbed her jacket. "I'll go with you."

The October evening was brisk, reminding them that winter was just around the corner in this part of the country. They strolled down the road, collars turned to the cold.

"Oh, that's better." Franny breathed, taking the biting air deep into her lungs. "Eating too much makes my brain go all foggy."

"Me, too. I've been so busy between work and volunteering, I haven't spent enough time with my music and fun stuff. I swear I don't know what I'll do if we have to put up with Reagan for another term."

"I'm with you, but..."

"What?"

Franny shrugged. "I just think there are too many people who don't think the way we do. That's all."

They walked for a while. Overhead, stars winked through the mostly-naked trees.

"How are things going?" Ryn asked.

Franny didn't answer right away. "Better." She bumped her shoulder against Ryn. "Thanks for the pep talk."

"No problem." Ryn grinned. "I owe you ten pep talks."

Franny gazed down at her. "Things are good with you and Henrietta." It wasn't a question.

"Yeah. They really are. The visit with my folks kind of turned things around for us. She is so much more open now."

"I'm happy for you, Ryn."

"I mean, we're still not... I share her bed most nights, but we just cuddle. I never thought that could be enough, but it is. It's weird, but it's easier, in a way. There's none of the trying to read her mind, like with my last girlfriend. Is she waiting for me to initiate something? Did she mean something else when she said that?"

Franny's voice was so soft, Ryn almost missed it when she said, "I remember that tension."

Ryn squeezed Franny's elbow, pulling her to a halt. "Fran, please don't think I'm judging your decisions or anything, but... Do you think maybe part of the reason you're having a hard time is because, you know... you want to be with someone? A human someone?"

Ryn held her breath, afraid she'd overstepped.

"I've thought about that." Franny linked arms with Ryn, and they kept walking. "In fact that was a big part of my retreat. Have you ever read *The Song of Songs*?"

"I don't think so."

"It's in the Old Testament. A love poem. Many of the verses are incredibly erotic and sexual. My retreat director kept giving me these passages to pray with. It was like she knew, and she was forcing me to remember what it was like to make love with someone, to feel a woman's arms around me. God."

Franny ran her other hand through her bushy hair. "You know going in, that you're giving that up. Freeing yourself from human entanglements and commitments so that you are able to say, 'Use me as you will.' But knowing it and doing it are sometimes two different things."

Ryn wasn't sure what to say. "Where are you now?"

Franny gave a half-laugh. "I'm on the proverbial fence. And it's as uncomfortable as it sounds." She heaved a sigh. "We should get back or your woman is going to think I kidnapped you."

They turned around.

Ryn smiled to herself. *My woman.*

⁓

STEPPING BACK, HENRIETTA FROWNED at the painting she'd never finished. It wasn't quite right. She turned to the large windows, staring down at the pond, trying to remember what that day had been like. Meryn in the boat—not yet realizing she'd brought the snake along for a ride—her guitar case on the dock on the far side of the pond, sunlight dappling the water through the trees, as it had only been early autumn and the leaves hadn't yet fallen.

The day my life changed.

She closed her eyes, no longer alarmed by the racing of her heart when she thought of Meryn or how very much she loved her. She pressed her hand to her chest, savoring the sensation.

When she opened her eyes, she saw what the painting needed. She'd never done it before, and she wasn't certain she wanted to, but this was to be Meryn's birthday gift.

Think of her, she told herself, reaching a tentative brush to the canvas.

The studio was rather barren, the deep stacks of completed canvases now much smaller. Nearly everything she'd sent to the gallery in Albany had sold. Since then, she'd had gallery reps from all over the Northeast contacting her, not for one-woman shows, but looking to take a few of her paintings. They'd been selling well, and Henrietta had decided to put all of that money into a long-term investment account with Meryn as the beneficiary.

In fact, she'd contacted her attorney and altered her will. With the exception of a set sum of money to go to St. Aloysius, everything else, including the house, would be bequeathed to Meryn. Henrietta had no idea if she would want to live here after Henrietta died, but it would be hers to keep or sell. She hadn't discussed it with the girl—anytime she'd tried, Meryn had accused her of being morbid. To Henrietta, it was simply being practical.

Despite the exercises, she was weaker, her breathing a bit more labored. She was under no delusions that she was going to grow old with Meryn. But she was determined to enjoy every moment she had.

She still had her doubts that Meryn was truly content without a more physical relationship, but Henrietta had finally set aside her constant questioning of that. If Henrietta was feeling under the weather—and somehow, Meryn always seemed to know—or if Meryn had to stay up late grading exams, she slept in her old room so that she wouldn't disturb Henrietta's sleep. But they spent more nights together than not. When they did, Henrietta often lay in the dark, just listening to the sound of Meryn's breathing beside her, shifting her arm over to feel the warmth of Meryn's body beside hers.

She'd forgotten what it used to feel like to sleep with Una, and she liked to think Una would approve of the happiness she'd found.

When she was done painting for the day, she cleaned her brushes and then went to the dining room, where a large stack of envelopes lay on the table.

"I will not call strangers to ask them whom they intend to vote for," she'd said, flatly refusing to participate in the local telephone campaign.

But she'd agreed to help stuff and stamp envelopes and address postcards. Personally, she felt this effort was in vain. She was certain Reagan was going to be re-elected. There were too many powerful white men in control behind the scenes, pulling Reagan's strings. But Meryn and Sandy and the others were so thrilled with having the first woman on a major party ticket, that she hadn't the heart to argue with them.

In fact, she kind of envied them their enthusiasm. "You're just old and jaded," she muttered aloud as she added another envelope to the stack waiting to be mailed.

Outside, the late afternoon light faded, and Henrietta listened for Meryn's key in the front door. When she heard it, her heart leapt.

"Hi," Meryn said with a big smile.

"Hi, yourself."

Henrietta knew she would never see anything that made her happier than Meryn's smiling face.

"You did all these?" Meryn set her backpack down and leafed through the stack of envelopes.

"They still need to be sealed, and I am not about to give my tongue a paper cut for Walter Mondale."

But Meryn wasn't put off by her grumpy tone. She grinned. "I'll seal them with a sponge. Wouldn't want you to sacrifice any body parts." She gave Henrietta's shoulder a squeeze. "Be right back."

She disappeared into her room to change her clothes. "What would you like for dinner?"

Henrietta thought for a moment. "How about omelettes?"

"Sounds good. Do you want coffee?"

"I'll make that if you'll do the eggs."

"Deal."

They went to the kitchen, working around each other in a choreography that had become routine.

"Andy and his wife invited us to their house for dinner this weekend." Meryn glanced over from the stove, where she was pouring the scrambled egg mixture into a pan.

Sometimes, it seemed to Henrietta as if her world kept getting bigger and bigger. It was hard to remember when she'd felt she was surrounded by walls that were closing her in.

"We don't have to," Meryn added quickly.

"They're nice people," Henrietta said. "I wouldn't mind."

Meryn placed her hands on Henrietta's shoulders, forcing her to look at her. "Are you sure? I don't want to ask you to do something you don't want to."

Henrietta placed a hand on Meryn's cheek. "As long as I'm with you, it's where I want to be."

~

THE SEMESTER WAS FLYING by so fast, Ryn sometimes wondered if she'd been sleepwalking through parts of it. Mid-terms were over after a marathon session of grading. Part of what made it feel so chaotic was the fact that she was spending nearly every spare minute volunteering for the Mondale/Ferraro campaign: going door-to-door every weekend, helping with the telephone calls during the week, pushing her students to vote—"remember those women who fought for your right to vote? Don't waste it!" she reminded them after they'd studied the suffrage movement.

It made her proud that so many of the young women on campus had been energized by Ferraro's nomination. She knew the men rolled their eyes, but she encouraged the women. A small gaggle of them followed her out of the classroom at the end of lecture.

They accompanied her across the quad to the steps of Rayburn Hall, all making plans to go together to the student union tomorrow to vote for the first time. She waved them off before climbing the stairs, where Beverly was waiting for her, holding a small cardboard box.

"Your fan club left you?"

"They're not—" But she stopped when she saw the mischievous gleam in Beverly's eyes. "Very funny."

Beverly shrugged, accompanying her down the corridor to her office. "You're one of the most popular instructors on campus."

Even if it was true, Ryn didn't like to think about it. She was pretty sure there were a couple of baby dykes in her classes, and she was being extra careful not to give them any encouragement of a personal nature. Geary's example was always fresh in her mind.

"What's up?" she asked when Beverly followed her into the office and closed the door. "And what's in the box?"

Beverly's expression sobered. "I don't know what's in it," she said, holding the box out, "but it's from Mrs. Feldman. For you."

"Vanessa's mother?" Ryn heart pounded as she took it and set it on her desk. Her hands were trembling so badly that Beverly took the scissors from her to slit open the packing tape. Together they opened the flaps and peeled apart the tissue paper inside.

"Oh." Ryn put her hand over her mouth when she saw Piglet lying there.

"There's a note," Beverly said gently.

Ryn blinked hard and shook her head.

Beverly opened the note and read,

"*Professor Fleming, I hope you won't think this is foolish, but I wanted you to have one of Vanessa's animals. As you can probably guess, she is gone. No matter how many therapists and doctors we took her to, she was never again the happy girl we used to know. You were the only one she spoke of fondly from her time at St. Aloysius.*

"*I so regret forcing her to go there. She must have been so lonely. But I'm happy she had you for a friend. Please accept this in remembrance of our girl.*"

Beverly folded the note. "Meryn, I'm so sorry."

Ryn couldn't see through her tears. "She was so beautiful."

Beverly reached up to pat her shoulder as she cried. "There, there.

You helped get some justice for her from that awful man." She rubbed Ryn's back.

When Ryn's tears slowed, she wiped her eyes. "It's so unfair."

"Many things in life aren't fair," Beverly said. "But we must push on."

Ryn nodded, tucking Piglet back into the box and packing the box into her bag.

"You go home now." Beverly helped her with her jacket. "There's nothing here that needs doing today."

Ryn zipped her jacket, embarrassed by her red eyes as she left the building. She walked quickly, preoccupied with thoughts of Vanessa. When she got home, she went straight to her room. She opened the box and gently placed Piglet on her dresser. Behind her, she heard Henrietta's crutches.

"I thought I heard you come in."

When Ryn didn't turn around, Henrietta asked, "What's wrong?"

But Ryn's throat closed up as more tears filled her eyes. She dropped onto the side of the bed. Henrietta came in and sat beside her.

When her eyes lit on the stuffed Piglet sitting there, she said quietly, "That girl? The one from the boarding house?"

Ryn could only nod. Turning to Henrietta, she buried her face in her neck while Henrietta held her, rocking her.

When Ryn's tears slowed, Henrietta released her. "Stay here. Play your guitar."

"I can't right now."

Henrietta stood. "You need your music now. Just as I'd need to paint." She bent to kiss the top of Ryn's head.

She closed the door on her way out. Ryn opened her guitar case and sat on her bed. Staring at Piglet, she played for Vanessa.

~

THE RESULTS WERE PREDICTABLE. Meryn had sat glued to the television as the election tallies came in. Henrietta had known Reagan would win, but even she wasn't prepared for such a landslide.

The extent of Meryn's depression had been alarming. She'd been sleeping in her room, hardly eating, barely speaking for the entire week. Henrietta saw her for only a few minutes each morning and evening. She knew part of it was the news of Vanessa's suicide. For Meryn, it was all tied together with her having poured so much of herself into the campaign and feeling as if she'd somehow let Vanessa down. Meryn took everything so personally. This was one time Henrietta was glad not to feel so passionately about such things.

Henrietta let her go until Friday morning. "Enough of this," she snapped as Meryn moved silently around the kitchen before she left for campus. "We've already lived through four years of this administration. Four more years won't be terrible."

"It's not just that," Meryn said heatedly. "This country is over two hundred years old, and we've never had a woman in the White House. Except as First Lady."

"Of course we haven't."

Meryn turned to glare at her.

"Do you honestly think the men—the rich, white men—who control things are going to let go that easily?" Henrietta scoffed. "Did you think the first time a woman was nominated, she was just going to skate in? I thought you taught about the suffrage movement in that history class of yours."

"I do," Meryn said in a stung tone. "You know I do."

"Then you also know how long they fought just to get the vote. How many times did they try and fail to get that amendment passed? And that's just the vote. What about the Equal Rights Amendment? When was it first introduced?"

Meryn looked slightly abashed. "1923."

Henrietta simply folded her arms.

The teakettle whistled. Meryn turned her back and poured hot water for her tea.

"And I know it's not just the election," Henrietta said.

Meryn carried her cup and a plate of toast to the table. "It's just not fair."

"Neither is polio," Henrietta said flatly.

Meryn could only stare. Henrietta poured her own coffee, and Meryn brought the cup to the table for her.

"Henrietta, I didn't mean to compare—"

"I know that," Henrietta cut in.

Henrietta's heart ached for the hurt in Meryn's eyes. "I've had my moments of wondering 'why me?'" she admitted as she sat down. "Why did Una have to die? Or Vanessa? There are no answers to these questions, Meryn. And you'll drive yourself mad if you continue to ask."

She reached for Meryn's hand, wondering if she'd pushed too far. But Meryn raised her hand to her mouth, pressing her lips against it for a moment.

"You're right," Meryn said quietly. "I'm sorry."

"Don't be sorry," Henrietta said. "Just don't allow yourself to be defeated. The loftier your goals, the longer you're going to have to fight to achieve them."

She spooned up some cereal. "You've had this week to sulk."

Meryn's head snapped up at the use of that word.

"If you feel this strongly, then do something. Start getting involved for the next election in two years. But for God's sake, stop moping about."

Her scolding had the desired effect as Meryn's mouth twitched into a grin.

"By the way," Henrietta continued, "we're having company tomorrow night for a cookout down at the pond."

"We are?"

"We are."

"What's the occasion?"

Henrietta shrugged. "Maybe I just need to be around people who will actually speak."

Meryn gave a sheepish chuckle. "Have I been that bad?"

"Yes, you have." Henrietta smiled grudgingly. "It's nice to hear you laugh."

"I'll be better. I promise." Meryn finished her toast and gulped her tea.

"Go on with you."

Meryn washed her dishes quickly and stopped to squeeze Henrietta's shoulder. "See you tonight. Love you, Hank."

Henrietta listened to her retreating footsteps and the sound of the front door closing. She closed her eyes and touched her lips to the back of her hand, to the place Meryn's soft lips had so recently touched.

"I love you, Ryn," she murmured.

～

THE POND RANG WITH laughter late Saturday afternoon. Ryn rowed Andy's two kids, Mike and Kelsey, around in the old boat. At the landing, Franny and Roberta tended the fire burning in the stone pit. The old card tables and folding chairs from the basement had been dusted off and brought down to the landing. One of the tables was loaded with bowls filled with pasta salad and potato salad and baked beans and Bonnie's homemade bread.

Bonnie and Beverly were there with their husbands, while Steph helped Sandy and Charlene set out stacks of paper plates and cups and utensils. Gordon and Andy carried down coolers filled with ice and drinks. Maxine accompanied Henrietta down the path, carrying a platter of hamburgers and chicken to cook on the iron grate that had been laid over the fire.

Up in the kitchen, a big pot of shrimp gumbo was bubbling on the stove, waiting to be brought down.

Ryn rowed up onto the bank. Mike got out to tie the boat to a tree and then steadied it for his sister. Ryn stood in the wobbly craft, wondering if she was going to fall into the pond again before clambering ashore herself.

"What can I help with?"

Franny handed her a folding knife and pointed to a stack of long, green branches lying next to the fire. "Sharpen those for hotdogs. We'll use them later for marshmallows."

Bonnie and Beverly sent their husbands up to retrieve the pot of gumbo and bring it down while Steph and Roberta got the burgers and dogs cooking.

The fire snapped and crackled as the afternoon faded to evening and the eating frenzy gradually slowed.

"More potato salad?" Bonnie asked Henrietta.

Henrietta shook her head, placing a hand on her stomach. "I'm so full, I couldn't eat another bite."

"Until the s'mores are ready," Franny teased.

"Those are different," Henrietta said with an indignant sniff.

"This was so much fun," Ryn said, pulling another blackened hotdog off a stick.

"Happy Birthday, Meryn," Beverly said.

Ryn lowered her hotdog and looked around. "What?"

"We're celebrating you, you goof," Roberta said. "Your birthday."

"Really?" Ryn grinned. "But it's not for a couple of weeks yet."

"We'll be in Uniontown with your family for your actual birthday," Henrietta said.

"And we have to leave next weekend," Steph said apologetically.

"So we decided to do this early." Maxine held up her drink. "How old?"

Ryn wrinkled her nose. "Twenty-five."

"A tyke," Andy said.

"A quarter-century," Ryn said.

Franny held up her drink as well. "To Ryn. Happy Birthday."

The others drank to her and then broke into a chorus of "Happy Birthday."

Ryn met Henrietta's eye, and her heart caught in her throat. *She did this for me. They all did.* There were still pangs of regret when she thought of Vanessa, and the defeat of the campaign burned in her gut. She looked around. *But this, this is here, now. This is real.*

Hours later, after the fire had burned to ashes and everyone had left, Ryn went to Henrietta.

"Thank you. What a great night."

"There's one more thing."

Henrietta led the way into the studio. Moonlight streamed in through the windows, lighting their path to one of the easels with a draped canvas.

"Turn on that lamp, would you?"

Puzzled, Ryn did as Henrietta asked, clicking on a gooseneck lamp that was aimed at the canvas.

"Now, lift the drape."

Ryn hesitated. "What—"

"Just do it."

When she pulled the cloth free, her mouth dropped open. "Oh, Henrietta," she murmured, staring at the finished scene.

She was in the boat, on a pond that reflected the clouds and the trees. But what really caught her attention was the figure on the landing, watching her—no crutches, no braces. She tried to think of something to say, but words wouldn't come. Her hand fumbled for Henrietta's.

For long minutes, they stood side by side.

"Thank you," she whispered at last.

"It's not realistic," Henrietta said.

"It's perfect." Ryn turned to her. "Just as I see you."

Henrietta's face was red. Ryn bent her head and gently touched her lips to Henrietta's.

Reaching for the lamp, she clicked it off, leaving them bathed in moonlight again. Down below, the pond glimmered, a silver disc.

"I wish we had a quarter-century together," Henrietta said.

"We may." Ryn wrapped an arm around Henrietta's shoulders.

"You know that's unlikely. By the time you're fifty, I'd be over eighty, and—"

"Hush."

"I'm not being morbid," Henrietta insisted. "I want to spend every moment of the rest of my life with you, no matter how long that may be."

Ryn sighed. "Me, too."

"You scared me this past week," Henrietta said quietly. "It was as if the light inside you, it just snuffed out."

Ryn suddenly thought of the candles that day in the chapel. "I didn't mean to worry you. I just didn't know what to do with all of that weight. It felt like..." She gazed down at the pond. "It felt like it was pulling me under."

Henrietta looked at her. "You didn't turn to me, Meryn. I'll be here for you, just as you have been for me. Don't ever let anyone or anything do that to you again. You don't know, you have no idea," she added fervently, "how much joy, how much light you have brought. Not just to me, but to everyone who knows you."

Ryn didn't know what to say. She could only squeeze Henrietta a little more tightly.

Henrietta nodded toward the pond. "That gathering tonight? All those people? The only thing they all have in common is you. You are the light that drew them together."

Henrietta leaned her head against Ryn's shoulder. "Promise me you won't ever let that go out."

404

Ryn pressed her cheek to Henrietta's head. It was a moment before words would come. "I promise."

Epilogue

November 9, 2016

LUE LIGHT FROM THE television flickered over the living room. With it muted, the only sound in the room was the soft sobbing coming from several of the people scattered in the chairs and on the floor. Phones pinged, but no one seemed to notice.

Ryn sat, stone-faced. Not crying. Not speaking. Her eyes glazed, unfocused.

On the screen, election returns popped up, rotating through states as they updated their vote counts. No one needed sound any longer. The impossible had happened.

"But how?" whispered one young woman.

They all turned to her, looking for answers she didn't have.

"Turn it off," she said hoarsely.

Someone clicked the TV off. She stood, rubbing her eyes.

"Dr. Fleming?" asked another young man. "What now?"

She looked down at them, all those young faces looking to her for reassurance. "It's almost dawn. Stretch out. Get some sleep. Then we get started."

The students glanced at one another.

"Get started with what?" asked one.

"With fighting that bastard with everything we have." She smiled grimly. "Don't worry. People will not take this without protesting. They'll start organizing immediately. And we'll be there with them."

Tearful eyes looked doubtful.

"We won't give up," she said forcefully. "But you're tired. Get some sleep."

She went to the foyer and reached for her jacket.

"Where are you going?" asked the first young woman.

"I need some air." She opened the door. "I'll be back soon."

Outside, the sky was just beginning to lighten through the clouds. The drizzle from yesterday was forecast to continue off and on but, for now, it wasn't raining. Across the road, the golf course was dark, but she could hear the distant roar of mowers. She set out for the village, drawing her collar up against the chill.

The cool air helped clear the fog of disbelief from her head, but that only left room for the ache in her heart.

The village streets were deserted. A few lights were on in houses she passed as she wound her way through town to the cemetery. Even without full sunlight, she knew where she was going. Unlike the village, the cemetery was full of activity. Squirrels hopped around, gathering acorns and walnuts that had dropped from the trees. The birds were noisy, hopping up to perch on headstones and chirp before pouncing on unsuspecting worms in the grass. A fat groundhog trundled along, pausing to watch her as she made her way to a gleaming white stone.

Ignoring the wetness that soaked into her jeans, she knelt, brushing away a few branches that littered the grassy surface of the grave.

Unable to hold her emotions in any longer, she bent double, letting herself cry the tears she hadn't wanted to shed in front of her students.

After what felt like a long time, she sat up, wiping her face. The sun was just visible over the horizon, a gauzy spotlight through the clouds as she heaved a shaky breath.

"It happened again."

She reached out to run her fingers over the smooth marble.

"I know I promised I wouldn't give up, Henrietta, but sometimes, it's just so damned hard. I wish I could talk to you."

As if she were listening, she cocked her head. After some minutes, she bowed her head.

"But I know what you'd say, don't I?"

She sniffed and pushed to her feet. "Got work to do, Hank."

Brushing her knees off, she turned back in the direction of the house.

As she left the cemetery, the clouds broke, and sunlight streamed through in rays that resembled an Italian Renaissance scene. One of the beams lit on the white stone, illuminating the deep carving there.

Meryn Grace Fleming
November 23, 1959 –
Invisible, as music...

Henrietta Marie Cochran
April 11, 1930 – July 3, 1999
...Positive, as sound

THE END

About the Author

BESTSELLING AUTHOR CAREN WERLINGER published her first award-winning novel, *Looking Through Windows*, in 2008. Since then, she has published fourteen more novels, winning several more awards. Influenced by a diverse array of authors, including Rumer Godden, J.R.R. Tolkein, Ursula LeGuin, Marion Zimmer Bradley, Willa Cather and the Brontë sisters, Caren writes literary fiction that features the struggles and joys of characters readers can identify with. Her stories cover a wide range of genres: historical fiction, contemporary drama, and fantasy, including the award-winning Dragonmage Saga, a fantasy trilogy set in ancient Ireland. She has lived in Virginia for nearly thirty years where she practices physical therapy, teaches anatomy and lives with her wife and their canine fur-children.

Website: *carenwerlinger.com*
Blog: *cjwerlinger.wordpress.com*
Amazon: *www.amazon.com/Caren-J.-Werlinger/e/B002BOI2ZI*
Facebook: *www.facebook.com/CarenWerlingerAuthor*
Audible: *www.audible.com/author/Caren-J-Werlinger/B002BOI2ZI*

Printed in Great Britain
by Amazon